THE
WICKED

THE WICKED

REBECCA JOHNPEE

BRAMBLE
TOR PUBLISHING GROUP
NEW YORK

This is a work of fiction. All of the characters, organizations, and events portrayed in this novel are either products of the author's imagination or are used fictitiously.

THE WICKED

Copyright © 2025 Rebecca Johnpee

All rights reserved.

A Bramble Book
Published by Tom Doherty Associates / Tor Publishing Group
120 Broadway
New York, NY 10271

www.torpublishinggroup.com

Bramble™ is a trademark of Macmillan Publishing Group, LLC.

EU Representative: Macmillan Publishers Ireland Ltd, 1st Floor, The Liffey Trust Centre, 117–126 Sheriff Street Upper, Dublin 1, DO1 YC43

Library of Congress Cataloging-in-Publication Data

Names: Johnpee, Rebecca author
Title: The Wicked / Rebecca Johnpee.
Description: First edition. | New York : Bramble, Tor Publishing Group, 2025. | Series: The wicked trilogy ; 1
Identifiers: LCCN 2025029525 | ISBN 9781250385857 (trade paperback) | ISBN 9781250385864 (ebook)
Subjects: LCSH: Organized crime—Fiction. | Thieves—Fiction. | Revenge—Fiction. | LCGFT: Thrillers (Fiction). | Romance fiction. | Novels.
Classification: LCC PS3610.O2854 W53 2025 | DDC 813/.6—dc23/ eng/20250715
LC record available at https://lccn.loc.gov/2025029525

The publisher of this book does not authorize the use or reproduction of any part of this book in any manner for the purpose of training artificial intelligence technologies or systems. The publisher of this book expressly reserves this book from the Text and Data Mining exception in accordance with Article 4(3) of the European Union Digital Single Market Directive 2019/790.

Our books may be purchased in bulk for specialty retail/wholesale, literacy, corporate/premium, educational, and subscription box use. Please contact MacmillanSpecialMarkets@macmillan.com.

First Edition: 2025

Printed in the United States of America

10 9 8 7 6 5 4 3 2 1

To Zahra, for you saw this first.

Caution

Zahra: Before we begin, we'd love to say—

Zahra and Elio: Welcome to our world.

Zahra: I'll start off by saying this story is about criminals. Dark, twisted, arrogant sons of—

Elio: We want to ensure you have the correct perception of the Mafia before you proceed. They are not to be glorified in any way, as they are way more ruthless, violent, and deceptive than you might have been led to believe.

Zahra: When it comes to the real Mafia—

Elio: And if you happen to spot them—

Zahra: You run like hell; they aren't playing around—who am I kidding? If I spot a real Mafia, and a hot one likes me, goodbye, world—

Elio: To make sure we have all grounds covered, here is a list of trigger and content warnings to look out for.

Zahra: All the violence you'd expect from the Mafia—

Elio: Look, we have to stay competitive!

Zahra: Intimate partner abuse and violence. (takes a breath) Mentions of past child sexual abuse and death. Not detailed.

Elio: . . .

Zahra: Depression, discussions of self-harm, and suicide.

Elio: Kidnapping.

Zahra: (laughs) Oh, so we're starting to spill our secrets? My kidnapping or your kidnapping? What about the torture?

Elio: There was only a little bit of that. (pause) And lots of intense sexual encounters.

Zahra: (winks) Also that.

Elio: Okay, I think that covers it. I'm done here. Want to find somewhere a little more private?

Zahra: (laughs)

THE
WICKED

Prologue

He was called "The Wicked" for many reasons.

Some were accurate, while some were drawn from mere hearsay. Some said he was the psychopath who murdered his entire family, others said he was a man who wiped out the bloodline of anyone who died with a bullet from his gun. Those who claimed to admire him would call him a tyrant, one who would do anything for power and the preservation of status, one who would betray his people if the result proved to favor his goals.

He wasn't loyal.

He trusted no one.

He was a man, made of assumptions and truths blended to create an abominable image—but the man couldn't be bothered about how the world perceived him.

They feared and respected him for all the reasons they hated him, and if he was being completely honest with himself, that was all that mattered.

The air was still and the smell of Cuban cigars slightly fogged the large office, courtesy of Elio Marino, whose cigar was locked between his lips while he relaxed in the visitor's chair. His eyes were half open, thick lashes casting shadows on his cheekbones; his suit jacket was long discarded, leaving him with his black button-up and well-knotted black tie, a uniform his father had locked into his personality long before he even held a gun. *"White doesn't suit you, son, why do you think I never wear anything with bright colors? You don't want to be stained with the sinner's blood and let it show, do you?"* his father had told him when he turned seven, and he'd worn only black since that day.

Elio's focus had not shifted since both he and Casmiro, his underboss, had stepped into the man's home—Basilio, a longtime Caporegime associate of the syndicate, who kept glancing in Elio's direction with fear in his eyes; The Wicked just gave Basilio the look he'd seen him give to people who were now six feet under.

"We didn't see them," Basilio said, forcing down a swallow. "They were like shadows. No footsteps were heard, but our soldiers fell noiselessly."

Casmiro's jaw clenched. "The security cameras?" he asked.

"Tampered with. We don't know how. My guys are working on getting back control—"

"You're still locked out?" Casmiro exclaimed in disbelief.

"Whoever these people are, they know what they're doing," Basilio said with a nervous smile, as though there was something amusing in the matter. He glanced at Elio, and his smile dimmed slowly.

The Wicked never smiled. He saw no use for it.

He could still remember it as clear as day, dragged to one of his father's many business meetings. He had dared to laugh when one of their associates made a joke. Nine-year-old Elio received the beating of his life when they returned home. He still had scars to show for it. They stung mentally each time he saw something potentially funny to smile at.

Basilio here, obviously, never got that kind of training.

"Six billion, Basilio," Casmiro said, "do you understand?" He stared pointedly at the man. "That's six billion . . . burnt like it was nothing. Revenue from the Marino Vault House under *your* care."

Basilio swallowed. "I know. One of the soldiers gave us very important information. These people call themselves 'Street.' We aren't the first ones to get hit like this. They take a little and burn the rest. It started about three months ago."

"I don't fucking care who they are, or when it started. They can fuck with other families, but not Marino. *Never* Marino. How the fuck did they get under your noses?"

Basilio shrugged with uncertainty. "It's still a mystery. I would blame it on the Nazaris, but this operation was different. It was . . . perfect. Like a blink—and money gone—Vault House burnt—men dead."

Elio could feel Casmiro's anger from beside him but said nothing. He kept staring at Basilio, whose gaze kept skittering away from him. The man was probably wondering why he was so quiet—well, Elio had other business to take care of, and if it weren't for Casmiro's insistence, he would have been dining with the dignitaries of Turin, thinking of new ways to sink his teeth further into the government.

All this felt like child's play, and the last thing Elio wanted was to deal with children.

Elio's tattooed fingers, gracefully ornamented with rings, lowered the cigar he had just taken a smooth pull on. He blew out a streak of smoke.

Casmiro straightened. "What makes you think the Nazaris have something to do with this? I don't think anyone would be foolish enough to start a war with us."

Frustration pulled down Basilio's brows. "Okay, then I say we take it to them; we make them pay for this hit."

"And what if you're wrong."

"No, believe me—I'm on to something—"

Elio drew his gun. There was a loud bang and the smell of spent gunpowder, mixed with the thick metallic stench of fresh blood, filled the air.

Basilio's lifeless head dropped to the table with a dull thud, causing a small oval puddle on the desk.

"What the fuck did you just do?" Casmiro yelled, briefly

forgetting who he was talking to. "We were getting somewhere! The man was right! We're targeted!"

Elio rose to his feet, pressing the lit end of his cigar into the warm blood. "And you think the Nazaris are possible suspects?"

"Rasheed Nazari knows better than to fuck with us like that."

Elio nodded once. "Do not go looking for trouble where there is none. I am not bothered about what we lost. Focus, Casmiro. They are children throwing tantrums. Hm?"

Casmiro hid his glare. "Why am I not surprised? You care less about the real business these days. Politics wasn't what our fathers chased."

Elio paused and regarded him for a bit before speaking. "I am not my father. I am not your father. I do not know what it means to care *less* about something. Besides, I chase and crave power, and only power, Casmiro. Politics is power. Have someone clean up this mess." He fastened the two buttons of his suit as he asked, "Where is Angelo?"

"Work."

"Hm. Extend word to his right hand to assign men to take over this place. I want business running here in a few hours," he ordered.

At this, Casmiro's jaw clenched. "The occupants? Basilio's family?"

Elio's indifferent gaze swept over his underboss. "Wipe it all away. The sinner doesn't exist if my bullet ends up inside them."

Casmiro gave a curt nod, getting to his feet as well.

About to walk out the door, Elio held him back by his arm. "Never. Ever. Raise your voice at me. The next time it happens, I will feed you your vocal cords. Clear?"

Casmiro didn't bat an eye. "I apologize."

Nodding, Elio let him pass, his gaze not leaving the man's back for one second.

His apology meant nothing; Elio would have been a fool not to see it.

He also knew the man disapproved of how he handled things—but Elio was okay with it; as long as Elio's father consented, no other opinion mattered.

CHAPTER ONE

Zahra

Was there such a thing as having too much money?

I shook my head, ignoring the single bead of sweat running down my spine as my gaze roamed over the pool table before me; the endless cash bundles shocked me while at the same time sending a thrill through my body that was hard to disguise.

This was the biggest heist we had ever pulled. What's more, with all five of us still intact, with no casualties, and no mistakes made. It was fucking fantastic, and my grin was about to split my face in half.

With gloved hands, I pushed my hair away from my face, my tongue running over my bottom lip in anticipation.

"Bloody fucking mental," Upper said in awe, his accent coating his words.

Dog blew out a whistled breath, soot-stained fingers rubbing his stubble as he looked up at each of us. "This is what I'm fucking talking about. I want to keep hitting the people who have more than they should."

"Yeah." Milk nodded in agreement, her pink hair still in a ponytail as she shrugged out of her coveralls. "I gotta say the thrill of hunting the people at the top of the food chain is—God, it's sweeter. So much money . . ." She clasped her hands in glee. "Our vacation is guaranteed."

Removing the black gloves from my hands, I picked a bundle of money from the table, fingers skimming through it, the smell going straight to my head—the smell of new, fresh, illegal money was like a hit of cocaine.

Familiar arms wrapped around me from behind, followed by a kiss on my neck. Devil. He was a good six foot one and towered over my five-foot-five frame. "We should listen to Zahra more often," he said, and I could tell by the sound of his voice that he was grinning from ear to ear. My own grin spread wider when I leaned into him.

We called ourselves Street. Growing up in the streets, surrounded by people who stole and killed to eat, we were built from the cracks and crevasses of neighborhoods too rough to survive in, but we made do through theft and trickery, break-ins and shoplifting.

Every member of Street, aside from me, went by a code name.

There's Dog. He was one crafty motherfucker; partially good with computers, but his humor sometimes was the very relief we needed when things went awry on a mission.

There's Upper, who was a mad genius with computers and all things coding and hacking. He was our eyes and ears and seldom played the role of our guy in the chair.

Milk, on the other hand, could talk any man or woman into doing her bidding, and it was a gift I would have killed for. She was approachable and beautiful. She compelled people with her smile and the seductive sound of her voice.

There's Devil, who had a mysterious aura. He always wore black and knew how to handle weapons like a professional. He was hard-hearted when it came to doing something none of us would approve of but would have to do.

And then there's me, Zahra—as it says on my anklet. I'd love to think I was the bravest. When you spend every waking minute of your life around people who can snuff the life out of you at any second, you learn to be bold and fearless, to never cower when there's a gun pointed at your face.

"I'll prepare the bill counter," Dog said, rubbing his palms together as he disappeared to the small storage room.

"And I'll get dinner; what do you fuckers feel up to?" Upper pulled off his overalls, took out his contact lenses, and carelessly flicked them to the ground for the next person who would bother to use the vacuum cleaner.

We lived in a studio apartment that was never tidied and would probably get us arrested if the cops were to burst in, but it was above an unpopular kitchen in the city, so the odds of us getting busted were slim.

Devil shot Upper a taunting smile, turning me around to face him. "Get us whatever, as long as it's not stolen."

"What the bloody hell do you mean by that?" Upper cursed, but there was a lightness to his voice.

"I'll go with him," Milk announced before dashing after Upper, who grabbed his glasses from one of the worn-out couches, slipping them on without bothering to clean the lenses. He threw his arm around Milk's shoulder as they walked out the door and out of view.

Devil grinned down at me. "How are you so amazing?" he asked, pulling me to his body, lips trailing down my neck, with his hands going down my back to squeeze my ass.

I pushed at him lightly with a smile. "Get your horny hands off me, I'm sweaty."

"Yeah, but that's us half the time."

I smiled at him, throwing my arms around his shoulders.

"You *really* are amazing, Zahra," he repeated.

I traced his jawline with my index finger. "I'm pretty sure when I was born, my mother or father said the word *amazing*. It grew with me, I guess."

"Mm-hmm," he murmured, pressing his lips to mine in a kiss. My lips parted, kissing him back.

While our relationship wasn't defined, he was one of my best friends, and we shared comfort and appreciation with, well, *very* intimate gestures.

"I'm pretty sure we pissed off some really dangerous people tonight." Dog's voice rang through the space as he dropped the bill counter on the table and pulled up a chair. "Ass off the table, Zahra."

I chuckled.

Life was going well—as well as it could for five skilled criminals who robbed other criminals. I didn't know how we managed to pull off this mission, but somehow, the forces that ruled the world seemed to be on our side.

And honestly, I wasn't complaining.

"I'm thinking . . . America," Milk said, her eyes dreamy as her hands waved apart an invisible picture of America. "I've always wanted to live that American dream. With all this money, I could even open my salon and spa."

I smiled, relaxing back on the bean bag as we thought about our next step after this. We'd always wanted to go on a one-year vacation away from Italy; we wanted to travel the world and see people and places we'd only heard of.

The money we had now could last us more than three years, and though I knew we could never have too much money, the break was something we all needed.

Hitting one of The Wicked's vault houses was the biggest risk we had ever taken; we had made a pact before we left that if we pulled it off, we would all go on a vacation together and live like royalty.

They deserved it, and if I managed to cross off everything on my list, I might deserve the break too.

I let out a silent breath, glancing at the wall clock opposite me before focusing on the conversation going around.

"Just think of all the places we could visit," Milk said.

"America, where dreams come true," Dog sighed. "Los Angeles, the city of angels, and Miami, the city of tits."

I laughed, shaking my head. "You're an idiot."

"You trained me well."

I flipped him off.

"Isn't America overrated?" Upper cut in, playing lazily with his Rubik's cube. "I heard it is."

"We could go to Hawaii," I chipped in. "I've heard it's beautiful there."

"And dreamy," Milk added. "All those men walking around with those beach shirts they leave unbuttoned to show off their chest hair."

"Yum." Upper grinned. "I would love to see—"

"Or maybe we could travel around," Devil interrupted. "Spend a month in each city, live like the world has always been in our favor. We don't have to overthink it."

I directed my smile at him this time. "Yeah," I backed him up. "I think we need to draw up a—"

Something shattered in the distance, cutting me off. We all sat up—alert, ultimately quiet for almost two minutes, listening for any other suspicious noise. But it was dead silent.

I glanced at the wall clock just as the sound of pounding footsteps reached our ears.

Dog frowned. "Guys, I think—"

Our door exploded with a force that had my heart almost beating its way out of my chest. Masked men rushed into our space before white smoke filled the air. My throat started to feel tight, my limbs weaker by the second; I couldn't see a single thing but blurry black figures all around me.

I could hear Devil shouting my name; I could hear gunshots, bone-breaking kicks, and grunts—more ear-numbing gunshots and Milk's terrified screams. I tried to reach for her, but my lungs felt so heavy I couldn't breathe, my eyelids fluttering furiously, fighting dizziness.

Come on, Zahra, get up.

Get up.

I fought to get on my knees and managed to open my eyes, only to find the hilt of a gun quickly approaching my face.

I didn't get to feel the pain before I was out like a light.

CHAPTER TWO

Zahra

There was a ringing in my ears when I regained consciousness.

My throat was dry, and my skin felt singed. I could feel sweat rolling down my face, beading at the skin between my nose and lips.

I tried to open my eyes, but a thundering headache had me wincing. My vision was blurry for the first few seconds, but I soon adjusted to the empty pale walls around me. No windows. No opening. Just walls.

I couldn't breathe properly. The air—it was hot, it was thick and dry, and I felt so dehydrated. I parted my lips, desperate for relief, but the thick, searing air filled my lungs like fire, and I quickly shut my mouth.

Why was it so hot?

I wanted to cry and scream at the same time. It felt like the air was suffocating me. I tried to move, but I couldn't, and with the pounding in my head, it took me a good while to realize my legs were tied to the chair I was sitting on, and my hands were bound behind me.

The room was too fucking hot, and I could smell the tangy odor of something dead, of piss, of dried vomit—of torture.

I continued breathing through my nose, short inhales, as sweat dripped down my chin. I moved my head to my shoulder, wiping the irritating moisture with my damp shirt.

Suddenly, a door opened, and I jerked up, completely freezing when I saw who approached me.

Fear gripped my bones for the first time in years.

I had seen his face in philanthropic magazines, the news, and the internet, but I never thought there would be a day I would come face-to-face with this side of him. The Wicked himself—the boss of the Marino empire—was standing before me, hands tucked into his pockets as his eyes scanned my form from head to toe.

"You are so . . . ordinary." His voice was deep and a little accented, tinged with irritation and muffled in a room that was supposed to echo.

I blinked up at him. "But special enough for the boss to come g-greet me himself," I croaked out.

Slowly, his brows pulled down in a frown as he tilted his head to the side, the tattoo on his neck peeking out of the collar of his dress shirt.

"If you're—just gonna stand there, might as well fetch me water."

"Thirsty?"

Yeah, no shit.

I sighed and nodded, lips burning.

"Is the room too hot for you?" he asked menacingly. "Does it feel like you're . . . drying up?"

Annoyance bubbled in my stomach and I clenched my jaw.

He bent until he was face level, eyes locking with mine. "Now you know how my money felt when that fire started," he said, tone calculated. "If you did not have the resources to take all the money, you could have just left the rest. Did your employer ask you to burn it?"

I remained quiet.

"Who is your employer?" he asked.

I locked my jaw, keeping my mouth shut.

He pressed his lips together, waiting a minute too long before nodding. "Okay," he said, rising to his full height. My eyes burned when I tried to follow his movements.

He brought his hands out of his pockets and clapped once.

Immediately, the door opened, and a man walked in with a

bottle of water, a gun, and a small evidence bag. The man handed the items to him before swiftly leaving the room.

I could see the tiny beads of sweat on his forehead as he looked at me again. "Water?"

The fight left me at the sight of the chilled water. "Yes."

He nodded, gently placed the gun on my lap, pocketed the bag, and uncapped the water bottle slowly.

Then he held my face in his hand, fingers pinning my lips together as he lifted my chin towards the ceiling, pushed it back, brought the bottle to my lips, and poured the water over my lips so that it didn't enter my mouth. His grip on my face tightened painfully as he raised the bottle to my nose, pouring the water into my nostrils.

I fought to escape the brutality, choking and gurgling. Tears fell while I struggled for air.

I could see how my struggle pleased him. He looked so relaxed while I fought to breathe. My chest constricted, my body took on a dull buzz, and when my eyes started to see him in a painful blur, he let me go.

I coughed hot air back into my lungs and bent to allow the water that hadn't gotten to my head to slip out of my nose.

"My hand slipped," his voice rang out again, calm and collected like he wasn't also feeling the lack of oxygen in the room. "It does that sometimes."

He threw the almost empty bottle to the ground and took his gun from my lap, disengaging the safety.

My head felt lighter, and my left ear rang so loud I feared I would never hear again. "What—what the *fuck* do you—want from me?"

He didn't speak for what felt like a minute before he began to circle me. "I want to know who you work for. Give me a name, and I promise only to put you in a coma and not kill you."

At this, I frowned. "What?"

He stopped right in front of me. "I hate repeating myself, it is tiring. This room is too hot, and the stench is repulsive. So, speak, and let us be done with this."

"We don't work for anyone."

He kept his eyes on me, bringing out the plastic baggie, and revealing my anklet. "How do you explain this?"

I eyed the jewelry, my heart hammering before I looked up at him, nerves crawling up my spine. "What does that have to do with anything?"

He studied my face as he spoke. "It was found at the scene of the arson. For such a careful operation . . . you must have wanted to be found."

Fuck . . . I dropped my head and blew out a breath. "It probably fell off, for fuck's sake. I didn't even realize until now."

"Do not lie to me."

"It's the truth. My crew and I—we—we work alone. Wait— Where are they?"

He let silence fall before he stepped closer to me and slipped the bag into his pocket, his gaze roaming my face. "Dead, alive, being tortured as we speak, it is of no importance to me. Tell me what I need to know and stop wasting my time."

"I already told you," I gritted, meeting his gaze. "We work for no one. We know no one but each other. If it's your money you want, as you already know, we took some and burned down the rest; we can return what we took—we can—"

"You do not want to lie to me; aside from the fact that I can see through it, I am a liar who hates liars."

My gaze locked with his. "Doesn't—doesn't that mean you're lying right now?"

He went quiet, blinked, then, "What?"

"If you hate liars—and you are a liar—doesn't that mean you hate yourself?"

His expressionless eyes stared into mine—if I weren't tied to a chair, probably about to die, I would have commended the way he stopped his thoughts from being highlighted on his face.

He nodded. "You think I am here to play psychology with you." He pointed his gun at me, and I heard a loud bang before I felt the pain spread from my shoulder to my whole body. It was as if my breath had been sucked out of my lungs. The cry that left my mouth was harsh and hoarse.

The bastard shot me.

For the first time, his eyes turned hard and he leaned in again, placing his gun-free hand on the shoulder he just shot, his thumb pressing against the wound. "Now, I ask again—" Through my blood-and-sweat-soaked shirt, his thumb dug deeper into the wound as if fishing to find the bullet.

"Gah, fuck!" I yelled. The pain was blinding, and I ground my teeth together as tears fought to leave my eyes while I held them at bay.

"Who paid you to steal from me?"

"No one!" I screamed between my teeth in anger and pain. "Please—please stop! I swear we did it alone—fuck!" My lips trembled.

"Truth, I need the truth."

He dug his thumb in again, and I squirmed and bit back a cry at the pain that had me lightheaded.

"Talk."

"Why—*why* would I fucking lie! You are The fucking Wicked. People fear you—more than anyone—in this—business—no one could pay me a million dollars to fuck with you—no one but myself. As we have done before, I trusted myself to do this without any casualties, and my people trusted me. No one sent my team or me—we did it of our own accord—because we could."

"How do you explain the tracking device on the anklet?"

I shivered in pain. "Safety purposes, I swear. Our job is dangerous; it was meant to be on me."

Then there was silence. A moment of him watching me and me breathing heavily while watching him.

Suddenly, he removed his hand from the wound, and I sagged in relief while he straightened and looked away, wiping his forehead. "This is a waste of my time," he muttered under his breath before looking back at me. "How can you all be so stupid to steal from someone like me? You thought you could get away with it?"

"We did," I said before I could stop myself.

"Angelo!" he yelled into the silence, and a young man walked in. Composure in place, his hair brushed back and curled at the tip, his brown skin tanned, lips pursed. His eyes moved to me for a swift second before they settled on The Wicked.

"Marino," the man—Angelo—said in greeting.

"¿Qué dije?" *What did I say?* The Wicked had a small edge to his voice that almost had me believing he was angry. "Did I not say they were lone rangers? But Casmiro knows best, no? Now I have wasted my time and my resources."

"I see . . ." His gaze flicked to me, then his boss. "Should I call Casmiro?"

"Leave it. There is no point in dragging out something that doesn't deserve the time and energy. Oversee this case. Have your people dispose of the others, make this one watch, and then dispose of her too. Before you do that, increase the heat enough to make the skin burn. It is only right to prepare sinners for what awaits them after death."

Angelo nodded, gaze sweeping in my direction again. His eyes showed no form of hesitation, and I knew he would follow through with it.

The Wicked handed the gun to Angelo, adjusting his collar as he began walking to the door.

No, I can't let it end like this. There must be something—anything—think, Zahra—think, think—

"You're making a mistake!" My voice rang out in desperation, and he halted.

Angelo's brows shot up in surprise.

Silence followed until slowly, ever so slowly, The Wicked turned to me, his brows dropped in confusion. I understood that expression.

Anyone in my position would be begging for their life, but me? I wanted to make a proposition.

He took a few steps back to me. "I am . . . making a mistake?"

I didn't take my eyes off his. "Yes," I breathed. "If you kill us, you'll be making a big mistake."

"Pray tell *why* you think this?"

I swallowed. "I can help you."

His gaze moved to Angelo's interested one.

"Help me?" he asked, eyes on me once more.

"Yes."

"Why would I want the help of a child?"

Despite the sarcasm in his tone, I bit out my response with a scowl. "I'm twenty-six."

"Ah . . . And here I thought you were a child, throwing a tantrum."

There was a short silence before he nodded. "Okay, Sport, I'll bite. What does that little head of yours think it can help me with?"

"My people and I are efficient," I started, "fast, and skilled. We can get in and out of a building without getting seen. I know your syndicate has a legal face, but you should know that sometimes, you must mix the legal with the illegal. We are like shadows, and we can slip into your legal spaces and turn things to your favor without anyone ever guessing you might have been involved—if you know what I mean."

He nodded. "Hm." He shoved both hands into his pockets again. "Everything you just said would have been a compelling reason to keep you and your people alive if you weren't tied up in a chair after being caught by me."

"That wouldn't have happened if I didn't leave something behind."

"Hm."

"I know my mistakes, and I know better than to make them again."

He looked like he was pondering hard, gaze searching my

face. "So, you agree to be indebted to me for the rest of your life?"

"If that is what it takes to stay alive, then yes."

"You speak for your whole . . . crew?"

"Yes."

He nodded as his gaze settled on Angelo. "Have your people turn up the heat until she can't breathe; record it."

Fucking hell.

"And the others?" Angelo asked.

The Wicked glanced my way, his eyes moving from my head to my toes before he spoke. "Make them watch."

I tried to wiggle my way out of the hold on the chair, my shoulder burning away with pain. "Please!" I cried out pathetically.

He turned, walking out of the room without a second glance. Angelo followed seconds after him.

I was panting, shivering in anger as the heat became unbearable. I groaned in pain. My shoulder wound was burning—and I was screaming and begging—again and again and again.

I used to think if I ever were in a situation like this, I would face it with equal confidence and grace; I used to think I wouldn't beg—I used to think I wouldn't fear death.

But here, in this room, alone, with no assurance of me or Street ever coming out of this alive, I was trapped. I had no solution. No quick thoughts. Our lives were in the hands of a man who was known for his inability to show mercy.

I was wrong. The universe wasn't on our side, it was preparing a wicked trap for us, and there was no escaping it.

This time, we were all going to die.

CHAPTER THREE

Elio

I settled the cigar between my lips and flicked open the red lighter, allowing the flame to light up the foot before flicking it shut. I sucked in the thick smoke, taking the stick from my mouth while swirling the smoke around my tongue, exhaling slowly and pouring myself a drink.

My lounge door opened and closed, but I didn't turn to see who walked in because I already knew.

"What were you thinking!"

"You forget yourself sometimes, Casmiro," I said, putting down the whiskey bottle, picking up my glass, and turning to face him.

"You're keeping them alive?" He ignored my statement, his eyes burning with anger and disbelief.

"What can I say? Being wicked was getting old," I told him while taking a sip, allowing the drink to warm me up instead.

"This isn't funny."

"I would be laughing if it was."

He took a step closer to me. "They stole from our family, and you let them live. Why?"

"They stole from me."

Casmiro frowned in confusion. "What the fuck does that even mean? I don't—"

"You think with your anger; that is why you don't understand things. I wonder how you made it this far with me."

Casmiro glared, taking off his jacket and carelessly throwing it on a couch before walking to the bar area of my home lounge, picking up a glass, and pouring himself a drink. My gaze kept going to the mess he made with his jacket, but I hid my irritation.

"What's going on, E?" he asked.

"I see potential in a partnership with them. Besides, they don't know I'm keeping them alive. I left them with their assumptions. It kills faster than death itself."

Casmiro shook his head, raising his glass to me. "Only you, Marino. Only you."

I shrugged. "They have guts—and determination. I could tell from the one I spoke to."

"Zahra?"

"Hm. Do you have the full name yet?"

Dropping his glass to the table, he nodded. "Her last name is Faizan. She was bought in Saudi Arabia and abandoned before coming to Italy. Couldn't dig up much about her."

"Parents?"

"Father unknown, mother disappeared right after birth. No other records."

"And the others?"

"I already sent you all the information you should need about them, but I know you won't read it, so—pink-haired girl who calls herself Milk is an orphan and was in foster care before migrating to a small biker group. The group is still active, but when we reached out, they refused all claims to her. Upper and Dog are no-name orphans. Devil's background is still unclear; the background check we ran on him was void."

"Void?"

"He's a ghost."

I brought the cigar to my mouth, inhaled once more before putting it out in the ashtray. "Hm. No childhood pictures, surveillance cameras, webcam images?"

"None. He's not in any database. Medical records are also zero, and criminal records are clear—no legal name to pin him to like the others. And we can't exactly run a check on a nickname. It makes it difficult because that face isn't in the system."

I nodded. "Interesting. We should keep an eye on that one."

Casmiro grunted. "I don't think we should be keeping eyes on any of them. They should be dead."

"They are useful."

"Useful in what sense? We have guys who can steal for you and would never be seen doing it."

"These people stole from those *same* guys and were not seen by them. They locked us out of our security system for two hours after they left. They had the guts to do all that and were still successful."

"We caught them."

"Because they left something behind. The jewelry. They know it too."

"I don't think this is wise, E."

"I think it is. They are under Marino's command now. They are not our people but assets we can use. Political assets."

"There we go," Casmiro mumbled.

"Think. These men in the big seats only listen to the command of power, Casmiro. You might not see the use of politics. But the Marino empire is legal, thanks to me. We can touch the government and political bodies and be so big that future accusations without proof would brush past the media in a swoosh no one would see. Our fathers never thought of this because they were old-fashioned. They were scared little men who didn't dare to branch out of their comfort zone," I said to him, drinking the rest of the whiskey in my glass and dropping the empty glass on the counter.

He was silent after that. I watched his jaw clench and unclench, still looking at the collection of whiskeys and wine before him as he spoke. "Then let me in."

I sighed, turning to pour myself another round, ignoring the pointedness of his gaze at the side of my face.

"But you won't." He turned fully to me. "You won't because you don't trust me—because, for some reason, you choose not to. I would have accepted that if there had been a time when I did something to break your trust in me, but I never did. You just stopped."

"I don't trust anyone, Casmiro. Don't make it personal."

"Fuck you, E. I am making it fucking personal."

"Cas—"

"I am tired of you treating me like one of your soldiers. It was supposed to be the two of us. Against everyone. But you fucking treat me like an outsider."

At times like this I didn't know what to do. Yes, we used to be close, but why couldn't he understand that things change? These days, there's no such thing as brothers, friends, or even family when it comes to the business. Why couldn't he understand that I would kill him if necessary? Friends do not think that about their friends, do they?

I am confused.

I watched him swallow the last of his drink, shaking his head and dropping the glass on the table as he began to walk away.

"Cas," I called, but he ignored me. He reached the couch where he had dumped his jacket and slipped it on before attempting to walk out. "Stop," I called out again, leaving my glass on the counter as I approached him. "Sit."

He looked at me and then at the couch. "I have shit to do."

"Sit down, Casmiro."

He hesitated but succumbed with a grunt.

Sitting down next to him on the couch, I watched a hard line form on his face. "You are like a child sometimes."

"I have every right to feel offended."

"Really?"

He threw a stern frown at me.

I nodded. "Useless emotions, Casmiro. This kind of heart you have isn't what this business needs."

"Did you ask me to sit so you could insult me?"

"No." I took in a sharp breath. "Listen. You cannot throw tantrums like this because we don't drink whiskey together and do things friends do. You said I treat you like a soldier. But I do not think any soldier would have the guts to walk in here and pour himself a drink. I do not think I would sit down with a soldier and talk to him like I am talking to you now. You assume I do not care because that is what you see."

"It's what you show."

"Yes. Because a time will come when I will have to choose between you and something I want badly, and I will choose that without blinking. It is not that I don't trust you. I don't trust myself. I cannot be a friend to you, Casmiro. I will mess it up, and you will hate me." This time, all I saw on his face was confusion.

"How can you be so certain you will mess it up?"

"Because I am sick. I am unpredictable, even to myself. I do not know consequences until they hit me in the face. This is me being very honest with you because I can tell my behavior is upsetting you."

"I hate your honesty sometimes."

"I tell you what you want to hear, and I know you wanted the truth."

He nodded and was silent for a few seconds before he broke it. "I still want you to let me in—"

"Casmiro—"

"Try. Let's take power together. Teach me. You can do it alone, but you don't have to. Not when I'm here."

I worked my jaw, refusing to give myself unnecessary time to think it through.

"Okay," I said. "You want to get inside my head. You want me to tell you things and trust you. You want to make a brother of me. Fine."

"Why do you make it sound so scary?"

"It is the accent."

There was a slight pause before Casmiro blinked. "I think you just made a joke—but your face isn't—it's not—"

"I know. I am funny."

"It's hard to tell if you're telling a joke or—just being *you*."

I stayed silent.

He sighed. "I just want things to return to how they were, you know? I don't want secrets between us. Whatever we're doing, we do it together, like brothers."

I nodded. "Okay, Casmiro. No secrets. But remember, I warned you. You do not get to complain that I am overbearing or talkative."

He scoffed. "Talkative is the last thing I would call you, E. Even when we were children, you only talked when it was necessary or when you were excited. I can't remember the last time I saw you smile or get excited about anything."

I nodded. "That is true. But I get excited about things." Then I pointed to the side of my head. "In my head. I also talk my mind off in my head. But now that you have offered your ears"—I got to my feet, motioning to the home office a few feet away from us—"let's talk politics."

CHAPTER FOUR

Zahra

My eyes snapped open, and I flinched, a sharp burn scraping down my arm. "Motherfucker." I groaned in pain, realizing I was lying on a soft mattress. My head rested atop comfortable pillows stacked up to ensure I didn't cause any discomfort to myself when I woke up—apparently, that hadn't worked.

"Hey." Devil's voice had my head snapping up; he was leaning on the wall next to the small table across from me, arms crossed against his chest, watching me like a dark shadow, dressed in all black.

I sighed in relief. "Hey, creep, why are you way over there?"

A small, strained smile tugged at his lips as he approached me, sitting on the side of the bed. "How are you feeling?"

My eyes took in the bruise on his cheek. Other than that, he didn't seem injured anywhere else.

"Like death." I groaned, trying to sit up. He was quick to help me, but I moved my arm wrong and winced at the spike of pain. "Ugh, fuck, this hurts like a bitch."

"I know. It's going to leave a scar. They took the bullet out, but it was difficult because of how deep it was in your shoulder; they had to tear—"

"Don't tell me. I'll probably ink it when it heals," I said, letting out a shaky breath. "How are you? Where are the others? Where are we?"

I took in my surroundings more clearly. It looked like a guest room. But none of this made sense. I shouldn't be alive—none of us should be alive.

"Where else would we be?" The sharpness in his voice had me frowning. He sighed, looking down at my arm in the sling. "Sorry, we're still hostages. We were given quarters in the compound. We're in Marino territory."

I slumped slightly, careful not to move my arm. "Fuck—the others, they—"

"Are pissed. Just a heads-up."

There was only one reason they could be pissed at me. I told The Wicked we would forever be at his service as long as he kept us alive. When he left me in that fucking oven, I didn't think for one second that I would make it out of there alive. He hadn't given me any guarantee that he approved of my proposal to be at his service, so it made no sense—or maybe my brain was still filled with the water he had almost drowned me in. Water—

It was almost like the thought of water reminded me of how thirsty I had been before I had probably passed out from all my pathetic screaming.

I cringed, embarrassed that I had let myself go like that—that I had forgotten how to be strong.

"Can I get water?"

Devil's eyes softened. He got up from the bed to walk to the table across the room. He poured water into a glass and brought it over to me. I collected it eagerly with my good hand before bringing it to my lips, drinking it all in five gulps.

There was a tense awkwardness in the air between us. It was unfamiliar, but I knew where it came from; it was probably why I felt ashamed.

"How did we get here? Was I the only one questioned?"

"Yeah. For some reason, you were the only one they wanted to talk to."

My anklet.

"I take it you watched—everything—me?" I asked, a little part of me hoping those bastards didn't make them watch how I screamed and begged. Devil was quiet, and it only confirmed my suspicion.

Carefully, I relaxed against the headboard. "Is that why you're being awkward? Because the *amazing* Zahra you knew would have never begged, cried, or screamed while she was basically being toasted alive."

His gaze snapped to mine in a second as he blinked his thoughts away. "What the fuck? No. Never—I don't—it's not you—" He breathed. "They made us watch. They tied us up and made us watch, and it was fucking torture, not being able to—" He swallowed. "To do anything. It was cruel, Zahra. I can still see, hear, and feel the anger. I hate myself for not seeing this happening and talking us out of going through with the Marino mission—we should have known."

I shook my head. "No, this isn't your fault. If anyone's to blame, it's me. I brought the idea—"

"And I egged you on. I provided the layout; Milk seduced one of the soldiers, and we got electronic access; Upper fucked with their systems and locked them out; Dog and I took the men guarding the Vault House down, one by one. This shit? It's on all of us."

"But they're pissed at me."

"Because you signed off all our lives to him, Z."

I blinked. "There was nothing else I could have done, Devil; he could have killed us all—he could have—we wouldn't be alive right now if it weren't for me. I did what I fucking had to do. Do you think if it were just me, I would grovel like a fucking pussy? My head, thoughts, mind, and heart were on all of you. I don't give a fuck about my life; he could put a fucking bullet in my head as long as I know you all are far away from him."

"I'm not blaming you for it, Zahra; I would have done the same thing."

"But apparently, those shitheads wouldn't—fuck this." I was already getting out of the bed, ignoring how heavy my body felt, and my arm throbbed.

But I was pissed; I was pissed because what the hell were *they* angry about? I was the one who had been tortured; I was the one who had been baked alive; I was the one who had saved their sorry little fucking asses.

"Zahra, slow down."

I was already out of the room; hearing their muffled voices, I followed the sound. It didn't take long before I found myself in a kitchen. "Okay, motherfuckers, let's hear it. Why whine behind my fucking back when you can say it to my face?"

I was met with silence, but I watched how Dog's expression turned into a hard glare; he had a cut on his brow that was already stitched up. Upper had a scowl on his face, but I could tell it was only directed at the situation. Milk had a bandage on her arm, but I couldn't read her emotions because she wouldn't meet my eyes.

"You wanna pick a fight?" Dog asked. "Cause I'm ready to give it to you; I don't care if you have a busted arm."

Devil came up beside me, sighing. "Guys, the last thing we need right now is a baseless disagreement."

"Baseless? We are fucked—we're all fucked!" Dog yelled.

"No more American dream." Milk's voice was quiet.

"What the fuck else was I supposed to do? He was going to kill you all—I had to do what I had to do, so yes, I spoke for us at that moment."

"Really? Who the fuck put you in charge? Because last I checked, we don't have a *boss* on this team," Dog said, coming closer. "This is your problem, Zahra; you always love to play the hero. It's probably why they picked you and shot you."

I scoffed. "We got caught because of me. That's why they picked me *and* shot me. I left something behind. They found it."

After I said that, it went very quiet around us, and I could see them all giving me questioning looks.

"Shit," Devil said from beside me. "I was wondering where your anklet ran off to."

"Are you bloody joking!" Upper exclaimed. "We made a mistake?"

"Funny how that's what you're worried about when we will never get to see America ever again," Milk directed at Upper.

Dog groaned. "Would you shut the fuck up about America for one goddamn minute?"

Milk stood upright with a frown. "Don't tell me to shut up. You're the one who's been whining about being chained up."

"Guys—" Devil tried to cut in.

"How could we have made a mistake? How could we have missed something? That never happens," Upper mused out loud.

"Miss Hero probably took it off herself so she could sell us all out and keep the prize money for herself," Dog said.

The accusation slapped me in the face.

"You're *so* fucking stupid, Dog. I am trapped too! There's no way I can sneak my way out of this compound without being shot in the head. Besides, why would they leave the money back at the studio? It belongs to them now."

"Guys, stop—"

"Just like we belong to them, thanks to you!" Dog yelled back. "I don't give a fuck if he could have killed us all—I'd die happy knowing that I didn't have to live my life committing crimes for anyone again."

"Me too; you also kind of did bring the idea to go for Marino, so . . ." Milk added.

I let out a humorless laugh. "Oh, you guys are ungrateful pieces of shit. I really should have just let every single one of us die because I can't believe I brought down my fucking pride, begging for our lives, only to survive this shit to see how fucking terrible the people I consider family are!"

Dog glared. "Don't you fucking pull the family card because that doesn't have shit to do with—"

"It has *everything* to do with—"

"I can't believe we made a mistake—"

"It was supposed to be our vacation time—"

"Time-out! Time-fucking-out!" Devil yelled, and I almost jumped out of my skin. "We have bigger fish to fry, okay? The last thing we should be worried about is the mistake we made, or the stupid vacation, or the life sentence, or our fucking pride.

We're here, and that's done. We should be thinking about how to keep our heads above water."

Dog shook his head, returning to stand behind the counter, rubbing his palm down his face as the quietness seeped in.

"I don't care what any of you think you know, but E—Marino—is not a merciful man. Do you think he would just send someone to shoot you if he wanted to kill you? No, he would send people to do it slowly and painfully until you beg for death. Zahra saved us from that shit—"

"I don't need you to—"

"Would you keep quiet?"

I glared.

"No matter how angry we are right now, I have no doubt we would have done the same thing if we were put in that position. It's who we are. We are family. We do our best to make sure we survive to see another day. Just because we're here now doesn't mean our life is done. We're smart; we're fucking *Street*. There's no way we aren't going to wiggle out of this. I can't guarantee our freedom if we turn our backs on each other now, if we point fingers, fight, and hold grudges. We need to trust each other now more than ever."

He was right, and I felt the anger that had been boiling in my blood dissipate. The solemn looks on everyone's faces also said Devil's word had hit home.

"So, what's next?" Upper asked from where he stood.

"We wait," Devil said.

I nodded. "Observe and listen."

"And after we've observed and waited?" Dog asked me.

"Then we do what we do best," I said, looking over at Devil.

Jaw locked, he said, "We scheme."

CHAPTER FIVE

Zahra

It was one thing to jump into danger when you were the one putting yourself in it, and it was another thing to be running—or in my current situation—walking towards the danger when you have no control of the situation.

Angelo—the guy The Wicked had called into the torture oven—had arrived a few minutes before at the quarters where we were kept. He led us to another building in the compound, and now we were walking down a very long hallway. Men were everywhere, coming in and out of rooms you would never have guessed were rooms.

"Just how big is this place?" Upper asked, breaking the tense silence.

"It's never-ending," Milk added, but her voice was small.

"We're almost there," Angelo said.

We had passed through a large hall to get here, and it was littered with soldiers walking around, all distracted with individual tasks. My eyes quickly scanned the layout of the space, mapping out every possible corner that could be used as an escape or a hiding spot.

Beside me, Devil wore one of those expressions that once had me raising my guard. I could tell he was prepping his front, but I didn't understand why he was so tense. Maybe he was scared? But putting Devil and that word together didn't make sense.

I wanted to hold his hand, squeeze it to let him know that we were all here, we were all still alive. But I held back because we didn't do that, and I would be a hypocrite because I was also in my head—for completely different reasons. I balled my hand up in a fist and steadied my breathing, calming myself.

Before I could register the faint sound of music, the men on each side of Angelo were pushing open double doors, and we were entering a different space and time. It looked like we had somehow teleported into a casino in Las Vegas. The club was bright, with white, red, and golden lights dancing around, different gambling tables, and seats filled by money-hungry people.

I felt warmth encasing my free, uninjured hand, and I tore my gaze from my surroundings and looked up at Devil. He squeezed my hand in his and bent to whisper in my ear. "You okay?"

I answered with a stiff nod. "Are you?"

He answered with an equally stiff nod.

"It's like a fucking sin bin," I heard Dog say, but I didn't turn around. My nerves were too raw to fully comprehend the chaotic surroundings. Angelo led us up a staircase, which led to a more secluded area that gave way to yet another hallway.

My anticipation grew, and my stomach tightened, but it was a feeling I could control, and Devil's hand in mine had me relaxing a little; I could only hope he felt the same relief.

Almost as if he had heard my thoughts, he squeezed my hand again before letting go the moment Angelo stopped in front of a door, using a key card to unlock it.

We walked into a large area that looked like a VIP apartment with an office, a boardroom, and a library. I noticed the men who followed Angelo had stopped at the door as we continued inside, the door closing behind us.

In the middle of the room was a long conference table surrounded by black leather seats. There was soft classical music in the air, smooth yet unnerving.

At the head of the table was none other than The Wicked himself, *Elio Marino*. He was holding a book, the hardcover a plain black. He wore reading glasses, and between his lips, a Cuban cigar rested, burning away slowly.

His black button-up had been rolled up to his elbows, showcasing the tattoos on his left forearm.

I couldn't tell what the drawings were, but they looked like flames. I averted my gaze to the man sitting by his side. His eyes had been on us the moment we stepped into the room, calculating and scanning us like he was dissecting us limb by limb, to see if it was clinically safe to be in the same space with us.

My eyes shifted back to Elio, whose tattooed, ring-bound fingers moved to take the cigar from between his lips. He blew out the smoke as he closed the book and set it on the table.

Angelo cleared his throat, taking his seat. "You can sit; the chairs don't bite."

Devil moved first, pulling out a seat, and we all followed, doing the same.

Milk leaned into me as she whispered, motioning to the shelf, "So many books with the same black hardcovers. It's creepy."

My gaze moved to the shelves lining the walls. The spines were all black, hardcover spines, similar to the one he had been reading.

"They are personalized versions of every popular book you can think of," Elio said, and my gaze snapped to him as Milk stiffened beside me.

His reading glasses were still on his face. The moment he pressed the cigar into the ashtray before him, he raised his gaze, his eyes locking with mine. My stomach jumped, but I didn't look away.

He shifted his attention to Milk, who still sat frozen beside me. "The color of your hair is pink, yes?"

She was like stone now, nervousness pouring off her in waves. Fuck. We really shouldn't have spent last night rehashing what this man was capable of. "Y-yes."

Dog looked irritated and I knew he was thinking that she was making us look weak. Upper just sat there stunned, probably waiting for the other shoe to drop. Devil was tenser than he had been before we got here.

Elio hummed. "Your hair is beautiful; what is your name?" he asked.

"Um . . . Milk?" she answered, confusion lacing her tone.

Elio's head tilted toward the other—which I guessed was the Casmiro who knows best—for confirmation of Milk's name.

"An alias," Casmiro confirmed, making me frown. "You want the real one?"

Milk's breathing quickened.

"No. I like Milk better. It's very . . . soft," Elio said, taking off his glasses and arranging them carefully beside the book before he looked at Milk again. "To kill your curiosity, *Milk*. My books are all black because I do not fancy colors and black is the absence of all colors."

"White is also the absence of all colors," I said before I could catch my tongue, and his gaze shifted to me, then to my arm as if to remind me what had happened the last time I contradicted something he said. But I didn't back down. "Green is also the absence of all colors; basically, all colors are the absence of all other colors, so how can you say you do not *fancy* colors in general?"

His right brow lifted. But he didn't break eye contact, and I refused to look away, either. I noticed the music in the background beginning to ascend slowly.

"Aside from stealing money from people who can kill you, you like physics too," he said.

"It wasn't a physics question."

"It sounded that way to me."

"You just didn't make any sense. I was only trying to understand you."

From the corner of my eye I could see Casmiro's eyes widen and Angelo shift uncomfortably.

"I didn't make any sense," Elio stated as if testing the words on his tongue.

"Yes, you—"

"Zahra." Devil's voice came out in a low hum of warning.

"What? I was only pointing out what I thought was an error of thought. Isn't that allowed around here?" I raised a brow, looking around like we had an actual audience, before meeting Elio's gaze again.

The silence stretched, and I was glad because I saw the shift in his eyes.

The man was . . . *angry*.

"Seriously, cut it out," Devil said.

I felt the fear I'd once harbored slipping away as control took over.

I counted up to five in my head before looking away from him, and the moment I did, Upper spoke up. "I think Zahra's right."

"Fucking hell," Devil whispered under his breath.

"The color green is the absence of all colors, pink too, brown, yellow—all of the bloody colors, so like—black, they all stand on their own."

"Isn't black a shade?" Dog piped up, and I smiled, leaning back on the chair, glad everything was playing out how my mind wanted it to. "I read once that black and white aren't colors but shades?"

"What the fuck is the difference, Dog?" Upper countered.

"I'm here wondering how Dog got that information," Milk added.

"Found some textbooks in a dumpster once. One was about all the fucking colors; I don't even know why I read that shit. I don't know why it stuck too."

"We're all gonna die," Devil muttered again.

"Black and white are augmented colors. Not like the other colors; they're like the parents of all colors," Milk said, nodding as if she was only just understanding what she said.

"Colors don't have parents, Milk. You're an airhead," Upper said.

"You're the airhead if you don't understand simple metaphors, Upper."

"I know bloody metaphors; I went to school, unlike you and these other shitheads."

"When the fuck did you have the time to go to school?" Dog asked.

"We're all dead." Devil rubbed both his eyes in defeat as he shook his head, the music in the background ascending even further.

"He probably climbed up school roofs and hid in their ventilators just to attend classes," Milk said with a smart-ass smile curling her lips.

Upper's jaw clenched. "Fine, you fuckers, I climbed up a few ventilators, so bloody what? I'm still fucking educated, better than the lot of you."

"I read actual books from the trash and still remembered deets from them—fuck. If I had finished school, I would have been one smart motherfucker," Dog said.

"You're pretty good with numbers," I mused.

"I'm a fucking genius with numbers," he corrected me, and the room went silent again, followed by the music in the background descending.

I sat up, finally looking back at Elio, Casmiro, and Angelo.

Elio still had a look of indifference on his face, but his gaze was sweeping over our little group with wonder. Casmiro's jaw was hanging open, and Angelo just sat there, eyes wide, a slight smile curling at his lips.

I cleared my throat. "There you have it, we're Street." Then I let my taunting stare settle on Elio as I said, "It is only right to prepare your family for what awaits you, as you've decided to consider my request."

Elio was silent for a few moments before he spoke. "What makes you think I've considered it?"

"I'm still breathing," I answered without blinking.

"And I'm beginning to think Casmiro knows best after all."

At the mention of his name, Casmiro cleared his throat. "I was wrong. I think they're perfect," he said.

"Just because that one crawled up a vent like a deranged rat?"

Devil sighed. "I think what Casmiro is trying to say is, because Upper crawled up a vent for years and got a full education without being *seen*."

Elio's gaze snapped in Devil's direction, and I saw that shift in his eyes again; the look was an obvious dare, almost as if he was daring Devil to speak again.

I could swear I saw Devil roll his eyes as he relaxed back in his chair, crossing his arms against his chest, looking straight ahead, his jaw locked.

What the fuck was that?

Elio's gaze rested on me. "Your introduction was comical but not appreciated."

My gaze flickered between him and Devil before I responded, "I beg to differ; if we're going to work together, you should know who you're dealing with."

Casmiro frowned at my tone. "Or maybe you have forgotten how you got here. You work *for* us now, not *with* us. There is a big difference."

"I know, but just because we work *for* you doesn't mean we change how we work. Or the way we communicate with each other; getting engrossed in a stupid argument when our lives are in danger is how we work well together."

"It's the only way we can function, honestly," Dog added.

Upper nodded. "Chaos is Street."

"And it's kind of fun"—Milk blinked—"most times."

Elio's gaze settled on each of us—except Devil—before he relit the cigar he'd discarded, placing it between his lips. I watched him take a long drag and let it out slowly, tormentingly, before he finally spoke. "Why don't we test that theory?"

CHAPTER SIX

Elio

I should have killed the short one when I had the opportunity. While audacious, she constantly placed her foot in her mouth.

Aggravating.

I looked away from her to take them all in individually. I could tell they had a tight-knit relationship, built on trust and relatable life experiences.

My gaze moved to *Devil,* and my stomach curled. Was this a feeling of irritation—or anger—or was I simply reacting negatively to the countless cigars I had smoked today?

"Should I proceed?" Casmiro asked, and I nodded once, my gaze shifting to the short one again when I caught movement from her end. Her face was pulled up in a tight frown, her posture rigid as Casmiro stood up to retrieve whatever case file he had put together about their first task.

I tuned him out, choosing some time alone in my own head to study these people, starting with the one who claimed to speak for this . . . band of thieves: Zahra Faizan, a twenty-six-year-old woman whose mouth spoke before her brain filtered the words, a woman whose eyes remained impossible to read. Her looks were deceiving, with a diamond-shaped face, and curly dark brown hair cut below her jaw; careless and uncared for, she looked too innocent for the character she portrayed.

It disturbed me. Her appearance. Her face, her hair—if my mother were here, she would have whipped out a brush and styled the hell out of it—though the color suited the warm undertones of her light brown skin and sharp brown eyes. That pointed nose and those full lips—her gaze caught mine, and her frown deepened, her upper lip turning up in an irritated snare as she raised a brow as if to ask why I was staring.

Quite fascinating.

The fear I saw the other day was gone. It made me question if that emotion had been fear or defeat. Over the years in this business, I'd learned that there was an extensive line between those two feelings.

"Marino?" I caught myself, blinking before looking away from Zahra to Angelo, who wore a cautious look on his face while Casmiro stared with slight concern.

"What?" I asked them, discarding the cigar.

"Oh." Angelo cleared his throat. "You were supposed to update me on Dion Juan Pablo's next visit to Lazzo Blu, but I never heard—"

"In three weeks. It should give the girl's shoulder time to heal so it won't raise suspicions."

From the corner of my eye, I saw her raise her hand like she wanted to ask a question, and this was a classroom. "The name's Zahra, in case you've forgotten. I know old age can be a bitch."

I paused.

Annoyance and irritation had me clenching my jaw.

I looked back at her. "Don't force me to make the unpleasant thoughts running through my head a reality."

She dropped her hand. "Maybe when you start addressing me by my name, you won't have to harbor unpleasant thoughts, or kill me, which would eventually result in you killing us all, and then who would help you with whatever you need to get from Dion Juan Pablo, who, mind you, isn't going to be at Lazzo Blu, but at Eden, because he probably knows people like you would want to pay him a little visit, hence why everyone who isn't us would think he would be at Lazzo Blu."

"Hold on; you know Dion Juan Pablo?" Casmiro asked.

"Uh . . ." the Upper one said. "He's kind of like a public

figure? You lot know what the gram is, right? He posts everything about his life there. We also happen to know through the gram that he is gunning for control over state affairs in Turin, and of course, we know it's for the Pablos, and they'll most likely handle private affairs; the people don't know that though, hence why there's massive support from them because he markets himself as a people person."

"Dion is also a very cunning and foolish man, getting high on his drug supply," Devil added, "while boning for the power at the high seats, just like Marino is. And we know how difficult it is to breach his walls."

"For your people, not for us," Zahra completed.

Then there was silence, save for the ticking of the grandfather clock behind me, as we all watched each other until—

"And we killed his dog."

"Oh my fucking God, Milk," Dog said.

"You just had to contribute," Zahra said.

"Why would you say that?" Upper said.

"Fucking hell, Milk," Devil said.

They all spoke in sync.

"What!" Milk whined in defense. "I thought we were all saying stuff we knew about Dion."

Zahra groaned. "Not that kinda stuff."

"You killed his dog?" Angelo asked with confused amusement.

"It was an honest mistake. I sincerely thought it was dog food, and the big guy was giving me the *I am hungry* eyes. *Please feed me, kind lady;* what the hell was I to do, leave it to starve?"

"Yes," they all chorused at the same time.

"That would have been cruel."

"And accidentally killing it wasn't?" Upper voiced.

"At least I tried to feed it; what did you do, Upper?"

Upper gasped. "He sniffed the bloody cocaine. How was I supposed to know dogs love sniffing things."

"You can ask the one beside you." Devil pointed to Dog, who allowed a small unfeeling smile onto his lips before raising his middle finger at Devil, who answered with an appreciative nod.

Milk scoffed. "Maybe the thingy in the can wasn't what killed it; the cocaine probably did, so technically, Upper and I murdered Dion's dog. Don't blame me because I'm the only girl in the group."

Zahra blinked in shock, shooting Milk a look of disbelief before Milk corrected herself by saying, "Yeah, and Zahra too."

Devil bit back a laugh, which earned him a glare from Zahra.

"Okay, so what I'm getting from this is that you all have seen Dion and have some kind of *personal* relationship with him?" Casmiro asked.

"No, man." Dog answered this time. "We have *seen* Dion, yes . . . but he's never *seen* us. No one ever sees us."

I shook my head at this *group*. "But, somehow, you managed to enter his home and harm his dog," I stated, very confused.

"We were pursuing a lead for a mission. But we did also go there for free food and the amazing bathtub he announced on his socials; we stayed for just two hours . . . wasn't anything personal," Dog answered.

"They're serious; they actually killed the dog. Dion held a funeral for it," Angelo said, his eyes glued to whatever article he read on his phone.

I took in a breath and then let it out. "I'm afraid your first mission for me would require some of you letting Dion see you. Are you certain Dion will be at Eden?"

"We are," Devil answered.

I nodded, thoughts filtering through my head before finally letting out the less obnoxious one. "Then that's where he's stationing for his stay. Dion is probably the only man with power who surrounds himself with incompetent soldiers because he is ignorant."

"That I can agree on," Dog said.

Angelo sat up. "Our people would need direct intel on him

and the entire Pablo syndicate. We want to see and hear everything, from their business meetings to past and present associations and collaborations, legal and illegal; everything. We need a chain, and we need them not to notice until we are done with them. This means an invisible non-existing server they would never be able to trace back to Marino. Can your team arrange that?"

"It's possible," Upper said, looking at Dog. "Right?"

Dog's gaze settled on Zahra, and I looked back in her direction to find her deep in thought before she looked up. "It is possible. But our method is to *not* be seen. I'm finding it hard to understand what you meant by Dion seeing some of us?"

My tongue poked the inside of my cheek as I thought about her question. "Dion's only going to see what we want him to. I would assume your team is well-versed in creating narratives."

"We are," Milk said.

"So"—Devil leaned forward, eyes locking with mine—"you want to get into Pablo's affairs. That can be arranged. We'll relay the plan to Angelo once we have it. But the sooner we can get started, the better. Permission to leave?"

"Permission granted," I said, and he began to stand before I added, "for everyone but you."

He winced, closing his eyes and letting out a silent curse before sitting back down and turning to a confused Zahra and an even more confused crew. "It's okay, guys. I'll catch up."

Zahra glanced at me, the frown still on her face.

"Z, I'll explain later—leave; I promise I'll come back alive."

"Don't make promises you can't keep," I said, eyeing the two of them.

Zahra's scowl deepened as she got up, signaling to the others to do the same.

I watched them all file out before looking over at Casmiro and Angelo and raising a brow.

Casmiro frowned. "Us too?"

"Yes, Casmiro."

His eyes shifted between Devil and me before he asked, "Is everything good?"

"Everything is perfect," I answered.

"Okay," Casmiro said, nodding to Angelo as they both walked to the door before Casmiro turned back to me. "Hey, if he tries—"

"If he tries to stab me in the neck, I'll cry for help; now leave." My knee was bouncing rapidly underneath the table.

Rolling his eyes, he and Angelo walked out. I allowed a minute of silence, closed my eyes, and let out a long, controlled breath before speaking.

"What the *fuck* have you gotten yourself into, Elia?"

CHAPTER SEVEN

Elio

I found out my father was having an affair when I was eight.

And when I was nine, I saw my half-brother for the first time. Father had named him Elia; he was so tiny, fragile, and innocent. I used to be angry that my father had forgotten his vow to my mother. I knew he lacked common morals, but I'd always respected that even though he didn't show it, he loved my mother—well, until the day I saw him kissing a dark-haired woman in his car.

My father told me that no matter what I did, I couldn't tell my mother, my sister, or my brother that we had another blood relative. I felt guilty whenever my father would take me to see Elia, guilty that my family didn't get to meet him, to see how precious he was, and guilty for denying Elia the opportunity to meet them.

I vowed that one day I would get my father out of my head, and I would make sure everyone knew about Elia. I swore that I'd give Elia a chance to know my family; but that was until my father decided he didn't want anything to do with Elia nor his mother after he found out Elia's mother had seen something she shouldn't have, and the next solution he could come up with was to get rid of them.

I was fifteen, and Elia was just six when we watched my father and his mother lash each other with words, a scenario that led to a bullet right between her eyes. It took me a good two minutes to remember Elia wasn't supposed to see that, but before I could shield his eyes from his mother's lifeless body, he'd seen it all. But I still held him, and my grip tightened when my father turned his furious and sick gaze to us, pointing the gun in Elia's direction.

"Step away, Elio," my father had said, his voice molded with hatred and determination. "I don't want you stained with the sinner's blood."

I remember how the gun resting at the back of my pants burned at my skin. I wanted to shoot him—to kill my father. The urge was strong, but I knew I couldn't do it. I'd never killed anyone; I didn't have the guts to do it.

"Move, Elio," he said with an impatience that had me blurting out the first words I could think of.

"I'll do it."

My father raised his brow in confusion and question. "Repeat that."

I gulped, my form rigid with panic and decision. "I will kill him myself." I lifted my chin and hardened my gaze. "No one betrays Marino and lives. The sinner doesn't exist if your bullet ends up in them."

My father studied me for eight damning seconds before lowering his gun and slowly walking over to me. He placed his hand on my shoulder, and I was baffled at how I didn't jump out of my skin.

He looked me in the eye as he said, "I renounce Elia as my flesh and blood. When you kill him, you kill the last of his bloodline."

I gave a single firm nod.

"I am proud of you, Elio. Make sure I see proof."

"I will, sir."

He nodded and looked at Elia in disgust. His gaze was hard enough that I visibly flinched, and then he was gone.

I released a breath, my ears ringing in alarm because I knew I wouldn't do it—but I knew coming to a decision about Elia was inevitable. I knew I had to provide proof. I knew I needed a bucket full of luck if I wanted to save Elia's life—and I did save him, but it came at a cost I knew I would never be able to pay, and a part of me I knew I would never be able to get back.

I learned three things that day. My father was a sinner, and like the many he killed, he also didn't deserve to live, but unfortunately, the same now applied to me.

"Good to see you too, Elio," Elia said.

I studied him. I'd kept tabs on him—discreetly—over the years. And I'd refrained from reaching out and compromising in my goals. Still, I felt a hollow, sinking feeling in my chest sitting across from him now.

I shot to my feet, stepping away from the table and turned my back to him. A tense silence lingered as I massaged the side of my head. "How long have you been in Italy?" I finally asked him.

"Does it matter? I'm here now." His voice was unconcerned. I heard his chair shift.

I turned to find him standing there, no expression on his face and both hands shoved into his pockets.

"Answer the question, Elia."

"I go by Devil now," he snapped, and I felt that coil in my stomach again.

"How *long* have you been in Italy?"

He squared his jaw. "Twelve years."

"Twelve—" I deflated, looking at him with disbelief. "*Twelve* years, Elia? How do I not know this?"

He shrugged. "According to your intel, I'm probably on my way home from work in Los Angeles. You're not the only smart person in the room, Elio."

"You think this is smart?"

He gave another nonchalant shrug; anger blinded me, and I was walking towards him. He stood taller, fear in his eyes as he inched backward. It was a small flinch, but I felt the effect of it roll down my chest. "You think I will hurt you?"

"I don't know what to think. I don't know you."

"Elia—"

"It's Devil," he gritted.

"You are not supposed to be here. Los Angeles was *perfect* for you. You could have it all, a normal life, a clean record—"

"I don't have any records; I'm practically a nobody. You made sure of that."

"To protect you, Elia. I did it all to protect you from this. And you—a common thief? Stealing from me? I would give you whatever it was in a heartbeat. Why did you have to pull up with this so-called *gang*? To rob me, your family?"

"You are not my family. As far as I'm concerned, that so-called *gang* is my family. They would never abandon or erase me to make things more convenient for them."

"I never abandoned you. I protected you from me, from this, from my father. You're my only living flesh and blood; I don't want you to walk the path I have walked, Elia. You deserve all that is good. A clean life. Not *this*." I shook my head in indignation. "I never wanted this for you."

"You don't get to *want* things for me, Elio. I'm not some dumb kid anymore. The last time I saw you physically, I was ten fucking years old. You were my brother, the only person I knew, the only person I loved, my only family, and all I asked—all I asked was for you not to let me go, and you fucking promised me you wouldn't send me away. You gave me your word. And then I woke up in Los Angeles—"

"Elia—"

"You don't get to fucking talk about family when you won't even tell anyone that I am your blood. When you're ashamed of me." He laughed humorlessly. "I used to make excuses for you, you know? I used to think, maybe he did it because he was scared of his father; maybe he did it because my life would have been in danger. But then I heard the news—about the fire. Lorenzo and Mariana."

Pain held and squeezed at my heart, and I waited for what came next.

"How you fucking burned them alive . . . and stabbed the mother you claimed to love. Then I realized maybe you are just like him—*worse* than him—and then I beat myself up every day for believing what could have been lies because the person I knew would never do anything like that. But then again, he would also never break his promise to me, but he did."

The silence that stretched between us after he said that was a long, tension-filled one, but after a while, I nodded, forcing on a look of indifference while taking steps away from him to the minibar on the side.

When I turned, I stretched my neck muscles from left to right, proceeding to pour myself a drink, and then leaned an elbow on the counter, drink in hand, as I watched him.

"You're angry."

"No shit, fucking Sherlock."

I nodded. "What do you want me to do about it?"

He frowned. "What?"

"You want me to apologize for abandoning you, hm? You want me to hug you and tell you how much you mean to me? To beg you to go back to Los Angeles, live your best life, and stay away from crime?"

He didn't respond, but his eyes flared.

"By all means, *Devil*. Carry on with your thieving addiction and the little minions you consider family. But remember that I own you now—not as a brother, but as a man who stole from me. You want to separate yourself from me, tell me you don't know me—fine, I have no problem with that because, honestly, it gives me one less thing to worry about."

"I'm good with that," he bit out.

Taking a sip from my glass, I began walking toward him again, this time getting in his face. He didn't flinch.

"I am glad you are good with it. Do you know why?"

His nose flared.

"Because I won't have to think of you when I put a bullet in the head of one of your *family*—when I kill them right in front of your eyes, slowly—very slowly because I would desire for you to hear them scream while their lives slip away from their eyes, and then after I've done that"—I inched closer to him, directing my mouth to his ear—"I'll point a gun to your fucking head and do what I should have done years ago. I'm sure your cunt of a mother would appreciate it."

He shoved me so hard that the glass fell from my hand, shattering on the ground. The shout of anger from Elia was the only warning I got before he pounced on me, and we both fell to the ground.

When his fist connected with my face, I let it happen. I let him hit me repeatedly, and when he yelled, "Fight back!" I didn't protect myself from him; I allowed him to inflict what little damage he could. I let him pour out his anger.

I let him take what he wanted from me.

Only a few seconds later did the sound of the door busting open reach my ears, and then Elia was being hurled away from me.

About a dozen men were in the room; Casmiro pointed his gun at Elia's head.

"Don't you dare!" My voice boomed through the space. Everyone except Elia looked confused.

I jumped to my feet like a madman; my heart was racing, my whole body vibrating with anger and—and *fear*. Suddenly I was fifteen years old again, and there was a gun pointed at my brother.

Quickly, I pulled him behind me, putting myself between him and Casmiro's gun.

Immediately, Casmiro lowered his gun, and so did the other men around him.

"Anyone who touches a hair on his head will not live to see the second after. That's a fucking promise."

My breathing was harsh, the panic inside me uncurling. Fifteen-year-old Elio was back in my body, and the image of my father was as clear as day in my head: his gun—Elia's small frame—the tangy smell of blood coming from his dead mother.

Elia yanked his hand away from my hold and bolted from the office without a second glance our way.

I tried to calm my breathing—I tried to count in my head like I used to do all those years ago—but I suddenly forgot how to count, I forgot numbers—I forgot everything. My name, where I was, who I was—everything. My brain was completely empty.

"E, what the fuck just happened? How—"

"Out." My voice was clipped, short, and unfamiliar.

"What—"

"Out—everyone, get the hell out. Now."

I heard footsteps retreating, followed by the sound of the door closing and then . . . silence.

I sank to my knees, unable to stand any longer. My hands shook and my breathing was short.

I squeezed my eyes shut, willing myself to remember how to count again—but I couldn't. I felt like a stranger in my own body, and I craved a sense of familiarity more than I craved air at this moment.

When I opened my eyes, my gaze came in contact with the first comfortable thing my brain could register.

I sighed in relief as I dragged myself forward and picked up a triangle-shaped shard of glass.

CHAPTER EIGHT

Zahra

"It's almost as if they stocked this place knowing I would come," Dog said, taking the fresh beef out of the freezer. Milk helped herself to sliced vegetables while Upper and I sat at the kitchen table.

Dog dropped the meat on the table, slapping it almost sexually, before giving me a silly wink.

"You're gross," I told him.

"You love it." He grinned.

"So according to my info, Dion has changed his bodyguards three times in the last two months," Upper cut in, adjusting his glasses as he clicked open another window on his laptop screen—they must have searched our studio apartment because we were provided with all our gadgets the moment we returned from the meeting with Elio.

I jotted down that information. The only reason he changed his bodyguards was because of the three consecutive attempts that had been made on his life in the past four months.

His paranoia was probably responsible for why he changed his bodyguards. He trusted no one—not his mother, not his boss, not even his right-hand man. Getting to him might be hard.

"That's suspicious," Milk said as she gathered chopped vegetables into a bowl. "Intuition tells me he wasn't just annoyed one of them had a mole on the face."

Dog nodded. "They probably weren't as guard-y as their resumes implied."

"Or he just didn't trust them," I contributed, toying with the pen in my good hand.

"They made him feel unsafe," Upper reasoned. "Can't be a coincidence Marino wants intel on the Pablos now. Dion's the weakest link, and Marino probably tried to take him out, hence the change in bodyguards? The *why* could possibly be a very bloody impending hostile takeover."

My tongue poked the inside of my mouth, knowing the threats on his life had nothing to do with Marino.

"That or Marino is interested in the same reason we paid Dion a visit," Milk said.

I halted my toying with the pen, my brows dropping. We had gotten a private mission months ago to find a painting, but after we got paid, the client disappeared, so we couldn't get more information about the mission, and Dion's lead was a dead end . . .

Dog frowned, shaking his head. "I doubt it. What the fuck would The Wicked want with some dumb painting of a chihuahua, and why would he kill for it? At least with Dion we know he's a big lover of dogs, hence why our lead for the painting got him on our radar in the first place."

"Marino doesn't exactly scream 'dog lover' to me," Upper said.

"So it's gotta be something else then," Milk concluded.

I blinked, coming out of my thoughts. "Who knows? It's better not to get involved in their shit and just get the job done."

"On a scale of one to ten, what are our chances of actually pulling this off?" Dog asked.

"A ten. It's not the hardest job we've ever done," I answered.

"But it's the only job where we'd be seen for the first time," Milk said.

"Disguise has never hurt anyone," Upper responded, looking up from the laptop with a double take towards the front door. His brows drew down in a concerned frown, and I followed his gaze to find Devil walking towards us. His features were tight, frown hard, and knuckles . . . bruised.

Silence settled as he walked past Upper and me, and then around the kitchen counter to the fridge. Wordlessly, he opened it, grabbed a beer bottle, uncapped it with his teeth, and took a big gulp before he walked out of the kitchen without acknowledging any of us.

"Something's up." Milk's voice came out in a whisper.

"Boy's fuming," Dog pointed out.

I got off the stool the same moment Upper did. "I'll check—" we said simultaneously, and I paused, frowning in confusion at him.

Upper blinked before gingerly sitting back down, clearing his throat, and adjusting his glasses. "I was—I was only curious. You know me. Sticking my nose in everybody's bloody business is my forte."

"No, it's not," Milk stated.

He blinked again, unable to mask his fluster. "Well—I'm making it my bloody forte now." He looked around the kitchen before his eyes settled on Milk. "Why . . . are you . . . wearing that pink shirt? Why didn't you wear another bloody color? See, that's me being in your bloody business—"

"Do you know you use the word *bloody* excessively whenever you're trying to lie your way out of something you don't want others knowing?" Dog said.

"I don't bloody do that," he responded, then blinked in a pause.

Dog's lips thinned as he nodded. "We'll pretend you didn't just prove me right."

"I'll go check on him," I said, ignoring Upper and his weirdness as I made my way to the room he shared with Devil.

The door was wide open, and he was sitting at the edge of his bed, head downcast, holding the beer bottle in a tight grip.

I knocked gently, and he raised his head, haunted eyes locking with mine. "I don't wanna talk."

I sighed. "It's unfair to tell me that when you look like you want to spill your guts, Devil."

He looked away, staring at the wall as if he were trying to burn a hole through it.

I walked into the room, sitting beside him, and letting out a shaky breath. "What happened?"

"Can't talk about it."

I shifted slightly. "Did he . . . make another bargain? Threaten us? If it's about—"

"It's not about you or Street. Just forget it; I can't talk about it, Z."

I was confused. What could they have talked about? What could Elio have said to Devil to get him in this mood?

Could it be . . .

"Wait—did he tell you shit about who you are? Because in that meeting, it seemed like they knew us—like they dug deep into our background and probably knew stuff we don't even know about ourselves. Is that what this is about?"

He closed his eyes, letting out a slow, steady breath, almost like he was trying to calm himself. "No, Zahra."

"Then what the hell happened? Why do you look like you're stopping yourself from punching something?"

"Drop it, Z. I said I didn't want to talk about it." His voice was heavy yet cutting.

"You can't expect me to just ignore—"

He turned sharply to me. "You know, just because we fuck from time to time doesn't mean you get to push when I *clearly* don't want to talk about something."

I backed up at the bite in his voice, ignoring how his words poked the wrong nerve, before speaking again. "I care, Devil; *that's* why I'm here."

"Then don't fucking care. I didn't ask for it; we don't have that kind of relationship, so what the fuck is this?"

His gaze searched mine, silently pleading for me to stop trying to get through to him, to turn around like I usually did. To pretend that I cared but not do anything about it because it would complicate things.

"Okay," I said softly, getting to my feet.

His jaw clenched as he watched me with glassy eyes.

I brushed my hair away from my face. "When you feel better, join us for dinner; we're looking over some details about Dion. Um . . . just—feel better because we need your head in the game."

When he didn't respond, I moved for the door, but his hand gripped my wrist, stopping me before I could walk past him. I turned to see him drop the beer bottle on the ground before pulling me to his lap. "I'm sorry. I didn't mean for it to come out like that. I just—"

"I know—"

"No—it's not as if I don't want to talk about it . . . I do; I really fucking want to tell you everything, to tell someone—it's just—he won't let me. I'm not allowed to; I've never been allowed to."

I was more confused but knew not to push it, so I just nodded and asked, "Is this thing—bad? Like, does it put you in any sort of danger?"

He shook his head. "No." Then he chuckled sadly before releasing a sigh. "I think it's the only reason we are still breathing."

"Is it . . . personal?"

He squared his jaw before nodding.

"Does it answer why you somehow know every nook and cranny of this whole compound?"

He hesitated before nodding again.

"Did you punch him?" I asked.

"Several times, yes."

I smiled sadly at him, wrapping my good arm around him in a hug. "Good," I whispered, and he held me tighter. I buried my head in the crook of his neck, breathing him in.

He didn't have to tell me. It was pretty obvious—either they were very close friends or . . . they were family.

There was only one way to confirm this, and it made me look forward to when it would be dark again.

"This won't . . . complicate things, will it? . . . Between us?" he asked.

I chuckled, raising my head to meet his gaze, my knuckle coming to graze his cheek. "I don't know why we're so scared of that. I mean, I care about you, and you care about me. This crew, we care about each other, and though we have other stuff going on, it shouldn't stop us from showing support when any of us are in need of it."

He nodded.

I brushed his hair back. "I know how these things work, how feelings could get mixed up, how we could ruin our friendship . . . but I just don't see it happening with us, do you?"

His lips curled in a smile. "No. You're my best friend, Zahra. I don't want to lose this too. Maybe that's why I don't want to blur the line. I need you."

I leaned in to press a kiss to his lips, before brushing my thumb softly against the bottom one. "I'm here," I whispered. "I'll always be here for you. I might not know the right thing to say, but I can listen, and I can hold you, and you can cry if that's what you want; I'd never tell anyone."

"But then you'd have something to hold against me."

I smiled. "I have to get you in line one way or another, Devil."

His forehead rested on mine as he closed his eyes, breathed, and swallowed. "You already have me in line."

Escaping the soldiers assigned to watch our building was the easy part. The hardest part was climbing up the stairs to the roof, where I had spotted Elio from Upper's—unauthorized—access to the Marino security feeds.

Who in their right mind would build a place as high as this, without an elevator or even a fucking stair railing for people who have fucking anxiety!

The moment I passed through the roof's door, I let out a breath of relief, willing my heart to return to its normal rhythm.

I stood still, peering through the darkness until I saw where Elio leaned against the bricked railing on the roof, his back to me.

He looked one with the night in his all-black attire. A black sweatshirt and pants.

The door to the rooftop closed behind me with a loud bang, but he didn't flinch, nor did he turn to me.

Was he careless or too confident no one could hurt him in his space?

It was cold up here, and I let a shiver run through me as I walked over to stand beside him.

He still didn't turn toward me, so I took that opportunity to study his profile. I watched as he blew thick white smoke into the air, the white streak snatched away by the wind, thinning as it danced into the dark depth of the night.

"Some would say it's foolish for a man like you to leave himself so vulnerable." I broke the silence, my gaze roaming over his face. He had a cut on his chin and a bruise underneath his eye.

Without so much as turning his head, he looked at me out of the corner of his eye. I could feel the impact of his attention even without the full force of it on me. I knew I wasn't all that tall, but even with that sideways glance he made me feel like a grain of rice atop his shoe. I couldn't help but take another step away instinctively.

He looked away, shaking his head as if he didn't have the physical or emotional capacity to entertain my presence.

There was something odd about his vibe; it made me want to leave him alone so he could continue to brood. Instead, I studied him, noting his dark hair, the same shade as Devil's, his full brows, the same curve as Devil's, and that nose, straight and perfect, maybe a little more perfect than Devil's. There was a resemblance, one I hadn't noticed before because I had no reason to try to find any similarities between the two men.

But it was apparent; they were family—brothers maybe . . .

half-brothers, because Devil's eyes were a dark brown while Elio's were an intense, smoky dark gray.

He cleared his throat, startling me.

"Your staring makes me very uncomfortable, and I am two seconds away from throwing you off this roof." He turned towards me fully, resting an elbow on the bricked railing. "How did you get up here?"

"The same way I stole from men like you without being caught all this time."

He frowned thoughtfully. "I can't help but notice . . . you have this . . . habit of repeating yourself. Is it a mental illness?"

"You asked me a question, I answered."

"Straight to defense. It's a sensitive subject, isn't it? You're ashamed of your mental illness. I understand, I won't judge you."

I fought the urge to catch his tongue and slice it off, but instead I shook my head, ignoring his sarcasm, and got straight to business. "You abandoned him, didn't you?"

I was hoping to get a reaction out of him, but his stare was blank.

"He told you."

"I figured it out. It was either an estranged friendship, exes with bad blood, or sibling abandonment. And seeing the distinct resemblance between you two, it wasn't hard to figure it out."

His face remained expressionless. He gazed off into the distance above my head for a beat or two before he looked me in the eye again. He brought the cigar to his lips, taking a long drag, which he never let out. As he spoke, puffs of smoke escaped his mouth. "Meddling in my private affairs will only get you killed faster than I initially planned. I'd suggest you forget everything you think you know and focus on why you're here."

"You hurt him; it's not something I can forget. He's my best friend and family—"

"You fuck your family?"

"And you abandon yours?" I shot back, unblinking.

Just one step, and he was towering over me, eyes hard. "I didn't abandon him; I was *protecting* him."

"There's a fat line between abandoning someone and protecting them. I don't know why you wanted to protect him, but you could have done that and still kept in touch; maybe then you both would welcome each other with a hug rather than a punch."

Something flashed in his eyes, and he backed up a step, shaking his head and turning to face the brick railing, bringing the cigar to his lips again.

It might be the wind, or maybe my eyes were playing tricks on me, but there was a slight tremor in his hands as he pointedly looked ahead into the distance.

I watched him blow out the smoke.

"You know those things tend to kill faster than weed, right?"

He glanced at me, took another drag, and muttered, "That's the point." The words were for himself, but I heard them, and I couldn't help but wonder what the hell he meant by that.

He wordlessly dropped the cigar on the ground beside him. He sighed, closing his eyes for a moment before looking at me, his jaw clenching and unclenching. "How is he? Still angry?"

I didn't know this man; I only knew *of* him. The whiplash I was getting from his behavior now was pretty concerning. The man I'd heard of wasn't capable of feeling; the man I feared wouldn't look so confused and—dare I say—lost. But the concern in his voice told me it wouldn't be wise to taunt him. Not now.

This has been a weird day—hell, this has been a weird week.

"I wouldn't say angry," I said, placing my good elbow on the brick railing too. "More like—sad. Hurt. Confused."

Elio nodded but kept quiet.

He clasped his hands together like he was in deep thought.

I stood there, wondering what the hell this was and why he hadn't tried to throw me off the roof or even told me to leave him alone. Then again, no matter how badly I wanted to stab him with a knife for shooting me, he looked even more disturbed than Devil. He was vulnerable, and this was an opportunity to get in his head . . . if that sort of thing was possible.

But I was going somewhere, now I knew he had a weak spot, a half-brother no one knew about . . . a half-brother I had wrapped around my fingers. Very useful leverage for the future.

CHAPTER NINE

Elio

I'd abandoned my brother.

No matter how much I tried to convince myself otherwise, I knew that was something I could never change.

I never considered how my actions would affect him. I was too blinded by revenge—too far gone in the grand finale I had planned, and I'd hoped he wouldn't care. Perhaps he would find his own life and wouldn't even shed a tear when everything was said and done. But I had been wrong. He cared, and it was a big problem.

Elia wasn't supposed to love me or hate me. How was I guaranteed that I could proceed with my plans without hurting the person I'd spent almost all my life protecting?

I felt her shift beside me, and I remembered I wasn't alone.

It irritated me, but all she had said was correct. Her accuracy was probably why I didn't bother to shield or deny anything.

"It wasn't my intention," I said into the silence between us. "All I wanted was to protect him from all of this. But then he met you and started to steal. And now he's here."

"Devil was the way he was before he met me. Hell, he was worse. He had so much anger and distrust. Street tamed him, tamed his anger, and you should be grateful for that."

I allowed my gaze to settle on her again; her hair was all over her face due to the light wind—so unkempt—but I couldn't look away. My fingers twitched to fix it. Clean it. Clean her.

"You shouldn't be here," I said.

"What?"

I watched her carefully, thinking once again about how fearless she seemed now, and something felt odd—misplaced—like I was missing something important. "You're here, talking to me . . . without fear after I tortured you. It makes no sense."

Something shifted in her gaze. "I'm tougher than I look, and now that I know what I know about you and Devil, I'm confident that I'm safe. Besides, I'm here because of him. Whatever argument the both of you had did a number on him."

"Do you have a hairband?" I asked before I could hold my tongue.

She raised a brow, clearly caught off guard. "What?"

"Your hair, it's distracting. Do you have a hair—hold on." I stood upright, digging my hand into my pants pocket, pulling out my packet of cigars, and removing the black band I'd wrapped around it.

The small band had been around a book whose hardcover had been falling off. I'd wrapped the band around my cigar packet when I glued it back. "Come here," I said, twisting the band around my fingers. I made a turning gesture with my hand.

"Why the—" She started to protest but stopped when I walked towards her instead. I made sure I was not too close for both her and my comfort.

She looked up at me with wide brown eyes, her lashes long and tangled, her nose and cheeks dusted with light freckles that suited her skin tone.

I ignored the heat between our bodies, the gentle hollow where her collar bones met the smooth skin of her neck, as I began to brush her hair away from her face; I tucked both sides behind her ears, catching the two-dotted birthmark on the shell of her left ear, and the tiny scar right below her right. Slowly, her frown eased.

I tilted my head slightly to the side as my fingers disappeared into her hair.

I was wrong.

Earlier, at that meeting, I thought her hair was uncared for—but I was very wrong. It had a fullness that made me bury my fingers even deeper.

It was soft, wavy, and, surprisingly, smelled divine, like—vanilla or amber; I couldn't decipher it, but I liked it.

A lot.

"What are you doing?" Her voice was coated in uncertainty.

"Caring for your hair." My gaze fell to hers quickly before shooting back to her hair. "It looks . . . a mess."

I pulled her hair up in one swoop, curling the band to keep it in place.

"According to my mother, it is important to care for your hair. To care for it like it is a child; because, like children, your hair is clueless on how to take care of itself," I said, successfully tying her hair in a tiny ponytail, as far high as the short length could go. "She says you can always tell about a person's neatness by the state of their hair. Now I know how messy you are. That is not information you want your employer to know." And then I stepped back, assessing my work and nodding. "Better."

She blinked at me, giving me a very familiar look. One I usually received from people after saying or doing something that didn't fit their assumptions of me.

I returned to leaning on the railing, watching her swallow as she shook her head.

"You're . . . very . . . weird."

"I am aware. To avoid situations like this in the future, make sure you're well-arranged before speaking to me. I can't control the urge to fix things. And I do not care if I offend you by my actions."

"Aún no tiene sentido," she muttered under her breath. *Still doesn't make sense.*

I blinked in clear surprise. "¿Tú hablas español?" Hiding the excitement in my voice was impossible. *You speak Spanish?*

She shot me a sweet but taunting smile. *"Sí, ¿por qué?"* *Yes, why?*

I raised my brows, nodding because I was genuinely impressed; her Spanish was clean, smooth, and accented. *"Where did you learn?"* I asked in Spanish.

"None of your business."

The look that flashed through her eyes told me it was indeed none of my business.

I still pushed the conversation in Spanish. *"What kind of relationship do you share with my brother?"* I asked.

She eyed me carefully, probably wondering why I continued the conversation instead of having her locked away for interrupting my peace. She was right to wonder because I was wondering the same thing. She was the opposite of a person I'd want to spend my time with. Nothing was captivating about her or her presence, yet she was still here.

"He's my best friend and partner in crime."

I frowned. *"That cannot be right. You two have another relationship."*

"What makes you think that?"

"I am not blind. Aside from the thieving addiction you both share with the other members, I know you and him have something more."

"So what if we do? What's it to you?" There was a defensive tone to her voice as she pinned me with a glare.

I couldn't stop my eyes from taking her in from head to toe and back to her head. *"He's my blood. It concerns me the kind of woman he chooses to get intimate with."*

She let out a humorless laugh. *"What the fuck is wrong with me?"*

I paused, trying to find what was wrong with her physically; when I couldn't find anything, I shook my head and said, *"You're a bad influence on him. You and the others."*

Her glare hardened, and she took two steps towards me, the wind sweeping the seductive smell of her hair toward me. *"Talk shit about me all you want, but leave the others out."*

"They are also to blame for who my brother is today."

"Maybe you need to grow up and realize that Devil is not a kid but an adult who can very well choose the kind of people he wants to fuck with."

I shoved both my hands into my pockets, looking around the vast expanse. I took a step closer to her, and she took one back. I sniffed slightly. I leaned down, my gaze pinning hers. "Or . . . I could kill you"—I switched back to English—"and the others, and then make my brother do whatever the *fuck* I want. Because I *fucking* can, and because it would give me nothing but joy to see him far away from you . . . criminals."

She watched me for a few seconds before she laughed. Laughed in my face until I was the one inching away.

"Not only are you fucking weird, but you're also funny."

"Indeed?"

"Yes. You call us criminals? Have you met yourself? What we do is steal to fucking survive. But you, you kill people for power, betray family for status; you don't give two shits about how your actions affect the lives of people around you. People call you The Wicked; for fuck's sake, you hurt innocent people just because they're related to those who offend you. You think that's not criminal?"

I allowed her words to sink in, and I took another step back. "What I do is not criminal. It's worse. I should die for it. I *will* die for it eventually. But my brother is the sweetest kid I've ever known . . . this life, this world that I live in, he doesn't deserve to live it. I have done . . . *things* just to make sure he doesn't have to live it, to give him what I never had. To give him happiness, and normalcy."

"Haven't you ever considered that he doesn't want that? Why are you projecting your idea of a normal, happy life onto him? He's not you, Elio. He's Devil; he's his own person."

Elio . . . My eyes roamed her face, wondering if she realized her use of my first name. It felt unfamiliar to hear a stranger speak my name out loud without fear, and it felt odd that I . . . wanted to hear it again.

"I know it's none of my business, but no matter what you think, Devil's my family too, and I'm only trying to look out for him. You should respect his own life choices—"

"You do not understand," I said. "I lived this life, I'm currently living it, and I don't want him to experience what I have. I don't care about you, but I still think there are better ways you can survive. You're young; you could find decent work, live a life where you don't have to watch your back every second."

Her brows lowered. "You think I don't want that? The same way you got into this business without a fucking choice is the same way I found Street. You don't know what it's like out there, the fucking horrors I've been through, so forgive me if I can't stomach the thought of being around *normal* people who would judge me because of my mental and physical scars."

Annoyed, I massaged my head. "You're missing the point, Sport."

"No, *Dad,* I'm not."

I cringed, irritation crawling up my spine. "What the—"

"Just because your father put a gun in your hand when you were just a little boy doesn't mean you try to push your opinion into someone else's life."

I kept quiet.

"If you want to build a relationship with your brother, try not to be controlling and be more accepting. If you're clueless on how to start with that, maybe begin by actually telling people that you're both related because if you don't know, that shit hurts him more than you abandoning him."

She turned to leave, taking a few steps away from me before turning and walking back to me, this time with a venom in her eyes that had me backing up. "And don't you ever, in your fucking life, call me *Sport,* or any other fucking derogatory nicknames, because I'll back that shit up with daddy jokes that'll make you feel like ants are crawling up your fucking ass. Don't test me." Then she was off; I blinked and watched her disappear out the roof door.

Silence encased me again, mouth dry, speechless... With my gaze still trained on the door, I shook my head, looking away and absentmindedly reaching for my cigar pack. I got one stick out and shoved it between my lips—pausing shortly after to stare at the roof door again.

I scoffed in amusement, shaking my head yet again.

CHAPTER TEN

Zahra

They removed the sling three weeks later and wrapped my shoulder with a smaller bandage. The pain had subsided a little, and the wound was healing but showed signs of scarring.

I locked my jaw to the side, watching the reflection of my fingers softly graze the sides of the bandage. I hated seeing it. It was a constant reminder that I hadn't completely washed off all the fear I thought I'd gotten rid of.

Anyone who had ever left a scar on me had never lived to tell the tale about it.

Every single scar on my skin had been paid for. *In blood*.

But that was then; the bastards on my list had been dealt with, and the one that got away was back on my radar.

Dion Juan Pablo.

A sigh left me. I couldn't touch him, not with everything right in the spotlight with Street and our job for Marino. I was already building up my mental shields, knowing I would be in the same room with that bastard. Hopefully Upper would fix me up in a position where I didn't actually have to be near him.

I hated lying to Street, but there were parts of my life none of them could know, starting with the stories behind my scars.

The first time Devil saw them, he had asked me what happened, and I told him I couldn't remember. To his better knowledge, half my past had been wiped from my memory because of how traumatic it was.

In some ways it was true. I used to get nightmares, but not

anymore; now my nights were mostly dreamless, and I was grateful for that. It only solidified my answers to where I got my scars.

I didn't remember.

I did.

I just couldn't afford to trigger it.

I pulled down my shirt, covering up as I locked eyes with myself in the mirror. I stood there, staring at my reflection for minutes before allowing a sharp, broad smile to appear on my face. I held it for almost a minute and then abruptly let it fall.

I sighed. "You've got this. When all is said and done, you'll be soaking up the sun on a beach somewhere in Mauritius with your best friends all around you, and they will understand why you did all you did because they're family," I said softly to myself. "And family sticks with you, through thick and . . ." I stopped, dropping my gaze, closing my eyes and drawing in a deep breath, holding for a few seconds before letting it out and opening my eyes. "Fucking hypocrite," I muttered, turning and leaving the bathroom to find the others.

They were all in the living room. Pizza boxes opened on the table while they strategized.

Milk was sprawled on the floor, reading a magazine about disguise. Dog was also on the floor, checking all the equipment Angelo had provided upon his request. Upper was on his laptop, and Devil was on his phone beside him.

"Wow, who would have thought there would come a day when we'd be all so serious about a mission?" I mused, dropping on the couch, stretching to grab a slice of pizza, and taking a bite from it.

"Wrong, Upper's on Pornhub," Dog said without looking up.

"Rot in the burning furnace of hell, Dog," Upper responded while Devil took a small peek at Upper's screen before returning his attention to his phone. "I'm checking if my eyes inside Eden are still intact. It's past one hour, and I'm still not getting live feeds."

"You think there was a mistake with the wiring?" I asked.

Upper glanced at me. "I never make mistakes." His concentration went back to the screen.

"Maybe you should take a break. You've been glaring at the screen for five hours now," Devil suggested, his eyes still on his phone.

"I don't remember asking for your opinion." Upper didn't lift his head.

"I don't remember giving a fuck about you not asking for it," Devil responded.

"Maybe mind your bloody business."

"Maybe don't be a fucking dick."

Silence.

The pizza was paused halfway to my mouth; Dog's and Milk's attention turned slowly towards Upper and Devil, who seemed *too* focused on their task.

Dog looked at me and mouthed, *What the fuck?*

I don't know, I mouthed back.

Milk sighed loudly. "I think we all need a break. We've been too focused on planning because this is our first job after the last one, which landed us here. We're on edge."

"No shit." Dog stopped his task, stretching his muscles.

"What should we do?" Milk asked.

"Well." I finished my slice of pizza, grinning and dusting my hands on my naked thighs. "I'm in the mood to cause some trouble."

Devil scooted away from Upper. "I don't know if you remember, but we're sort of . . . in danger already?" Devil objected.

"We won't be harmed," I assured. "We have so much more leverage than you think."

"What are you talking about?" Devil asked with a frown.

I shrugged. "If Marino wanted us dead, we would be dead. The first mistake he made with us was keeping us alive."

"That sounds like a fucking blessing to me," Dog countered.

"I didn't mean it like that. What I meant is that he kept us alive because he needs us. That means, as much as he wants to put a bullet through our heads, he has to wait until we are useless to him."

Devil eyed me suspiciously.

I knew I sounded so assured, as if I knew something they didn't.

Devil's connection to Elio was the only thing keeping us alive. We were Devil's family, and if Elio touched any of us, he'd lose the only family he had left. We were pretty much set to wreak havoc as long as Devil was by our side.

"Everyone and everything is replaceable to Marino; don't be fooled," Devil said.

"I doubt that," I said, my eyes searching his. "Look at us; we're treated like guests instead of prisoners. I mean, we're eating fucking pizza. We have access to our phones and the internet. What hostage eats pizza and accesses the internet? That should tell you something."

"Yeah, or maybe he's got a fucking pet crocodile, and he's treating us good because his crocodile loves fresh, well-fed, happy meat. And by happy meat, I mean us," Dog said.

Milk lightly slapped his arm. "Who has a crocodile for a pet?"

"You'd be shocked, Pinky Brain," Dog said.

"So." Upper sat up. "You wanted to cause trouble, what did you have in mind?"

I curved my lips into a sly smile.

The loud music from Elio's casino was the relief my body needed, and from the looks on the faces of my beloveds, it was exactly what they needed too.

"This better be a good idea," Devil muttered beside me.

"Do you smell that?" I asked him, and he frowned, sniffing the air.

"Weed?"

"No. It's the smell of a great idea."

"Nah," Dog said. "I just smell another bullet coming; this time, I don't think he'll miss."

"I love it," Milk said. "I want to get very drunk and steal some money."

"No stealing," Upper chided her, but his eyes were filled with mischief. "We're gonna cheat ourselves some cash, and I might find myself a hot guy who will buy me beer."

Devil shook his head, his frown hardening.

I ignored his low spirits, feeling the rise of excitement in my stomach. "This, guys . . . is our zone. Let's make as much money as we can. And maybe we might be lucky enough for it to end in a huge casino fight, cross that off our bucket list."

Dog threw his arm around my shoulder, careful not to hurt my arm. "I'm a zombie slut for that genius brain of yours."

"Hm, talk dirty to me." I leaned into him as we began walking amongst the crowd, who didn't pay heed to us. Yet. Soon, they'd notice.

"How long do you think until they realize the soldiers assigned to watch us are no longer watching us?" Milk asked.

"An hour or two," Upper said. "Should supply us enough time to cause some trouble."

"That is if we don't get reported to the boss himself, seeing as we are simply walking into his turf like his *guests*. Wonderful," Devil said.

We stopped in the middle of the club, and Dog distributed some cash he'd stolen from the wallets of every soldier we'd encountered before reaching the casino. "The goal: use these to win big."

"I'll hit the tables," Upper said, going east.

"You guys are gonna get me killed one day," Devil muttered.

"I call roulette, my specialty," Milk said, already heading in that direction.

Devil sighed, backing away. "I'll be at the poker tables, *away* from all of you."

Dog and I looked at each other, speaking at the same time. "Blackjack?"

An hour later, we had more than fifty eyes on us. We were winning, we were loud, and we were pretend-drunk as fuck.

The exhilarating feeling of winning and pissing so many people off never gets old. We had bagged so much money and almost caused a massive fight in the casino, but it was settled thanks to Devil.

We had been noticed. There was a lot of whispering amongst the soldiers, and I was sure someone had gone to inform the bosses of the chaos we were creating.

Two hours flew by, and we were still winning; Milk was already worn out, and that was our cue to leave.

"All right. Let's wrap it up," Dog said, Milk appearing by his side as Upper joined Devil and me.

"Yeah, we did good," I praised.

Upper held the bags of money we had collectively won for the night. "I think it's pretty weird that no one—"

Silence slowly stretched through the casino, cutting Upper off.

People's attention automatically shifted to the stairs. Devil was the first to turn. "Shit," he muttered, "he came down himself."

I turned to see Elio descending the stairs at a leisurely pace in his usual all-black outfit. Two soldiers followed behind him, with one holding a black briefcase in hand.

My back straightened as they walked directly towards us. I was nearly sober just by the sight of him; the last time we'd seen each other, I had mouthed off like an idiot. I didn't know what to expect, and the thought alone made me nervous.

The intensity of his presence doused the room of whatever fire had gotten people going before. Some faces around us paled as he stopped before the guys and me.

The DJ had even lowered the volume of the music.

I could sense fear in the air, but none of it was coming from me. Maybe it was the fake alcohol or the fact that I had pictured a thousand ways I could deal with him, but I found myself looking him in the eye.

And . . .

Why does he have pretty eyes? He was a terrible person, and terrible people shouldn't have pretty eyes . . . He didn't look too bad either . . . He didn't look bad at all. Fine. The man was something, all right, I admitted it; and the challenge in those dark grays seemed to look even deeper tonight.

"Fine evening . . . *Street*. My people tell me you have made big wins tonight," Elio said, his face expressionless.

"It's a really lucky night," I answered.

"Isn't that just fabulous," he stated, eyes quickly running up and down my form. "I am pleased to see that you are all enjoying your *freedom* in my compound. It must feel like a *vacation* for you."

"You have no idea," I responded.

Devil stepped forward. "We don't want any trouble; we just wanted a break from—"

"It's okay," I cut him off, smiling. "He knows we don't want trouble; he's only commending us for how lucky we were tonight, right?" I threw the question at Elio, and his left brow twitched, but he nodded.

"Indeed. It's truly outstanding, this thing called luck."

I laughed in mock wonder. "Right? So crazy."

Elio's gaze remained solely on me, my brows, eyes, nose, forehead, lips, jaw . . . his staring made me even more anxious, aware that he was singling me out. It took everything in me not to shift on my feet and give away the fact that he was getting to me.

Finally, he nodded. "Yes, in fact, I was so inspired by this luck of yours that I decided, why not come down to see if I can interest you in a small game of chess, nothing serious."

I watched him as I locked my jaw. We didn't break eye contact for about a minute, and I knew he dared me to say no. He wanted to teach me a lesson.

I knew that look so fucking well.

Tilting my head a bit to the side, I asked, "What's the catch?"

With his eyes still on me, he signaled to the soldier who held the briefcase, and the man stepped forward, opening it. I almost doubled over at the sight of the clean stacked bundle of cash arranged perfectly in a mouthwatering way.

Fucking greed.

Elio straightened. "We play five single rounds. Best-of-five winner takes your earnings for the night and the briefcase."

It took a lot of willpower to drag my eyes from the money.

It was risky; we could lose all we'd earned tonight if I agreed.

"And if I don't agree?"

His jaw clenched, and he paused two seconds before taking a step closer to me. I sucked in a breath, raising my chin a little so I could meet his gaze as he buried both hands into his pockets and gave me that degrading look again, the one where it seemed like I was only a grain of rice on his shoe.

"Allow me to reiterate, *Sport*. You do not have a *choice* in this proposal."

"Fuck," Dog cursed.

I stepped closer to Elio, looking up at him with determination. "If that's the case, allow me to add a new catch."

His gaze flickered between my eyes. "What would that be?"

"A chance to renegotiate the terms of my and my people's service to you."

He thought about it for only a few seconds before nodding. "Okay. I would also like to add a *catch*."

"I'm listening."

"I get to tie you up, shoot your good shoulder and kneecaps, and then throw you off that roof. In simpler words, I kill you."

I didn't flinch.

Devil shook his head. "Zahra, don't—"

"Deal."

Elio's eyes widened a bit, and I briefly saw surprise in them before it was masked with indifference.

He exited my personal space, and I let my breathing flow freely once more.

Straightening his suit, Elio outstretched his hand in the direction behind me. "Very well. Let's play."

CHAPTER ELEVEN

Elio

The silence was deafening.

Beyond ridiculous was the perfect way to describe my actions. The chess, the bargain. It was out of character. I never behaved this way. I never stooped to such levels to allow myself an opportunity to kill someone.

Never once had I tried to prove to myself and some amateur that she couldn't undermine me. Her little warning on the rooftop grated on me. It was a petty feeling. Immature. It shouldn't matter. But it did.

Maybe that was the reason I was pissed. She had snuck right underneath my skin. She compelled a wave of unnecessary anger from me, and the distaste of that feeling was far from appreciated.

She had no right to mess with my focus the way she did, and now cheating in my casino, gambling with thievery. It was egregious.

I was irritated by it.

The whole buildup had led to this very moment, with her sitting across from me, the chessboard between us, my people behind me, while her friends stood behind her.

An aura of uncertainty lingered in the air around us, and judging by the look on her face, she would most likely lose every penny she had stolen. Her stubborn eyes lifted from the chessboard, and our gazes locked. She didn't look away, and neither did I.

It was unnerving how she portrayed the stance of being in control. Jaw set, eyes hard and calculating. It made me curious to know how she had groomed herself into doing it.

Curious, she made me *curious*. Her personality was *intriguing;* it was so like mine, familiar but unfamiliar.

I had gone out of my way to dig up information about her life after the move to Italy, but there was nothing very useful. I knew she had been sold, so my search was restricted. I still had questions: How was she here? How had she escaped whoever had bought her? If she was bought from Saudi Arabia, why hadn't she attempted to go back home? Why was her mother's record wiped clean? Why did she feel . . . made-up? Who was my brother sleeping with?

She was a frustrating mystery. I do not like mysteries.

She looked away first, her focus settling on the board as we began.

All eyes were on us.

And I watched her.

Her long fingers hovered on the board, and her confidence dwindled. A few seconds into it, her face finally hinted at what and how she was feeling. Her brows were drawn down in a frown, almost as if she was unsure of the first move to make.

When she made it . . . I relaxed.

She was an idiot.

I found her eyes on me when I looked up.

In Spanish, I spoke while making my move. *"If you didn't know how to play, why did you agree to my terms?"*

"I have never been known to back down from a challenge," she responded before looking down and making another dumb move.

I shook my head, already mapping out my first win with my next move. *"How did you survive this far with such low thinking capacity?"*

Move after move, she was losing.

A smile curved at the side of her lips. *"I have been told countless times how amazing I am. I think that quality serves as the charm of my essence."*

"I'm afraid I don't see it," I responded, switching to English as I made my next move and said, "Checkmate."

She sucked in a breath, sitting up as she watched the board.

Dog leaned into Zahra's side. "You should fucking quit this."

She was quiet, studying the board before answering him without looking away. "Didn't you hear? I have no choice. Not only is our money on the line, but my life is too."

We started the second round, and it was the same thing. She made lousy moves, throwing herself off. I would have suggested she did it all on purpose if I didn't know better.

"At least make an effort to pretend like you know what you're doing," I said.

Her brows came down in a frown. *"Stop talking,"* she responded without looking up.

She made her move, opening the ground floor for me to win the second round.

"You realize if you lose this, you're dying."

Her fist clenched and unclenched. "You made that very clear."

After three more moves, I called checkmate, and the look on her face was the definition of unsettled.

"Let me take her place," Devil said, seeing that the odds weren't in her favor. "Same terms."

"No."

"It's clearly a rip-off; she doesn't know how to play the game—"

I shot him a glare. "Not another word from you. Stay out of this."

"This is fucking—"

"It's okay," she cut in. "I can handle this."

Upper shook his head slowly. "You're losing, love. Embarrassingly."

She looked back at the board as I arranged it. "We still have three winning rounds. There's still hope. I love my kneecaps too much to risk them," she said, her smile taunting.

I was irritated by the unseriousness in her voice. The control.

We started the next round. Her first move was a disappointment; I almost felt sorry for her.

She was the most terrible chess opponent I'd ever had. Her confidence should be giving her a good dose of embarrassment now. I wasn't in her shoes, but I knew I would have called it quits at this point, with all the eyes watching us. But she kept going, and I kept clearing her pawns off the board. With my eyes closed, I could take a hundred to none wins from her.

I shook my head when she made a move that elicited groans from the people behind her.

As we made move after move, I knew there was no way she was winning this.

She was an insult to the game of—

"Checkmate."

My thoughts seized, and I stopped short, allowing my mind to replay her move as my eyes studied the board.

When I caught my mistake, my jaw clenched.

Someone whistled.

"Where's your mind?" she asked me, voice leveled.

When I raised my head, I caught her gaze, shimmering with a smugness that pulled out a glare from me.

Her smile widened.

I sat up. "Next round."

I reset the board again, and we started.

Her demeanor changed completely, making my ability to read her next move nonexistent.

For a casual game, this round surpassed forty minutes, and thoughts were placed into moves.

The tension around us escalated by the long minutes. Move after move, my anger flared. I became utterly uneasy, and I loosened the tie around my neck.

"You are too open." Her voice pierced through my concentration.

My gaze shifted across the board, and I thought hard before

making my next move. She couldn't see her win. It was covered. Only a professional would spot it.

If she made the wrong move now, I would win the round with only two moves.

Her brows fell in a frown, taking the bait. She let a breath fall through, and then she made her move.

My eyes snapped up the moment she raised her eyes from the board.

She smiled before saying, "Checkmate."

"Fucking diabolical," Upper said, heaving a breath.

She relaxed back. "This is fun?" A grin split across her lips, and Devil scoffed in amusement. "I'm having so much fun," she continued, ignoring the look on my face. "Last game, champ?"

After the last round, I sat upright as the briefcase was handed to the hollering demons behind her.

She had won.

Not for one second did her eyes leave mine to celebrate her victory with her friends; there was a taunting smile playing at her lips as she raised a brow at me, extending her hand for a handshake.

My gaze dropped to her hand, before lifting to her face again.

I swallowed my immature pride, joining my hand with hers and . . .

Warm and small.

Her hand was warm and small. It held a sense of delicateness that didn't suit her abrasive character or the foul words that fell from her lips each time she opened her mouth.

Her fingers were long with chipped red nail polish.

Messy. Like her.

She visibly took in a breath, her smile faltering a little, an action that made me wonder what had passed through her mind at that second.

"Good game," I told her, and her smile widened at the comment.

"Of course, this thing called luck, right? It's been blowing my mind all night, and now this? I don't—I still can't—wow."

My jaw clenched. "You are twenty-six, you shouldn't be this annoying."

She frowned. "I didn't know being annoying came with an age limit. I thought anyone of any age could be annoying, did I miss something growing up?"

"Oh, I'm sure you missed a lot of things growing up, common sense being one of them."

She nodded thoughtfully. "Yeah, probably, it's why I get myself in these situations, you know. But honestly, if we truly look at it, in a way, you came to me for a game, and you said it was going to be nothing serious, so you shouldn't be too beat up about it, right? It's just chess. Some people are better than some. It's unfortunately the way the world works."

My gaze flickered between her eyes. "I truly don't like you."

Her eyes twinkled and her lips twitched in a smile. "But you sure do like holding my hand."

I stilled. My attention dropped to our hands, still held together. I lifted my eyes to meet her purposeful stare before jerking my hand back and shooting to my feet. I buttoned up my suit, righted my tie, and cleared my throat, looking everywhere but at her. "Come with me; let's see about that renegotiating you discussed."

"Gladly," she said, and I watched from the corner of my eye as she stood, her bare stomach on display for a second before she pulled down the half-shirt-like cloth she wore.

Someone cleared their throat rather loudly, and I tore my eyes from Zahra to find one of her friends . . . the Dog one, staring at me with a slight frown. It was obvious he'd caught me staring. "Just to be clear, we're not getting in trouble for this, right?"

Zahra's attention was on me once more before she looked at Dog with a frown. "Of course not. What are you doing? Trying to remind him that we should be in trouble?"

Ignoring them, I moved to leave. "Someone will bring you up. Don't keep me waiting."

"I'll come with," Elia said.

"No." I pinned him with a stern look. "She'll come alone."

Elia frowned; there was a warning in his eyes that had me grunting another addition to my statement. "She'll return alive," I said with a twinge of disinterest, but he didn't budge. I almost groaned when I added, "Unharmed."

His features relaxed as he looked at the woman, who didn't seem fazed by our exchange.

"Z, if—"

"It's fine," she told him. "I can take care of myself."

"You're sure?" he asked her, an undeniable concern shining in his eyes. "I can take care of it if you—"

"I'm sure, Devil. I can handle him."

My insides clenched, and I looked away when I realized I wasn't just looking at Elia and . . . her, I was staring. "Escort her up," I said to one of the men who'd accompanied me downstairs before walking away, more troubled than I'd been before I came down.

CHAPTER TWELVE

Zahra

He was alone when the guard opened the door to the room where we'd discussed Dion Juan Pablo. It was the same as the first time I was here: way too clean with everything in its place.

When the door closed behind me without so much as a *good luck* from the guard, I turned my attention to Elio, who was placing an expensive bottle of red wine alongside two wineglasses on the table. He began to clean the two glasses.

I noticed he had discarded his jacket and tie; his sleeves were rolled up to his elbows, revealing the tattoos on his left forearm again, but unlike the first time, there was a small bandage on the inner part of his forearm. It had happened sometime between the meeting day and now.

I hoped it hurt like a bitch.

He glanced towards me the moment I started making my way to him.

"Don't touch anything; just come forward," he said, then looked away.

"What's with the command?" I asked, now standing opposite him, with the minibar counter separating us. "I was already *coming* without touching anything."

Either he didn't understand my statement's double meaning, or he decided to ignore me, but his face showed no hint of discomfort.

"No one can tell with people like you," he said, face void of emotion. "You think they're going to go one direction, and they end up going the other."

I eyed him, noting how he was entirely focused on the very unnecessary cleaning he was doing.

My gaze landed on his lips; they had that rich, attractive fullness that made me stare a little too long. His face was—perfect. His eyelashes were full and pretty long for a man who was supposed to be wicked. My stare trailed down to his neck, catching a glimpse of the tattoo there. I wanted to know—

"You're staring again," he said without looking up.

I placed my hand underneath my chin. "You're a hot guy with a pretty face. I can't help myself."

He looked up at me, dark eyes filled with apparent surprise. I batted my lashes, giving him a sweet smile. He looked away again, dropping the glass, clearing his throat, and picking up the second glass. "Do you get off from annoying people around you?"

"No . . . but I could totally get off on that face of yours."

His cleaning ceased, and our eyes locked again. "Stop," he warned.

I smiled. "What? No one's ever flirted with you before?"

"You're making me uncomfortable."

"Hmm." I nodded. "Good uncomfortable or bad uncomfortable?"

He stared at me for a few seconds before shaking his head and returning to cleaning the glass, probably realizing he was going to get nowhere in an argument with me.

I got more comfortable. "You've been cleaning that glass for minutes now. Do you have OCD?"

He averted his gaze, cleaning delicately, while his rings clinked on the frame from time to time.

"Do you have—"

"No," he answered.

"Then pour the fucking wine, and let's talk business."

He steadied both glasses in one hand while he used the other to wipe the counter slowly and delicately before placing both glasses on it; then neatly, he folded the cloth and tucked it away.

Fucking weirdo.

He poured wine into both glasses, pushing one towards me.

Reaching behind him, he pulled out a gun, and my eyes followed as he carefully placed it on the counter. He picked up his drink and swirled it softly as he walked around to stand right next to me.

"We apparently don't like each other," he stated, "so I'll skip the necessary pleasantries I offer to people I have business with."

"Oh, it wasn't the wine?"

He leveled me with his stern stare, which quickly flickered to my messy hair before coming back to my face again. Ignoring my statement, he said, "I'll consider renegotiating your case only when I know whom I'm negotiating with."

"That wasn't our deal."

He took a sip from his glass. "Did we make one? I don't remember signing any document or agreeing to anything legally with you. I think you must be confused; you did have a lot to drink tonight."

I took a step closer to him. "You fucking bastard, I should have known your word meant nothing."

"I never said it did."

"Then what am I fucking doing here?" I hissed, turning to leave, but he grabbed my wrist, pulling me back. I tried to wrench my hand free, but his grip was firm.

"I didn't dismiss you."

"Oh, sorry, Principal Marino, I didn't know I had to ask for your permission before getting the fuck out of your face."

He let me go instantly. "I told you I would reconsider your case."

"Yeah, I heard that part, but it came with a little clause I don't think I want to fulfill."

"So, you'd rather subject yourself and your friends to me for the rest of your lives than tell me who you are?"

"You already know who I am. I'm Zahra, a very rude and expensive thief who fucks your brother. What else do you wanna know?"

He placed the glass on the table and shoved one hand into his pants pocket; the other rested on the table as he drummed with his fingers. "What happened after you were sold?"

I flinched. He noticed, but didn't say anything.

"Look who did his research," I said. "Didn't know I was *so* important. Honestly, I'm flattered. No one has ever cared that much about me."

His stare remained blank, pointed, patient.

I sighed. "I can't remember."

"Liar."

"It's not a *lie*," I snapped.

"From one liar to another, it's best not to evade my question with a lie. I'll spot it."

I reached for my glass of wine, brought it to my lips, and downed it to the last drop before setting it back on the counter.

The silence stretched as he waited for me to speak.

I crossed my arms against my chest. "What would you do if I didn't wish to disclose my *life's journey*?"

"I'll kill you for wasting my time."

"Earlier tonight you promised Devil you wouldn't hurt me."

"I promised I'd never leave him, and I did."

My gaze flicked to the gun on the counter, and he mirrored my action.

Our eyes locked again.

He read my mind, and I read *him*, and then we were both diving for the gun, but I was faster. I grabbed the weapon, flicked off the safety, aimed it at him, and pulled the trigger.

He knocked the gun from my hand before the shot faded, the weapon clattering away into a corner. He gripped my arm and twisted it. A raw scream of panic escaped me as a sharp pain shot right through my wounded shoulder. He took that opening to grab my other arm, twisting it behind me and swiftly flipping our positions, shoving me against the counter, my back to his front, the wood digging tightly to my ribs.

Before he had pinned me, I caught a glimpse of blood on his upper left arm. His dress shirt was torn, and a flicker of satisfaction flowed through me because the bullet had grazed him just like I intended. I was still in his hold—locked between the hard plane of his chest and the unforgiving sharp edge of the counter, the wound on my shoulder burning with pain.

"Let go of me!" I let out almost breathlessly.

"That was an idiotic move, Sport. You're lucky I instructed my people not to interfere no matter what they hear—you'd be dead if I hadn't taken that precaution." His breath brushed my ear.

Close.

I pushed back, ignoring the pain. "Let me *fucking* go!"

"What could be so important that you would try to kill me?"

Too close.

I thrashed, pushed back, bucked my hips, anything to squirm free of him—the dark was closing—I was fighting.

He pushed me further into the edge of the counter. "Keep that up and you'll break all your ribs."

"Fuck," I voiced breathlessly, blinking rapidly as I felt the stitches on my shoulder tear open. His hold remained strong, tethering me back to the here and now, but I was slowly falling, zoning out, stuck. I felt stuck, suffocated, trapped—"Let me go!" I screamed, but he only tightened his grip on my wrist.

I couldn't move, couldn't escape; I had no control, no space to breathe.

My chest tightened, my breathing quickened. "Let go of me, Elio!" My voice shook.

I was winded, trapped by the walls of his body. *No, not walls . . . cage . . .* he was morphing into a cage.

No. *No.*

I threw my head back, hoping to knock him in the chin, but somehow, I missed, I was trapped. And there was no escape. No escape. I couldn't breathe.

"Let me go!"

He released his hold but kept his arms on both sides of me. "Stop fighting me." His lips were right by my ear.

My chest heaved. "Let go or I swear to God . . . I swear to God—"

"Breathe." His voice softened, but he still held me, and alarm bells rang in my head.

"Just let me go!"

"Not until you remember how to breathe."

"Fuck you!" I heaved, collecting air into my lungs, and realized I wasn't entirely pressed into the counter anymore.

"Breathe."

My pulse was still racing, and I was trying to regain control of my ringing ears, but I was breathing, trying to calm my racing heart, breaking down the iron walls that had quickly mounted themselves around me. I wasn't pressed to the counter, his hands weren't almost breaking my wrists.

Space.

There was a lot of space.

"Are you calm?" he asked.

"No."

It took four minutes until the ringing stopped, until I could breathe properly again.

I drew in a breath and released it with my response. "I'm calm now. Let me go."

He did, and I wasted no time turning and pulling back my fist to aim at his face. My fist slammed into his stupid fucking perfect nose, and I was disappointed that I didn't hear a crack, but I must have hurt something because he swore, stumbling back while cradling his nose as blood poured from his nostrils.

Good.

I held my shoulder, the pain making my knees weak.

He hissed, swiftly wiping the blood away. "You throw a good punch, I'll give you that."

My eyes shifted to the bullet graze on his arm before looking at him again. "I aim to please. I'll also ensure I don't *miss* the next time I shoot you."

"Your aim is pitiful. I'm not worried."

I let out a humorless laugh. "I never fucking miss. The only reason you're alive is because Devil fucking cares if you're breathing."

"Amazing, because that's the only reason *you* are breathing."

"Yeah, you can try to kill me; I promise you won't succeed."

"You're so certain."

"Oh yes, I am." I took a step back. "I was shoved in a room with twenty horny armed men, and I was the only one who came out breathing. My luck doesn't *end* with gambling."

His face hardened. "Who the fuck are you?"

A smile curved at the side of my lips. "Wouldn't you like to know?" Then I turned, opened the door, and walked out.

He didn't stop me.

I walked straight ahead, hearing the door close behind me as I rounded the corner.

I spotted Casmiro walking towards the room I'd just left, and I didn't stop when he spotted me, complete shock and horror in his eyes.

He'd heard the gunshot and probably thought it meant I was dead.

My smile widened as I brushed past him. "Hey, Cassie, you might wanna check on your boss," I threw over my shoulder without stopping. His curse and footsteps as he rushed to his boss resounded in the hall. "*Amateurs.*"

CHAPTER THIRTEEN

Elio

It wasn't the fact that she put up a fight. Her stealth and the absence of hesitation when she raised the gun and pulled the trigger was the thing that threw me off. I couldn't for the life of me stop thinking about that—about her.

Why had she occupied more space than Elia had in my mind? Why was I having an inner monologue about a woman? Not just any woman; the one who should die for even pointing a gun at me. A woman who didn't even know how close she was to razing my whole plan. If that bullet had killed me, my soul would have never known peace.

"The girl has to go."

Angelo's gaze rose to me. "We had a deal with them. We can't exactly go back on our word."

"I can."

He sighed. "Your word is law, remember?"

"I relieved you of your duty years ago, remember? I don't need your advice, Mancini."

He shook his head, sticking a needle in to sew the wound on my arm. "I will still offer it as long as I'm here, Marino."

I looked at him. "Then *leave*."

He nodded. "And give you the chance and space to off yourself? Yeah, no. Not going to happen on my watch."

This time, when he pressed the sharp point of the needle into my skin, I flinched.

Angelo made me very uncomfortable. It never used to be that way before he *saved me*. He usually just did his job and managed his affairs with his men. He was the only other person who understood how politics worked, and he would have been fun to talk to if he didn't watch me like a hawk every time we were in the same space. It didn't help that he was probably the only one who didn't believe I had an ounce of wickedness inside of me.

It was unsettling.

I frowned. "I've given you a good opportunity for a life outside this business; why won't you just take it and get out of my way."

He met my eyes. "Because this is my life, and you have no control over what I choose to do with it."

"That's why you came to stitch me up instead of calling our medic?"

"Yes. If our people find out you were shot by a *woman,* who is supposed to be your *hostage,* they will kill her and question your leadership. We can't have that now, can we?"

"I want her dead."

"Okay, that can be arranged. *After* they do what they're here for. As much as their presence brings chaos, we need access to the Pablos. The intel on that painting is required, and Street is the best bet we got."

Silence followed after he said that. He put in the last stitch, applied ointment, and dressed the wound.

I broke the silence when he pulled back to cobble the first aid kit together.

"You thought I did it to myself, didn't you? That's why you came running."

With his back to me, I noted how his form grew tense, but he didn't respond.

"You should stop worrying about that," I said, picking up the well-folded shirt beside me and slipping it on. "It's never going to happen again. I'm over it. I'm fine. I've got too much to live for, and it was a mere slip-up. A mistake. You shouldn't use that as an excuse to remain in this business."

He let out a sharp breath before turning and pinning me with a pained expression he tried to mask but couldn't. "You know I lost my sister to suicide, right?"

I watched him as I buttoned up my shirt. "Yes, I'm well-informed about that."

"Before she finally . . . left, I'd saved her; I think—three, four times. It was never fun. It was traumatizing, and I still have nightmares featuring scenarios of the many ways I could have saved her if I had been there in time."

I blinked at him, unsure if I should mention how proud I was of his sister or apologize and do the "I am sorry for your loss" thing.

"What does that have to do with me?" I asked instead.

"Your excuse and your 'I'm fine' is something I've heard before. The rise and fall of your voice showed the false reassurance you just tried to give me. I'm not a fool, Marino."

"You're a fool for wanting to remain here with me, Mancini. I'm not worth it. You should go live your life."

"No . . . no, *you* should live your life. Leave the four walls of this—this *cursed* library—leave the freaking books with their fake words and lies woven to twist your mind into a fucking web of unrealistic scenarios and fucking socialize. Talk to real people. Go to real places. And for once in your life, don't be a mastermind." He breathed, watching me as if pleading for his words to sink in.

The silence stretched for a few seconds before I responded.

"I'm good."

His shoulders sagged. "You need therapy."

"Please." I got up from the stool and walked to the nearest shelf. "You see these books, Mancini? They're the only therapy I need. Whenever I read them, it's like my sister's here, reading them to me."

"But she's not." Pity softened his voice.

I ignored it.

"Mariana loved reading books. She'd spend so much money on the little books she could get without our father knowing. He never liked them. Thought they were silly. My mother never objected to his reasoning. She never objected to many of his twisted thoughts and actions. It was probably her only flaw. Aside from that, Mother was perfect," I said, picking up a book from the shelf.

"I always teased Mariana because she loved filling her head up with these romance books. As you called them . . . fake scenarios, I did that too. And she would glare at me so fiercely I'd cower."

"Marino—"

"When Mariana died, I created this little library. I bought every single book she had ever wanted to read." I brought the spine of the book to my view. "And engraved her name into the spine of these hardcovers. I swore to myself that I'd read it all on her behalf." My thumb grazed the spine before I placed it back on the shelf and turned to Angelo.

"I don't have time to socialize, to make friends, and to talk to real people. I'd rather spend every free minute reading words Mariana would have loved to read. So yes, you have nothing to worry about; I am not dying until I read every single thing on this shelf. I will have slip-ups. I will make mistakes." I raised my sleeve to my forearm, pointing to the bandaged wound. "I'll hurt myself because, for me, that's my normal. That's my life and the way it is. I'm not spiraling; it's just me. It's normal for me."

Angelo sighed. "It's not normal to want to hurt yourself, Marino. Or to give yourself a death date . . . or a fucking timeline. It's—you need help—at least, get it for the books you might not be able to read if you slip, make a mistake, and never come back from it."

"That won't happen."

"It almost did. And if it weren't for me, you'd be dead."

"It won't happen again."

"That's what my sister said the first time she attempted it. And it happened again, and again, and again until she didn't live to give me the same excuse."

I am not his sister.

"Listen," he said, "I don't want to pretend to know what goes through that head of yours. I don't even want to imagine how it must have felt to have everyone who's ever heard your name believe you're some killer. But I want you to know I understand what it feels like to be too late. The guilt. The pain. The grief you can't bring yourself to feel. You were too late, and I know how your father twisted the whole shit in his favor. But you've got to know that none of it was your fault."

"Your advice means nothing, Mancini. I am not your sister."

"I know—"

"I'm not talking about this anymore."

"You have to come to terms with—"

"I am *done* talking about this."

Almost as if the universe were listening, Casmiro walked into the room with a scowl, shrugging off his jacket, and throwing it carelessly on the table. "The amount of money lost today is fucking unforgivable. These Street people have no control," he said, helping himself to a drink at the bar, sneaking a glance at Angelo.

I walked to the table, picked up his jacket, and hung it on the clothes valet.

"Have you tightened the security?" Angelo asked him.

"Yes. Those rats knocked them clean, locked them up, and stole from them. They didn't deserve that briefcase."

"She won." I walked to the bar area.

Casmiro got two extra glasses, filling them up for Angelo and me. "I don't trust her."

Angelo hummed in agreement. "I know her kind. Always searching for ways to mess with people for their gain," he said. "What I don't understand is how she almost killed our boss."

They both looked at me, waiting to hear how I had let that happen.

I looked between them before shrugging. "She was faster than me. It was quite impressive."

"There aren't many who would have the guys even pick up a

gun in your presence, let alone shoot at you or punch you in the nose," Angelo said.

"She's the one we need to watch. We know nothing about her, and I have a gut feeling that the little we know is—staged; it's what we're meant to see when we do our research."

Casmiro sighed. "They're useful, but they're trouble."

I took in a breath. "Here's what we can do. Their security will have to be assigned shifts to avoid any familiarity. We keep a close eye on them. No cameras. Physical watch only. No one touches any of them. No matter what."

"We could take one of them. An example to keep the rest in check," Casmiro suggested.

"No."

"How do we control them, then? You lost the chess game, giving them the right to return to the casino."

"Let them."

Casmiro glared. "What exactly do these people have on you, E?"

"Don't question me."

"It's hard not to."

I sighed. "Is it that you are blind, or you've just decided to block your sense of reasoning for the night? Mancini, please explain to this dumb friend of mine why we can't make an example of one of them?"

Angelo put down his glass. "Because they complement each other; hurt one, hurt them all."

"So what the fuck do we do about them? We can't let their intrusion at the casino go. I have double my task tomorrow thanks to them. People were angry; bets were lost. The casino was chaos after they left."

"It will be handled."

"How?"

"We just need a scapegoat, one provided by their own hands."

Casmiro frowned. "What do you mean?"

"I have seen them interact," I told him. "I have them under

my roof, and they have a job to finish for me. I know one of them is messy and impulsive, and I have a gut feeling she is bound to make a mistake at some point."

"She makes a mistake, then what?" he asked.

I picked up my glass. "Then I intervene," I said, downing the drink and dropping the glass back on the table, leveling him with a stare. "And make her a scapegoat."

CHAPTER FOURTEEN

Zahra

Devil was quiet as he helped redo the stitch in my shoulder. His form was tense, his jaw clenched, and his brows were drawn down in a frown.

It was clear that he was upset with the state I had returned in. Yet another promise to him broken.

"I'm okay, you know," I told him as he cut the thread, proceeding to get out new bandages. "Everything that happened tonight happened because I let it. You know that, right?"

He didn't look at me or respond as he unwrapped the bandage.

I sighed, placing my palm on his thigh. "Hey."

He paused.

"What is it? Talk to me," I said quietly, trying to catch his gaze until he succumbed and looked at me.

"He could have killed you," he said. "I can't believe I trusted him with you—"

"I'm fine—"

"No, you're not. You have bruises on your wrists. You tore open your wound. He lied. And I—" He stopped, letting out a shaky breath.

It was quiet for almost a minute until I broke it.

"You're angry at yourself," I pointed out. "That you believed him when he said he wouldn't hurt me." I wondered if I should add or keep the next part to myself. But he looked like he needed to talk to someone, and what was the point in hiding the fact that I knew they were related? "You're angry that you believed him despite how it turned out the last time. How he abandoned you."

Devil flinched, his eyes widening in shock as he watched me. "How did you—"

"I figured it out, and he confirmed it for me."

He blinked at me. "He—he told you we were related?"

"More like I hinted it, and he didn't deny, just . . . leaned into it."

His shoulder relaxed a bit. "Now I know what you meant by leverage." He eyed me. "You plan to hold me at gunpoint demanding all the money we stole from him?"

My smile was small. "If that's what you want, we can go for it."

He shook his head, looking away. "Like he would even care," he muttered under his breath.

"Oh, trust me, he would. Everyone thinks Elio Marino is incapable of loving anyone just because they don't know you exist, but I can assure you, if there's anything that man loves more than power and being a fucking psychopath and killer, it's you. You come first to him, above all else."

"And you know that, how?"

"I saw it."

"You saw wrong. When we spoke the other day, he washed his hands clean of me. He told me he would kill me. He said some fucked-up shit that keeps playing in my head nonstop, and I—I want to hate him. I want nothing more than to see him dead for everything he's done, to me, to his family, to innocent people. I want to see him suffer, but at the same time, I don't." He swallowed. "And I don't know if that makes me every bit as bad as he is."

"No." I scooted closer to him, my fingers diving into his hair as I massaged gently. "You're not a bad person. We can't choose our family, Devil. We can't choose who we love, and we shouldn't hate ourselves for it."

"I don't know what to do," he confessed. "Despite everything he's done . . . I still—I still want a relationship with him. Believe it or not, that man leading this whole thing used to be the greatest person I knew. He was . . . he was *good*."

"That's very hard to believe."

He chuckled. "I know. When I look at him now, I just—I see a stranger; I see someone else. The person I know is long since dead, and this is just a very wicked ghost of him. The day we talked, I thought I saw a flicker of what he used to be, but I'm not sure after tonight."

"But you still want to try?" I asked.

"Yes," he confirmed. "Not for this version of him. For the one I remember as a kid. The one who would protect me and tell me how loved I was, the one who I shared dreams with. The one who hid me because his fucking dad wanted me dead. Elio, he's—God, he's been through so much. I don't even know if he remembers now that he's in charge of . . . everything."

"What do you mean?"

"He was all over the place. Being groomed to become like Ricardo, caring for me, his mother, and his siblings. Sometimes he'd come to me, beaten and bruised; he never told me how he got them, but I knew they were from his father. He never liked to talk about it and the things he'd done." Devil looked far away as he spoke. "I remember how sunken his eyes always were, dark and tired like—like he never slept.

"One day I asked him why he always looked like a zombie, and he said he was a zombie because zombies didn't sleep. I remember laughing because I didn't really understand. He would smile at me, but it never really did reach his eyes, almost like—it took everything in him to move that muscle.

"One night, he rushed in, gave me food, and apologized because he had to leave. He said his mother had been sick. It was the first time he'd been honest about literally anything that had to do with his family. He always talked about them, but only the good parts.

"The next day when he came by, I asked him if his mother had a cold or the flu, and he said he wished that were the case. He looked sad and defeated. I hugged him because he looked like he needed it. And then he cried. He cried so hard and held me like I was the only thing keeping him together. Then he fell asleep for hours. I thought he was dead. He looked so . . . different, peaceful.

"That was the first time I ever saw him cry, and it was also the last. At that moment, I badly wanted to protect him from what made him cry. I hated it. The tears. It hurt me. I wished he never went back to his father. I hoped he would stay with me because—each time he went out and came back . . . something was always missing. With each visit, something died. At first, it was his smile, then his affection, and then—basically everything."

Devil let out a breath, looking at me again. "I know it might not be worth it, but I want to try. For that boy who cried as I held him, the one who needed nothing but company and good sleep." He breathed out a small laugh.

"Well fuck," I said.

"What?"

"I can't kill him now."

He flicked my forehead, and I scrunched up my nose.

"Like you could hurt a fly," he said, proceeding to finish bandaging my shoulder.

A comfortable silence fell between us until I broke it. "For what it's worth, I think he's still there. The brother you once knew."

"How are you sure?"

"As I said, I saw it."

It was slow, but a smile broke out on his lips as he resumed his task, looking a lot more relieved than he had minutes before.

It had been two weeks since the casino incident, and our security had doubled since then. I'd been waiting for the other shoe to drop, for actions to be taken about the casino stunt we pulled, but they had surprisingly left us alone.

I joined the rest of them in the living room. Upper had a whiteboard already littered with information. A thin drumstick was in his left hand, and I didn't even want to ask how he got it.

"Lovely of you to finally grace us with your presence," Upper said, looking away as he stood beside the board. At the same time, I found a space next to Devil, opposite Milk, whose eyes scanned the board as if trying to take it all into memory, and Dog, who divided his attention between Upper and the laptop in front of him. Our comms were splayed out beside the laptop while he worked on them.

"All right, so we move tomorrow, and the plan is quite simple as we have devised over the past couple of days," Upper said, pointing at a space in the whiteboard, a miniature van drawing. "This is Dog."

"The guy in the chair this time," he muttered, not looking up.

"Yes, he'll be our eyes and ears, the mission's omniscient body. The van contains three computers showing live feeds from all corners of Eden."

I nodded in agreement.

Upper continued. "Devil and I installed cameras in all wings of the building the other day, tracking devices on anything that could be lifted and carried away, and also chips that can enable us to listen in on conversations that might aid us, or deliver important information we might need."

"Are Angelo's people tracking our activities? Is there a chance to snag up some info for ourselves?" Milk asked.

"They're tracking everything; Dog might be our guy in the chair, but a good number of guys in chairs are backing him up. This is important to them," Upper said.

"Way forward," I said.

Upper pointed to the club entrance, at two stick drawings with spaghetti hair. "This is Milk and Zahra. Your entry is through the front. We already obtained VIP tickets so the bouncer will swipe you in without questions or the unnecessary ID checking."

"How did we get VIP tickets?" I asked.

"Milk has a brother who's a new bartender in the bar. He's popular, handsome, and can sneak in to collect VIP tickets. Illegally."

"And this brother of mine is?" Milk asked.

Upper pointed his drumstick at the drawing of what looked like a table, with a stick person behind it holding a glass. "Devil is your brother; although he won't be there when you and Zahra walk in, he'll be opening the kitchen vent for me, and you'll have another bartender tending to you. He's normal people. I think Patrick was his name, if I'm correct. A man-whore for boobs, easily distracted. He's eyed four women who have been later called to join Dion, so the odds are in our favor there."

"And what's that?" Devil pointed to the two stick figures in a corner, entering another room.

"That's you and me; I'm leaving the kitchen after drinking too much and stealing food. I'm on the verge of throwing up and causing a small scene, but you're dragging me out through the back, where people think you're going to throw me into a dumpster or something, and if my timing is right, it would be about the same time Dion is getting too distracted by Milk's beauty and charm to notice the unusual chaos."

"So, there's a back door around the back door?" Dog asked.

"Yes." Upper's drumstick trailed from his and Devil's stick figures to a line trailing up what looked like stairs. "Inside the back room, there are two doors, one leading outside the club and the other leading upstairs to the VIP rooms. It's used as a quick escape route for these men in case there's an attack and they can't leave through the elevators."

"Got it," Dog said.

"So, Devil and I will go up these stairs quietly. Dion bought the whole rooms, and most of his boys are stationed there."

"How do you get past them," I asked.

"Our guy in the chair." His stick went back to the van. "There will be six guards stationed in front of each door; we would need to get rid of them to enter their tech room. So, our guy in the chair is to hack their comm devices and tell them that a stranger is coming up the elevator unauthorized; it's enough to raise their guard and divert their attention to the threat they can see; meanwhile, the coast is clear.

"Devil waits for me while I find the janitor's closet, get into a vent, and head straight to the tech room with a mask to cover my nose from the fogless sleeping gas, which lasts about thirty minutes, so we're going to have to be quick if we don't want to be seen. When the guards are out like a light, I enter the room and unlock the door for Devil, who closes it behind him, and it's like nothing ever changed."

"And in a situation where we exceed thirty minutes?" Devil asked.

"You knock them out before they can open their eyes and realize what's happening."

"That sounds like a plan," Dog said.

"So," I said, "back to the stranger in the elevator, that's me, right?"

"Adequate," Upper said, pointing the drumstick to what looked like an elevator with six stick figures pointing guns at it. "They're going to see a cute, freckled face, confused woman who looks terrified to see six guns pointed at her. Your name will be Fernanda Valez; she was a guest there before Dion. Your excuse, you wanted to retrieve a small locket you thought you lost weeks ago, and you used the opportunity since you were back in town to visit where you stayed last, or some shit lie, and then you're probably going to stall by making them uncomfortable. You're very good with that."

I rolled my eyes.

"Great," Upper said, "back to Milk and Dion. Milk, you're an essential part of this whole thing. Dion always carries his phone with him, and his phone holds all his passwords and time counts for access to the Pablos' server wall for classified documents, business passes, illegal dealings, and everything the Marinos need. We can't exactly ask him to give us time access, so you'll be given a device; the moment you get close to him, the device automatically gives me access to their servers. You might need to keep talking to him until we get all we need."

"Doable," she said.

"Once all that is set, and Devil and I get what we need, we communicate through our comms. Zahra leaves Dion's floor, Milk keeps talking to Dion for maybe thirty minutes tops, Devil goes back to bartending, I go to Dog at the van, and Zahra goes back to clubbing. We circle back here at ten."

"Okay," I said, dissecting everything in my head, looking for flaws and mistakes. "Milk and I walk in together, right? How is a sophisticated guest walking in with a bartender's sister?"

"You walk in as friends, all giggling and girly stuff. Devil will resume work with a duffel bag holding a change of clothes for himself, except there's one for you too. The duffel bag will be dropped in the third stall of the bathroom; the moment Milk is gone, you head there, change, and get into character."

"Change from . . . my usual self or . . ."

Milk sat up. "Not your usual self; we're going as Valentina and Isabella."

"Who the fuck are they?" I asked.

Milk smirked. "My personally created disguises."

I sighed. "I do not like the sound of that."

CHAPTER FIFTEEN

Zahra

Milk and I stumbled into Eden, laughing and looking as if we had just left another club to see what was happening in this one. Acting wasn't my strong suit, but it was easy to fall into character with my blond wig, made-up face, and short red dress that Milk had forced me into.

Men's eyes followed us, and I smiled to myself because that was all Milk's doing. She didn't even have to try. She didn't have to throw suggestive smiles, she just had to be herself, and men would start crawling to her.

"I see you." Dog's voice resounded in our ears, where the invisible comm rested.

"Do you see them?" I asked with a grin.

"Yup, up on your six. He's getting fucked up," Dog said.

"Just how we want him," Milk said as we reached the bar, smiling at the bartender. "Hi there." Her voice went down a pitch.

"Cringe." Upper's voice filtered through.

Milk kept her gaze on the bartender as she spoke. "Can we get something sweet and . . . hard?" she asked the man, who couldn't get his eyes off the swell of her cleavage as he nodded wordlessly. "Thank you. What's your name?"

"Pat—Patrick. But people call me Pat."

She eyed him with an appreciative look. "Can't wait to taste what you mix up for us, Patrick."

"Gag," Dog said this time.

"Y-yes, coming right up."

Her smile widened, and she turned to me with a wink.

I let out a laugh, spotting Devil from the corner of my eye before he disappeared into the kitchen. "Is it me you're trying to seduce, or Pat?"

Milk's gaze settled on my face slowly, her eyes searching mine before her attention dropped to my lips. "Could be both," she said, her tongue discreetly sliding down her bottom lip as she made eye contact again, a slow, seductive smile curling at her lips.

I swear my heart skipped a beat, and I forgot how to swallow. All amusement of the situation ceased, and I was attuned to her. She stepped closer to me, and my heart thumped. Anticipating. Her body heat kissed mine in a slow caress, and I forgot the mission.

Suddenly her usual smile broke through, and she tapped my cheek, chuckling. "Snap out of it; I'm messing with you." She stepped back.

I forced out a nervous chuckle. Somehow, she'd just played with my mind. "I'm still convinced your past is made up of you going to some kind of offshore women's school where they teach you guys how to seduce men . . . and women."

"*Like fucking sirens,*" Dog said.

"I could teach you if you want," Milk said.

I scoffed. "I don't have a seductive bone in my body. I mostly use my charm."

"*And it works like a charm, worked on me.*" Devil's voice warmed my ear, and I smiled, shaking my head.

"You have the voice," Milk said. "In fact it was the first thing I noticed about you before we even started talking. You had this dominating voice, and you didn't always use it much. Then I made sure to befriend you because, well . . . you were cool, and there could be a lot to gain."

I grinned. "Here I thought it was because you thought I didn't smile much."

"That was also part of it, and I can't say I didn't succeed. When I came into your life, you got to experience what it's like to have smile lines, and your style, *while it still needs an interven-*

tion, has improved. I became your first female friend, and you love me."

"I remember the story differently, but sure, I do love you."

"*Now years later, the two polar opposite women, now best friends, begin a very dangerous criminal organization where they trap men and suck them dry of any penny they had. The end, motherfuckers.*"

"Thanks, Dog, I was beginning to wonder what was happening," Upper said.

Milk shook her head with a chuckle, looking around and moving her body to the Spanish rap music playing in the background.

"You're welcome," Dog responded. "*Anyone else notice how fucking amazing the sound frequency in these comms is? Makes the ones we used before seem like toys. Rich people do have it all, don't they?*" I paused, listened closely, and frowned when I heard the honk of a car and voices at his end.

My brows drew down in confusion; why did it sound like he was . . . outside?

"*Where the fuck are you, Dog?*" Devil beat me to asking.

"*Went to get some hot dogs . . . There was this food truck not far from me. I couldn't resist the aroma.*"

"*So, who's watching the bloody van filled with computer systems showing live feed from a club down the fucking street!*" Upper yelled.

"*I locked it, Jesus, calm the fuck down. I didn't go far.*"

"Who is watching our backs, you fucking idiot? Go back now," I said with gritted teeth, forcing a smile on my face.

"*Not without that hot dog,*" Dog said.

"*I'm gonna fucking kill you if this whole thing goes to shit for a hot dog,*" Devil said.

"*Relax, it's my turn to order now—hey, beautiful, can I get three hot dogs to go, and uh . . . hmm . . . let me see . . .*"

I shook my head, and Milk sighed.

"*Hmmm . . .*"

"I swear to God, Dog—"

"*One Coke, please, and thank you.*"

There was shuffling in the background, and the person he was talking to said, *"There you go."*

"Thanks, sweetheart. Is that a One Direction wristband?"

"Yeah," the person responded, no doubt with a shy smile.

"That's rad; I was a huge fan. I find every One Directioner sexy. You know, there was a time I thought I could audition and join them because people tell me I sound like an angel when I sing?"

"Wait, really?"

"Mm-hmm. In fact, take my card, in case you wanna listen to my voice sometime, you can call me."

"Oh, of course . . . Derek."

"Will be waiting to hear from you."

We all waited, holding our breath as we heard some scuffling, footsteps, and a few street noises before the sound of a door jamming shut resounded.

"Okay, I'm in."

I exhaled, and Milk returned to Patrick, smiling as he dropped two shots before us. She thanked him before turning to me, handing me one of the shots.

I knocked it back without asking what it was.

It burned, but it was perfect, and I nodded at how fruity it tasted. It had a little bit of bitterness, but not too much.

"I love this," I said, smiling at Patrick. "Can I get four more of these?"

He nodded with a smile my way before walking down to the other end of the counter.

"What's your stat, Upper?" I asked.

"We're in position."

"Dog?" Milk inquired.

"Six guards. They're about to leave; give me a sec. Zahra, incoming."

I frowned. "Wha—"

A hand snaked around my waist, and I faked a flinch as the person whispered in my ear. "My boss wants to have a word."

My frown deepened, and my gaze snapped to Milk's surprised one.

"What the fuck?" Devil cursed.

"Your boss? Me?" I asked to be sure.

"Yes, follow me."

"Talk about a change of fucking plans. Zahra, you know what to do; Milk, remain in position until I tell you to move," Dog said, and I suppressed a groan.

Milk nodded to me with an encouraging smile, handing me her purse, where the device was, and I followed the man, who'd already turned.

"Upper, Devil, you're clear," Dog informed.

"The elevators?" Upper asked.

"Zahra can't fuck it up; I need Milk's eyes on her. Leave the elevator part to me; I'll handle it," Dog said.

"What do you mean, you'll handle it," Devil asked.

"Just trust me."

The man led me up a set of stairs, and I spotted Dion and some of his men. They were seated on a long red curved-edged couch, women flanking them.

Dion directed his crooked smile at me, and I wanted to carve his lips from his face. I'd never seen or known a more shameless fifty-three-year-old man in my entire existence; sure, I'd encountered older men with sicker minds, but Dion . . . Dion was one sick motherfucker, and I wished I were here alone, I wished everyone I considered family weren't somewhere around this damn club; I'd have been able to carve out that mouth and shove it down his throat.

"Come here, doll." He tapped his lap.

No way in fucking hell.

"I've got eyes on you. Do whatever he says," Dog said.

"Okay, Zahra, I need you close to his phone," Upper said.

"Don't worry, you're good. He'll touch you, but he won't rush. Smile," Milk encouraged.

Fuck.

I let out a breath, allowing a small, timid smile to slip onto my lips as I complied, walking to him and sitting on his lap.

"Ah, you are pretty, like a fine flower."

"Run your fingers through his hair, and thank him," Milk said.

My jaw clenched, but I did as instructed, leaning more into him and sliding my finger into his oily salt-and-pepper hair. "Thank you."

"Yes." His rough hand squeezed my upper thigh, and I wanted to gag as unwanted flashes plagued my mind.

I'm too fucking sober for this.

Almost like he heard my thoughts, he brought his stubbled face to my neck, breathing me in as he pressed a kiss to my flesh. "Would you like to loosen up, baby?"

"Say you're fine," Milk said, but I did the complete opposite.

"Sure, what do you have?"

"Stall him; I'm in, and we have just twenty percent left to get all we need from his phone. It slowed for some reason," Upper said.

"Oh, I have magic, baby." Dion reached inside his suit jacket. He brought out a small packet of blue capsules and shuffled one out. "Open up."

"Don't swallow," Devil warned.

I leaned forward, allowing him to put the pill in my mouth.

"Ten percent."

Dion pressed kisses down my neck, rough stubble scratching my skin, while his hand caressed my waist before slipping between my thighs. I felt the press of his hard cock on my leg, and my skin crawled.

"Five percent."

I can't do this sober.

His other hand moved to my breast, and he squeezed as his tongue licked my neck, sucking hard enough to leave a hickey.

Fuck this.

I swallowed the pill.

CHAPTER SIXTEEN

Elio

With one bag of late-night greasy food in my left hand, I filtered through the bundle of keys in my right, inserting the correct one and twisting until I heard a click.

As always, I looked left and right down the hallway and then at the security cameras before pushing the door open, entering the room, and kicking the door closed behind me.

I was at a washed-up motel a few miles out of town, away from protection and my last name.

The first time I had come here, I thought it would serve as a breath of fresh air, but it didn't. It never did. Because he was here. The man currently sitting in a rocking chair facing the window was none other than Ricardo Marino—the former boss of the Marino empire.

My father.

"You opened the windows again. Were you missing the outside world?" I asked, shrugging off my suit jacket before dumping the keys on the small wall shelf by the side of the door.

He didn't respond.

I kicked off my shoes, stretching my neck from left to right before walking to stand beside him. The wind that blew in from the netted window was chilling, and it made me let out a breath. "I see why. It's peaceful out there."

I moved to sit at the windowsill, outstretching the food bag to him, which he eagerly collected. "Slow down; you haven't eaten in a day. I can't afford you choking yourself to death—as much as I'd love to see it."

I studied the starved man in front of me. His pale skin, chapped lips, and red-rimmed eyes. He looked so much older than his age. The wrinkles on his face and the sagging of his skin had worsened. He looked like a dead man with life. It was irritating, but it pleased me.

Despite my warning about him rushing his food, he still gobbled it, and I shook my head, watching with pity.

He had stopped fighting me years ago, now he just... complied. If defeat were a person, it would be him.

"Not long now, Father. Everything is going according to plan. It would have been sooner, but there was a bit of a holdup."

Dread smeared his face, and a whimper escaped him.

"I know, it's infuriating," I said with a sigh of distress. "Elia showed up with this band of thieves. The foolish boy has been in Italy for years, can you imagine that? He's been committing petty crimes just for the fun of it. I wouldn't say he did it because he was hungry and needed the money. All the legal funds of the Marino empire will be going to his name. I had his entire life planned for him. He was settled, and all that remained was Casmiro and Angelo because they had worked so hard to be left with nothing. But then—Elia showed up; I can't burn it all with him in it. It makes all these years of planning useless."

My father whined. It was scratchy and irritating to hear when he spoke. "Just—kill me."

I sighed. "Have you heard a word I've been saying, old man? I can't do it yet—I kill you, and I kill me too, and I can't die until I am sure everyone else won't be affected by it. I need to make sure Elia is happy and away—far, far away from Italy. When that is done, you and I, we're going to have a lot of fun," I told him.

"You—you need help, Elio—please get help," he said. His eyes drained as he looked at me with pity, shaking his head slowly like he actually cared.

An image of me wrapping my hands around his throat, squeezing until I killed his body and his fucking soul because it didn't deserve to be judged, popped into my head. His soul deserved to rot as his flesh would.

Instead of putting my thoughts into action, I nodded. "You should have told my mother to get help. She needed it more. Who knows, maybe we wouldn't be here, and you wouldn't have to watch everything our predecessors have worked so hard for—"

"Kill me, boy." He jerked from the rocking chair. "I don't want to see it—I refuse to see you destroy my name—our legacy. Just kill me and be done with it, isn't that what you want?"

I observed him a bit, before looking away out the netted windows, seeing the light droplets of rain showering down, headlights shining and dimming.

"You don't even know me," I said, but it was so low I barely heard myself. "You did this to me . . . I'm fucked up because of you and you still don't know what I want. That's not fair."

Silence stretched, and I swallowed.

Since I took over the syndicate, I'd worked my head off to bring our name to insanely incredible heights. We were legal; we were in the political spotlight. We were gigantic, made for life. The family's inner business ran smoothly. No complications, no hiccups.

"I don't just want to kill you, Father. I want to make you *suffer*. I want to drive you *mad,* and I want to see you weep when you watch it all burn. You're so lucky because I'll be standing by your side, holding your hand. At least you'll have me as company. The sinner you created. The best fucking poetic justice. Mother would be proud of me."

He whimpered.

I looked back at him. "Would you be proud of me?"

He kept quiet.

"Speak, or the next time you'll see me will be weeks from this one."

"What do you want me to say?" he snapped.

"Tell me you're proud of me."

Silence stretched, and his eyes filled with pity and something else I refused to cling to. "I am proud of you," he said.

I breathed, holding my head high as relief flooded through me. "Thank you, Papà."

I looked out the window again. "This gang Elia brought about will allow me to cover more ground. I want to start with Pablo. I will discover what he knows about Arturo's painting, and then destroy our alliance and create a war."

My father shook his head. "You can't ruin decades of alignment with the Pablos, Elio. Y-you can't do this to the family."

"I can. I want to do it. I crave destruction. I crave to see the look on your face when it happens. The one thing—the *only* thing you have ever cared about, falling to pieces all around you. Ah . . . the bliss that would bring."

"Just kill me," the man whimpered again, looking on the verge of tears, and I wanted to smile. I so badly wanted my lips to curve up in a smile, but that invisible force kept them firm, denying me that relief.

It reminded me that though I had control over my father, his actions in the past still had complete control over my mind; there was still an inkling of fear when I looked at his face, a small piece of want for his approval in everything I did.

It only fueled my determination to finish what I had started.

And I would . . . soon.

Angelo approached me at the gazebo by the poolside; his stance held a stiffness that told me I was about to be given bad news. I refilled my whiskey glass, taking my eyes off him as I placed the bottle on the small table that held three lit scented candles, my cigar box, lighter, and a book.

The last thing I needed was any sort of disturbance. I took my "me" time very seriously, and Angelo might just be at the receiving end of however my response would come out.

Depending on whatever it was he wanted to tell me.

"Marino," he greeted when he reached me. "Looked for you earlier. Where did you go?"

"Monitoring my movements now?" I asked him, taking out a cigar and lighting it.

"You left the compound without security," he stated in displeasure.

I took a long drag from the cigar, blowing it out before settling my gaze on him. "What business do you have with that? Hm? Can't I leave my own home without soldiers tailing me like flies to shit?"

"Where did you go?" he asked again, eyeing me suspiciously.

Surprise had me widening my eyes. "Where did I—" I paused, shaking my head. "I went to a motel to see my dead father; what else would you like to know? The food I ate on the way? A greasy, unhealthy burger. Would you like to know if I stopped by the side of the road to piss and refuel my car?"

Angelo sighed, clearly not believing a word I said. Elio Marino would never eat greasy roadside food. He would never be so foolish as to drive alone; he would never stop by a shady gas station to refuel his car; there was no way he could see his father because Ricardo Marino had been dead for years.

"I am only asking because you shouldn't just leave like that—at least let someone know your whereabouts, and it's not a must if you have soldiers tailing you; they can stand back and only come to you when you need help." Angelo sighed. "Also, if you would just get a phone, so maybe I can call next time you choose to disappear."

"No."

He cursed under his breath. "You need a phone—"

"No. I carry too much with me. There is no space for a phone."

"Marino—"

I frowned in mock confusion. "I feel like I'm being repetitive. I feel this sense of déjà vu—like—like we have had this conversation before, and my response was exactly the same as the one I'm giving you now. Do you feel it too?"

Angelo dropped his head, a small chuckle leaving him. "No phone . . . got it."

"Excellent. Anything else?"

He stood straighter. "Yes"—he cleared his throat—"Street returned from the mission an hour ago."

"That was today?"

"Yes," he answered, his features suddenly tight.

"I take it we have what we need, then."

"Yes, we do."

I raised a brow. "But . . ."

"There was a little deviation from their original plan, and they—"

"Who died?" I asked, hoping it sounded like I cared as I dragged in a lungful of the smoke, leaving it in my body for a few seconds before letting it out. "One of the Street people?"

"No," Angelo said.

"One of Dion's people?"

Angelo cleared his throat again. "No. Dion Juan Pablo is the one who's . . . dead."

I paused and frowned. My gaze sharpened on him. "I beg your pardon?"

"She said it was a form of self-defense; he was pumped full of drugs and he tried to hurt her, so she protected herself."

"Which girl? The pretty one with the beverage name?"

Angelo shook his head.

I raised both my brows, nodding. "Ah, the other one." I mused aloud and sat up, pressing the cigar into the ashtray. *Finally* . . .

"Nobody knows they did it."

"It doesn't matter. Their mission was to steal. Not to kill. There is no excuse for carelessness. Have her brought here."

"Marino, she was almost abused—"

"Have her brought to me. Where is Casmiro?"

"Handling it. Dion's boss, Edoardo himself, will be seeking

answers. Casmiro is making sure those answers don't lead back to us."

"If it does lead back to us . . . a betrayal of this kind is unforgivable. This will most definitely give me a decent amount of inconvenience. Somebody has to pay for it."

"She was a victim."

"I was a victim; you were a victim. Did the world go easy on us? No. They lack discipline. She, in particular, needs a reality check. I am happy to deliver it."

"Dion was—"

"Have some soldiers bring her here. Do not let other members interrupt. Especially Devil. And tell Casmiro to meet me at my home lounge in an hour," I said, getting my gun and checking the chamber before swiftly cocking the weapon and flicking the safety back on.

"What do you plan to do?" Angelo asked, eying the gun in my hand.

My thumb rubbed against the surface of the gun as I responded. "Kill a sinner and everyone they share blood with. It has been a while."

CHAPTER SEVENTEEN

Zahra

I wasn't born like the other kids were.

I thought I was until I realized the things happening to me didn't happen to normal kids.

From age five to twelve, I lived with two adults—no, they were not my parents, and it wasn't foster care; it was worse than that. They were my Handlers. From the little I remember, and from what I know now, the gruesome things they made me and the other children do were not things children should have been doing.

But it made them money; older men and younger men alike would pay thousands of dollars to have their way with us . . . no penetration, just gratification, terrible, terrible things we had to do with our hands and mouths . . . If I closed my eyes, if I let the capsule I had taken win, I could go back to that house, I could remember the way it smelled, like detergent, one Miss Handler had used to scrub the floors every night after all our visitors left. I could see myself, an innocent little girl, standing in front of Mr. Handler, scared out of her mind from the alcohol on his breath, worried that she had done something to offend one of her favorite people in the world, scared that he would hurt her like the other men did.

If I really stopped to remember, I would hear my own voice, shaking and scared as I asked him, *"Did I do something wrong?"* Then I would see his eyes, blue like the sky, watching me with what my little self hadn't registered as deranged obsession. I would listen to him tell me how much he wanted me and how much he felt sick for wanting me. I would feel his lips on mine and his tongue inside my mouth. I would watch him take me to his bed, whispering filthy things I'd often hear the other men say, repeating his endearing nicknames he reserved just for me, *"Amore mio," "my Zahra,"* and I would watch myself cry in relief when Miss Handler interrupted him with a shout, pulling me from his grip and his touch.

I would hear his voice whisper, *"I don't know what I was thinking, Amore mio, please forgive me, my Zahra."*

Manuel Conti.

The reason I wished I had died a long time ago, and also the reason I was alive today.

Girls like me were called Plants, born and groomed to attract men as treacherous and disgusting as Manuel, the man who raised me since I was five. The man who wanted me when I was twelve. The man who saved me from sex slavery when I was sixteen, the man who took me to Sicily, made me his equal, gave me power and respect.

I had trusted him then. I once thought I loved him . . . He ended my trauma, but it was almost too late before I realized he made it worse.

Girls like me . . . we didn't have the petty wish of that magical first kiss, or the awkward first time. Girls like me were born into this world for the sole purpose of pleasuring men, and sometimes women. Girls like me were created to gratify the fetishes of people old enough to parent us. I didn't have my light brown skin because two people of different races fell in love and decided to have children; I had my skin because there was someone out there who wanted to fuck someone like me.

It was *why* I was born.

My past was why I didn't like Dion's lips on me. Not entirely because he was a sleazy bastard, but because it brought back trauma I had buried a long time ago.

My night wasn't going how I pictured it would. I was out of it, laughing and chuckling my head off. That goddamn pill Dion gave me was messing with my head. It was only five minutes ago that he had whispered in my ear, saying we should go somewhere private. I nodded like an idiot and let him pull me with him. We got into an elevator, and somewhere at the back of my mind, I heard a voice.

"Zahra, the fuck are you doing? Leave him now. Make an excuse and go to the washroom, I'm on my way."

I was dazed with everything around me, and when the elevator closed, Dion held my face in his hands and crashed his lips to mine in a kiss, pulling my waist to meet the bulge in his pants; I giggled when he dropped his head to lick and kiss my neck.

"Devil, Zahra's in trouble."

"Just helped Upper out of the club; I'm on to her now."

The elevator dinged open, and Dion led me out. We stumbled down the hallway, to a door he led me into. He closed it behind me, pushing me to the flat surface, his body pressing against mine, erection hard against my stomach while he kissed me.

"Zahra, I've lost visuals of you. Are you okay?"

Dion sucked on my neck. Eager.

"Mm," I moaned. "Slow down, tiger."

"I wanna fuck you, princess."

"You will; patience is a virtue," I whispered breathlessly.

I smiled at him when he looked at me.

"Get on the bed, Dion. Get naked."

Dion scrambled off me, turning to take off his clothes hurriedly.

"Remind me to drug you more often because you sound like a fucking horny teenager. He's almost twice your age, Zahra." Dog's voice reached my ear, the recognition shocking me for a second.

"Oh, hi, Dog," I whispered with a smile, watching as Dion's naked body rushed to the bed, his cock hard and ready.

"Oh, now she fucking answers—"

"Bye, Dog."

"Wai—"

I discreetly took the comm from my ear, dropped it to the ground, and stepped on it till it broke underneath my heel.

"Come over here, princess."

I walked to the foot of the bed with a smile, my tongue grazing my bottom lip.

He had his hand around his shaft, stroking it.

I tilted my head, watching him.

"Come on, baby."

My hand went to undo the zipper of my dress, and then I slipped it down my body, leaving the red lace panties and bra on display.

Dion groaned. "So fucking sexy. How did I get so lucky?"

I grinned, faking shyness as I bit my bottom lip to stop the grin from spreading. "Do you have a knife?" I asked him, and he frowned, still stroking his length.

"A knife? What for?"

"I was thinking . . . I could . . . cut off my bra, tie you up with it, then cut off my panties and gag you with them while I ride your cock. Red would look so good on your wrists."

"Top drawer to the left," Dion said like a happy dog waiting to be fed by his master.

I moved to the drawer he gestured to and smiled to myself, spotting the knife there. It was small and handy.

Just perfect.

I made my way back to the foot of the bed before I climbed on slowly, crawling up his naked body and pressing myself down to his hard cock.

"Ah," he grunted, his jaw clenching. He rocked his hips, trying to dry hump me through my thong.

"Shhh, patience."

"Ride me—fuck—I'm so hard right now."

"Poor thing, you wanna see something interesting before we start?"

He nodded hurriedly.

I raised my knife-free hand to the wig and pulled it off with the small wig cap I wore underneath it, whipping my short hair left and right, my fingers brushing the curls free.

I felt Dion's cock soften almost immediately, looking at me with wide eyes, the recognition shining like a bright light in those dimmed, intoxicated pupils.

"Oh fuck . . ." he muttered.

"You recognize me?"

Fear flashed through those eyes, and I smiled.

"Of course you do, Dion," I said, dragging the knife down to his chin from his cheek. "What?" I shot him a taunting smile. "You don't wanna fuck me anymore?"

His chest heaved. He was scared. Lying beneath me. Trapped with the knife to his throat. It had been a while since I felt the effect of my power.

"Look, Zahra, I paid off Manuel; I have nothing owed to you."

"You don't?"

"Just let me go; if you kill me, Edoardo will—"

"Do nothing; you know he'll do nothing, Dion. Even if he wanted to, Manuel or I would be the last people he thinks of."

"What do you want from me?"

"Your life." I smiled. "Remember that time in Sicily, the last time we saw each other? I told you I would dig a knife down your throat." I pressed the knife to his throat. "What was it you called me? Manuel's whore?"

"Manuel cut off my fucking finger for that—isn't that payment enough?"

"How about the little girl you killed? Maya. You fucked her—raped her, and killed her. This was before the incident with Manuel. Do you remember? Your words were, 'Throw her body in a fucking river somewhere; she didn't even make me *come*.' She was a *fucking* child."

"That was—"

"The moment I knew you would die by my hands, Dion."

His body shuddered beneath me.

"But before that happens, I have a question. What business do you have with Marino, and why would they want intel on the Pablos?"

The man frowned, chest heaving. "What the fuck are you talking about?"

"Does it have to do with the flash drives?"

"What fucking flash drives?" He looked even more confused, clueless.

"So you know nothing, then."

"Wha—"

"A waste." I raised the knife, but he, *obviously,* saw it coming so his blow to my forearm wasn't completely unexpected; the knife falling right out of my grip, though, was something I didn't see coming.

He gained the upper hand, pushing my body off him with as much strength as his drug-filled mind could muster. I landed with a sharp thud, my middle connecting with the nightstand as I fell. I held my stomach with a groan, grinding my teeth as I watched him stagger towards the locked door.

Swiftly, I got to my feet, ignored the pain in my ribs as I slid my hands behind me, undoing the clasp of my bra before rushing to him. I jumped on his back, wrapping the bra around his neck before he could reach the door, my legs circled and held tight around his waist as I pulled the bra tight, choking him with it.

I breathed heavily, teeth gnashing as the sound of him choking and staggering backward filled the room. His hands swung, trying to hit my face, anything to break free of my assault. He caught my hair in his fists as he pulled, running backward until his body slammed me against a wall, the force of it knocking the breath out of me, and the glass vase that had been on a table onto the floor. It shattered as the bastard's elbow connected with my stomach, and the bra fell out of my grip. He turned sharply, gripped me by my neck, and slammed my head against the wall. "You fucking bitch!" he spat, saliva hanging from his lips as he gripped my hair again, pulling me from the wall, and dragging me towards the bed.

I stumbled over my own feet, dropping slightly to my knees,

my fingers wrapping around steel as he forcefully pulled me up, throwing me carelessly on the bed, as if I weighed nothing.

He breathed, stalking closer. "What did you think, that you could kill me?" A smirk pulled at the corners of his lips. "*You?* A fucking rogue *Plant?*" His knees hit the bed. I pushed my body upward as if trying to escape him. "That's one thing with you fucking Plants; give them a bit of attention, and they think they are worth something." He crawled up above me, his eyes locked on my breasts before jumping to my eyes again. "You think you are Manuel's equal . . . no, you've only been one thing to him." He brought his face closer, until I could smell his rancid breath. "His. Fucking. Who—"

I plunged the knife right into the base of his throat with a yell. His eyes widened in shock as his blood pumped out, spraying and pouring on my chin and chest. I gritted and groaned, twisting the knife as I pushed him off me, straddling his waist and looking him dead in the eye: "Told you what would happen the next time you called me that, you fucking motherfucker." His eyes were wide in death as he choked on the gurgle of his blood, his bloodied tongue sticking out.

I twisted the knife again, bringing my face near his. "Rot in hell knowing a fucking *Plant* ended your miserable life, you fucking piece of shit," I spat, watching his life slip out of him, his legs weakly kicking out behind me, until his struggle slowly stopped, and his chest stopped moving.

I stayed like that for about a minute, breathing heavily before I pulled out the knife, heaving a sharp breath as I let go of the weapon, throwing my head back, and closing my eyes tightly. "Shit," I hissed, looking down at the mess I made. "Fucking hell, Zahra."

Quickly, I got off him, paced for a few seconds as my brain worked a mile a minute before I rushed to the bathroom and washed away as much blood as I could. I ran back into the room, picked up my bra and dress, and slipped them back on.

The door burst open brutally, and I gasped, turning to see

a fast-breathing Devil. "Zah—" He stopped short as his gaze shifted to Dion's body on the bed.

His wide eyes shifted to me and then to Dion. He rushed into the room, and before he shut the door, I spotted unconscious bodies on the ground.

"What the fuck happened?" he whispered in a yell, raking both hands through his hair. "How the—why the—"

My body shook, and I hugged myself. "He tried to hurt me. I—I was trying to defend myself, and I—I don't know what happened—I was—I was high—I wasn't thinking—I didn't know—"

"Hey, hey." Devil rushed to me, wrapping his hands around my body, and placing a kiss to my hair. "I'm sorry, it's okay; I'm glad you're okay. Fast thinking is always important," he assured, breaking away from me. "Are you hurt anywhere?" he asked, his eyes roaming all over me as I frantically shook my head.

"No, no, I'm not."

"Good, good," he said, before rushing to Dion's body and picking up the knife from beside him. "We gotta get outta here," he said as he rushed towards me, grabbing my wrist. "Come on."

Before we left, I picked up my wig and my ruined comm device from the ground and glanced at Dion's lifeless body.

My lips curved to the side.

CHAPTER EIGHTEEN

Zahra

One more, just one more act, and I could carry on with my day and self-reflect on my actions. No matter how many times I'd done it, there was still that hollow feeling that came after taking a life—the feeling of emptiness and wrongness.

They were terrible men; they deserved it because they hurt a lot of people. But who was I to pass judgment? There was no way to regain the little pieces of myself and the conscience that I lost after I ended a life.

The only thing keeping my head in check was the awareness of right, wrong, necessity, and the limit to how far I took my revenge.

Manuel would say there was a lever in every human, one you should always pull when you feel like you're drowning in the emotion that comes with getting justice for the wrongs committed against you. If you didn't pull the lever, you'd sooner forget where it was in your mind, and you'd be no different from the people you wanted dead.

I tried not to forget that. Each time I took a life, I'd take a moment to myself and pull back from that dark place.

The two soldiers that had been ordered to bring me to the poolside maintained their distance after I'd urged them to touch me and see what happened. I already knew it was a matter of time before the boss himself asked for me.

I hardened the frown on my face as we reached the poolside, ignoring the dull ache at the side of my head as my gaze shifted to Elio, who stood at the foot of the pool, both hands tucked into his pants, his suit and tie nowhere in sight. And, as always, he looked like someone dressed for a funeral.

I sighed, walking towards him, wishing I had changed into something else. This dress had overstayed its welcome.

He didn't look away from the pool as I stood beside him. "Thinking of taking a dip?" I asked. "Because I could totally sleep off tonight's chaos and leave you to it."

He didn't respond.

The silence toyed with my head, and I shifted from one foot to another, the cold outside sending chills down my spine.

"I can't remember the last time I swam," he said, still looking at the large pool, voice raspy. "It's been . . . years. I think I was still a teenager then." He breathed in deeply, and then out. "I feel this little twinge of fear whenever I see this pool. But for some reason, I can't stay away."

I looked at the pool and then at him. "I really don't give a fuck about anything you've just said."

He turned his head in my direction and then looked away. After a few seconds, a frown caused a slight pinch to his brows, and he looked back at me again, eyes scanning me from head to toe. "What in the world are you wearing?"

I looked down at myself with a frown and then met his gaze blankly. "Do you not recognize it because it's in a different color? It's a dress, Elio. Like . . . a cloth? People wear clothes to cover their nakedness? Cause it's . . . clothes?"

"I know what—" He stopped, blinking and shaking his head. "Angelo told me you deviated from tonight's original plan by killing Dion Juan Pablo. He says it is because he almost abused you."

"Yes."

"Indeed? You don't look too shaken up for a person who was almost sexually assaulted."

I frowned. "Dion was high out of his mind, he tried to hurt me, and I defended myself. I didn't mean to kill him, but I guess the knife touched the wrong vein because my good luck sometimes is a curse." My voice shook, and I felt tears rising like bile in my throat. I stood straighter, struggling to get ahold of my emotions, and I continued. "I couldn't exactly push him off me because he was twice my size. So, I did the next best thing I could do. I didn't think—think that he would . . . die."

Elio's brows drew down in a frown.

"My whole team is worried about me, and I fucking hate it when people walk around me like I'm an eggshell they don't want to crack." I let out a humorless chuckle, looking away from him. "As much as they don't like to admit it, they look up to me. I'm not about to make them see me as some weakling."

Looking back at him, I hardened my features even though I could feel the tears building up in my eyes. "I am shaken up, but I am also angry because I just *killed* a *person,* and the last thing I want to do right after is talk to the man who sent us on the goddamn mission in the first place. I just need to get under the damn covers and wait for the nightmares I can already feel coming; so sorry if I'm not a fucking weeping woman, but don't expect me to cry amid my enemies," I said in one breath.

Elio watched me, his eyes assessing and the frown leaving his face before he spoke. "Why do you even try?"

"What?" I feigned confusion.

"That . . . was a pathetic attempt at lying. It's the worst you've come up with for as long as I've known you."

"You think . . . you think I'm—"

"Enough. I see right through it."

I kept the act on for precisely five seconds before I drew on a blank look. "He got what he deserved," I said at last. "He wasn't a good person."

"So, killing him makes you better?"

"Yes."

"I will ignore your delusion and return your attention to what I wanted from this. It was not to kill him, but to get access to their system—"

"Which we did."

"You do not cut me off when I'm speaking, Zahra."

"Oh, so you do know my na—"

"Not only were you reckless," he said, cutting me off, "but you also put the lives of your companions at risk; you put the life of my only *family* at risk. And that is something I can't forgive."

"Well, head count says Devil is alive, and everyone else is fine."

"It doesn't answer the what-if question."

"There doesn't have to be a what-if question. Dion was a fucking bastard. I had a score to settle with him. I saw an opportunity to settle that score, and I did. No one was hurt, and no one knew it was us. The world is still turning."

"¿Qué cuenta?" he asked. *What score?*

"That is for me to know."

He turned away from me, facing the pool. "You have no remorse or regret for what you've done."

"I don't see a reason to."

He nodded, and I hated that I couldn't read him right now. Somehow, I had been the open book tonight; he wasn't giving anything away.

I took a step back from him just to be safe.

His throat worked. "My father used to drown me . . . here, right in this pool." His eyes were trained on the water like he could see it happening.

He took his hand out of his pocket and pointed to the gazebo. "Right over there is where my mother used to stand, watching him drown me." He dropped his hand back down.

I swallowed, remembering all Devil had told me weeks ago. "Why?"

"I was stubborn. I lied a lot. Kept things from him. Spoke English to him. Forgot something he told me I shouldn't forget. Did something other than what he wanted," he said, taking his other hand out of his pocket as he began to undo his cufflinks slowly. "He called it baptism. Whenever I did any of those things, he would call me a sinner and bring me here. And I would beg him, pathetically. I thought maybe this time he'd listen; he'd show mercy and let me off with just a warning. But he never did."

He slipped the first cufflink into his pocket, proceeding to undo the second one. "I would shout, but then, he'd dip my head under the water, cutting me off; I would fight, but he wouldn't let me go; I'd run out of air, and he would keep his hold firm. He did it until I would drown, and then he'd pump my chest until I woke up." He slid the second cufflink inside his second pocket and began rolling up his sleeves.

"When he wasn't satisfied with the lesson, he'd do it again. The feeling of fear . . . of dying, the number of times he made me feel it, had me defying him at every turn . . . just so he would bring me here and do it again. Just so I could revel in the dazed look my mother would give us. Just so I could imagine what it would feel like to just—watch."

He turned to me. "But more than anything, I wanted to know how it felt to be the one doing the drowning. I wanted to be the one pushing my head under the water. I didn't know why at that time, but now I do."

"Because you're a sick fucker who needs serious medical attention?"

"Part of the reason."

I took another step back, and he took one forward.

"The real reason was the relief of knowing that I would lose consciousness. I found that the better version of myself is when I can't be myself. When I get to escape, even for a few minutes." He sighed. "And my mother . . . after it all, she'd hold me, and take care of me, but I could always tell she waited eagerly for the next time we'd take another visit to the pool. She loved to watch it. Me drowning . . . but soon I found myself waiting eagerly as well."

"That's fucked up."

"She was sick. It's hard to blame her."

"Oh, so it's genetic," I said, stepping back.

"Hm."

"Why are you telling me all this?"

"Because you're a sinner, like me." He took one step towards me, and I took two back. "In clearer words, Zahra, because you're about to die."

I stood still, and it felt like everything paused around us for a moment.

We watched each other, and he waited for me to make the first move. It was bait. But it meant two things: I either fall for the bait and survive to see another day or put up a fight and die by his hands.

I chose the first option, turned, and bolted down the curved corner of the pool. I should have known there was a problem when the guards didn't make a move to even stop me.

Running from him was stupid, a guaranteed failure, but I still attempted it.

I reached the only exit door and tried to open it, but it didn't budge.

"Fuck."

I looked behind me to see him walking towards me like he had all the time in the world, calm and collected. "No cameras, no rules, no helper . . . it's just you and me now, Sport."

I looked around me. This was an open area, which was well fenced with bushes around. There was a building there, but the only way to enter it was through the exit doors and the window.

I rushed to the window and tried to pull it up.

"Locked." Elio's taunting voice reached my ears again.

It was made of glass; if I could punch a hole through and reach the lock—

"You can't break it." His voice rang out as if he were in my head.

I swallowed, feeling sweat bead on my forehead.

The fence.

"It's useless. I'm taller than you are, and even I won't be able to make the jump. Trust me, I tried." His voice was closer.

I turned sharply, and he was closing in on me as I had guessed. I moved to run again but didn't get far. He caught me just at the pool's edge; I tried to squirm out of his hold. I failed pitifully at trying to elbow him in his stomach.

I dropped my head to sink my teeth into the skin on his forearm and reveled in the bliss that came from his groan of pain. I dipped my teeth further until I tasted blood. He forcefully pulled his arm from my mouth, and his grip loosened.

When I thought I had the running opportunity, his leg swept mine from underneath me, and I was falling towards the pool. On reflex, I grabbed his shirt collar as I went down, and we both hit the water with a massive splash.

For about five seconds, I was underwater, but I pumped my arms and legs furiously until my head broke the surface again. I coughed, my chest heaving.

Elio surfaced right after me, his hair wet and pressed against his forehead as he angrily brushed it away, his gaze furious and dead set on me.

"You don't want to do this," I said with trembling lips.

He swam towards me, and my attempt to swim backward was a total failure. I tried to fight him off again, trying to move my legs to hit him, but I was too slow, and somehow, he was faster, like he had mastered the act of moving stealthily underwater. I moved to hit him with my hand in the open air, but he caught it, his other hand wrapping around my neck.

"You . . . you don't want to do this," I stuttered in a shiver.

"Why not?" he seethed, not even shivering as violently as I was, but I could see the goosebumps on his forearm as his grip tightened around my neck, almost cutting off my airflow.

My last resort was my leverage.

"Devil—he'll never forgive you."

He blinked, amusement filling his eyes as he responded, "Surprise . . . that's *exactly* why I'm doing this."

"You piece of shi—" My words were swallowed the moment the water swallowed my head and my entire body.

CHAPTER NINETEEN

Elio

It was simple.

I needed Street. They were skillful. Chaotic in the face of danger, but still conceivably effective. But I had never been one to rely on people before making my next move. I was beginning to lean on the idea of them, becoming perturbingly dependent on their presence to get things done.

There was the fact that I wanted Elia far away from me, from this country, but a lingering sense of peace seemed to fill me, knowing he was close by. The urge to keep him safe and shield him from danger was like a bow to a violin—still, him being close was messing with things. And him being attached to a person who attracted danger like a moth to a flame was worse than him being close to me.

I didn't know who she was, but I knew she was someone. Someone bold enough to kill the second-in-command of a pernicious family and show no remorse or fear—it put me on guard. It was a symptomatic sign that I had to cut her off. She was a threat. A threat to me and a threat to my brother's life.

She had to go.

Zahra's hand pulled at my wrist in an attempt to break my grip on her neck. Her face scrunched tight, trying to hold her breath and survive. The sheer determination she gave off was impressive. She'd been trained for this too. It was painfully obvious how she'd lasted this long, but I knew she was at her breaking point.

I allowed her a chance for a little hope, and she sprang up to fight me, resurfacing a couple of times, but I pushed her back under, her hands tangling with mine, her body slow from the fight and pull of the water.

A struggle she was failing to keep up.

My grip tightened, and her eyes widened, mouth falling open.

"There we go," I whispered, watching the bubbles from her mouth rush up and fade. "Don't fight it," I said, holding firm through every jerk of her struggle until it stopped. Until her grip loosened from my wrist. Until no sound of struggling or rippling water was heard, and it was just . . . silence.

I looked up, blew out a breath, and yanked her body back up to the surface, signaling to one of the soldiers as he rushed towards me. I grunted, lifting her heavy unconscious body from the pool, the soldier assisting in pulling her out completely, laying her beside the pool.

I brushed my hair back with both hands before getting out of the water, drenched and dripping from head to toe, my clothes sticking to me like a second skin.

I signaled to another soldier. "Turn the cameras back on," I said before turning to the other soldier, who had assisted in lifting her body from the pool.

"Make it seem like she drowned, and you tried to revive her. Do not exert effort; I want her to stay dead," I said to the soldier, who dutifully went to his knees, pumping her chest with little effort.

With one hand working on the buttons of my shirt, I made my way back to the gazebo, skin biting with irritation at what I'd just put myself through, at the unconscious step I had taken towards being exactly like my father.

My skin crawled, and the distinct need to punish myself pulsed through my veins.

I shook my head of the sickening thoughts just as coughs and sputter sounds came from behind me, followed by strings of panicked curses from the soldier.

I halted, a frown dragging down my brows as I slowly turned

towards the pool. She was awake, coughing up water, her hand pressing at her throat as the soldier watched in surprise.

Anger. Burning, flaming, hot, obdurate anger flooded my veins. "What part of 'do not exert effort' don't you understand, estúpido!"

"I didn't—she just—I—"

Groaning, I headed faster for the gazebo and grabbed my gun, walking back towards them.

"Step away," I gritted, and the man removed himself immediately.

I stared down at the nuisance. Her breathing was ragged as her eyelids fluttered shut and open in a battle to stay awake.

"I hoped the water would kill you, but I guess your lungs aren't as weak as I thought," I said, pointing the gun directly at her forehead.

Her gaze flickered to the gun, and then to me. "What is this—more foreplay?"

"In honesty, part of me was hoping that I'd get to kill you this way."

She watched me through half-closed eyes, her lips lifting to the side with a breathy laugh. "Aw, c-can't do it like Daddy, or is this you stalling?"

I detested the little truth in her observation. "I am not my father, and I am not stalling."

"Okay—cool, anytime now."

Provoked, I disengaged the gun's safety, seconds away from pulling the trigger when the exit door burst open, and Elia stopped short at the sight in front of him.

I sighed, shaking my head.

"This thing called . . . luck," she whispered with a scoff.

Ignoring me, Elia rushed towards us, immediately getting to his knees and lifting Zahra's body so her back was to his chest. "Hey, are you okay?"

"Peachy," she answered weakly.

"Get away from her, Elia. She's not who you think she is," I said, still pointing the gun at her head.

Elia raised his head, and I was met with a fury similar to mine. "Fuck off," he gritted.

"Do not make me repeat it."

Ensuring Zahra was okay, he got to his feet, his anger-filled eyes dead set on me. "First off, don't talk to me like I'm a fucking child, and secondly, how the fuck could you do this? What the hell did she do to you?"

"She killed without reason, put you in danger—"

"Are you listening to yourself? Dion almost hurt her; it was self-defense," he bit back, and I almost pulled the trigger then and there, hating how she had manipulated him, how she had him wrapped around her little finger.

"Elia, she has you fooled, believe me—"

"Believe you? Why the fuck should I believe you?" he yelled. "What reason do I have to believe any *fucking* word that comes out of your mouth." He shook his head, staring at me like I was a stranger. "You shouldn't have done this—you shouldn't have touched her, you sick bastard."

"Open your eyes, *Elia;* you're dancing to her tune. She confessed to me. She told me she killed him because she had a score to settle with him. I have only ever been honest with you, except when it concerns your safety. Otherwise, I would never directly put you in harm's way, and that is what I would be doing if I let her live. She is bad for you, Elia."

He shook his head. "I would take her lies over yours any day, anytime. I would take her bad over yours even in fucking death. There is absolutely nothing you could say to change my mind."

I hardened my features, knowing I couldn't be soft on him. It had never worked.

"Move out of the way, Elia."

He stepped closer. "I'm not letting you touch her."

"Okay." I raised the gun, pointing it right at him; the shock in his eyes had my arms feeling too weak to even hold up the gun, but I held firm. "You either step away, or I kill you first and then kill her right after."

Elia's gaze shifted to the gun in my hand and then to my eyes. "Bullshit," he said.

I tilted my head to the side. "I adore your faith in me, truly, but the last thing you should do is test me, Elia."

"You can't do it," he said.

"You think?" I asked.

"I know," he seethed. "You're all fucking talk when it comes to me. Weak and incompetent."

"I'd watch my mouth if I were you," I warned.

"You could never do it," he continued. "All those years ago, you couldn't do it—"

"Stop. Talking." The gun shook in my hand.

"Why? Because it's the truth? Because deep down, you're still that weak fucker who got beat around by his dear old dad?"

"Shut up, Elia." My breathing spiked.

"What did it?" he asked.

"Devil, stop." Zahra's attempt to stop him was a failure too.

"Tell me, what made you completely flip over? What turned you into him? Was it the thrill you got after murdering your whole family? Did you love your mother's scream while you stabbed her? Or Mariana's and Lorenzo's tortured wails while you fucking burned them alive."

My grip tightened on the gun. "Stop."

"Why? Be fucking honest with yourself, Elio; killing me would be your last tipping point, so fucking do it because I know you want to." He stepped closer to me. "I don't know why I didn't see it before, but it's clear now that me being alive is the only delusion you have of being a good person, but you're not. You're the one who needs to open your eyes, Elio. You didn't kill me, but you were ready to let me die just so you could please *him*. You think I don't remember what you did to me? Admit it. I'm alive because I'm the only physical trophy for the one good thing you have ever done."

My hand shook again, his words reaching straight to my heart. "Don't fucking degrade it," I said, my chest burning. "Don't fucking make it sound meaningless!" The yell racked my whole body, and I dropped the gun. "It took everything from me, you ungrateful bastard—everything!"

It was foolish doing this in front of Zahra or the soldiers who lingered by, but I was too riled up, hurt by his words and assumptions of me.

"It took my whole life from me! I didn't kill you, but what I did"—my voice broke, my eyes burned—"the lengths I went to for *your* protection, took my whole life from me, so don't fucking stand here and make my life more meaningless than it already is!"

Elia took a step back, a stunned expression on his face.

"Talk nonsense about me burning Mariana and Lorenzo alive; talk about me stabbing my mother; I'll take it all, but don't you dare question or degrade what I did for you. I'll take it from anyone but not you. Not you, Elia."

He did not attempt to say anything.

My gaze flickered to Zahra and then him. I blinked away the sting in my eyes, and sniffed, "Go . . . take her away. When she turns out to betray you, don't say I didn't try to warn you." I turned my attention to Zahra, remorse and the same regretful look in her eyes. "And you, stay clear of me because I swear to God, one more fucking problem from you, and this little drowning thing will seem like a walk in the park."

With that, I snapped my fingers to one of the soldiers, and he rushed to me as I made my way towards the exit. "Drain the pool, and clean it thoroughly. Take my things from the gazebo and bring them to me."

"Yes, Marino."

I stopped. "Everything that happened here stays here."

"The cameras were on, sir; it directly sent feeds to your home lounge, sir."

"Wipe it. No use."

"Sir, Casmiro was in your home lounge, sir."

I clenched my jaw. "Make sure those two get to their quarters without trouble."

"Yes, Marino."

I walked away without a glance at them. The need to punish myself had vanished—no, it had been sated. The only person I loved hated me; the only person I lived for saw me as everyone else did.

That was the worst punishment I could ever get. It was both physical and emotional, and I held on to it, held on to that feeling like it was the very ice the burn in my chest needed.

I held on to Elia's hate for me. It was all I'd ever wanted anyway; I just never thought it would feel even worse than the thought of dying.

CHAPTER TWENTY

Elio

Taking over the Marino empire had been one of the hardest things I had ever done. It was easy faking my father's death, effortlessly slipping into his shoes and taking over from where he left off. But even with the "Wicked" persona he had created for me before he "died," I had still struggled with our associates and other higher-ups who didn't see me as experienced enough to fill his shoes and run the business smoothly.

I was too young compared to everyone who answered to me.

Even now, though they didn't outrightly complain out of fear of offending the psychopath who would likely wipe out their whole existence, there were still murmurs. The old ones were still too traditional with their ways, fearing to take things to the next level and strengthen their families.

Old ones like Edoardo, who firmly believed in bond and family, detested betrayal and could ruin the reputation of any house if he so much as called a meeting with his little oldies. The sixty-seven-year-old man was a grumpy, uninterested traditionalist who still led by old laws.

Delusional men.

I was the lawless one, toying with politics and being almost legal. I was the one who betrayed and two-timed. I was reckless because I was young and didn't know actual loss and the love of family.

I agreed. My conscience and the feeling of right or wrong were gone. All I had to do now was complete this goal, and if having a sit-down with Edoardo in this very bright and un-sanitized city restaurant would help me accomplish that, then so be it.

I looked at my watch for the sixth time, watching people enter and exit the restaurant. Impatience curled in my stomach. "So unprofessional. How can a man like him disrespect time?" I complained, and Casmiro merely glanced at me with a slight lift of his shoulders, his eyes glued to the newspaper he was reading.

I sighed, reached for my cigar packet and my lighter, lighting one up and placing it between my lips, eyeing Casmiro. "How long will you keep this up, hm?"

He didn't respond, and I shook my head. It had been three days since I returned home from the pool to an empty home. No Casmiro. He had apparently seen the footage; he knew what Elia meant to me but hadn't said anything about it.

In fact, he didn't say anything at all. I hadn't seen much of him. If he had a message to pass across to me, he'd send one of his men to deliver it. I gave him his space and time to process it, but it was apparent he needed more time to wrap it around his head that my father had another son, and he was Elia. And I hid it from everyone, including him.

"We have work to do. We should be in agreement," I said, blowing out the smoke and nodding my head at the explosion of vanilla flavor. I rechecked the pack, reading what the stick was made of. "You should try this; it has a wonderful flavor." I extended it to him.

Slowly, he looked up from the newspaper, a scowl on his face as he watched me with disbelief. "I quit smoking, E. Three fucking years ago."

I dropped the pack immediately. "I remember that."

"Right, you do," he muttered, shaking his head and looking back at the newspaper, completely shielding his face from view.

I sighed, relaxing back in the chair, my fingers drumming on the table, my knees bouncing up and down, feeling even more restless than I did before.

"After this," I said, "I will be visiting a gallery for an art exhibit. Mayor Artyom Smirnov invited me. There will be lots of political talks and many things you can learn fr—"

"I'll be busy."

"Busy with what?"

"I'll be overseeing some shipments of petroleum, oil, and gas."

I nodded. "The one housing five thousand barrels?"

He shook his head. "That shipment will come six months from this one. They shifted the date to accommodate two added containers."

I frowned. "More barrels?"

Casmiro shrugged. "It's a shipment for the MCSS. We're only aiding. I signed off on it because I didn't want to have to go to their headquarters or bother you with it. It only delayed the shipment by six months."

The MCSS, Marino Caporegime Sovereign Society. A tight-knit, decades-old society in the body of the Marino empire. They had several associations with different Caporegimes from different families, inside and outside Italy. The society had been created under the supervision of my great-grandfather, and they brought in the second most significant illegal funds, from whatever criminalistic business they depended on to keep the association standing.

Although I had a vague idea of this business, I didn't care enough to investigate further. They were sovereign, only in my name. They could do whatever they wanted. I was just supposed to make sure they did it without hurting the family name, which I didn't care about.

They took 30 percent of the gains, gave the official Marino empire account about 30 percent, and the remaining 40 percent, for some reason, went directly to my account.

They'd been trying to rope me into their little cult. Every month, I got emails about the proceedings. They kept me in the loop like I was their god, and each email was like a prayer for me to answer.

I never gave them the time of day because I had more important things to worry about—like burning it all to the ground.

"So, which shipment are you going to oversee?" I asked Casmiro, bringing my mind back to the conversation at hand.

"A thousand oil barrels are coming from associates in South Africa."

"Oh." It clicked in my head. "Payment for the favor I granted."

Casmiro nodded, concentrating on the newspaper.

The silence dragged on until I spoke again.

"But that was almost four years ago; I didn't ask for a return," I said.

He sighed in exasperation as if my voice annoyed him. "*Nobody* wants to owe you favors, Marino. The oil barrels were an out *from* the favor. They managed to gather it as payment."

I nodded, impressed. "Fair enough," I said.

He rustled the newspaper pointedly, indicating he didn't want to talk to me.

"Where in heaven's sake is that old man? I am very compelled to leave."

Casmiro ignored me.

I pressed the cigar to the ashtray. The silence made me uncomfortable. It was unlike Casmiro to keep silent when we were in a space together. He always liked picking my brain, wanting to engage me in conversations.

It seemed he was intent on continuing this . . . malice. We had even taken separate vehicles to get here. It was unsettling and borderline childish.

This was why I preferred to avoid forming relationships. I should have never agreed to involve him in my matters and become his "friend" again. We worked better when our childhood shenanigans were only a memory, never to be remembered. But he had begged me to let him in and trust him, and I had been candid with him. It appeared he thought my warnings were nothing and that there was no way I could mess up our friendship.

"You can ask someone to cover the shipment overseeing for you. The exhibit is a medium for you to learn more about how politics work. Isn't that what you wanted?"

"It is. But I have to oversee things myself and report back to you. That's my *job*," he said, and I didn't miss the bite in his tone.

It was silent again, and my drumming increased. His grip on the newspaper tightened at the sound, and I decided to make the last push.

"What is so interesting in tha—"

He cut me off by slamming the newspaper on the table, and a few heads turned towards us. "So this is what you meant by being overbearing and talkative?"

"You agreed to lend your ears."

"Well, would it help if I said I don't feel like talking to you?"

My eyes remained on his. "But you have to."

"I don't."

"Are we bickering?"

He stared at me blankly for a while before confusion settled on his face. "What?"

"That's what friends do, right? They bicker. They fight. They argue, but at the end of the day, they circle back and talk about the issue like mature, levelheaded adults."

His jaw clenched. "I don't know what you're talking about."

I sighed. "I need us to work together to get Edoardo off our back and turn this whole thing into another one of our favors. That can't happen if you are secretly plotting my murder."

He scoffed, muttering something incoherent under his breath.

"I'm here, aren't I?" he continued. "You have your fast-thinking, problem-solving underboss right where you need him. I don't know why we're having this conversation."

"You—" I stopped when I spotted a familiar head of pink hair at one of the tables with a stranger, talking animatedly. "Is there a reason why Milk from Street is only a few tables away from us?" I asked, and my question brought a frown to Casmiro's face.

He started turning. "What—" He stopped when he spotted her too. He turned back to me and stopped short again, his eyes zeroing in on the entrance. "Not just her."

I followed his line of vision and saw Dog walking into the building. A lit cigarette was between his fingers as he looked around, not once glancing at our table before heading to the counter.

I frowned when I saw Elia's figure right outside the building. He was leaning on a sleek white 2014 Chevrolet Impala, wearing a black jacket and jeans, talking to Upper, who was pointing at a building by the side of a mini mall, explaining something to Elia, who just stared at him with boredom or disinterest; I couldn't quite place it.

My eyes swept from them, and I looked around for *her*, but she wasn't inside the building or outside.

"What the fuck is going on with our damn security?" Casmiro asked in wonder.

About to look at Casmiro, I caught a figure approaching from the end of the street outside the glass window.

Her short hair was pushed back by sunglasses, and she chewed gum mercilessly as she walked. She was wearing a sleeveless shirt that didn't cover her navel and shorts that were too short and made it seem like she had long legs.

Her skin was exposed to the sun—clear and glowing like she had spent extra hours caring for it before leaving her house. She looked like a foreigner who left her travel crew to shop around for items she could use in decorating her room back in Los Angeles, where she probably lived in a studio apartment with a boyfriend who had *gigs* at low-rated bars in town. The tote bag she carried played off the role so well.

I blinked, unable to take my eyes off her as she walked past Elia and Upper like they were random strangers. The people in question didn't even glance her way as she entered the restaurant, turning heads.

She took the gum from her mouth and threw it in the waste bin closest to her, and I cringed at the carelessness of her actions.

As Dog had done, she looked around, but this time, her eyes landed directly on our table, a determined smile curling at her lips as she walked towards us.

She reached us. "Oh—"

I got to my feet and placed my hand around her wrist. Before she could even start the sentence, I was pulling her away.

She yelled over her shoulder, "Hi, Cassie, bye, Cassie!"

I pushed past the door to the back room of the restaurant. Having glanced at the layout of the building in the car, I set my pace for the second door on the left, pushed it open, and shoved her inside, her back hitting the wall.

I locked the door behind me and turned.

She was looking at me with surprise, and that was when I realized the room wasn't exactly as large as the layout had shown, but it was big enough to put a five-foot space between us.

"Wow," she said breathlessly, leaning away from the wall. "Talk about taking me back to high school."

"You never went to high school."

"That's a very keen observation, *Dad*. Thanks for reminding me that I had a pretty shitty childhood."

"Don't call me that."

"You called me Sport at the poolside; now we're almost even, unless you call me Sport again. I make no promises—"

I closed the distance between us, my palm slamming on the wall, an inch above her head, and a gasp left her, wide eyes staring up at me. The bright light in the storage room popped out the freckles on her cheek. I could smell whatever treatment she used on her hair, and in a swift moment, I was back on that roof with—*Matter at hand.*

"Did you forget what I told you the last time we saw each

other? If you caused any problems for me, the drowning would seem like a walk in the park?"

"You're the one who dragged me in here like you wanted to fuck my brains out."

That made my thoughts cease. "No, I did not."

She relaxed, her lips curving in a smile. "We're in some kind of supply closet." She inched higher, standing on her toes as her gaze lowered to my lips, and I mirrored her action like her eyes had controlled mine. "And you're so close; you're towering over me." Her teeth clamped on her bottom lip swiftly before releasing it. "Now you can't even stop looking at my lips like you want to kiss me."

I felt the heat between our bodies. Warm and subtle, as I locked my gaze with hers.

When I didn't pull away, the amusement died in her eyes, and this time, when her gaze flickered to my lips, it wasn't deliberate.

I pulled back, keeping as much distance between us as I could, mentally knocking myself in the head and shoving both hands into my pockets to avoid unintentionally getting them anywhere close to her.

It was almost as if I'd lost all sense of reason when I saw her outside that window because I couldn't remember what I'd been thinking when I decided to pull her in here with me.

"¿Qué quieres?" *What do you want?*

She cleared her throat, standing straighter. "Ayudarte," she answered. *To help you.*

I raised a brow. *"With what?"* I continued in Spanish.

"With Edoardo," she said, reaching into the tote and pulling out a flat brown paper bag. *"In here are documents proving Dion's illegal dealings outside the knowledge of their whole syndicate. Embezzling, cover-ups, and selling out close family secrets to rival families."* She responded in Spanish, so fluent that it filled something empty in me. I was just as impressed as I'd been the first time she had spoken it at long length, but unlike the last time, when I didn't care to press on how she learned, I was now inquisitive.

She waved her hand in front of my face, and I blinked, taking my hands from my pockets and collecting the file before removing the papers and skimming through them. I glanced at her before looking back at the documents and asking, *"How did you get this?"*

"Some secrets are mine to keep, Elio." She smiled.

I frowned. *"This whole back-and-forth secret affair thing you have going on is starting to irritate me."*

"That sounds like a *you* problem. Get those papers to Edoardo and tell him you found out Dion was a sleazy bastard, and you took care of it because he was about to mess up one of your projects together. He'll thank you and forever be indebted to you because Edoardo is traditional like that. Don't ask me how I know."

I eyed her; the need to ask pinched at my insides, but I dropped it. "Why are you giving me this?"

Something shifted in her eyes, and she swallowed.

I sighed. "This is not for free, is it?"

Her lips thinned as she sucked in a breath. "While I would have loved to give you those papers for free because I caused this mess, and I always fix up my shit . . . we need your help."

"The audacity you have is incomprehensible."

Frustration lined her brows. "I know we were supposed to stay indoors like good little obedient hostages. But this is pretty important."

I knew I should walk out and ignore how tight her tone had gotten, but instead, I asked, "What do you want?"

"Almost four months ago, we were paid for a job that's supposed to happen today; we lost contact with the client for a long time, and they only just reached out two days ago."

"I thought you worked on your own terms."

"It was a hard time for Street."

I frowned. "I'm listening."

"It's to steal a painting." She fished inside her bag, brought out a phone, scrolled for a bit, and turned the screen to me. "It's a really weird painting of a chihuahua. It's not the prettiest thing, but—it's something these people want."

With a clench in my jaw, I looked away from the picture as she dropped the phone back in the bag. "I'm still not following how I could help you."

"We happen to know that in a few hours, you'll be going to the same exhibit as—"

"Forget it." I started stuffing the papers back into the paper bag. "Not happening in this lifetime."

"Oh, come on, this is important."

"And I should care because?"

"Your brother is involved."

Maybe if I had shot him, this form of blackmail wouldn't be possible.

"Your people remain under my protection; even if you don't steal the—weird—chihuahua painting, they cannot reach you if you *stay* indoors."

Something changed in her demeanor, her eyes widening in a plea. "We collected the money, and when we asked to refund, they refused. It's just one job, one stupid painting, and things will go back to normal. It's our fucking reputation on the line. We've never disappointed clients."

"If you think I give an ounce of care for your reputation, then you are very ill-informed about me."

"I know you don't care, but those documents in your hand could open the door for you. With Edoardo."

"I can as well do that on my own."

Her eyes searched mine, and I knew she was trying to find a way to get me to agree. "Okay, fine, do this one thing for me, and I'll answer one question. Anything you wanna know about me, I'll answer truthfully."

"Indeed?"

"Yeah, anything."

"Hm." I thought carefully about the question, keeping my eyes on her. "How are you related to Manuel Conti?" I asked.

Her eyes widened as she stumbled back a step. "How—" She stopped; the horror in her eyes told me I had hit the nail on the head with that question, and my curiosity grew. That name had come up during my intense research on her background, but there wasn't enough information on their relationship.

She took a shaky breath and raised her chin a little, a stance to show courage. "I used to work for him."

"What work?"

"I answered your question," she snapped.

I remained quiet for a few charged seconds before I spoke. "You understand that many important people will attend the exhibit tonight."

She sighed in relief, her shoulders dropping as the tension slipped out of her. "Yes, we had a whole plan to get in and steal the painting after the show, but—Angelo has confiscated a lot of our equipment, and we can't go in blindly with just comm devices and wits, and since I've gathered putting your brother in danger is unforgivable, you're my best shot at this."

"I am not stealing a—chihuahua painting."

"No, you're not. You're just getting one of us in as your plus-one; you can go back and merry away with your fellow buddies and talk about the weather when we do our thing."

"Who am I taking along?"

She let out a breath of relief. "Any one of us. Milk is more—"

"The dress code color for women is white. Please look responsible."

She blinked at me. "Oh, I'm not volunteering; I can't be among social gatherings like that."

"Can't?"

"I mean, I can, bu—"

"Good, I'll be done here in an hour; be ready by then. If you're not, I'll leave you." I began to leave, but she held me back by my arm.

"Wai—whoa." She squeezed my arm, and I stood there in

confusion. Her gaze flickered to mine and then back to my arm. "You've got—real solid muscles. Do you work out?"

I wrenched my arm free from her hold. "Do you fondle people randomly? Because if you do, you must get that in check before tonight."

"I don't—why are you taking me? We can barely stand each other as it is."

"I disagree. The last few minutes are proof that we can."

"That's because there are catches to be gained from being civil."

"I don't care about the catches. It appears that after recent events, killing you is more hassle than it's worth."

"I did warn you, but I still want to know why you're taking me with you."

I searched my brain for a concrete answer before standing straighter. "Because I would rather take the muscle-fondling demon I know than the one I don't. There's also the fact that you speak good Spanish, and I'm impressed."

She momentarily looked surprised, but shook it off and released a sigh. "Fine. Guess I'll see you in a few hours."

I gave a nod and walked out of the supply closet, straightening my suit jacket the moment a female chef came out of the room opposite the one I stood in front of.

Zahra walked past me, offering the girl a wink before walking away with a confident sway to her—

Matter at hand.

I averted my gaze back to the girl, her cheeks growing red as she scurried away with assumptions about things that had never happened.

I took a sharp breath, shook my head at my situation, and returned to Casmiro.

CHAPTER TWENTY-ONE

Zahra

"Okay, Zahra, we've got you all covered," Dog said, handing the comm to Devil, who fixed it inside my ear. "Turn on the comm anytime you want to talk to us. The tracking device inside should let us know where exactly you are. Only when it's turned on."

I nodded.

"It should be turned on at all times," Devil reaffirmed. "On *no* account should we lose contact with you. Your phone should be in your hands because if something happens, or the comm stops working, that's our next means of communication," he said.

"Got it."

"Right." Milk brushed her hands together. "Shall we go over the plans one last time?"

"Attend the event with Marino," Upper said. "Mingle and talk for a bit, familiarize yourself with the security around the space. Dog will handle the security cameras from the little cafe at the other side of the street when you go off to *explore*."

"The painting," Devil took over, "is kept in a vault-like safe; the unlocking device sitting pretty in your purse will be able to rig the system without setting off any alarm."

"It's tested and trusted," Milk cut in with a proud smile.

Upper nodded. "You get into the vault, and I'll be there inside the vent tube, waiting for you to vent me in."

"He gets in with his computer," Dog continued, "disables the alarm so that when you open the safe where the painting is kept, the security won't get alerted and storm the place."

"You grab the painting, hand it over to Upper, he gets back into the vent with it and meets me and Dog at our getaway car a street away from the museum," Devil said. "Meanwhile, you get back to the event, and stick to Marino's side until he leaves."

I nodded. "Okay, should be easy enough."

Dog eyed me with concern. "You sure you're okay with doing this? After the thing with Dion—"

I smiled at him and then at all of them staring at me with worry. "Guys, come on. I can do this; I'm perfectly okay, mind and body."

Devil shook his head. "It's not that. It's the person you're going with."

My gaze locked with Devil's. "I can handle him," I said with assurance.

"Like you handled him when he tried to drown you," Dog muttered. "That bastard."

"It would take more than a little foreplay at some pool to drag me down. You guys have nothing to worry about. Let's just get this over with, close the deal with this damn painting."

"I still hate the fact that we're doing this for such a little amount of money. Do you think we should have demanded more since they want it so badly now?" Milk said.

Devil shook his head. "No. I want us to be done with the client. I don't have a good feeling about it. I mean, they reached out to us months ago, sent the money, and disappeared, and then out of nowhere, they pop up again, wanting it *tonight*?"

Upper frowned. "And weren't we supposed to have it in our possession for like a week before delivering? But now all of a sudden, they need it . . . Something doesn't sound right about that."

I nodded. "Yeah."

"Maybe they had a change of plans?" Milk considered.

"That could be the case, but what about the radio silence all this time?" Upper chipped in.

There was a hard knock on the door, followed by a gruff voice. "Marino's here; get out."

"Watch your fucking tone!" Dog yelled at the soldier outside our door. "Rude fucking motherfuckers," he muttered, beckoning to Upper to recheck the sound transmitter for my comm device.

I sucked in a breath, channeling my social spirit, my pretense aura, and my alter ego.

"Hey." Devil held my elbow, gently pulling me towards the door. "You sure you can do this?" he asked quietly.

"I am. I was serious when I said I knew how to handle him. He doesn't scare me."

"I know, but—it still doesn't stop me from worrying, Z. I don't want you to be in the same space or even country with him at this point. I don't trust him with you."

"Then trust me."

"I do," he whispered, fingers running up my arm in a sweet, nerve-awakening brush. "I trust you to come back to me in one piece—" His gaze lingered on mine before it traveled down to his fingers on my arm. "Because . . . when you come back, there's . . . something I wanna tell you."

I frowned. "What is it?"

He smiled, meeting my eyes once more. "Good, now you gotta come back to me in one piece, so you can hear it."

I smiled, shaking my head at him. "You're a devil."

His hand on my arm moved to hold the side of my face as he leaned down to press a kiss to my lips, careful not to ruin my lipstick, before pulling away and speaking. "If he tries anything, I give you permission to shoot him."

I chuckled. "Of course, if that's what you *really* want."

His smile was sad. "You should get going; we'll start up here." He pulled back.

I turned towards Upper and Dog on the couch, catching Upper's stare on us. His eyes held an emotion that had me frowning slightly. But it disappeared as quickly as I spotted it, and he forced a carefree smile. "Be safe. I'll see you on the inside."

I nodded. "See you guys soon."

We bid our goodbyes, and I forced away the thoughts that swept through me after that look from Upper.

As I approached the vehicle, the driver opened the door with a slight bow, and I thanked him with a smile.

When I got into the back seat, Elio was at the other side, holding a black hardcover book in his hand, his reading glasses on his face as he flipped the pages and spoke without looking at me. "Good evening." He greeted me politely, an action that made me pause.

"Uh . . . yeah, evening?"

He looked dangerous, wearing a black trench coat and a men's turtleneck shirt with black slacks and shoes. All colorless. His silver watch glinted in the light from the car as we started moving. His rings on tattooed fingers also complemented his wristwatch's twinkles, drawing me to how lithe and well-kept his fingers were.

I swallowed. "Aren't you hot?" I asked.

"No," he responded, but still didn't take his eyes from the book.

"I know the aircon is on, but you could at least take off the trench co—"

"This idiot girl," he muttered, slamming the book shut as he closed his eyes, letting out a controlled breath.

I frowned. "Excuse me? If you didn't want to remove the trench coat, you could have just said so. You don't have to be rude about it."

He opened his eyes again, sighing. "I was not talking to you," he said as he turned his head to look at me. "It's the book—why are you wearing a nightgown?" His gaze spelled shock, lingering on my exposed thighs, then my cleavage, before settling back on my face.

"Ha! He called it a nightgown, guys, he called it a nightgown." Dog's voice reached my ear.

I looked down at the length of the dress: It was a thin-strapped white silk dress that stopped mid-thigh. I opted to wear a waist-length straight brunette wig, which was parted in the middle and tied into a low ponytail. It was sleek and classy, and it made my face pop, accentuating my cheekbones and the dark brown lipstick I wore. My makeup was minimal; Milk had hidden my freckles and paid attention to my eyeliner, which was dark and sharp, giving me a cat-eye look. I looked less like Zahra and more like a sophisticated rich escort.

"It's not a nightgown; it's a dress—"

"Where's your hair?" Elio asked with distaste in his eyes.

"Under the wig? I wanted a disguise because I can't be seen as myself on a job."

I watched his eyes take in my face before he looked away, shaking his head as he muttered, "Ridiculous."

That made anger blossom in the pit of my stomach. "I didn't dress up seeking your validation."

A muscle ticked in his jaw. "I specifically asked you to look responsible."

"This isn't responsible enough for you?"

His head turned in my direction again. "No. You look like an unscrupulous escort."

Dog spoke. *"I really want to rearrange his face. It's like a burning urge. Let us find time to tie him up and fuck up that face like we did to that biker dude a year ago."*

"Ignore him, Zahra; focus on the mission," Devil said.

"He clearly doesn't have eyes," Milk muttered in annoyance.

His gaze shifted to my ear, where Devil had placed the comm, and then he looked back at me. "If you and your little choir group ruin today for me, I will ensure you don't return alive."

"Is that a promise?" I asked with a smile, and he looked away from me, a frown on his face as he opened his book again and didn't look up once or respond to me until we got to our destination.

When we pulled up to the front of the gallery, the door was opened for me by one of the chaperones; I smiled at them, looking up to see paparazzi taking endless pictures. I spotted three more cars pulling up behind us, Marino soldiers filing out of each, guarding the perimeters as if the security provided at the gallery was a joke.

"This is a big event," I whispered.

"We have to be more careful, but we don't have that much time since the buyer was specific about delivery time. The docks. Ten P.M. sharp," Devil said.

"Ten P.M., copy that," I responded.

"Just got to the cafe, all set and ready to go," Dog voiced.

Even with my disguise, I still tried to hide my face from the camera flashes, and when Elio came to stand beside me, now without his reading glasses, giving me his elbow to put my hand through, I smiled up at him, and he looked away, not returning it, as I would've expected.

Come to think of it, I'd never seen this man smile. He was either indifferent or annoyed half the time, and right now, he looked neither indifferent nor annoyed, just blank.

The inside of the building was bright and had the perfect temperature; warm, homey, and relaxing. There were people in twos everywhere, men wearing black suits and women wearing white dresses, chatting, drinking expensive wine, staring at sculptures or paintings, snapping pictures of themselves, and laughing like they were having the time of their lives.

I looked up at Elio, a smile curling on my lips. "Isn't it wonderful?"

He looked down at me with a frown. "What?"

"Us . . . being here together. Anyone looking at us right now wouldn't know you tried to drown me in your pool just a few days ago." I laughed, shaking my head.

He watched me intensely. Completely unnerving because he just stared, with no expression, word exchange, or response; he just looked at me, and when my laugh died down, I cleared my throat, looking away from him. "Weirdo," I muttered.

"Marino?"

"Por favor." *Please.* He groaned under his breath; a woman hurried towards us with a drink and a dashing grin on her maroon-painted lips. "Grace," he said, a cheer to his voice that didn't reach his eyes or tug a smile to his lips as he detangled my hand from his elbow and turned towards the woman.

She was gorgeous. Her white dress was lacy and looked like the industry's most prestigious designers fashioned it. The material hugged her curvy, voluptuous body like it was sewn to her skin. Her eyes were the brightest brown, complementing her long curly light brown hair, which added to the shine of her delicate dark skin. She would have intimidated the old Zahra, who felt inferior in the presence of other women with a normal childhood and upbringing.

And if I was being honest with myself, there was still a twinge of that feeling, but I suppressed it and turned my head to study my surroundings.

"What a pleasant surprise," Grace said.

"Indeed," Elio said, taking her hand in his and kissing her knuckles like a gentleman. The need to snort gripped me, but I held firm, watching the exchange.

"I really wish we could have gotten visuals," Milk said. *"That voice sounds like it belongs to a beautiful person."*

"Yes." The woman blinked in a blush, looking like there were stars in her eyes after Elio dropped her hand. "You never attend these gatherings; it's quite the shock to see you here."

Without warning, his arm snaked around my waist, warm and strong as he pulled me to his side, so affectionate, I couldn't hide my shock in time. "Blame my woman," he said with such fondness, his behavior supplied me a healthy dose of whiplash. "She has longed to attend this event for months; a certain painting caught her eye, and she wanted to see it for herself."

My woman?

Grace's eyes shifted to me, a smile on her face. "Oh, hello."

She extended her hand, which I shook. "I'm Grace Alden, a pleasure to meet you."

"Layla Rahal, a pleasure to meet you too, Grace," I said, dropping my hand from hers to place it on Elio's chest, feeling his muscles tense underneath my palm, though he made no move to show his discomfort.

"It's beautiful, isn't it?" Grace said, gesturing around. "I've also wanted to see this for months now. I flew in from London three days ago. I tried to get in touch with Marino, but sadly, he was unavailable at that time."

I frowned. "Three days ago . . ." I looked up at Elio, feigning confusion. "Honey, wasn't that the pool party day?"

His jaw clenched, but he nodded. "I think so," he said, playing along with whatever this was. "I apologize, Grace, we had people over, and many things were going on simultaneously—"

"Yes, and I almost drowned," I blurted.

"Oh dear," Grace said, genuine concern on her face. "That must have been terrible. Are you okay?"

"Yes, fortunately, Elio also happened to be in the pool, and he saved me." I looked up at him, our gazes locking.

"I did." His tone dropped. "I would have hated for you to miss all that I have planned for you, querida." *Darling.*

My mouth grew dry, almost like the intensity of his gaze sucked every single drop of liquid from my body. The press of my side to his became more prominent in my senses. He was warm against me, and I felt a tantalizing shiver sweep through my body.

His gaze dropped to my cleavage shamelessly, and it felt like someone was blowing softly at my nipples; I felt them press to the material of my dress.

Elio's grip tightened on my waist, his gaze briefly rising to my lips before he broke the connection, looking back at Grace, who seemed to have just witnessed something private between us.

"I am sorry to cut this short, Grace, but we have places to be after this, and I need to say hi to the mayor; it was a pleasure meeting you again."

"Yes, of course, take care," she said before turning to me and going for a hug.

I moved away from Elio's side to hug her, knowing people like these preferred hugs to handshakes.

"He looks at you like he wants to eat you. Keep him," she whispered to me, and I cringed, knowing the rest of Street could hear it.

I smiled at her when she pulled away with a wink before walking in the other direction.

"Who was that?" I asked, looking back at Elio and immediately remembering how he had touched me with his eyes. The last person I should feel any sexual attraction to was him. Yes, he was sinfully attractive and oozed an unhealthy dose of sex appeal, and there was that pull between us . . . so damn strong that I was almost positive I wasn't the only one feeling it.

Elio cleared his throat. "A person I know," he stated. "Go find your painting; and don't cause any trouble."

I smiled. "When have I ever?"

He shook his head, and without another word, turned and walked away.

"Okay, guys, let's find that naughty chihuahua."

"Am I the only one thinking it?" Milk asked.

"Thinking what?" I asked, walking casually while eying the door I was supposed to walk into, and the guard that stood right in front of it.

"Is it possible to feel tension without seeing it, like just from sounds and quietness that's a bit static?" Milk said.

"Audio porn?" Dog inquired.

"Yeah, but like, between people who don't like each other—"

"Quit it, Milk. Do you see the door, Z?" Devil asked.

"Yup, I'm approaching now," I answered, walking towards the door and the guard, whose frown hardened when I reached him.

"In position, waiting on you, Zahra," Upper said.

I smiled tightly at the guard. "Hi—"

"This hallway is reserved for VIPs only."

"I know, but—listen, I heard there was a fully equipped female bathroom somewhere in there, and I need to go."

"There is a guest bathroom at the other aisle by your left—"

"I know, sir . . ." I said with an apologetic smile. "I just—this place is closer for—for the little problem I have? If—if I have to walk all the way to the aisle, it might—it might be very *bloody*."

The man frowned. "I beg your pardon?"

I stepped closer to him, looking around before beckoning him nearer. He leaned forward. "It's that time of the month. I didn't know it would be today, and I can feel it—the cycle blood, pouring out of—"

He stepped aside, holding the door open for me. "Just go."

"Thank you, sir, I don't know how to—"

He averted his gaze completely. "Just go, go—"

I rushed into the hallway, and the door slammed shut behind me before I could thank him again.

"You are one cruel motherfucker," Dog said. *"I'm disabling the security cameras now, shouldn't take me . . . Done, you're on loop. You have about fifteen minutes before the system rewrites the codes and the cams are back online with real-time feed."*

I began walking to the elevator, getting in and pressing the button for the floor where the vault was. "I won't need fifteen minutes," I said as the doors jammed together and I started going up.

In no time, I was out of the elevator, heading straight for the vault. "Okay, Milk, I'm standing in front of the vault lock. It's like the picture we saw, there's a huge box and a rotary mechanical combination lock in front of it."

"Great, take out the device."

I took it out. It was a black cylindrical box. "Is this filled with water?"

"Nope, just an illusion of what water should feel like," Upper said.

"Water would work just fine too, but this device is more effective with sound and resistance recognition."

"Place it on top of the box," Milk said. "You're looking for a light click, two resisting clicks, three thick clicks, and one light click to get it open."

"Twelve minutes," Devil's voice cut through.

I got to work, picking the lock with the instruction Milk provided. It took two minutes to hear the final click and get the vault open. "I'm in."

"Ten minutes."

I rushed into the vault, seeing the sensored safe in the middle of the room, big enough to hold the painting. I looked up at the vent and grinned. "Hey, Upper, what are you doing up there?"

"You know, just, hanging around," he said as I went to the vent-lock key swipe by the side, digging through my purse for the key card I'd nicked off the kind guard who let me into the hallway. I swiped the card and the vent gate pushed open on its own.

I shook my head. "I still don't understand technology. In my days, vents were pegged tight with screws."

Upper jumped down, landing on his feet as he opened the laptop in his grip. "You're twenty-six, not sixty-eight," he said, typing furiously on the keyboard.

"Seven minutes," Devil called out.

"Hacking into the systems now . . . lucky for us, I recognize this build, it might take a few—oh." Upper scoffed as he typed. "It's either this painting is worth nothing or the people who built this system didn't care enough to make this challenging—security alarms disabled, password, 556745."

I typed that into the safe lock; it clicked and I twisted it open and—

"What the bloody fuck?" Upper said, staring at the same thing my eyes were locked on.

"What is it?" Milk asked, alarmed.

"It's empty," I said, my shoulders slumping.

"Fuck, you think someone got to it before us?" Dog asked.

"*We're the only ones hunting this thing, right?*" The wariness in Milk's voice didn't escape me.

"The client was vague with their email. They didn't exactly give anything away, just that we needed to get it," Upper informed.

"*It's 9:49, Zahra,*" Devil said. "*You have to leave that vault in three minutes.*"

I stood there, at a loss for words. "I don't know what to do, maybe we should—"

"Sport."

I turned immediately, seeing Elio standing by the vault door. "Let's go," he said.

I frowned. "It's empty, I can't just—"

"You"—he gestured to Upper—"back up the vent you crawled in from. I bought your team some time—if you want to leave, now's the chance." Then he looked at me. "You, follow me," he said, turning and walking out of the vault.

"*What the fuck is he doing? You can't leave without that painting,*" Dog said.

Upper had his eyes on me, waiting for instruction.

I sighed. "Go, I'll handle this."

He nodded, shutting the laptop and going his own way.

I rushed out of the vault, shutting it behind me.

Elio was already walking down the hall to the elevator, his strides so long that I found myself walk-running after him. "I can't leave without the painting," I gritted.

He walked into the elevator, and I groaned, stepping in after him. He pushed a button for the underground parking lot when the doors closed, and we started going down.

"*We cannot fuck this up; I will lose my shit if we fuck this up,*" Dog said.

"Why are we leaving?"

"It's almost ten, no?"

"Yes, but—" The elevator stopped after a short while and slid open again; he walked out, and I rushed out after him; he dug his hand into his pocket, bringing out a key and pressing a button. A car beeped to life in the distance, and someone leaned away from it quickly; she was wearing a waitress uniform.

My eyes widened as I took in the ride. "Holy mother of fucking Lambor-huracán-ghini," I whispered.

"You're shitting me." Upper's voice reached my ear.

"I shit you not."

"Please sneak a picture, please, Zahra, please."

I pulled out my phone, took a quick picture, and sent it to him. His squeal of excitement almost made me deaf.

The car was matte black and smooth on the eyes. It was so low that it almost kissed the ground. I just knew I was looking at millions of dollars.

The waitress straightened, holding a painting in her hand. "Sir, as you wanted."

"The painting . . ." I trailed off, watching him collect the medium-sized frame wrapped in secure transparent packaging.

The twisted chihuahua stared at me. Why the fuck would anyone want this? I'd scream Bloody fucking Mary if I had to wake up to this hanging on my wall.

The waitress shot a stiff nod to him and then to me before leaving.

Elio handed me the painting. "Come on; I have places to be," he said, already walking around towards the driver's side, none of his security in sight. I rushed to the passenger's side of the car, entering what smelled and looked like leather heaven.

"Why did you tell me to go find the painting when you had already found it? Do you know the kind of risk we took?"

He started the engine, and the car roared to life.

He glanced my way. "Your presence was beginning to get insufferable," he said before pulling the car out of the parking spot and driving towards the entrance.

I stared at him, dumbfounded. "You really are a shitty motherfucker."

"That is an incestuous remark. I don't think I appreciate you implying I had intimate relations with my late mother," he responded, entering the main road.

"What—I—you weren't supposed to respond to that—it's one of those statements where you just *don't* respond."

"Whose law was that, querida?"

"No, we're not doing that. Don't call me that."

Still driving, he looked my way. "What. You don't like Sport; you don't like Darling—"

"Darling is fucking cool; I'm all for it, but when *you* say it, it's like you're mocking me."

"That is exactly what I'm doing. *Mocking* you."

"Anyone ever told you you were an asshole?"

"No."

"You're an asshole."

The car swerved suddenly, tires screeching. My heart jumped into my throat.

When the car settled again, I was heaving. "Motherfucker! Just because you have a death wish doesn't mean I do too."

He glanced my way, looking very calm as he said, "Seatbelt."

I scoffed, securing my seatbelt. I was ready for this night to be over.

Elio drove like he had extra lives, and in order to swallow my fear and hold on to my pride, I didn't utter a word because he got us to the meeting point at exactly 9:59 P.M.

I unhooked the seatbelt and wasted no time getting out of the car, a gag rising in my throat at how wobbly my legs felt. I brought out the painting and dropped my bag on the seat, slamming the door. The sight of the boats rocking atop the water by the docks, and the cold breeze, helped quell my urge to throw up.

Elio got out of the car, looking pointedly at the black SUV a few feet away from us. "Your client?"

"Should be," I answered, looking around us.

It was dark, save for the dim lamplight around the boats and the small cabin a few feet away. An unsettling feeling came with the atmosphere, and it made the hair at the back of my neck stand at alert.

"Let's get this over with," I said, walking towards the SUV.

"Wait, something is not right . . . or just walk right into the pending danger." He sighed. "Estúpida," he muttered, but I heard his footsteps fall in right behind me.

I reached the SUV but stopped short when I saw the person inside the car. His head was on the headrest, eyes wide open, with a bullet wound between them.

"Shit, he's dead," I said.

"What the fuck?" Dog's voice rang out in alarm.

Elio pushed me aside and approached the body, hand touching his skin. "It's still warm. It just happened."

"Guys, the mission has been compromised."

"Are you bloody shitting me? Three times in a row? Somebody fucking jinxed us!" Upper exclaimed.

Elio's gaze snapped to a spot behind me at a slight click sound, and he groaned in annoyance. "Great."

He suddenly and forcefully pulled me down, and the next thing I heard was multiple shots firing directly at us.

CHAPTER TWENTY-TWO

Zahra

Adrenaline pumped through my veins as Elio and I ran around the car to take immediate cover. The bullets didn't stop, slamming into the black SUV, shattering its windows.

I hissed as the glass rained down on us, light, sharp, and graceless. Elio was covered from head to toe, unlike me, whose skin was exposed to any little graze. My breathing was harsh and my heart was racing. "What the fuck is happening!" I yelled as Elio reached behind him, seeming very calm as he pulled out his gun.

"It's an a–mbush, th–at's w–hat," Devil said.

"Conne–ction's failing, fuck . . ." Upper said, his voice a distant static, but I could still pick out its tight edge.

"I still don't get it. An ambush for a painting?" I said, breathless and annoyed.

Elio shifted beside me, lifting his head a little to—I guess—see who was shooting or how many of them were there.

Another string of bullets came, slapping against the car in sharp thudding noises that had my blood running hot. Elio ducked immediately, cursing while sending a stern glare my way. "There are about six of them, maybe more. We have one gun, and I am in no mood to kill anyone tonight."

My eyes widened. "Well, if you haven't noticed, they're kind of in the mood to kill us."

He looked around before his gaze settled on the Lamborghini a short distance away, and then he looked back at the SUV we were shielding ourselves with. "Okay, I'll cover you."

"Wait, wh—"

"On my signal, you'll open this door and check the glove compartment for weapons."

"What—" The side mirror shattered beside my head, and I cursed, ducking further down as I whisper-yelled at him. "What if there aren't any weapons? Got any other smart ideas?"

He grunted, almost as if he couldn't deal with me, and then in urgency, gave me the gun. "Cover me. I'll do it."

"What the fuck—" He was already opening the door as if people weren't shooting at us. "Crazy motherfucker." I got in position; the gun was heavy in my grip as I shot back at them, bullets flying blindly in the direction of the boats, and I caught dark figures ducking.

As fast as he had raced to open the door, Elio was back beside me, a gun in his hand, which he quickly checked for bullets before clicking in place.

"How did you know—" A shot wheezed past my ear, and I groaned, swiftly getting back in position to find the fucker who had shot it reloading his gun. I set the angle, targeting the side of his head, before pressing the trigger. His body dropped lifelessly to the ground.

I retook cover, only to find Elio's eyes on me.

"Some—ahh!" I winced in pain as the comm in my ear sent out a sharp noise that had me rushing to take it out. The device was hot against my hand, and I quickly threw it to the ground, my ear burning. I grazed the spot and brought my shaking fingers to my view, blood staining them. "Motherfucker!"

"We have to get to the car." Elio's voice reached me, and I realized he hadn't been shooting back. "First, we need—"

At the sound of tires screeching, I turned to see a bunch of black SUVs pulling up roughly without formation, men filing out of them like fucking ants. "Are those your people?"

Elio watched the new change, confusion dragging down his brows. "No."

One of the men stopped by our ride, checking it carefully before stepping back and shooting at the windows and the tires of the Lamborghini, in other words, killing our means of escape.

The shooting doubled now, no longer aimed at us but at the people who were once shooting at us.

"Throw it in!" somebody yelled, followed by an engine revving.

"Oh God," I muttered as two SUVs came slamming at the Lamborghini, making it shift forward violently. The SUV riders didn't seem to care about the damage the hit did to their cars because they were now reversing, stepping on the gas and colliding into Elio's car again; I watched it groan and tumble before falling into the water with a thick splash.

After that, the space between Elio and me went quiet.

I blinked, turning ever so slowly to Elio, who sucked in a deep breath, lips pressed tightly together.

"I am genuinely sorry. I felt that right in my heart. The beauty didn't deserve to go down like that."

He swallowed. "That apology should be addressed to Casmiro if we ever see him again."

"That was his car?" I asked in a wheeze.

"No. That was his baby."

"Shit."

Elio moved past me swiftly, showing me his back as he scanned the area. "Our cover is about to be blown."

I gripped the gun tightly. "What the fuck are we gonna do?"

"We have to be quick."

I frowned. "What do you mean by *we have to be quick*?"

He looked back at me. "We are going to run."

I searched his eyes for any hint of a joke. There was none. "No, we can't—"

He grabbed my wrist. "Come on, on the count of three—"

"No, wait, we're not—"

"Two."

"We have no fucking cover, E—"

He was on his feet, pulling me along with him as we sprinted down the open area towards the SUVs.

From the corner of my eye, I saw one of the boats filled with men taking cover and shooting at the other party that had just arrived.

What the fucking hell is happening?

Elio pulled us down again behind one of the SUVs. He blew out a short breath, his eyes doing that sharp movement thing again as he looked around. "Were you shot?"

"No, I wasn't, but you'd love that, wouldn't you."

He ignored me. "We're taking one of their cars, they'll probably chase us, but you have an outstanding aim, so we should be fine."

I swallowed, leveling my breathing. "What the fuck is in this painting? They literally brought a whole goddamn army."

"How much were you paid to retrieve it?"

I hesitated, sucking in my pride as I spoke. "Five thousand dollars."

His head snapped towards me sharply. "Five thousand dollars?" he almost yelled.

"It was a moment of weakness; trust me, we regret taking the job."

"Nobody would send this many people to kill for a painting worth five thousand dollars," he stated, his stern gaze locked on mine.

We stared at each other, my head roaming with thoughts, mind racing, gears shifting.

"Well fuck," I finally said, cocking the gun. "Now four parties are gunning for this fucking twisted chihuahua."

"Four?"

"Yeah, the person who paid us, the people who shot him, the people currently shooting at the people who shot him, and now us, the people who stole it."

Elio shook his head in disbelief. "Greedy fucking thief."

I smirked. "Psycho fucking killer."

He let out a frustrated sigh. "Come on." And then he was moving again; I followed him swiftly.

We quietly maneuvered through the maze of cars, ducking when we came in line with some of the men standing guard while the others shot at the boat people.

I held tighter to the painting, knowing that whatever it was had to be something big. Big enough to cause this amount of chaos in such a short period.

"Hold," Elio said, stopping, and I froze behind him.

Scoffing, I tsked. "Acting like you were in the army," I muttered.

"I was," he said without looking back. "A year. It was enough to learn that when a superior says hold, you shut your mouth and hold."

I did shut up, stretching my neck to see him eyeing a car by a near end; a man stood there, alert, gun in hand, looking for any unusual movement, presumably.

"We're taking that one," Elio said, voice low, calm, and precise.

"Okay, sure, what's the plan? Walking up to him and asking to borrow his car because we have to run away from him?"

Elio's form stilled for about three seconds before he suddenly stood upright, turning to me as his head tilted to the side, eyeing me from head to toe.

I took a step back. "Whatever you're thinking? It's a bad idea."

"Scream," he commanded.

"What?"

"Scream. Now."

"I'm not just gonna fucking—"

His hand wrapped around my throat, and he slammed my body into one of the cars, causing an instinctive shriek from me.

His body pressed to mine, all rugged ridges over my soft curves as he whispered to my face, "Now, was that so hard?" His hand gripped my ponytail, pulling off the wig and removing the wig cap. My hair fell free, and then he was gone, disappearing behind cars. It all happened within seconds, and I didn't have time to catch myself or to hear the footsteps before they reached me; the man who'd been guarding the car was standing there, gun in hand, confusion on his face as he stared at me, holding the painting for dear life.

"Um . . ." My voice shook. "I don't know what's happening, but I was asked to deliver this, and then people were shooting, and now there are too many cars and too many dead people"—something shifted behind the man—"and I just wanna go home because I'm so scared"—fake crying—"I didn't plan to do this, but my fucking boyfriend said it would be quick, but now it's messed up. One minute I was dressed up for our date together"—fake heave—"and the next, he gives me this ugly painting and tells me his friend Marcus would be here, and then he had a bullet in his head, and then the gunshots and I don't wanna die because I have college and fashion school and my whole future." Fake sob.

"Miss—" He couldn't complete his statement because Elio was bashing his head in with a—a stone potted plant that shattered on impact. The man fell with a dull thud to the ground.

My stare was blank. "A potted plant, really?"

"Why not?"

"I don't know, maybe because you have a silencer in your hand?"

"I told you I wasn't in the mood to kill anyone tonight." Then he bent and searched the man's pockets, got the SUV keys, and walked in its direction silently; I followed behind him as he unlocked the car.

We got in, locking the doors softly. "I don't get you. One minute you're a psychopath who kills innocent people, and the next, you're not?"

His jaw clenched as he turned sharply towards me. "What do you want from me, Sport? Should I get out of the car and go back to kill him, take his wallet and find his ID card and then hunt down his wife and children and put a bullet through their heads?"

I swallowed, blinking. "Now that I think about it, the potted plant was more creative."

"Good."

"Can I at least get your phone? I need to let Street know that I'm still alive."

"I don't have a phone."

I stopped short, blinking at him. "Who doesn't have a phone?"

"Me. Are you slow?"

"How do we contact help?"

"In some situations, you must be all the help you need."

He shoved the key into the ignition, and the moment the engine roared to life, we heard a shout. "Hey! Kto vy?" *Who are you?*

I froze. My blood ran cold, and shivers flowed down my spine in waves as my gaze locked with Elio's.

"Russians?" we said at the same time.

"Ya nashel ikh!" *I found them!*

"Shit! Go, go, go, go!" I was practically jumping on the seat as the men fell back from shooting the boat people, rushing towards us and firing at the car.

Elio stepped on the gas and maneuvered the car out of the maze, hitting some of the other vehicles as we finally got out, cutting into the road with blind speed; the vehicle bounced a bit, swerving from left to right, Elio holding the steering wheel, muscles clenching as he tried to steady the car.

With one hand, he adjusted the rearview mirror, glancing at it. "We have company."

"Sweet." I exhaled sharply, getting his gun from the console; I cocked it and then proceeded to grab mine too. "Almost out of bullets on this," I said.

"Glove compartment," he said, expertly overtaking some cars—one hand working the steering, the other working the gear, focus dead set on the road.

The road, thankfully, was a little bit free; other cars around swept by with speed, not wanting to get in the crossfire.

I glanced in the side mirror, seeing the cars chasing after us.

I reached for the glove compartment. "Why do you always assume there's something in the glove—oh." Two packs of bullets and a gun sat there, and I nodded. "Impressive."

"Thank you."

I clicked on the car music.

"What are you doing?"

"A little music; it helps me focus."

"It doesn't help *me* focus," he gritted.

"Your problem."

Familiar music blasted through the speakers, and a smile curled on my lips as I bobbed my head. "The Russian dude knows good music. 'Hello Cherry Bomb' by the Runaways. Oh, Dog is going to freak when I—"

He made a sharp turn, and I held my seat to keep in place, shooting him a glare.

"Motherfucker," I muttered, shaking my head at him while I carried my weapons with me to the back seat.

"Again, what are you doing?"

"Shooting through the windows is a bit inconvenient. They're not shooting yet, which means I have the element of surprise. And I have good aim."

I caught him shaking his head. "Tell me when to duck."

"I might," I taunted, raising the gun to the rear tinted windshield, and fired three shots at it. The cracks invited me to break through, which I did, hitting the gun to the fragile glass and watching it shatter. The wind whipped at my face immediately, blowing my hair all around my head.

I grinned, reloading the bigger gun, seeing our chasers lose composure for a second.

"Hello, boys!" I yelled, aiming the gun at the tires, swiftly shooting the nearest car, which swirled to the side with a screech, the driver losing control.

With my other hand, I grabbed the second gun, aiming at

their windshields as I blasted bullets at them, and they drove unfocused, turning and slowing down to avoid the attack.

Two cars were tailing each other.

I moved to the side, shot at one of their mirrors, took his attention off the road, and then aimed directly at him with the second gun.

Blood splattered—and the car behind, not anticipating the unconscious turn of the vehicle, slammed into it, and it went tumbling.

"Elio, left!" Our car swerved left, missing the other car's tumble by mere seconds.

The crash was massive, and unfortunately, some innocent cars got involved.

"Are we clear?" Elio yelled, and I grabbed the guns, going back to the seat beside him.

"Yes, cut to the market at the next intersection; it leads to the highway, they'll regroup in no time, but we can shake them off that way."

Elio glanced at me. "You're awfully excited."

"I am."

He shook his head, focusing on the road again. "You're unhinged."

I nodded with a grin. "I am."

He cut through the intersection, driving a few distances before entering the market. People were out, all right. It was busy, with sounds of chatter and music in the air as people shopped while some got out of the way, seeing our bullet-designed car—speaking of bullets, they ricocheted in the air once more.

"Fucking Russians," Elio cursed.

I reloaded. "Like a fucking bone in the throat," I added, angling myself towards the window, and shot back at them. "Get out of the way!" I yelled to people as Elio stepped on the gas again, knocking out some food stands by the road. "Get out of the fucking way!"

My gaze shifted to the side mirror. "Duck!" I yelled to Elio when bullets came flying into the car from behind.

"Still think breaking the rear windshield was a good idea?" he asked.

"Shut up!" My adrenaline spiked high.

I risked shooting out the window again, getting my aim right as I fired at the car's front tire, missing the first time but getting it right on the second try.

The pursuer's car lost balance, ramming into a market stall, but another one was on our tail.

The guy was quick, firing three shots at once. Two missed me, and the other would have gotten into my arm had Elio not turned at just about the right time.

"Shit," I cursed, pain sweeping past my arm as I got into the car again, blood oozing from the wound.

Elio's gaze shifted from the rearview to me. "It got you?"

"Just a graze."

He groaned in frustration. "Can you handle the wheel?"

"Not as good as you."

"Can you handle the fucking wheel, Sport!"

"Yeah, yeah, I can."

He left control of the car, and we switched positions with mild difficulty, and briefly, just briefly, my mind acknowledged that we—kind of—worked well together.

He worked the guns with ease, entering into his element. Then he paused, staring at the weapon in his hand.

"What the fuck are you doing?" I held the wheel steady, eyes alternating between the market road and him.

He sucked in a deep breath. "Slow down."

"What?"

He looked at me. "Slow down." His voice was calm, too calm.

I slowed down, and he angled his body to the window, completely exposing himself while aiming the gun at our attackers, concentration lining his brows.

One shot.

Two shots.

Three shots.

Chaos.

From the rearview mirror, I caught the cars behind us ramming into each other, and then there was fire; people were screaming, fighting to run away.

No.

No, no, no, no, no.

Dread painted my stomach, making it dip with a sense of urgency and regret. I stepped on the gas, and our vehicle sped forward, my heart hammering as I tried to get us away before—

Boom!

I flinched at the explosion, and Elio slipped back to the seat, stretching his neck from left to right, looking like he hadn't just . . .

Wasn't it—wasn't there another way? How many innocent people were caught in that explosion?

I drove us out of the market, entering an unfamiliar road, the car steady again. Quiet.

The music from the speaker had long since stopped, probably damaged like the car was.

I didn't know how long we drove for, but I felt my body calm down from the adrenaline.

I glanced at Elio to see that he still held the gun in a tight grip. His knuckles were white, but he looked ahead with a calm expression.

"You okay?" I asked, but was met with complete silence from him.

I concentrated back on the road, letting out a breath.

We reached the highway, and the wind blowing inside the car calmed my nerves as I drove away from our pursuers.

Trees littered the sides of the road, and I was pretty sure we had lost the fuckers.

After what seemed like thirty minutes, the car started slowing down—its movements jerky, like it wanted to fall apart.

Soon after, it slowed to a stop with a jolt, headlights flickering off, the night enclosing us like a thick black blanket as the engine stopped, and quietness followed.

"Shit."

"I'm guessing your phone is deep inside the water with Casmiro's car?"

"Yup."

"And no one knows where we are?"

"Yup."

He nodded, his head falling back on the headrest as he closed his eyes, Adam's apple bobbing up and down when he swallowed and cursed.

"Fuck."

CHAPTER TWENTY-THREE

Zahra

Elio was the first to get out of the car, and I followed suit. No other vehicles were passing by, and the road seemed like a dead end from where we stood, so I was guessing we would have to walk a great distance before we found a motel.

I exhaled, hugged myself, and walked around the car to Elio's dark figure on the other side. The moon painted fine shadows over his features, and I let my eyes drink it in.

"Walking or waiting out here for a travel vehicle would be careless when we have the Russians on our tail," Elio stated.

"I thought we lost them."

"We stole their vehicle; it's only a matter of time before they find us. We're calling it a night."

I shifted on my feet. "I'm all for . . . calling it a night, but there is literally nothing out here for miles, and I don't reckon you have any money on you?"

"We don't need money to start an open camp in the woods."

I almost choked on my saliva. "I beg your pardon?"

"You're not deaf," he said, already walking towards the tall trees that cast shapeless shadows. A shiver of wariness ran down my spine.

When he noticed I wasn't following, he stopped, turning to me. "Are you coming?"

"Nah, I'm good. I'll wait for a car to fly by and hitch a ride."

I could feel his eyes roam up and down my body as he walked back towards me, determination in his strides. "Stay here and die. Follow me and survive on a maybe. You should be smart enough to know the good choice there."

"The woods aren't exactly safe either."

"They are, for the night. By morning, we'll leave because they'll likely double back when they don't find us at the nearest motel. When they're on their way back here, we'll be on our way to the compound."

"The car is practically parked outside the woods," I pointed out.

"Your smartness seems to have faded with your adrenaline." He sighed. "The key is in the ignition, the two front tires are blown, and the car is bent to a very odd angle. It's obvious that it broke down, and the two people previously in it have hitched a ride or walked to the nearest motel because there is *obviously* a tracker in the vehicle we should be running from."

My brain caught up to what he was insinuating. "Nobody in our position would stay behind instead of running away, okay, smart . . . But what about the painting?"

"We're leaving it underneath the seat."

"Excuse me?"

"It's not safe to take it along. And we're not stupid enough to leave it behind either."

"What if they check the car? Listen, I risked my damn neck for that painting, and I got a bullet graze that hurts like a bitch because of it. There's no way I'm letting them find it after all the trouble."

"Risks are better than consequences. On the off chance that we get found out by whoever these people are, they'd kill us and take the painting, but if they find us without the painting, two things. They can kidnap and torture until we deliver updates as to who has it and who doesn't, or we make a bargain. And I have a gut feeling they won't waste time searching the car when we are supposedly with the painting and would never be as foolish as to leave it behind."

"But—"

"We are doing the exact opposite of what anyone should do in our situation. I will not ask you to trust me because it isn't a foolproof plan, but I will ask you to follow my lead. I am never wrong."

I gritted my teeth, looking around the lonely area before my attention settled on him again. "Fine. You might have a point."

"I'm glad your brain still works. You had me worried there for a second."

"You don't have to be rude."

"That was not me being rude, merely observant," he said, turning again, and this time I followed him.

"And here I thought you were a man of action and fewer words."

"I am."

"Well, you talk an awful lot when I'm around."

He let a few beats pass before he responded. "A significant mystery I plan to unearth."

I snickered. "It's okay; I have that effect on people. It's like one of my charms."

He remained silent.

We walked into the woods with only the light from the moon to guide our path. I commented on getting lost, but Elio simply pretended he didn't hear me, walking like someone who knew exactly where he was going. My joints ached, and the pain on my arm from the grazing was numb due to how tired I was. I could feel fatigue catching up to me, but I willed myself to remain alert.

We reached a clearing in the woods. The space looked like an area where people would pitch their camp tents and huddle around a fire.

I shivered slightly from the cold as we stopped.

"We'll settle here for the night. I'll get some wood and start up a fire," he said, glancing around until his gaze settled on me with a pause. "You're cold."

"If you haven't noticed, it's freezing out here."

"No, it's not. It's what happens when you wear a nightgown out of the house."

"It's not a—" I paused, doubling back with the conversation. "You know what? Fuck you. I own what I fucking wear out. Nightgown or fucking lingerie, it remains my choice."

He took me in, something dark passing through his stare. It

made the gray in his eyes seem darker as he advanced towards me, like a predator approaching its prey.

I swallowed, standing my ground and raising my chin as he stopped before me. "Look at you, Zahra," he said, voice barely above a whisper, an edge to it that had my stomach sinking; flashbacks of moments before we fell into that pool plagued my mind, but I held firm, refusing to let him intimidate me. "Dressed in the most revealing outfit," he continued, "alone in the woods with a man who tried to drown you . . . a man that wants you dead."

He took one more step, closing whatever distance remained between us. I sucked in a breath, one that was filled with his scent.

"No one is here. I can do"—his eyes searched my face—"anything I want to. You could scream, and no one would hear you or rescue you. You are wounded, tired, bruised, and weak, entirely at my mercy. I won't try to control what you wear, no. I have no care in the world if you decide to roam the streets naked. All I'm saying—is I have eyes; I see how attractive you are and how you love to flaunt it on occasion, but one thing you should never do is be careless. And right now, Zahra, you are. Being here with me this way is the most careless you've been.

"You're smart, but you lack wisdom. You know how to protect yourself from people who threaten you, but you do not know how to protect *yourself*," he said, leaning away from me as he took off his trench coat, wrapping it around my body before his gaze locked with mine, and he spoke. "I could have been anyone else." He stepped away. "Stay here. I'll get wood for a fire."

When he left, I let out a long breath; it was shaky and cold, but I quickly slipped both my hands inside the arms of his trench coat, hugging it to my body; the warmth gave the distinct feeling of how intense it felt to be standing close to him.

As I do with every piece of advice I have ever been given, I held on to his, seeing my mistakes and making sure never to repeat them.

Elio was . . . confusing. His threats somehow managed to seem like advice, a warning, and a guide at the same time. He had no reason to stick with me at this point; he could have gone on his way, but he was still here, and I doubted it was because he wanted to know what was really in the painting.

I wouldn't delude myself and think he was here because it was kind of the right thing to do. The only reason I could think of right now was Devil. He was sticking around because his brother would want that.

I sighed, looking around me, trying to find a stone or a log to sit on. I arranged something not even close to comfortable, but my legs were killing me so I sat down and relaxed against a tree, the roots supporting my sitting material as I tried to get as comfortable as anyone could in a situation like this. I rested my head against the tree, sighed, and decided to rest my eyes.

The crackles from a fire and the distant howling of what might have been a wolf had me jerking awake, my brain confused for a moment before I remembered where I was. The smell of burning wood and wet earth lingered in the air, and opposite me sat Elio, gaze steady on the dancing flames.

I relaxed back against the tree, ensuring I didn't make a sound while I moved, not wanting to draw his attention because he seemed very far away from this space, and I couldn't help but watch him.

He didn't have any mask on; that was the first thing I noticed. He didn't wear a blank look of indifference . . . rather, he looked . . . sad and tired. His hair was also slightly wet. There were dark circles underneath his eyes, very visible.

I cleared my throat, and he blinked away from whatever daze he had been in, gaze rising from the fire to me.

"How long have I been out?"

His stare shifted from me to the fire. "Four hours," he said. "It's five A.M. now. We'll leave at daylight. You can go back to sleep."

I sat up, stifling a yawn, feeling more refreshed. I didn't know time would go by like that. It didn't even feel as though I'd slept that long.

"No," I said, hugging his coat to me and maybe sniffing it a little because it smelled good. "I'll keep watch. You should get some sleep."

"There's no point," he said. "It's already morning."

"You look tired. You've kept watch all night. Why didn't you wake me?"

"There was no point," he repeated, and I watched him in the silence that followed, wondering if I should let my questions out or keep them to myself, but I was very curious, and the worst he could do was ignore me, right?

I cleared my throat, waiting a few beats before speaking and breaking the silence with a question. "Why did you hesitate?"

His gaze flicked to me, and I took that second to appreciate how pretty his eyes were. His eyelashes made the color even more pronounced, designed to draw you in and keep your attention. When he looked back at the fire, he responded, "I don't understand your question."

"You hesitated before you caused the explosion. Why?"

He let the silence drag on before answering. "I told you. I wasn't in the mood to kill anyone."

I frowned. "I don't understand, you kill people all the time."

"I do?" he asked.

"Seriously? You tried to kill me a few days ago."

"I had a reason to. I don't kill people without a valid reason. I don't hurt people I don't know."

I scoffed. "Right, what about the families of the people you killed? Did you know them?"

He went silent, and I thought he wouldn't answer until he . . . did. "No," he said. "But I know grief. I danced with it. Lived with it. I kill them for their sake. The grief of losing a loved one is . . . brain-damaging. No one deserves to go through that."

I shook my head, watching him closely. "You can't just choose to kill innocent people because you think you're saving them."

"I know; that's why I don't shoot anyone without a valid reason. If I do shoot, I don't shoot to kill. The healing scar on your shoulder is proof of that. If I need someone dead, I have people around me who can do it. Well—unless I'm in a mood, then, you can guess the rest."

"So . . . all those people yesterday . . ."

"It wasn't my intention." He filled in, "I'll pay for it one way or another."

"What does that mean?"

He raised his gaze to me again before looking away, not answering the question.

When silence came again, I had the urge to fill it.

"You know . . . it's not your fault. I believe in reasons. Everything that went down yesterday happened because it was meant to. No matter how bad it was. If we weren't there, somehow a fire would have started, and there would still have been an explosion, maybe even worse than the one we caused."

This time, when he looked up, he didn't immediately look away. He just stared at me.

I felt my stomach clench with the feeling that came with his stare, and I sucked in a breath, swallowing to ease my suddenly dry throat.

"What?" I asked.

He shook his head. "Nothing," he let out before looking away, adding wood to the fire.

"Was that a moment?" I asked.

He frowned, side-eying me.

"Did we just have a moment there?" I repeated, keeping my tone light.

"No."

"That was definitely a moment; I know a moment when I see one—"

"Do you ever shut up?"

"Yes . . ." I let a soft edge enter my voice, calling his attention. He fully looked at me now, waiting for me to complete my statement. "Only when there's a dick in my mouth."

"Okay." He moved to stand and walk towards me, and a laugh bubbled out of my chest.

"Wait, wait . . . sit down," I said between laughs. "I was just fucking around. Calm your tits, *Dad*."

He settled back down, shaking his head. He didn't smile, but he didn't look annoyed either.

I shifted my position, wondering why the hell the thought of *that* actually happening didn't sound so bad. I mentally shook off the images my brain supplied, and the sudden awareness of the heat his coat supplied to my body.

"Where's your sense of humor?" I asked, hoping my voice didn't give anything away. "If Street were here, they'd get the joke."

He didn't say anything to that.

I rested my hand on my cheek, watching him with interest.

"Do you have friends, Elio?"

I don't know why I asked that . . . but I continued because where's the fun in silence?

"I mean, aside from Casmiro . . . like outside your whole syndicate circle . . . do you have a group of friends from, like, college? Oh, and you said you were in the army for a year? Did you have friends there?"

His brows drew down as if he were thinking, and then he locked eyes with me briefly before speaking. "Friends are another level of weakness. When you have friends, you're open to betrayal, inessential drama—"

"Less loneliness," I cut in. "I could totally be your friend if you stop trying to kill me." And then I backed up. "Why are you trying to kill me?"

"Many reasons."

"Okay, I turn you on, next?"

"That is not part of—" He sighed. "You stole from me," he said.

"See, that's where it gets confusing. I wasn't the only one who stole from you, yet you singled me out. I don't see you trying to drown my friends, and we've registered the fact that Devil joined Street of his own free will."

"You still manipulate him, and you will eventually end up hurting him when he finds out you're not who you say you are."

"Devil and I aren't in a relationship. He's my best friend, and I know little about him, just like he knows little about me; it's mutual."

"Well, there's the fact that you seem to be too skilled for Street. You've only caused me headaches since we met, and you have managed to disobey direct orders, undermine me in front of my people, and act like you have once obtained the same role as me."

He wasn't wrong. "That's my personality. You want to kill me because of my personality?"

"No."

"Then . . ."

"You talk too much. You make me talk too much."

"Talking is good, but that's not reason enough to kill me."

"I just don't like you . . . your presence . . . it's—for reasons best known to me, I'd prefer you dead. Let's leave it at that."

I tsked, shaking my head.

"Why do *you* want me dead?" he asked.

I shrugged. "You shot me, left a scar on me. Nobody does that and lives. Because of Devil, I'm lenient. Getting your name on my shit list would only take one action. I hope, for both our sakes, your name never gets on it."

"There it is, that tone. It's why I want you dead."

I laughed, eying him before relaxing back on the tree. "Get used to it, *Dad*. It's not going anywhere."

He didn't respond, and I no longer tried to fill in the silence. I closed my eyes, replaying the whole conversation in my head.

Elio's personality confused me, and I could feel my obsession to fix things tingle, but I reined it in. Despite all he had revealed, he was still The Wicked. He still shot me and tried to drown me. He couldn't be trusted.

And yes, I was proven right when I woke up to a bright day, the fire quenched with light smoke erupting from the ashes, and the man in black nowhere to be found.

I cursed, got to my feet, and called out his name, but I got no response.

He didn't just leave me here, did he?

I looked around and noticed the morning fog dissipating and the sun rising in the distance.

"Motherfucker," I muttered with grit, shrugging the trench coat off my body in anger. "That bastard."

I turned on my heel the moment something sharp whizzed past me, landing with a soft thud on a tree. I turned to the tree, squinting my eyes to see a small red syringe—"Ouch!" A sharp pain pricked my neck, and I quickly moved to pull out another syringe, bringing it to my view—

"Oh, fuck me."

I lost control of my legs and fell straight to the ground, dizziness tugging at my eyelids as echoing footsteps reached my ear.

From my blurry vision, I saw them dressed in all black, with masks covering their faces.

One of them bent down and took off their mask . . . I spotted a grin as he said, "Dors bien."

I might be crazy, and my knowledge of that language might be rough, but that sounded so much like—French for . . . *sleep well?*

My vision blackened, but I heard someone else speak.

"Carry her; let's go."

It was too late, but it dawned on me that the Russians weren't the only ones hunting for that painting . . .

What the fuck have we gotten ourselves into here?

And then I felt my body lifted from the ground, and I was thrown over a shoulder, the earth zooming in and out in a stomach-turning way. My tongue was heavy, my body numb, and I finally . . . finally gave in to the darkness.

CHAPTER TWENTY-FOUR

Elio

Control, unpredictability, and the ability to make decisions for the sake of the greater good have always been my strong suits. Some of my father's many lessons and why I had lasted so long in this business, in this world. I didn't throw temper tantrums; I didn't do things incapable of benefitting me; I didn't go off my self-made script. I was always ten steps ahead of a situation.

For example, the ugly but priceless chihuahua painting. It didn't look like much, just a square-framed blue-and-gray picture of a chihuahua with too-wide eyes, a crooked mouth, with her head bent at an odd angle, a head I'd had the pleasure of patting once . . . Many people wouldn't believe it—but that chihuahua, though odd-looking, was one of the sweetest pets that had ever gotten to grace this world.

Arturo Garza, the owner of the chihuahua, a dark-skinned, burly man who was untouchable to the point that he had the pleasure of dying at an old age, had been quite influential during his reign. This man knew everyone who was anyone. He could answer any question with the right incentive—a nutcase on his best days—but I still admired him.

Why? He had been the mastermind of all masterminds. There was also the fact that he was the first man my father had cowered in front of. I was eighteen when we first traveled to Mexico to find him. Then, I didn't know why, but my father had said Arturo was a man never to be crossed; he said he could squash us with just a snap of his fingers.

When we'd gotten to Arturo's manor, my father had been

sweaty and shaky. Though I waited outside, I could hear my father's angry voice, yelling at Arturo, trying to intimidate the man, but the man's response was always level, not shaky or lacking composure.

My father had opened the door, and I caught a glimpse of Arturo, a cigar between his lips and a small dog in his arms; our gazes connected before the door closed, and my father pulled me out with him.

On the way back, my father had been reeling with anger, and I just watched him. Feeling some peace from seeing him so unsettled.

At twenty-six, a few years after I'd taken over the empire, I took a trip to Mexico, seeking Arturo.

The man recognized me, and the dog perked up at the sight of my figure, tail wagging from left to right. I had crouched down, patting her. I liked her; she was odd but confident.

She reminded me of myself, and I temporarily forgot where I was until Casmiro discreetly kicked me.

I looked up, catching Arturo's interested gaze as he ushered me to his study.

He told me I was the first to look at his dog for over a second. *"People are always threatened by things they don't understand,"* he had said, and he had been right. He sounded so wise and made me feel comfortable enough to ask him anything.

I had gone straight to the point, telling him I needed his help to pull my family's name to the ground. I needed his information on us to do it myself.

Apparently, I had taken him by surprise because he stared at me like I was from a different space and time.

When he asked me why, I told him I wanted to see that look again—the one my father had worn after exiting his home.

He had a question in his eyes that clearly asked how possible it was to compel a facial expression from someone who was supposed to be dead. He didn't ask it. Instead, he told me he would have loved to help me, but he had his own plans, and that I would be informed of them when *everyone* else was informed.

The moment I received a letter after his death, I registered the man as a crazy person, even though I partially understood his motive.

His dog had been his only family, and everyone avoided it like the devil's spawn.

What better way to seek justice for the chihuahua than having people hunt for it like it was their salvation?

So, he had an artist paint her. Created a map. Turned every single one of his assets into gold, roughly 300 million pieces of solid gold. He gathered dire information he had gotten about six of the most prominent criminal families and world governing bodies, turned it into software copies, and placed them on custom-made flash drives. Then, he duplicated the painting into ninety-nine reproductions, inserted a map to find the gold along with those flash drives inside the frame of the original artwork, and then distributed them around the world.

This was his way of making people hunger for the painting of his dog; the dog they'd feared and made fun of was now the very thing they had to find to get their hands on the gold . . . and those flash drives.

Although 99 percent of the people gunning for the painting were there for the gold, only a few like myself needed those flash drives; this was because people who were hunting for the gold had no clue about the flash drives.

Therefore, whoever found the original painting first got the gold, the flash drives, and the key to being as powerful as Arturo was in our world.

The ultimate power. The final key to my puzzle. I'd find it. Let my father know that I had achieved the power to make anyone bend to my will. I would dangle what could have been right in his face.

Then I'd burn it all.

When Zahra had mentioned the painting in that supply

closet, I knew it was the same one perilous people were looking for. When she showed me the picture, it took everything in me not to snap her neck right there, kill the rest of Street, and send Elia far away from the chaos.

But I reined it in because I knew the painting that would be in the gallery was a fake. I had checked even before it arrived at the gallery.

The people who sent Street to retrieve the painting had cheated them. But I would have done the same. There were so many fakes and one original.

Each of these paintings was treated with equal attention and importance.

It was clear how Arturo had achieved all that he desired and more through this ridiculous quest.

The more paintings were released, the more crafty and dangerous people got in on the quest. A decent example of this was how we were ambushed and how curiosity had made Zahra fight to keep the painting, to get in on whatever it was about.

I knew I was close to finding it. This was precisely why I couldn't afford any distractions. Zahra was a distraction, and that would not do.

I couldn't kill her. *But that didn't mean I couldn't let her get herself killed.*

Having left the clearing to get the painting and bring a car to get us back to the compound, I genuinely didn't think there would be such a huge turn of events.

She had been asleep when I left, and I couldn't bring myself to wake her. Sleep was a luxury I didn't get to have in abundance. I admired people who could do it without restlessness and the need to make it permanent.

On getting to where the car broke down, I stopped when I saw a white van by the side of the road, a small distance from where I stood.

I'd shoved both hands into my pockets when I caught movements at the corner of my eye.

Leaning casually on the SUV, I watched about five men in black clothing and masks emerge from the woods and walk towards the van.

One of them held an unconscious Zahra over his shoulder, and the other quickly opened the back of the van, where they filed in, dumping her body.

They spoke in another language. I couldn't hear much from my distance, but I knew it was a language I didn't understand.

They locked the back doors, started the engine, and swiftly drove away.

I stood there for a couple of minutes, just watching them disappear down the road.

Well . . . it's not as if there was anything I could have done.

I pushed away from the SUV, grabbed my gun from the console, and shoved it into the back of my pants.

A few minutes later, I was getting in a red open-roof Beetle, hitching a ride back to town with a blonde who looked at me like it was the first time she was seeing another human being.

I politely ignored it.

"I gotta admit," she started, her voice sweeping with the wind, blond hair flying all around but tamed by a small scarf, "when I left my house this morning, the last thing I expected was to give someone as unreal as you a ride."

I frowned in genuine confusion. "Unreal?"

"Yeah! You got pretty eyes, a pretty face, and that body, whoosh." She glanced at me. "Are you a model or something?"

"No." I didn't like compliments, they made me uncomfortable, but the least I could do was be nice, seeing as she was giving me a ride. "But—thank you?"

She chuckled, all bright and sunshine. "How are you that hot, with a rough edge that screams walking red flag, and also so cute at the same time?"

Should I thank her again?

"Do you have a girlfriend?" she asked.

"No."

She glanced at my fingers. "A wife, then."

"No, I do not."

She smiled. "I like your rings; they look cool."

I brought my fingers to my view, turning them back and front. "Thank you . . . I like rings; they're . . . a mystery."

She chuckled. "Like you . . ."

"Hm." I watched her. "I like your hair."

Her eyes widened in surprise, but a grin broke through. "That's sweet, thank you."

I nodded, looking away.

She glanced at me, then back to the road. "You know you give off the vibe of a serial killer, right?"

I slowly looked back at her. "Do I?"

"You're dressed in all black, standing by the side of the road at the crack of dawn, you've got this mysterious aura, and you talk like you're testing out the words before you say them; you have this odd calmness to you . . . It's kind of unsettling."

"Yet, you offered to give me a ride."

She glanced at me and shrugged. "Maybe I have a death wish."

It was silent for a few beats.

I broke the silence. "I'm Elio."

She grinned. "Gemma."

"Put your mind at ease, Gemma; I have no reason to kill you. I just needed a ride."

She laughed, showing off a dashing set of straight teeth. "Well, if you did have reason to kill me, I'd ask that you don't mess up my face. I want to be a hot corpse—don't wanna traumatize anyone in the open casket ceremony." She grinned. "I'm glad I could offer you the ride, Elio."

She was still chatty as we drove, talking about how she was taking a road trip in three days because her grandmother wanted to experience it before she passed, and then she spoke about her grandmother, who was her only family. She asked me about my family, and I told her I had none.

It wasn't far from the truth. I was dead to Elia.

We arrived at a convenience store a few minutes later, and I told her I'd find my way from this point. I wished her and her grandmother well and watched her drive off.

I walked into the building and made my way up to the counter; a boy in a beanie with headphones around his neck eyed me wearily. My gaze shifted to the phone in his hand. "Can I use your phone, please?"

He blinked before slowly outstretching the device to me wordlessly.

"Thank you," I said, dialing Casmiro's number offhand.

He answered almost immediately. "Before you say anything, I want you to know that I will never forgive you for hurting my baby. Destroying her like that." His voice rang through, and I was pleased that he knew off the bat that it was me. He knew I would find a way to contact him.

"Glad to see you had a comfortable night in a comfortable bed, Casmiro. My night was fine too; I spent it in the woods, very comfortable, sleeping underneath the open sky. I didn't miss my bed, and I was far from danger. Did you have breakfast? Because I didn't, and I've just remembered that I didn't have dinner. How wonderful the last twenty-four hours have been for the both of us."

He sighed in resignation. "Are you okay?"

"Yes."

"Good, I found your artist. Where are you? I'll send people over."

"No need for that. I'll be at the compound shortly; I have somewhere else to visit."

"Where's Zahra?"

My fingers drummed against the counter. "She got kidnapped about an hour ago."

There was a slight pause as if he was trying to detect a joke. "Is that a joke?"

"No."

"Hold on, I—what? What is—what do you mean kidnapped?"

"Hm. It's none of my business; I'm sure she can handle herself." I flexed my fingers. "Hopefully, she can't and does me a favor by dying. I don't really care."

"Her team members have been here, seeking info."

"Tell them she was—"

My gaze shifted to the transparent doors of the store, and held.

You've got to be kidding me.

"Elio?"

I blinked. "Tell them she was kidnapped, but it has been taken care of," I said, watching the familiar white van move beside a fuel stand. A masked man in black hastily rushed out to fuel the van.

I knew it was empty now, and he was the only one inside the van; no one was in the passenger's seat. They'd dropped her off somewhere—at a site. Who knew. Hopefully the van had a location installed.

I shook my head, closing my eyes as I rubbed the space between my brows. The luck this woman had was . . .

"What do—"

"I'll be back soon." I took the phone from my ear, blocking and deleting the number before handing it to the boy, who was now staring at me with wide eyes. "Do you have cigars?"

He shook his head wordlessly.

"What do you have?"

"Cig—cigarettes."

"How can you not have cigars?" I sighed, rubbing my neck in tiredness. Then I gestured hastily with my hand. "Give me the cigarettes."

He rushed to fish for a pack, placing it on the counter.

I picked it up, watching the van as I took out a smoke, placing it between my lips while I checked my front pocket for a lighter. I flicked it on and lit the cigarette. Returning the lighter, I sucked in the smoke, blowing it back out.

"Do you believe in luck?" I asked the boy while watching the van.

"Huh?" he squeaked out.

I turned to him again, shoving my hand inside my other pocket and pulling out a small bundle of money, placing it on the counter.

"Luck, do you believe in it? Do you think it exists?"

His jaw was dropping at the sight of the money on the counter.

"I—I guess?"

"Hm." My gaze shifted to his side, and then I pointed to the baseball bat resting in the corner. "Is that yours?"

He quickly looked to the side, nodding. "Yes, sir."

"I need to borrow it. You can get yourself a new one."

He blinked before quickly reaching for the bat and handing it to me. It was strong enough, perfect for my grip.

"Thank—"

"Sir, this money is—even if I got a baseball bat with it and paid for the cigarettes, it's still too much, sir."

I blinked at him. "It's for the phone bill. Also, you need to stock the store with cigars, preferably flavored ones, in case I happen to visit again."

He gulped. "Yes, I—thank you—I will—thank you, sir."

I nodded, exiting the store as I walked towards the guy in the mask, watching him close the fuel tank before going around the van.

"Hey," I called, slipping the cigarette between my lips.

The moment he turned, I forcefully swung the bat at the side of his head. His body dropped to the ground, and he passed out on impact.

I twirled the bat, nodding. "Hm. Perfect."

Then I got in the van, satisfied to see that the location he was heading to had been channeled into his mobile device resting on the console. I started the engine, set the car gear into drive, and proceeded to save the woman.

How . . . inconvenient.

CHAPTER TWENTY-FIVE

Zahra

"*A more mio . . .*"

His gloved hand softly stroked my left cheek, warm and tender. His hot breath fanned my face, and I shifted uncomfortably, dread tugging at my stomach.

That voice . . .

"*My Zahra . . .*" The side of his face brushed mine, clean-shaven and smooth; his lips hovered above my ear, and he whispered, "*Wake up.*"

My eyes snapped open with a short gasp.

I was alone.

Relief flooded through me, but it ceased when I realized I was hanging . . . hanging from a ceiling.

"What the . . ."

My arms were stretched above my head, with my wrists tied to an iron hook at the top. My feet were far from the ground—and *God, I was aching*. My eyes burned as I looked around the space. It looked like an abandoned shed, and I could tell we were well into the afternoon and approaching evening from the light sneaking in through the small window at the end.

"Fuck . . ." I groaned in annoyance.

My ribs burned from the strain when I tried to twist my wrist free, but whoever tied the knot knew what they were doing. I drew in a deep breath before swinging myself back and forth three times, lifting my lower body and then my upper. It only lasted about three seconds before my body dropped in a painful protest.

I ground my teeth together, holding in the sharp pain that

shot through the joints in my shoulders at the drop. I had probably been hanging for hours.

Voices had my ears perking up; I was breathing hard as the door opened. Two men in black walked in, one rolling in a table with what looked like an electrical torture machine.

"Oh, come on, for a chihuahua painting, really?" I asked, my voice tired.

One of the guys approached me while the other rolled the table beside him. The one watching me had a buzz cut and a brutal healed scar slashing from his brow to his cheek. His lips were lifted in a sneer.

"Hi?" I voiced.

"You have a mouth on you." His French accent shot thickly through his words.

"Doesn't everyone have a mouth on them?"

His hand roughly grabbed my chin, turning my face from left to right.

"See something you like?" I asked. "Is it the freckles? It's always my frec—"

The back of his hand swung, connecting with my cheek in a hard slap. My head whipped to the side at the force of the hit, and I tasted blood in my mouth.

My breathing shuddered as I licked it off my lips. I turned to the buzzcut motherfucker; he was smirking at me.

"Learn to keep that mouth shu—"

I spat in his face before he could complete that statement.

He closed his eyes, pausing a few seconds before slowly digging his hand into his pocket, bringing out a handkerchief, and wiping the spit off his face. He opened his eyes again, this time with a glare that had me wondering if he would kill me now.

The other man turned on the machine, clearly pissed at how I'd insulted Buzzcut.

"My boss was right," Buzzcut said, throwing the handkerchief away. "You *are* her."

I frowned, my thoughts freezing. "Her who?"

"Manuel's whore."

I swallowed, my blood running hot. "I don't know what you're talking about. Who's that?"

"You want to play dumb?"

"Bitch, I thought I was here for the painting."

"Oh, you are." He stepped back and picked up a pair of jumper cables. My breathing changed pattern as I caught the jagged metal teeth gleaming in the dim lighting of the space. With a flick of his wrist, he scraped them together, causing a crackling spark that cut through the air.

My eyes alternated from him to the metal clamps as he faced me once more.

"Buddy, just—just calm—"

He jammed the metal clamps to both my ribs, and a searing, sharp, burning sensation swept through my body like knives; it felt like every organ inside me grew sharp pointy edges, stabbing me from the inside out. The pain had my body shaking violently; the electric current was slicing my muscles apart one by one. A strangulated scream left me, and he drew back the clamps.

My breathing was nothing but short gasps, and I felt warm and cold at the same damn time. "Well"—my lips trembled—"that's one way to shut me up."

It had been years since I'd felt torture like this. It wasn't unfamiliar. I'd undergone what Manuel had called necessary training. He'd shown me pain. Different kinds. He needed me to be strong. Ready to stand by his side, rule with him. I knew this pain, felt worse than this pain—but I wasn't prepared for this, and that alone made the pain hurt more than it was supposed to.

"Manuel Conti sent you to find the painting. Why?" Buzzcut asked.

"Who the fuck is Manuel Conti—" The clamps were back on my ribs, and my body shook in spasms, my teeth pressing together as I tried but failed to suppress my groans of pain. He released me again, and I gasped out, my breathing noisy and labored.

"This time, I want you to answer me with the truth; I will increase the voltage if you don't."

I let out a shaky breath, my body growing weaker with each passing second.

"I was paid f-five thousand fucking doll—ars to retrieve the painting for an unknown client. If this"—I swallowed—"if this person is Manuel Conti, whoever that is, I don't know them. No names were—were given when I passed information across to them."

"I know your face. I know you know him. And he sent you. Manuel Conti doesn't care about gold. So, there must be something else, and we want to know what it is."

What?

"Gold? There's—there's gold in the painting?" I asked, my surprise rocking some strength back into my body.

"Don't act like you don't know." The man sneered, rubbing the clamps together.

My gaze dropped to the clamps.

He moved closer. "Talk."

"Just c-calm down, okay? You don't think I was fucking surprised when I was sent five thousand dollars to retrieve that ugly painting? I thought I hit the jackpot, but now you're talking about—about gold? I was cheated."

"Quit playing dumb. We want to know why Manuel Conti wants the painting. What else is there with the gold?"

I sighed, confusion gripping me. "Who the fuck is Manuel Conti? Whoever you think I am, I promise—I promise you've got the wrong girl."

"Increase the voltage," the man said with a no-nonsense tone.

"Oh God, I'm fucking serious; I don't know what you're talking abo—ghhhhh." My body locked on tight as it shook violently; I felt the sharp, painful, blood-draining zap from my head to the soles of my feet, my toes curling, the strain on my arms—the pain gripping my insides so fucking unbearable, I didn't bother to hide my screams this time. My throat burned, my chest squeezed—

He released me again, and my body slumped, my head lolled to the side, and my breathing grew faint.

His hand came underneath my chin, raising my head.

"Talk now, or I kill you," he said.

I smiled, then a broken chuckle left me, and then a laugh; though weak, it still sounded like I was deranged.

I licked my bottom lip. "What do you . . . think, Buzzcut, that you'll . . . you'll shock me a few times, then I'll, what—cry and tell you all I know about Manuel Conti?" I drawled.

An unsettled look flashed in his eyes, making my smile widen as I said, "You don't . . . you don't know who you're fucking with. I humbly suggest you go back to your boss and tell him to leave Manuel to his business."

"So, you admit you know him."

I didn't respond, and his eyes scanned my body from head to toe. "You admit you're his . . . whore?"

My jaw clenched as he dropped the clamps, his finger coming to trace my jaw, down to my collarbone, then to my chest.

My hand formed a tight fist above me as I tried to level my breathing. "Get your *fucking* hands off me," I gritted.

"What does Manuel Conti want with that painting?"

I leveled him with a glare. "I don't know, and even if I do know, I sure as fuck won't tell you."

His fingers trailed down to the swell of my breast, and I jerked weakly away from his touch. "I swear to fucking God," I said, "I will chop your fingers off one by one if you don't keep them to yourself."

He laughed. "Making threats when you're tied to my ceiling." Then he looked at the other guy, who had a crooked smile on his face. *"Crazy woman."*

"Try me," I said, and both of them stopped laughing, attention back on me.

Buzzcut looked like he was seconds away from snapping my neck. "Millions of gold bars are not enough for Manuel Conti to send people out for the painting. You know something. Not just

Manuel, my boss suspects other families are on the hunt for it. What we don't know is why. Surely it can't be gold; these people are richer than sin. What else aside from gold connects with the painting?"

I frowned, dissecting his words, as a separate kind of suspicion arose in my mind. I tucked it aside for later, leveling Buzzcut with a glare.

"As I said, stay the fuck out of Manuel's business because if he doesn't hunt you for meddling, I will."

He smirked, and I watched his hand travel down my cleavage, but before he could wander further down, a loud clash from outside got their attention. There were shouts and grunts of pain and loud, unending, piercing gunshots.

Buzzcut and the other man exchanged a look at the chaos that seemed to have erupted outside.

My joints curled tightly in alert when the shooting lessened.

"Go check," Buzzcut said to the other man, his voice strained while the other guy left his position.

The shooting stopped completely.

I briefly wondered what the hell was happening, but I stopped wondering when the door to the small shed barreled open, a baseball bat swinging right into the face of the other guy who had been approaching it to go check.

The guy went down immediately, disoriented, as Elio swiftly twirled the bat, holding the handle and jamming its end into the man's face. He went out like a light.

And then Elio looked up, face stained with violent sprinkles of blood that I knew weren't his own, red splatters dotting from face to neck—he was wearing a button-up, which meant he had left me to change his shirt. The sleeves were rolled up to his elbows, revealing dots of blood on his forearms and the hand that held the baseball bat.

Elio's gaze swept up and down my body, completely expressionless, while he stood there, looking like a fucking psychopath who had just survived the zombie apocalypse, before he settled his gaze on Buzzcut, who looked like he had seen a ghost. He knew who stood before him. I could spot the moment fear took over his form; he quickly grabbed the clamps again, increasing the voltage to the highest setting as he aimed it at me.

"Don't come any closer, you—you come close, I fry her," he said.

Elio's gaze fell to me again before looking at the buzzing clamps and then back to Buzzcut.

"Okay." His voice rang through as he pressed the barrel of the baseball bat to the ground between his legs, both hands holding the knob as he spoke. "Go ahead."

"You think I'm bluffing?" Buzzcut said, inching the clamps close to my ribs, eyes sharp. "I will fucking do it."

Elio's expression didn't give anything away. "Was there a stutter to my previous statement?"

Buzzcut swallowed but didn't make a move to do anything.

"Are you going to do it, or should I approach?"

My insides tied knots around themselves. If Elio had really wanted me dead, he wouldn't be here, but why the fuck was he urging this fucker to fry me?

A few beats passed, with Elio staring intently at Buzzcut. When nothing was done, he nodded, lifting the bat, and started stepping forward, but the moment he did, Buzzcut found his senses again, about to press the clamps to my body. I was one second away from being electrocuted to death, but it seemed as if that one second was enough for Elio to reach behind him, whip out a gun, and aim it right at Buzzcut's head, pulling the trigger.

Buzzcut's blood splattered on me, and the clamps clattered with him as he fell to the ground.

He just . . . killed someone.

Elio dropped the bat, gun still in hand as he approached. He didn't look at me. Not once. He just went straight to the machine supplying currents to the clamps and turned it off. The silence grew between us, and it stretched even further when he raised his gaze, locking it with mine.

My breathing was loud, while his, as always, was controlled.

"Well, *Sport,* how's it hanging?"

I scoffed out a weak laugh. "Wow, *Dad,* how long did it take you to come up with that—that one? Real original."

"It is?"

"Very."

"I'm glad. The moment I saw you hanging, my brain immediately searched for a befitting response to your condition."

"Really? I'm happy you're finally learning to give a good sass."

"Hm. It seems the negative influence you have on my brother is beginning to rub off on me."

"Maybe we spend too much time together."

"Maybe."

And then silence fell, his eyes lingering on mine before falling to my cheek and then my lips. "Are you okay?" he asked, lifting his gaze to mine again.

"As okay as a person hanging from a ceiling for hours could be," I said.

"Right."

He came closer; his warm, firm body pressed against mine while one of his arms went around the backs of my thighs, a little below my ass, as he lifted me so that I wasn't hanging from my own weight anymore. I suppressed my sigh of relief when he untied the knot at my wrists; the numbness in my hands slowly vanished with the sharp pin-like stabs I felt in my fingers as blood rushed back into them. He placed me back on my feet, which were bare.

I dropped my arms, my body pressed flush against his, with his arm still around me.

Our gazes locked again. "You can let me go now," I said.

I lost my balance the moment he did, but he snaked his arm around me, pulling me back to his body. "Steady," he said; somehow, his voice had grown soft, or maybe I was just reading too much into the gesture.

I pressed my hand against his chest, feeling his muscles beneath my palm as I pushed slightly. "I can stand on my own; I'm not a damsel in distress."

His gaze roamed my face. "I did just save you."

"I was handling it well on my own."

"You were? It's odd, but I seem to remember untying you a few seconds ago."

"I would have untied it myself, even if you hadn't shown up."

He was still holding me. "A little thank-you doesn't hurt, Sport."

"I have nothing to thank you for, *Dad*." I pushed away from him, standing on my own two feet, ignoring the tiny wave of dizziness that hit me, ignoring how I felt less warm, being away from his body. "You left me."

"Not exactly. I would have returned for you if you hadn't gotten yourself kidnapped."

I blinked at him. "So, you—you saw them taking me away."

"I did."

"And you didn't do anything?"

"This is ludicrous and will never happen, but would you have stopped them from taking me away if you were the one in my place?"

I couldn't answer because, yeah, he was right.

"There's my answer. Come on, I have somewhere to be, and we need to look at your arm before returning to the compound. I honestly wonder how you're standing after all they seem to have done to you," he said, walking past me to Buzzcut on the ground.

Ignoring his remark, I asked, "Did you shoot anyone outside? The gunshots—"

"They shot themselves while I used them as human shields. Broke a few faces with the baseball bat. The usual."

I frowned when he bent, fishing in his pocket for a handkerchief; he covered his hand with it as he searched Buzzcut's body until he recovered a wallet and pulled out an ID card, examining it before slipping it into his pocket and throwing the wallet back on Buzzcut's corpse.

"Let's go," Elio said, brushing past me.

My stomach ached as I followed behind him. "You didn't take that ID card because you want to—" I stopped short when somebody came rushing through the entrance. The boy was in the same uniform as the other guys, but he had a striking resemblance to Buzzcut, mainly because his hair was also a buzzcut. He didn't look like he was more than nineteen.

His frantic eyes swept past Elio and me to Buzzcut's body, and he screamed, "Papà!"

Elio's gaze swept between Buzzcut and the boy.

No . . .

"Elio, don't—"

The shot rang through before I could even complete that statement; the boy's body dropped to the ground with a crumpling thud, blood running from the wound on his head.

I stood in shock, my body completely frozen, as Elio slipped the gun back into his pants. "Come on."

I couldn't move. I couldn't bring myself to. I felt sick to my stomach.

What the fuck.

What the fucking fuck.

A groan left Elio, and I caught his figure approaching from the corner of my eye. "I don't have time for this," he said, grabbing my good arm and pulling me with him.

My head was cloudy, the sound of the gunshot still ringing in my ears, even as Elio reached a black car and opened the door, pushing me inside the passenger's seat, and rounded the car to the driver's side; I stared into nothing.

The car started moving, and as we drew further and further away, my breathing became sharper.

Once on the familiar highway, I felt unable to breathe properly. My hands were shaking, and thinking was beginning to feel difficult . . . The torture, the lack of food, the shocks from the metal clamps, and then this . . . what I'd just witnessed.

This man had just—he had just . . . he was—I can't—I can't—

"Stop the car."

"What?"

"Stop the car, now."

"I do—"

I picked up the gun he'd dropped on the console and pointed it at the side of his head. "Stop the fucking car, or I'll blow your fucking brains out."

He glanced at me, annoyance glazing in his eyes as he navigated the car to the side of the road.

The moment he stopped, I was dropping the gun, ignoring my exhaustion and my worn limbs, staggering out and away from the car, taking a lungful of breath, my fingers raking through my hair in frustration.

"Fuck, fuck," I chanted, trying to calm myself.

The sound of the car door opening and closing had me looking up at Elio, who came to stand outside, leaning on the side of the car hood in my direction as he watched me before fishing in his pocket for a cigarette and a lighter.

He lit it and put everything back in place while he smoked and watched me. There was no remorse in his form, almost like he hadn't just shot a teenager.

"You didn't have to kill him," I said, my voice heavy with anger.

"I did."

I was thrown back by how direct he sounded—like—like he was in the right. "What the fuck—he was just a fucking—he couldn't have been more than nineteen! He was innocent!"

He brought the cigarette to his lips, sucked in, and blew out smoke calmly. "Sins are passed on from a parent to a child as long as they share blood. People need to live much better lives, so when they meet their fate, their families don't have to pay for it."

I took steps closer to him now, poking at his chest. "That. Is fucking. Bullshit! It's bullshit twisted in a way that only makes sense to you!"

"I know."

"Yet you still fucking do it!" I yelled in exasperation.

His brows dropped, and he looked irritated. "It had to be done. If they die, anyone who shares blood with them dies too."

"Oh, for the love—says who!" I yelled.

"Says me!" he yelled suddenly, and I had to step back momentarily. He wasn't one to lose his cool, but he just did. He threw the cigarette to the ground and closed the space I had created, getting into my face. "It is my fucking law, and if you keep running your mouth like this, you and your blood relatives will share the same fate. You know them, or you don't."

"Oh, please—"

"Don't be a hypocrite, Zahra. I have seen you kill people without batting an eye. You don't think they have family somewhere who would grieve them?"

"That's different!"

"How is it different? Because they're above twenty? A life is a life, no matter how old they are."

My breathing was harsh as I shook my head, looking at him with a newfound hatred. "I hate you; I have never hated anyone as much as I hate you."

"Okay."

"You will rot in hell."

"I know."

"The world will be a much fucking better place without you in it!"

"As I have devised."

I wanted to pull my hair out at how unfeeling his voice was. "You're a fucking murderer! A fucking psychopath and serial fucking killer, a sick unfeeling fucker! A twisted monster! Child-murdering bastard—" His hand gripped my throat as he switched our positions and slammed my body against the car.

"And you're beginning to get on my nerves." He seethed, his

eyes a deadly mask of anger and something else I didn't even care to put a name to.

I tried to struggle out of his grip, but he held firm.

I ground my teeth together, looking him dead in the eyes. "I will kill you. Mark my fucking words, Elio, you've just made it to my shit list. Watch this fucking face because it will be the last thing you see when you breathe your last."

"I'm honored to have made it to your list, but I already called *dibs* on killing me. Genuinely sorry to disappoint."

I stayed silent, my eyes flickering between his, his words loosening in my head, the meaning clear as fucking day.

"Get off me!" I yelled, pushing at him. He let me go, stepping away with his eyes still dead set on mine. "You're fucked up," I said, straightening. "I knew you had a few screws loose, but boy, are you messed up in that fucking head of yours."

His jaw clenched, and he shoved his hands into his pockets.

I raked my hair from my face, and his eyes followed the movement.

"You're so gone beyond redemption, and you can't even see it, Elio," I said, shaking my head. "Devil deserves better than having you as the only family left. You don't deserve him."

He remained quiet, eyes hardening, brows twitching, showing how my words had hit him.

Well—good fucking riddance.

"I don't know what you think you're waiting for?" I stepped closer to him. "But you need to hurry the fuck up and get the fuck out of everyone's faces. No one needs your bullshit, neither do they want you here."

He remained silent for a while before he swallowed and responded, "Okay."

I scoffed, shaking my head in disbelief before walking away from him and back to the car, needing to get out of there and away from him.

CHAPTER TWENTY-SIX

Elio

"A man like you shouldn't feel."

"Love is only a sentiment, boy. It is a weakness. Take out your heart and paint it black, a man like you shouldn't love."

"Be ten steps ahead of your enemies and your friends, boy. Never show remorse. Never show regret. And most importantly, never show weakness."

"Chin up, soldier; everyone you shoot today will deserve it."

"So what? You lost a few men. Get back on your fucking feet! I didn't send you here to make friends."

"Elio, I wish I could help you, but the voices in my head won't let me see your pain, my love."

"If you keep this up, you'll be dead as soon as you take my place. Bold, Son. Be bold."

"You kill a father? Make sure you kill everyone he has fathered; you don't do it? They'll come for you."

"You are like your father! You're never here; you're always shadowing him! What about me? What about your mother!"

"I'm scared, Elio."

"Family is only necessary when they're useful."

"I hate you!"

"I need help, Elio; help your mother."

"They were screaming for you; where were you?"

"Open your eyes, Elio! This world is not black-and-white. It's whatever color you paint it."

"Lock him up until he comes to his senses."

"He's a monster; he murdered his whole family; best not cross him."

"You are not my family."

"What reason do I have to believe any fucking word that comes out of your mouth!"

"Weak. Incompetent. A fucking failure."

"Did you love your mother's scream while you stabbed her? Or Mariana's and Lorenzo's tortured wails while you fucking burned them alive."

"The world will be a much better place without you in it!"

"You're so gone beyond redemption, and you don't even see it, Elio."

"You need to hurry the fuck up and get the fuck out of everyone's faces. No one needs your bullshit. Neither do they want you here . . ."

Words.

They were simple alignments of letters to form something meaningless or meaningful, depending on how they were used.

You'd think a man like myself would be accustomed to taking things in stride.

But I was impressionable when it came to compliments, advice, or reprimands. I couldn't help it. I was built that way.

It was probably abysmal that I had to share this idiosyncrasy with a clinical depression that I'd never bothered to treat since I was diagnosed years ago. It was the same illness my mother had. The same one my father had ignored.

When I got symptoms, I'd hoped to God that I hadn't inherited it, seeing who she became down the years . . . I was scared of what I'd become with the kind of hand I was brought up with.

My childhood hadn't been normal. It was replete with abuse, verbal, physical, and emotional.

I'd done things I would never forget or forgive myself for, things I had punished myself for.

But sometimes, the punishment was never enough. Nothing was ever enough.

Angelo would tell me to go for proper treatment, but there was no point in treating myself; I didn't deserve to get better, not after everything I had done in the name of revenge. In the name of *care*.

Deep down, I knew I was just a sick bastard. I was delusional. I didn't know consequences. I grew up learning to forget the meaning of that word. I didn't care for useless emotions because I knew how my life started and how it would end. There was no point in building relationships or dwelling on something less than its worth.

There was no point to me.

Why was I stalling in the name of revenge . . . on the father who didn't even give a shit, on a brother who hated me—on some false delusion of poetic justice. Did I even deserve that?

No one really needed me here. I was alone with the books most of the time anyway.

A waste of space and valuable oxygen just to fulfill a promise made to a dead sister who probably would have wished for my death if she were alive.

Until Zahra mentioned it about an hour ago, I didn't realize all I was doing was stalling. Because even when it came to finishing this, I still couldn't do it.

How meaningless could I get?

I shook my head, gripping the steering wheel tightly, dark thoughts spinning and dancing around my head.

They meant business this time. They were merciless. Uncontainable. I needed to be alone.

I neared the drugstore, itching to get out of the car—away from the woman beside me.

In my periphery, Zahra's head rested against the window, but her eyes were trained on me.

I should have known.

I should have known she'd alter my streak from the moment she opened her mouth when we first met. I always stayed away from things that drew unwarranted emotion. Things that made me feel. But her . . . this woman.

First, she provoked curiosity in that torture room; anger in the boardroom; irritation and competitiveness with the chess game; regret on the rooftop; lust in the supply closet and the exhibit; impulsiveness in the car chase; desire, denial, and remorse in the woods . . . care in that shed . . . then acceptance and realization by the roadside.

She made me feel useless emotions; somehow, I'd grown comfortable thinking I'd found someone like me. The more unrestricted, open-minded version of me. If I hadn't returned to find her after the amateur kidnapping, I was almost positive she'd have found a way out of that position because *I* would have found a way.

Somewhere between the supply closet and the shed, I'd thought maybe I wasn't the only one without morals.

It turned out I was being delusional: even *I* was fucked up to someone like *her*.

"I could totally be your friend if you stop trying to kill me." Her voice echoed in my head.

Guess now that wasn't an option.

I pulled into the parking lot by the drugstore just out of town, turning off the engine.

"Why are we stopping?" Tiredness coated her voice as she stretched.

"There's a change of clothes in the back seat," I told her, unbuckling my seatbelt without looking her way, even though I could sense her stare. "By the side of the building, there's a washroom. You can freshen up; I'll get things for you to clean your arm wound. There's a local mobile restaurant near here; since you've not eaten anything all day, we'll stop by."

Her gaze shifted from me to the back seat, probably seeing the folded clothes and the fake chihuahua painting, and then she looked back at me. "When—when did you have time to get the clothes and check the area?"

"Before I reached the shed. I'll be back." I was already opening the door and getting out, making my way into the drugstore. A mild headache paid a visit as I picked out the little things she'd need to take care of the wound. I knew I was about to scare the person behind the counter due to all the dried blood on me.

Or . . . I might be scaring the person humming and turning towards the shelf I was standing in front of.

I glanced in the voice's direction and frowned, doing a double take at who emerged, my attention focused on pulling out a drug from one of the shelves.

"Gemma?" I called.

Her blond head snapped in my direction, eyes widening as she froze, staring at me. Her gaze took me in from head to toe—surprise, confusion, and caution shining in her eyes, but there was no trace of fear.

"Elio? What a coincidence."

"I don't believe in coincidences. Are you following me?"

She blinked out of the daze she seemed to have been in. "No? My grandma and I decided to hit the road early. I'm refilling her meds . . . Are *you* following me?"

"No."

She swallowed. "Is that . . . blood on you?" She eyed the things in my hand. "Oh my God, are you hurt? Or did you hurt someone, and now you're trying to help them? Are you—are you really some kind of serial killer?" She whispered the last part.

"No."

She nodded. "So . . . what—what am I looking at here?"

"If I told you it was paint, would you believe me?"

"Nope."

I nodded. "My . . ." I trailed off, wondering what to refer to Zahra as. I couldn't exactly use *hostage, friend,* or *woman* like I'd used in that exhibit to get Grace off my back. So, I went with my generic answer when I didn't want to expatiate. "Someone I know is hurt."

Her lips formed an "O" as she nodded. The warning bells that usually alerted me to be cautious didn't go off in my head. "Well . . . this must be the universe . . . Maybe it wants us to exchange numbers," she said with a grin.

"I'm covered in blood."

"What does that have to do with numbers?" she said, fishing through her purse as she approached me.

"You still want to talk to me?"

She smiled, confusion dancing in her eyes. "Of course I want to talk to you. Why wouldn't I?"

"You are not . . . scared . . . of me?"

"If you wanted to kill me, you'd have done it earlier today." She outstretched her phone to me. "Type in your number."

"I don't have a phone."

"Ah . . . you're one of those types." I watched her search inside her purse for a pen and a piece of paper, and then she quickly scribbled a phone number on it, extending it to me. "There, you can text or call me whenever you get a phone?"

"What if I never get a phone?"

"Then, if the universe wills it, we'll see each other again." Wide eyes shone with amusement.

I took the paper.

She walked backward, a teasing smile on her face. "If you do get that phone, don't be a stranger."

"Okay."

She chuckled, shaking her head and muttering, "So cute," before she turned and disappeared down the aisle, away from view . . . I memorized the number before slipping the paper into my pocket, continuing my hunt for the last item, which was cotton wool, and then I paid a frightened teenager and exited the store towards the building out back.

Walking into it, I trekked the short hallway to the female washroom.

I raised my hand to knock. "Spo—" I stopped, closing my eyes for a second before opening them back up, my knuckle connecting with the door three times. "Zahra, I got the materials for your arm."

"Come in." Her voice was muffled, and I twisted the handle, pushing the door open, and walked in . . . The moment I raised my head, I paused, unable to stop my eyes from taking her in.

Her hair was wet, and she wore the black sweatpants I had chosen. Her shoulders were naked, and her hand held the black sweatshirt over her chest in an attempt to cover her breasts, but I could still see the swell, barely covered underneath her naked arms.

I was staring. Of course I was staring.

She was the first woman in a year and a half who had piqued my interest sexually.

The reason why was still a mystery to me.

I found her attractive. I find a lot of women attractive, but Zahra, while not my usual type, managed to challenge me in every way.

I didn't like loud women. She was loud. I didn't like careless people. She was the definition of careless. I didn't like people who talked back when they were not supposed to. She talked back—*every* time. I didn't like women with short hair. She wore her hair short, though it always smelled excellent, pleasant to the point that I was impressed with the effort she put into it to make it smell—see? My thoughts derailed again.

She was like me—except she held all the characteristics of myself that I habitually hid to keep up the façade that was my whole life.

It was scary. It intimidated me in a way I had never thought probable.

I liked a challenge, but this time it came in the form of a woman I couldn't have.

A woman I don't want to have.

"I would have asked if you liked what you're seeing, but the last time I asked someone that question, I got slapped." Her voice made me blink, pulling me back from my head—*both my heads.*

I approached her, taking my eyes away before placing the items on the counter. "That's all you'll need."

This scourge of a woman wouldn't take her eyes off me, even as I turned to go back outside.

"Elio," she called. I stopped. "Help me."

"I'm assured you know your way around sewing your own wound."

"I do, but not from this angle. I might do more damage than good."

I clenched my jaw, pulling on the blankest expression I could muster in her presence before turning to "help."

Without looking at her, I washed my hands clean in the basin, then put on the gloves I had gotten, cleaning the surface area of the cut.

"You won't even look at me," she stated.

I continued my work, ensuring the needle was sterilized properly before connecting it with her skin.

She winced, and I glanced up, catching her stare, which was able to hold mine for about five seconds before I focused on what I was doing again.

It was quiet for a while before she spoke again. "Fine," she snapped, sounding agitated. "Your whole quiet broodiness is making me feel like shit, so I'll be the bigger person and . . . try to . . . a—apolo—fuck. I'm sorry, I shouldn't have said that after you told me you wanted to off yourself. I was just tired and pissed because you didn't have to shoot the boy, and you showed literally no remorse."

I carefully put the third stitch in, remaining quiet.

My silence disturbed her; I could feel it each passing second her words hung in the air after her forced apology.

"So you're not going to say anything . . . maybe something along the lines of, *you're right, I shouldn't have shot the kid?*"

I put in the fourth stitch, trying to block out her voice.

"Listen . . . I never apologize to people, okay? So, this is kind of a big deal for me, being the bigger person, because I'm petty as fuck."

I put in the second-to-last stitch, concentrating.

"Oh, come on, Elio, I'm trying here."

"I have no use for your apology," I stated, my tone flat.

"That's not what you're supposed to say to someone who apologizes to you."

"I have no reason to acknowledge your courtesy."

"Okay, Your Highness."

The ick in my stomach had me losing focus for a second, and she flinched at a wrong movement from me.

My gaze snapped to hers. "Fucking stay still, Sport."

Her lips curved upward, drawing my gaze to them. "I'm perfectly still," she said, and I looked away, back to her arm.

My blank look was a failure because I couldn't help a frown from drawing my brows together.

Her stare made me uncomfortable, as always. Not that I didn't like it when people looked at me, she just had this—thing where she lured the victim of her stare to reciprocate the action.

It was unnerving.

Her eyes . . . her freckles . . . her face. Terrifyingly sinful.

I avoided sins. Especially the ones woven into the body of a pretty face.

"For real, today has been terrible. I was legit shocked from direct electricity, and then your actions—but with all that, I'm still trying to salvage this little partnership we've developed—"

"Don't delude yourself."

"Okay . . . friendship?"

"We are not friends."

"Frenemies?"

"That's not a real word."

"Enemies, then?"

"If I considered you an enemy, you'd be dead."

"Okay . . . what do you consider me—"

"Nothing."

I finished the stitching, dropped the materials by the sink, and removed the gloves.

"Nothing?" she asked, doing that thing with her voice, the one that compelled attention.

I fell for it . . . again. Pausing before looking back at her.

A taunting smile played on her lips.

She lowered the sweatshirt.

I dropped my gaze.

Fuck.

Piercings. Her nipples were pierced. Erect. Brown against full breasts.

Was I impressed by it? Yes.

Was there an uncomfortable aching in my tongue and cock? Yes, which I concede is a normal reaction. Did I need this reaction? No. This was useless . . . this was . . . *temptation.*

She pulled the sweatshirt down the rest of the way, covering herself and raking her fingers through her wet hair.

I raised my gaze again, catching a smile from her, her stare flickering from my eyes to the strain against my pants. She took two steps closer to me, just enough for me to get the now distinct, distracting smell from her hair, enough for me to feel what warmth from her body would have felt like—enough to take me back to that shed, where her body pressed flush against mine.

She tilted her head. "I admire your control, Elio. It makes me wanna . . . *challenge it.*" Then she subtly scrunched her nose to show her pending excitement for challenging my control. "I'll wait for you in the car," she said. "I could eat, and then we'll talk about today . . . Don't take too long." And then she reached behind me, purposefully brushing her chest with mine as she grabbed the nightgown she had been wearing before heading out of the washroom.

I released a breath, closed my eyes, and moved my neck from left to right, willing for a semblance of control.

It wouldn't matter . . .

In a few hours, it wouldn't matter.

Focus . . . *those piercings* . . . focus.

I hissed, snapping my eyes back open and glaring at the wall. "Fucking witch."

CHAPTER TWENTY-SEVEN

Zahra

Elio got into the car, all clean from the blood on him, making it a point to avoid looking at me.

I fed off attention and control. In whatever position or situation I found myself, I always made sure the rein of control remained firm in my grip. Losing it would shove me right back into that scared sixteen-year-old girl—the spineless Zahra who chose the wrong person to hold her hand under the guise of freedom.

With Elio, I held the reins, but there were just times when my control flickered. Flashing him hadn't been my plan to get his attention. A part of me just wanted to see his reaction, and boy, was it priceless. His eyes had been lust personified.

It excited me.

It shouldn't. It shouldn't because after I left that damn washroom, I felt guilt cloud my senses. What would Devil think if he discovered this new development?

I couldn't want this man beside me. But I did want to play with him.

I was itching to tease him till he was at his brink—but God—that expression on his face when he walked in and saw me half naked.

The control that had been at the top of my palm. The reaction it had elicited.

After leaving the clutches of those sex traffickers, I'd made all my sexual encounters ride on my terms. We had an equal say. Don't grab. Don't own unless I ask. I never did. The fear of giving my trust to a man and letting him take me was not something I liked experiencing. But damn it to hell if I didn't—somehow—like the way Elio had arrived at that shed and shot Buzzcut, holding me firm to his body afterward.

My pride seemed to be nonexistent.

While I liked to be the one in control most of the time—my gaze shifted from the road to Elio, who had an elbow resting on the window while his tattooed fingers rested on his cheek and his lips, his other hand controlling the steering wheel—I wondered how it would feel to be owned by a man like him.

I wanted to drive him to the edge, make him lose control, let go of the reins, and see what he would do to me.

I had never wanted this . . . I would probably never go through with it, but it wouldn't kill to wonder, would it?

Minutes later, Elio pulled up at the mobile restaurant he had talked about. It was small, but a few travel cars were parked around.

"So, how do we pay for the food? You don't look like you have a phone or an ATM card."

He turned off the engine before turning to look at me like he was surprised that I'd asked that question. I just knew in my gut that he was about to respond with an indirect insult. The mock concern in his eyes was a dead giveaway.

"I remember we spent hours away from each other, and you seem like a person with a good memory, like the fact that this was not what I was wearing yesterday. Who knows? Maybe after I left you with your captors, I went to get clothes for you and myself . . . and I never told you I didn't have any money on me if I recall correctly," he said with a cautious stare, one that made me feel like I was intellectually inept.

"Well, at least you're talking to me."

Seconds passed before he shook his head, getting out of the car. I got out after him, following behind as he walked towards the restaurant entrance.

I spotted a pay phone by the side, making a mental note to ask if it was still in order.

When we entered, the smell of roast beef and late-night greasy food filled my nose, and my stomach grumbled. There were people in booths here and there, but overall, the building had a cozy, secluded, homey feel. I just knew the food was going to be great too.

"My God, I'm so hungry; it's been years since I've gone this long without eat—"

"I'll find a booth," Elio cut in rudely before walking away from me.

I shook my head, ignored him, and ordered a variety of food, sending the plates to the booth where Elio was before rushing outside to use the pay phone, which I had confirmed was thankfully still in order.

I borrowed a few coins, assuring them the man dressed in black would cover it.

Entering the phone booth, I placed a call through to Dog's private cell, and he picked up at the third ring.

"Who the fuck is this?"

"Zahra—"

"You're not dead?" His voice came with a twinge of relief and mock shock, and then I heard footsteps from the other end. "Guys, she's alive. We can't use her bedroom for the orgy anymo—hey!"

There was a quick scuffle, followed by Dog's protest, and then Devil's voice reached my ear. "Z, are you okay?"

I smiled, leaning on the booth wall. "Yeah, D, I'm okay."

"Where are you?"

I looked around. "Some restaurant out of town, but I'll be back soon. I was a little hungry."

I heard him sigh. "You had me worried—you had all of us worried."

I chucked away my guilt. "Sorry, did you guys find anything about the painting and why I was fucking abducted by really hot French guys? Also why they were asking about some . . . gold?"

There was a mini silence before I heard Milk's voice from a distance saying, "Put it on speaker."

"Where are you calling from?" Upper asked, and I knew from the lagging in his voice and the distant keyboard tapping that he was trying to track the device.

"Some pay phone?" I said, confused.

"Hold on," he said, and then there was complete silence, a little bit of static, and then, "Can you hear me?" His voice was clearer.

"Yeah? What's going on?"

"I rerouted transmission to something more private. Safer that way."

"Okay? So . . . I take it you guys know what's going on?"

"Yes," Milk said. "Dog was able to find the location of the person who's been exchanging emails with us for months. We traced them to Australia."

"Australia? A lot of people want this thing," I said.

"It's fucking gold. Three hundred fucking million bars. Of course people are gonna kill for it," Dog responded.

"The painting originally belonged to some dead rich dude, Arturo Garza. Feared by most made men," Devil added.

Ah . . . I see.

"He made a map, placed it in the original frame, and made about ninety-nine copies of the painting, and sent them out. It's basically a quest for gold, and obviously something else," Milk said.

"We haven't figured out what that something else is," Devil said, "but if bosses of criminal families are also hunting for it, it's gotta be big."

"Probably intel," Milk said. "Groundbreaking intel is the only reason these men would want it."

"The power . . ." I said. "This is huge. People are getting informed of this quest every day. Forget the intel, and think about how many people out there are killing to get their hands on that gold."

"I want to get my hands on the gold," Dog said. "We'll be made for fucking life if we find the original painting."

"I'm guessing the one sitting in our car right now isn't the original. Do we know how each painting is released?"

"It's spontaneous. Arturo was a mastermind. He wanted this quest to last for a long time, and it's working; everyone is barreling down, following the same patterns. While there's probably a quest twist somewhere, we have to brainstorm, think like him . . . that's the only way we can win this . . . if we all want the gold, that is," Upper said.

"I want the gold," Milk said. "And I love quests! It'll be fun."

"And I want to know what's got these powerful men cowering," I said.

"I'm curious too," Devil joined in. "We can't talk expressively about this over the phone."

"I'll be on my way as soon as I eat."

"Can you pack something for me too? I'm starving," Dog said.

"You literally just ate," Milk said.

"Did I?"

I chuckled. "Okay, guys, are we telling Marino?"

"If this painting is as popular amongst criminals as we've found, then he already knows about it," Upper said.

Of course he had no reason to tell me even if he knew. "I'll go now; see you guys soon."

I hung up, making my way back into the building. I walked towards our booth, almost doubling over when I saw the food on the table.

Spaghetti with oil and garlic—*aglio e olio*—sauced meat in a full bowl, spicy vegetables that smelled divine, three pieces of tomatoes and onion-sauced chicken, and yummy-looking French fries to go with it. I was practically drooling at the sight, wishing I had a phone to take pictures and send to Dog so he'd cry.

I slipped into the booth, rubbing my hands together as I looked over at the man opposite me, whose gaze was trained on the window beside him, arms crossed against his chest, lost in his world. He didn't even look over when I arrived.

I dug into the food immediately, diving straight for the water before picking up the fork, rolling the delicious pasta onto it, shoving it into my mouth, and moaning at the taste. "God, fuck yes, this is so good."

When he didn't turn my way, I lightly hit his leg from underneath the table, and he turned to me, raising a brow of inquiry.

"You've got to try this; it's heavenly. Why didn't you order?"

"I'm not in the mood to eat."

I scrunched my nose. "Do people have to be in a mood before eating?"

"I am not *people*."

I shoved another forkful of spaghetti into my mouth, speaking with my mouth full. "Did you stop by here to eat something when we were apart?"

"No."

"So you've not eaten all day as well?"

"Yes."

I grabbed a piece of sauced chicken, tearing into it like a starved woman, knowing my mouth was as messy as my hands, seeing that Elio's blank stare had quickly turned into one of irritation as he watched me eat.

Yes! A reaction!

"You're not avoiding food because you're ashamed to eat in front of people, are you? Cause that's just pitiful," I said, one of my hands rolling spaghetti onto the fork, shoving it into my mouth, while my other hand brought the chicken to my mouth, tearing a bite as I chewed the spaghetti and chicken together, melting at the combination.

"You're an animal," he stated.

"Stop flattering me; I might just fall in love with you."

"That was not a compliment," he gritted.

I swallowed, picking a piece of sauced beef with one of the toothpicks. "I have this disorder where every insult I get materializes into compliments in my head; it's like—so rare and incurable."

"There's no such thing."

"Do your research," I said, digging into the vegetables and pasta to find what combination they would form in my mouth. "Oh yes." I threw my head back. "I'm having a literal food orgasm right now."

Elio relaxed in the booth, shaking his head like he was done with me. I smiled inwardly; at least he wasn't looking out the window with that wary expression anymore.

"This place is perfect! They bring tradition into the taste of their food. Dog would love it here. I'll bring him sometime to have food orgasms together."

"You lack table manners."

"No. I just love being free, not uptight and proper like you." I grabbed another chicken wing, waving it around him as I said, "I know there's a food craze in there somewhere; you just gotta let loose."

"Like you let yourself loose to the extent of"—his gaze flickered to my chest—"piercing your nipples?"

"There, there, is that what's bothering you? Can't get it out of your head? Is it making you hard again? You should have looked away."

"You didn't give me a choice. How did you sit through that? Who put it on you?"

Dropping the bone of the chicken wing, I smiled coyly at him. "A man. A hot, sexy, tatted, and pierced man. He was really good with his hands. His name was Julio."

The man opposite me just shook his head. "Why would you put yourself through that?"

"You got an opinion about my preferences, I don't wanna fucking hear it. My body, my choice."

"I'm not trying to give an opinion. It looks painful, and I wondered why you would endure it?"

"The pleasure that comes with it is worth it." I smiled, pulling the French fries towards me. "Besides, I was a sex worker, as you might already know, if you've pieced the whole being sold thing together."

He frowned immediately. "They forced it on you?" The edge to his voice had me clarifying.

"Nope, I saw some other girls getting it; I liked it but didn't dare to do it then because I was young. But I did it after I left; one of the best decisions I ever made, and from your expression earlier, I could tell you liked it."

"I didn't."

"Pfft. Right, you didn't." I picked up the glass of water, bringing it to my lips as I stared at him from underneath my lashes, ending my statement with, "But your cock did." I drank.

"I'm not talking about this anymore."

I chuckled, setting the glass down. "You raised the issue."

"It was clearly a mistake. You need to work on your conversational skills because, somehow, everything you say has to end in some sexual comment. It's worrying."

"Aww, you're worried about me?"

"No . . . you make me want to plant a bullet in my skull," he said, turning his head back to the window, his dull demeanor settling in an instant, like every conversation we just had never happened.

My stomach bottomed out with guilt at his response, and I dropped the topic, sitting up and raising a new one. "So, my captors were asking for information about some gold. Apparently, there's a lot of gold to be gained by whoever finds the painting . . ." I said, gauging his expression.

He hesitantly looked away from the window to me, looking indifferent. "Is that so," he stated.

I sighed. "You knew, didn't you?"

He didn't respond.

"Why didn't you say anything?"

"I had no reason to."

"Seriously? I almost got shot because of a fake painting. That's enough fucking reason to."

"How do you know it's a fake?"

"Street did some research, and they discovered all about the quest shit, the gold, and Arturo's little chihuahua."

"Congratulations," he said.

"You're so nonchalant about this. It's infuriating."

"Okay," he mumbled, looking out the window again. He looked like he was physically here, but his mind was elsewhere.

"Can I have the ID card? The one you took from the buzzcut guy?" I asked.

Without looking at me, he lifted himself a little, searching his pocket for the ID card and dropping it on the table.

I cleared my throat. "Thanks. I still don't think there's any need to hunt down the rest of his family."

"Hm," he responded.

Deciding to use Spanish, I asked, *"Where's your mind?"*

He turned his head towards me, staring for a few seconds before he answered, *"Everywhere."*

I sat up, knowing I was not good at this, but I still had to let him know, one way or another, why I was mad. "Listen, I appreciate that you killed that guy. He would have killed me if you hadn't done it. But the boy—he was still young, and I know your logic is to kill them so they wouldn't have to go through grief, but . . . you're not only stopping them from grieving . . . you're stopping them from a future they could have had. A life. Maybe even better than the one we have."

When he didn't reply, I continued, "I know this business comes with a lot of blood on your hands, but sometimes, it's better to have a limit so you don't completely lose yourself. Draw the limit at hurting children, or hell—any innocent person. You can kill a father, but you don't have to kill the child. Grief is normal. It hurts, but it's normal. You can't stop people from feeling it by killing them. You're only causing more damage to yourself."

"Thank you," he said, shocking me.

"Are you just saying that so I'll stop talking?"

He shook his head. "I understand where you're coming from. You've opened my eyes to many things today."

I blinked blankly at him before frowning. "Right, glad you . . . yeah. Good talk."

He nodded, looking out the window, locking up his posture in a way that told me he didn't want to talk anymore.

I sighed, grabbed the ID card from the table, and continued with my food.

The ride was quieter on our way back, and I felt pretty uncomfortable . . . he had barely said a word to me after everything I said about the boy. He seemed locked in his mind, and I wondered what was going through that head.

It wasn't until after he pulled up at a shady motel that I leaned away from the window, looking over at him. "Why are you stopping here?"

He unbuckled his seatbelt, and I watched him grab the gun from the console, opening the chamber as he said, "You're going to drive back to the compound alone."

I stifled a yawn. "What are you talking about?"

He removed all the bullets, leaving just two inside. "You'll drive back to the compound alone," he repeated. "There's something I have to do," he said, finally meeting my confused gaze.

I frowned, looking out the window at the worn-out building. "What do you have to do here?"

"Nothing you should concern yourself with," he said as I turned back to look at him. "I know you have no reason to help me do this, but when you get to the compound, please find Casmiro, tell him to go to my bedroom and check the floorboards in my wardrobe. I left something in there for him and Angelo."

All the sleepiness slipped from my eyes, my senses alert. "What the fuck are you talking about?"

He opened his side door, about to leave me there, but paused. "I can't believe you're the one I'm asking to do this . . . but—tell my brother I'm sorry and that I tried."

"You tried what—"

He was already getting out of the car, closing the door behind him.

I sat alone in the humming vehicle for a few seconds, watching him walk around it towards the motel, wondering what the hell just happened.

Two bullets . . . obviously he's going to kill someone . . . He wants me to deliver a message to Casmiro and tell Devil he's sorry?

Two bullets . . . one for the person he wants to kill . . . whoever that is, and the other for . . .

Realization dawned like ice water down my spine, and I was dashing right out of the car after him.

CHAPTER TWENTY-EIGHT

Zahra

"Hey, motherfucker!"

My voice rang out into the night as I rushed after him.

He stopped, shoulders slumping, head dropping as he turned with a glare.

I let out short, sharp, tired breaths, stopping right in front of his imposing figure, straightening my spine with determination even though my limbs begged for relief.

"If you have a message to pass to your underboss and brother, you do that shit yourself." I led with that, my eyes dead set on him.

"It's a simple task—"

"Do I look like a suicide note?" I was livid. I wanted to bash his head in. Anything to ease the fucking guilt lingering in the pit of my stomach. "We're gonna get our asses back in that car, and you're gonna drive us to the compound and deliver your fucking message yourself."

He actually looked like he was considering it before shaking his head. "That will be inconvenient."

I threw my hands up and dropped them down in frustration. "Are you fucking kidding me?"

"Drive back to the compound, and just do as you're told for once."

"Like hell I will," I said, baffled at what was happening. "You're crazy if you think I'll leave you here after your little speech in the car."

With his hand that held the gun, he moved to rub his brows, closing his eyes for a second as he shook his head before opening his eyes and pinning me with a glower that had me stepping back a little.

"Allow me to get this straight," he said. "You told me, just a few hours ago, to hurry up and do what I need to do, and now that I'm trying to do it, you want to stop me—"

"But I already apolo—"

"Shut up."

"—gized. I'm not going to leave—"

"Shut up."

"—you. This is fucking insane, Elio! You can't expect me just to let you—"

"Shut up!" He took a step closer to me. "Shut up." Another until he was standing right in front of me. "Shut the fuck up, Zahra!" he yelled in my face, and I inched back; his breathing was harsh, and so was mine. "Stop messing with my head. I am impressionable; words aren't just words for me. They're affirmations. You apologized—thank you for your apology, but it means absolutely fucking nothing to me."

I gulped down.

"No matter what you say," he continued, "or how much you apologize, I will never forget every word you said by that roadside. It'll always be in my head. I'll always hear you repeat it over and over again. When I see you, that's all I'll think about; when I hear you speak, it's all I'll hear because that's how my brain works."

I stepped closer to him. "But I didn't mean it. I was angry because it has been a long fucking day," I sighed. "No matter how much we don't like each other, I would have never said that to you if I had known you would take it seriously."

"Well, this is the situation I find myself in. Don't feel guilty. This was my plan all along; I'm only making it quicker."

I shook my head. "No."

"Yes."

"No," I countered with a confused frown, stepping away from him. "That's not how tonight's gonna go."

"Go back to the car, Zahra."

I stretched my hand. "Give me the gun."

His gaze slipped to my hand and back to my face with a stern glare. "Go back. To the car. Zahra," he repeated, a warning in his voice, one filled with so much venom, so much hate and frustration, but I couldn't leave him like this.

I stood straighter. "Give me the fucking gun."

He shook his head slowly. "Don't push me."

"Just give me the gun, and then we can talk. Just—" I swallowed to ease the tightness in my chest. "You know I'm not gonna let you do this."

It took a second. Just one second for his whole demeanor to change. The anger slipped from his eyes, his breathing calmed, and his eyes, completely vacant, were watching me in silence. It was like a switch had been turned off inside him, and I grew even more wary.

"Elio?"

"I love it," he said, voice flat and unfeeling.

I frowned. "What . . . what are you talking about now?"

"The fear my presence compels in people." He examined the gun in his hand. "The smell of blood, and death, and suffering, and tears." He closed his eyes as if he could see and smell all he just listed. "It's like heaven. Chaos, massacres." He opened his eyes. "I crave it like oxygen. I fucking love it, Zahra, shooting that boy, it felt so fucking good."

I locked my jaw. "You're lying."

He scanned my body from head to toe, slowly, tentatively, until his intense, vacant gaze locked with mine. Then he moved, closing the space between us enough for me to crane my neck, looking up at him, my breathing unsteady.

He raised the gun, trailing the barrel's mouth from my forehead, past my brows, down my cheek, and to the surface of my bottom lip, where he stopped, and raised his gaze. "One thing you should never do, Zahra, is make a hero out of me. I have killed men, women, . . . people I care for. I have lost count of people who screamed my name before I ended their lives, I have taken and taken and taken more than I should, and I don't regret any of it. The most beautiful thing is that the business is just a cover-up for how fucked up my head is, for how much I love what I do." He pressed his forehead to mine, closing his eyes as he swallowed and said, "How much I *long* for it."

My throat worked. "You're just saying that."

"You don't believe it? I'm not surprised. People love to underestimate me and make assumptions based on my actions. *He's kind sometimes; he's calm. He doesn't care; all he wants is power; he's all talk and no action.* Do you want to know why that is? It's because the people who are supposed to confirm the action are either six feet under or fish food. The stories you hear about The Wicked are just a scratch in the surface of what I'm capable of."

He drew back from me, still in my face, as he opened his eyes. "If you don't want to know, firsthand, what I'm truly capable of, how I could ruin you and serve you your worst fears on a silver platter, you'll walk back to that car and drive away from me."

I swallowed, grinding my teeth together as I said, "No."

His jaw locked. "Don't make me kill you, Zahra."

"You've tried several times before; it didn't work."

"Go."

"I'm not leaving here without you," I told him. "Everything you just said might be true, but I've seen you hold off from shooting and killing people just because you didn't want to hurt the ones related to them. Maybe you're not so far gone."

He shook his head. "You don't understand. Nobody ever understands—that explosion, the chaos we caused, the people who might have died. It drove me to the edge; I was gripping that gun so tight because of how much I loved it and wanted to make sure no one survived it. Make sure I finish the job. If I'm being honest, I don't want to like it, I don't want to do it, because when I do, it's the *best* feeling in this world . . . That's how sick I am, Zahra. And that's why you're right. This world would be a much better place without me in it."

"All right, but give me the gun."

"If I don't go in there and kill my father, everything you told me in that restaurant will mean nothing to me. If I leave here, go back to the compound, alive, I will be worse than I am now. Is that what you want?"

I paused, watching him with confusion. "Your . . . father?"

"Yes, my father."

I blinked at him. There was no sign of a joke in his eyes. He was completely serious right now. "Your father's dead, Elio."

He remained quiet.

I bit the inside of my cheek, changing my approach and asking him directly without making assumptions from what I'd heard. "Is your father dead?"

"No."

I took in a shaky breath, taking a step back. "What do you—"

"He's alive. In this building."

"All this time?"

"Yes."

I watched him for a long time, my eyes flickering between his as I said quietly, "I think you need help, Elio."

"I'm well aware."

Something cold ran down my spine as I turned to look at the motel and then back to him. "Jesus Christ . . . you need serious help, Elio. Why won't you get help?"

"Because I'm . . ." He trailed off, seeming confused. ". . . Undeserving of it . . ."

I swallowed, nodding slowly. "Okay, w-well, nothing you say will make me leave here without you. I don't care if you're a sick psychopath who doesn't wanna get help; I am not leaving unless you get in the car with me."

Staring at me for a moment too long, he sighed, dropping his head like he was running thoughts through his mind, and then he looked back at me and outstretched the gun towards me.

I didn't let my shock last, grabbing the weapon and letting out a breath of relief. "I know my words might mean nothing right now, but I really didn't mean what I said, and I'm sorry. I really am."

Without another word, he walked past me towards the direction of the car.

I sighed, watching his retreating form.

In about half an hour, we reached the compound, and Elio pulled over right in front of the quarters where I stayed with Street.

Still uneasy, I bid him good night and got out of the car; his gun was still with me, and I knew it was useless because I was pretty sure he had more guns in his possession.

Looking around, soldiers were guarding the area here and there, and I walked towards the house.

The sound of the car door opening and closing had me stopping and turning to see Elio approaching me. "I'm not giving you your gun back," I said, clearing that up.

"You can keep it," he said, now standing before me.

"All right." I nodded, turning to leave, but he grabbed my wrist.

"Wait."

His hold on my wrist was warm, and the feeling somehow managed to creep up my skin in a way that had my heart pumping blood to my body with the main purpose of making me flush.

"What," I stated in question, unable to stop my gaze from flickering to his lips.

Elio mirrored my action but made no move. "You won't tell anyone about my father."

I couldn't even hide the pity in my eyes. "There's nothing to tell . . . Your father's dead. He's been dead for years; everyone knows that."

He was about to say something when the door to the house pulled open, and Devil rushed out, beelining towards us.

"Devil—" Before I could complete my statement, Devil was yanking Elio's hold from my wrist, shoving him hard on the chest, and landing a blow to his face. Elio stumbled back at the impact. Soldiers rushed towards us, and Elio quickly waved them off.

I quickly intervened when Devil wanted to charge towards his brother again, getting between the two. "That's enough, D. Rein it in." His chest was heaving, a deadly glare aimed directly at Elio, who worked his jaw with his hand, making no move to attack back.

"That was for watching her get kidnapped," Devil said, trying to inch closer to Elio, but I held him back. "Fucking touch her again, and see what I'll do," he finished, grabbing my wrist and pulling me with him towards the house.

I turned briefly, just in time to see Elio, shoving both hands into his pocket, his eyes on the both of us. Something flashed through them, but Devil pulled me inside the house before I could name it, slamming the door shut behind us.

I pulled my hand from his grip, stepping away from him with a glare. "That was so uncalled for. Why the fuck did you hit him?"

"Are you seriously asking me that question?"

"Yes! It's not his fault that I got kidnapped, Devil."

He looked at me with disbelief, eyes running down my body as if just noticing my change of clothes. "He watched you get kidnapped. He stood there and watched them take you."

"I know, but that's not important anymore because he still came for me. Stop being such a controlling jerk."

"Controlling?"

A shuffle from a corner made us turn to find Upper watching us, leaning on the kitchen entryway. "Oh, sweet Devil," he taunted. "Always trying to control things he doesn't possess."

"Shut the fuck up and mind your own business; this has nothing to do with you."

Upper scoffed, glancing briefly at me before looking at Devil. "Right, nothing to do with me at all."

I frowned.

"Glad you're not dead, Zahra," Upper said, and then he flipped Devil off before disappearing down the passage, a bedroom door slamming a few seconds after.

I blinked in the direction Upper had gone before returning my attention to Devil, who had an unreadable expression on his face.

"What the fuck was that about?"

"Nothing," he said.

"I'm not an idiot, Devil. Upper's pissed; Upper is never pissed."

"It's nothing," he snapped.

I shook my head. "I'm just gonna go to bed; I'm too tired for this shit."

"Zahra—"

"Don't follow me," I told him before heading to my bedroom, knowing Milk and Dog would be fast asleep already; we were deep into the morning, and I knew I should probably question why Upper and Devil were still up together. I knew Devil would wait up, but like Dog, Upper liked his sleep, so it was weird.

The moment I fell on the bed, I groaned in tiredness, my grip still on Elio's gun.

I shoved it under the pillow with a tired sigh and passed out after a few seconds.

"Make one for me?" I said to Upper as I yawned and stretched, entering the kitchen as he was making coffee. He nodded at my request without looking at me, his form tense.

I frowned, about to comment when Milk's voice cut in.

"Morning, Zahra!" she yelled from the living room. "I stopped by your room early, and you were dead asleep, mouth open and all."

"Creep," I muttered.

She chuckled.

Now in a simple tank top and shorts, I sat atop one of the kitchen stools, placing my hand on my cheek as I watched Upper work on the coffee machine, rubbing sleep from his eyes.

Second to Dog, Upper was the one I warmed up to after we first met. He was always smiling, observant, and loved talking about things he claimed to know nothing about. Upper wasn't a mystery; he was an open book that held so many hidden secrets between the lines I would have loved to unearth.

When I'd asked him about his accent years ago, he'd told me it was learned, but I wasn't stupid. If the others believed that shit, I didn't. His accent had that unmistakable refinement of—I don't know—British aristocracy? The kind drilled into people raised in royal circles. It was too natural . . . too second nature; coupled with his posh mannerisms, it made him seem dignified—like he wasn't the same as everyone else.

He would often act a certain proper way, catch himself doing it, and adjust to being brash.

I never spoke on it or pointed it out; if the others caught it too, they said nothing.

We stayed away from broaching the "extra personal" in our lives. We kept our past to our past and functioned well with our present. There was a possibility we would perform better if we knew where we each came from, but none of us were willing or eager to let that information slip. But we still trusted each other, and it was healthy.

I worked my shoulders, trying to free my coiled muscles.

"I have a feeling you're being hostile with me," I said, watching his back tense up, but he continued what he was doing. "You know you can talk to me about anything if I did something wrong or said something that upset you."

He let out a shaky breath, turning with a fresh cup of coffee for me. I collected it, watching him avoid eye contact.

"Upper—"

"It's not you," he said, his bright hazel eyes raising to look at me. "You didn't do anything."

"So why are you being weird?"

"I—"

"Baby Zahra." Arms hugged me from behind as Dog slammed a kiss to my cheek. "I missed you!"

I tried to push him off. "Get off me, you clingy beast."

He tightened his hold and whispered harshly in my ear. "Where are my fucking pills?"

"Hidden."

"I can take that. My fucking pot is what I can't take; I was going crazy last night, you motherfucker," he gritted with a strained smile.

"I told you, you're not getting high without me to monitor you, *motherfucker*," I gritted with a strained smile too, and Upper eyed us warily.

"You could have at least left a joint, *bitch*." His grip tightened.

I was choking for air as I ground out, "Again, not getting high without me. You wanna get stoned, we get stoned together; that's how this relationship works, *cunt*."

"This relationship works how I say it works; a joint wouldn't make me an addict, you fucking *snake*."

"Your action right now is fucking proof you're on the brink, you fucking *dog*; maybe I should throw the fucking pills away."

"Do that and die a very miserable death in the Karakoram."

"That's oddly specific."

"I can make it happen—"

"What the fuck are you guys muttering about? You're scaring me," Upper said, mug paused halfway to his lips, eyes wide.

Dog released me, slapping my shoulder twice. "Just catching up," he said, walking around the kitchen, his eyes on me. When he crossed behind Upper, his glare rained, and he slashed a thumb to his throat, a premature gesture of him doing the same to me with a knife.

I rolled my eyes, drinking Upper's fantastic coffee.

When Devil walked in, Upper immediately took his leave, joining Milk in the living room, leaving Devil staring after him with an annoyed frown.

Something was going on between those two. But Devil wasn't into men . . . or was he?

All day, my head was filtering through thoughts, and even as they debriefed me on the painting with information that could be useful and resources we might need, my full attention wasn't on it.

Three things swarmed through my head.
Upper and Devil, what could be going on?
The painting and everything attached to it.
And finally . . . Elio.

What happened to make him that way? A heartless man with a heart. How many cobwebs were in his wardrobe?

Angelo had stopped by earlier to get a little debriefing about what my captors had asked me. I had kept Manuel's name out of it, but the man could tell I was hiding something else. Before he left, I hesitated but asked him about Elio because, if I was honest with myself, I was a little worried about him and how we had left things last night.

It was probably the guilt eating me up at his revelation of how deep my words had cut him.

Angelo had looked at me weirdly, and I didn't blame him; it was weird. I shouldn't care.

But I was relieved when he said Elio was doing okay but had left the compound with Casmiro quite early for business. Then he asked why I was asking, and I just shrugged, not giving him an answer, which I was sure made my behavior even more suspicious.

He dropped it, though, and I was glad he did. Hopefully, he wouldn't tell Elio I asked. That would be embarrassing.

After a small game of cards with the group, I retired early, still not well-rested from the last few days' events. I wore one of Milk's short satin nightgowns, one of the many that had somehow stumbled into my wardrobe. I could swear the girl was slowly changing my choice of clothing because each time something new was mysteriously added, a piece of my comfort clothes she had disapproved of would go missing.

I settled in bed, slipping my hand underneath my pillow, and brought Elio's gun into my view, examining it.

My fingers brushed across the muzzle of the gun, the same one that had touched my lips the other night. An action that should have made me wary of the impending death that could strike me if a shot was fired instead made me bristle with desire.

I hated that I was attracted to him, hated that his body had a huge part to play in it, but his mind and manners also drew me in. Hated that I was . . . maybe . . . potentially . . . already developing a silly crush. He *was* handsome, and there was something regal about the way he walked, and something stomach-flipping about the way he talked, and that . . . that thing he did with his eyes whenever he looked at me or anyone, or anything . . . the way he'd squint a little and then how his eyes would harden, or the way his lips had that permanent downturned tilt that made him look like he was not impressed with anything around him.

There was just this way about him . . .

My fingers brushed the hilt of his gun, and I stopped when I found his initials at the bottom of it.

E.M.

I scoffed. "Pompous fucker."

I slipped the gun back underneath my pillow and turned to my side, closing my eyes, trying to find sleep.

It didn't come. I tossed and turned, looking for a comfortable position, but nothing changed.

Groaning, I sat upright.

I could use a pill.

I got out of bed and out of the room. Milk and Dog were still awake, seeing as I could hear their voices from the living room.

I went down a small corridor opposite Devil and Upper's room, stopping before the fire extinguisher. I opened the case where it was mounted, reaching behind it quietly and grabbing a stash of pills.

"What the bloody hell, Devil. How does that even sound to you?"

I paused at the sound of Upper's agitated voice. Quietly, I closed the glass to the extinguisher and walked towards their bedroom door, leaning to press my ear against it.

"It sounds perfect. I like her, and we've been doing this for almost a year now, and I want it all with her; I know she does too.

I'm going to ask her." He sounded like he was trying to convince himself.

"Okay, fine, I'm not against it, nor will I ask you not to ask her. But I care about Zahra too, and I won't let you half-ass it with her. You must tell her about us. She deserves to know your reservations before you string her along."

My brows jumped.

Us?

"For God's sake, Upper, there's no us. There never was. I'm fucking straight."

Upper scoffed. "I'm not about to help you define your sexuality, but I can assure you that a straight guy wouldn't exactly give a gay guy a bloody hand job or receive a bloody blow job from a gay guy and then kiss him afterward, just saying."

What the fuck?

"It just happened, Upper. It didn't mean shit to me. You don't mean shit to me; Zahra does. And you—don't give me that fucking look; you came on to me."

"I came on to you?" His voice shook. "That's the worst fucking thing you could ever say to me. Listen, it was mutual; you had every right to forfeit the dare and not give me a hand job. If anything, you started it. But you don't see me saying that or accusing you of coming on to me."

Devil sighed. "Upper, I didn't mean it like that—"

"No, you're confused and so fucking toxic and problematic, and you rub it off on everyone who dares to even come close to you. I didn't ask for this shit. I didn't ask you to tell me shit you've never told anyone and make me feel like we were something special when it obviously meant shit to you, just like you said." He sounded so hurt, and I wasn't sure if my heart was aching from the not-so-betrayal or for Upper.

"Upper—"

"And now you're about to use Zahra to, what? Fuel your denial? She doesn't deserve that shit."

"That's not what I'm trying to do. I genuinely care about Zahra; I think I'm falling in love with her—"

"You think. You're not sure. You're leading her on, on a maybe . . ."

Deciding I'd heard enough, I twisted the knob and pushed open the door, startling both of them.

The look on my face probably spelled the fact that I'd overheard their conversation due to the horror on Upper's face and the curse Devil muttered.

I couldn't help but feel a sting at the sight of him.

He was my best friend and the first guy I'd been with more than once after leaving Sicily. Devil and I downplayed what we had almost every time, trying to stay within our limits, but there was something there, which was why I felt a little hurt and betrayed by this new reveal.

"So that's why you both have been acting weird around each other?"

Upper plopped down on the bed, resting his elbows on his knees as he covered his face with his palms, almost as if he couldn't believe this was happening.

"Is anyone gonna answer me?" My voice went a pitch louder, and Upper flinched.

Devil sighed. "It's not what you think, Z."

"Don't even fucking try, Devil; everything I heard is exactly what I think. It's exactly what this thing is?" I gestured between them.

Devil walked, trying to reach out to me. "Zahra, please . . ."

I took a step back. "Don't fucking touch me."

From my periphery, I spotted Dog and Milk right outside the room, watching the scene cautiously.

"At least let me explain what this is," he said, fear lingering in his eyes.

"What's there to explain? Look at him! Look at me; look at yourself. Look at the fucking situation we're all in. It's all self-explanatory; there's nothing you can say that would make more sense than this."

"Okay, fine, you're right, but that doesn't change anything . . . It doesn't change how I feel about you, or—I—fuck." He was so confused. I could hear it in his voice, see it in his eyes, the way they flickered between me and a distraught, probably traumatized Upper, almost as if he couldn't tell who to comfort or make feel better. "I don't even know anymore," he muttered, his voice hurt and defeated.

As a friend, I wanted to hug him, make him explain his feelings, but as a—as a what? We were nothing.

I shook my head, blinking. "I know we didn't put a label and shit, but I thought this—I thought we—" I sighed. "This is so messed up, Devil."

He dropped his head. "I know . . . I'm sorry."

My gaze shifted to Upper, who had both hands gripping his hair, not once looking up.

"I'm out of here," I muttered, turning on my heel and walking out of the room. I brushed past Dog and a wide-eyed Milk, who threw me a sympathetic look that I ignored.

They knew. They all fucking knew.

I was almost out of the house when Dog caught up to me. "Hey."

"Not now, Dog."

"I wanted to give you a jacket."

I turned to him, forcing on a smile as I collected the jacket and slipped it on, pocketing the stash of pills before he could catch a glimpse of them.

"You good?" he asked.

"Not really."

He nodded as if he understood. "Are you gonna go out there and cry?"

I scoffed. "The day I cry over a *boy* is the day I stab myself in both eyes. I just need a breather."

"Kay, use the kitchen window; there are a few soldiers standing guard outside tonight; it would be difficult to slip out."

I hugged him with a light squeeze. "Behind the fire extinguisher, I hid two joints."

"How do you know that's why I'm helping you?"

I laughed, pulling away before flipping him off and making my way out back.

Somehow, after maneuvering the guards outside the compound, I found myself climbing the killer stairs to the rooftop. The anxiety of falling was still present, and when I finally reached up and passed through the door, I breathed a sigh of relief.

"What kind of a psychopath is this man to structure those stairs like that?" I winced in a whisper to myself, the cold wind from up high easing my muscles as I walked towards the railing, sucking in a deep breath with my hair whipping around my face.

The quietness calmed me, and I replayed the whole event in my head.

It would most definitely be awkward between us all now. But did I even have the right to feel like I was cheated on? We weren't even in a relationship—but I thought we were exclusive.

I knew Devil was confused. Despite his denial, I knew he felt something for Upper, but he was scared to lean into it; I knew he felt something for me too, but what he had with Upper was stronger. I knew it; I saw it. And I was partly mad that he had treated Upper that way.

None of us deserved this situation we were in, but hell, if the god of situations cared what we did or did not deserve at this—

"If you're—"

"Motherfucker!"

"—looking to jump, I suggest the left side of the railing. It's steeper. One hit, you'll crack your skull on the cobblestones, death on impact. I've experimented and found that it's more efficient."

My heart was beating ten times per second; I'd almost jumped out of my skin. I turned to see Elio sitting on the ground, his back against a carved stone chair, with a bottle of cheap beer in his grip. He had his attention on me as he asked:

"So, are you jumping, or would you like a push?"

CHAPTER TWENTY-NINE

Zahra

"You know what? I'll take the push."

Elio paused as if trying to see if I was serious, and when I didn't counter my statement, he breathed out in relief. "Oh, finally." He attempted to stand, but I quickly responded.

"That was a joke! Jesus."

The man groaned in annoyance before he sat back down, looking away from me.

I chuckled at how he'd almost become shiny with excitement at the prospect of getting to push me over the railing. "Why are you so eager to kill me?"

"It is one of my many fantasies."

"Ooooh, you have fantasies about me?" I pressed my back to the brick railing, my front facing him.

"I didn't say that."

"Sorry, my mind already drove me down that route, and now I'm curious to know more about these fantasies you seem to be having."

He shook his head, not responding as he brought the beer bottle to his lips while he took a swig, his throat working as he swallowed.

I knew I'd gone out of that house to be alone, but somehow, I was more comfortable in his presence.

"You don't look like a beer kinda guy," I voiced into the silence.

"I also don't look like the suicide *kinda* guy, but here we are," he said casually while I flinched at the word, shifting uncomfortably.

"You're so nonchalant about it."

"Hm."

"Why?"

"Can you shut up?"

"What?"

"I do not appreciate the screech in your voice. It doesn't help my migraine. So I would appreciate your silence."

I threw my head back and laughed, my chest vibrating from how amused I was by his response. Looking back at him, I caught his eyes on me, intense and a little guarded as his gaze swept up and down my body.

The heat from his stare made me shift on my feet, and my laugh simmered down while I made sure to ignore the faint flutter that came with his attention.

"Do you not have normal clothing?" he asked.

"No." I curved my lips. "It's all silk and satin in my wardrobe," I lied. "I think it's sexy."

"Of course." His gaze lingered on my exposed thighs for a second too long before he looked away.

I chuckled, leaning away from the railing as I walked towards the stone chair, eyeing the space beside him and debating whether to sit on the chair or settle beside him on the ground. The ground seemed a better option, and I settled down next to him, leaving just a few inches between our bodies, but I was still close enough to feel how his posture grew tense with me sitting close.

I waited for him to complain, but he didn't, so I relaxed further and broke the uncomfortable silence.

"This is actually a nightgown, by the way. The other one was a normal dress."

"I didn't ask."

I rested my back against the stone chair, looking up at the dark sky filled with stars. The moon was bright and welcoming, and I couldn't fight the urge to soak it all in as I closed my eyes and took a lungful of air before releasing it in a calm breath and opening my eyes.

I felt Elio's stare, and I turned my head to catch his gaze on me, unwavering. He did not attempt to pretend he hadn't been staring at me, and I did not attempt to look away either.

The gray of his eyes was darker yet softer, like he was in his most relaxed state and had no thought in his mind. The haunted glint I'd found in his eyes the night before was missing, and I secretly wondered if it was the beer that made him seem so approachable.

His eyes . . . they showed a lot when he allowed it.

I hated that I liked it so much. That the allure of his gaze could suck you in without even intending to do so, and that's where I was, sucked in.

He didn't look away.

I couldn't look away.

I hated that my heart rate had spiked again.

I hated that the silence had somehow become a comfortable one. I hated this. Whatever this was.

His gaze roamed from my eyes to my cheeks, over to my nose, then to my lips. "You have an impressive face."

I frowned in confusion. "Um, wh—"

"I like your hair."

I blinked at him. "Are those compliments?"

He looked away. "Observations."

"Oh . . ." I shifted. "Thanks for the . . . observations?"

He nodded, taking another swig of the beer, the remaining contents inside the bottle a drink away from being empty.

"Why are you here?" I asked him, wondering if he would—

"Couldn't sleep," he answered.

Devil's voice filtered through my head from the time he told me Elio looked like someone who never slept. I was curious to know more about it . . . about him.

"And you don't have sleeping pills to aid?"

"I do."

"Why don't you just take them?"

He was silent, and I watched his brows draw down in a debating frown like he was unsure if he should continue talking or ignore me.

I wouldn't be surprised if he ignored me. We weren't exactly friends. I mean—I'd seen him in a terrible state, and I'd talked him out of his head once, but I didn't think that side of him was something he showed to people. I didn't want it to seem like I was prying because I cared, and I knew I shouldn't care about him because he tried to drown me, but—when you survive a shoot-out with someone, you tend to form a survivors' bond with them.

I guess that's what this was . . . and yeah, the unwanted physical attraction.

"I can't be near those pills. I'm not in the proper state of mind," he answered after the prolonged silence.

"How many people know that you—that you're like this?"

"Hm," he hummed. "No one aside from Angelo . . . and now you. If you're thinking of spreading the word, don't bother. No one would believe you."

"I'm not," I injected immediately. "Why doesn't Casmiro know? You two are close, right?"

"I already have Angelo to worry about, therefore, I don't need Cas on my throat too."

"But I know . . ."

"I don't have to worry about you since you hate me and want me to do it faster."

My stomach dipped. "I d—"

"Why are *you* here?" He cut me off. "You shouldn't be here; you shouldn't even be out of the house."

I looked away from him. "I couldn't sleep either. I—" I cleared my throat. "Needed a break from . . . everyone."

"Okay."

I glanced at him. "You're not gonna ask why?"

"I don't care enough to."

Right. So it was just me, then.

The silence stretched between us again, and I broke it with a prying question because, yes, I couldn't help myself; sue me.

"So your sleeping problem, is it—where's it from? Did something happen to you?"

This time, he turned his head and met my gaze with confusion. "There isn't some grand story behind it if that's what you're thinking," he said. "Christ, you sound like a book character, one of those prying, annoying ones. I have clinical depression, and the sleeping disorder is one of the hiccups that comes with it."

"Oh . . ."

"I either sleep too much or don't sleep at all. Often, I find myself not sleeping at all unless I take something and force it," he said. "Tonight is one of those nights when I don't want to force it. Does that answer your question?"

"Not really . . ."

"Should I interpret it in Spanish?" he asked.

"No, I—" I sighed. "That's not what I meant. I'm just confused because you know what's wrong with you, yet you won't fix it. It doesn't make any sense to me."

"It's good that it doesn't. Because I'm not going to explain. I already told you the other day that I am undeserving of it. Now quit prying and being unnecessarily annoying."

I rolled my eyes, fishing for the stash of white pills in my pocket. "If you're trying to wear yourself out, the cheap beer won't do the trick," I said, dangling the stash in the space between us.

He eyed it and then me. "What are you insinuating?"

"You wanna get high?" I asked with a grin.

After a bit of silence, he spoke. "Does my brother do drugs too?" There was an edge to his voice that had me shaking my head.

"Nope, he doesn't even know. It's just Dog and me; we don't do it often, but sometimes, we get high and smoke joints because life is shit, and you just gotta escape it for a few hours."

"It's not healthy, Sport."

"I'm not a kid."

"You could get addicted."

"I know my limits."

"It's—"

"Do you wanna get high? Or not?"

He eyed the pills and then me. I watched him struggle with a decision for a few beats before he outstretched his palm towards me.

I grinned, slipping out a pill as I said, "I knew there was a crazy in there somewhere." I placed one in his palm, and he eyed it.

"How strong is it?"

"One won't tip you off the edge, but it's enough to weaken your limbs and make you feel lighter . . . also, maybe a little . . ." I watched him put it in his mouth and swallow before I completed my statement. ". . . horny."

He didn't freak out like I expected.

I popped one in my mouth and swallowed, keeping the rest in the jacket pocket. "It's the kind that dissolves into your bloodstream immediately after taking it, so it takes about a few seconds to kick in. It's really good stuff."

"I hope I don't like it too much."

I scoffed. "It's just one pill."

"I know. I have APD," he said casually.

I paused. That didn't sound good. "What does . . . APD mean?"

"Addictive personality disorder. It's not intense, but it's there. I get attached to things easily . . . people too. And when I don't control it, it turns into an addiction. Like books, killing people, cleaning, and . . . what else? Ah . . . yes, cigars."

I stared at him, my eyes growing wide in apprehension. "What the fuck, Elio? Why didn't you say anything?"

He looked at me with a raised brow. "I said I hope I don't like it too much."

"How the fuck is that supposed to tell me *anything*?"

He shrugged like he didn't care as he downed the remaining contents of the beer bottle while I sat there, feeling the effect of the drugs and feeling like shit.

"It's like you've made it your mission to fill me with guilt at every turn," I said, annoyed.

"I refuse to take responsibility for what you feel; it's . . . oh." He paused. "I feel it."

My limbs grew weaker, and I felt lighter, but I wasn't feeling the feeling, not after what he had just told me.

"It's . . . outstanding . . . wow . . . what's the name? Where'd you get it?" His voice came out raspy as he dropped the empty beer bottle.

"I'm never telling you that . . . God, it's fucked up; I feel like shit."

"I don't." He released a breath, dropping his head on the stone chair with an open-mouthed sigh before he looked up at the sky. "I feel so light. The stars are dancing; it's beautiful."

I groaned, allowing the pill to take effect by wiping off my annoyance.

"The moon is so large; I think it's smiling. Can you see it?" he asked.

I looked up to see the moon grow large, a soft smile curving at the bottom. It also had eyes that looked down at us with a calmness that made me sigh.

"Yeah, I see it."

And then . . . it was silent.

A comfortable one that I didn't feel like breaking, and I don't know how long we sat there for, but it felt like minutes. Long minutes.

I felt the air grow colder, felt our surroundings grow quieter, as though everyone had gone to sleep, and we were the only two people awake.

"I finally figured it out," Elio voiced after a while.

"What?"

"Why I talk a lot when I'm around you."

I turned my body to the left so that I was facing him, and my side rested on the chair. My movement, though, felt sluggish. "Yeah? Why's that?"

"We're alike," he said. "In many ways. And I'm talkative. I like talking."

"I figured that one out," I said with a chuckle, and I realized we were closer than before; I could smell him now. He had this distinct smell of sweet vanilla spice rum, I guess from his cigars, and then there was a whiff of expensive cologne with a hint of orange blossom, and . . . there was something else . . . Was it lilies? God, he just smelled terrific, or maybe it was the pill.

"You like talking too," he said. "You talk a lot, and it makes me want to respond. I shouldn't respond because I'm supposed to be a man of few words."

"You are very good at pretending you are."

"I know. I've been doing it my whole life. I like it sometimes . . . just being quiet."

"Me too," I said, wondering what the point of this conversation was. I didn't really care.

"I like talking to you," he confessed. "I like that you annoy me." His voice came with a hint of a slur.

The faint flutter attacked. "With my screechy voice, as you call it?"

"Okay, maybe it isn't all that screechy, just slightly screechy."

"Right, got it."

"Hm. I want you dead too. Preferably when you're talking, I'd like to slit your throat and watch you choke on your blood," he said. "It's one of my fantasies too."

I laughed instead of being wary of his confession. It was funny, and the pill made it funnier.

"You hate me that much?"

"Hm."

I watched him for a long time, for some reason, wishing he would look at me.

"Why aren't you like—married? You're old enough," I said.

"So are you."

"I still have time, but you're like . . . twenty-eight—twenty-nine? Or . . ."

"Fishing for my age, Sport?"

"Curious."

"I'm thirty-three."

I jerked up, watching him with wide eyes. "No way, you look younger."

He turned to look at me. "I don't know if you know this, but thirty-three isn't old."

"Yeah, I know, but—like, I'm just surprised. You're so handsome and young and hot."

He looked away, his body shifting uncomfortably.

"Okay, so, still prying . . . why don't you have a girlfriend?"

He shrugged. "I do not know."

"Have you ever had a girlfriend?"

"No."

"How often do you have sex, then?"

He sucked in a breath. "You have no filter."

"I blame it on the drugs," I said, allowing my tone to grow sensual as I asked, "So . . . how often?"

I welcomed the heat from his body and how we'd drawn closer to each other. The lightness in my head turned heady, and I leaned into that heat.

"Not often." His voice was hoarse.

The pace at which my heart thumped had doubled, but I still pushed. "When was the last time?"

He stopped to think. "A year and a half . . . maybe more."

"Dude, that's—that's ballsy."

"Intimacy is sacred for me," he said.

"Is that so . . . ?" I said softly, raising my hand to trace my index finger down his forearm.

He turned his head to me again, his gaze falling on my hand on his arm while his muscles grew tense under my touch.

"So, like," I continued, "you like every woman you fuck?"

He raised his gaze, and our eyes locked. The tip of his pink tongue ran over his bottom lip, and I had the strongest urge to kiss him.

Yes. I'm horny as fuck right now. Pill's doing a good job.

"Hm, yes," he responded. "But I don't necessarily like them; I have to like something about them before I get intimate with them. And it's always a one-time thing. Because of my at—"

"Attachment issues. When was your first time?"

"Seventeen . . . yours?"

"Same." He knew that was a lie but didn't care enough to call my bluff. "First kiss?"

His eyes searched mine before he swallowed and said, "I don't have one."

I won't deny it; that caught me by surprise. "That's a lie."

"I have no reason to lie."

"But you've been with women—"

"You can be intimate with someone without kissing them, Zahra."

"And they don't get offended?"

"I don't think they realize it. They're always pretty distracted with other parts of me."

My lips curled, and my hand moved from his arm to his thigh. He tensed up even more at my touch, but he didn't ask me to stop, and I didn't. "Would you like to kiss me, Elio?" I asked, breathing through my slightly parted lips, my anticipation growing.

"It's too intimate," he said.

"Well, would you like to fuck me then?"

His pupils grew large, lust covering the dark, somber sense his eyes had carried earlier, and I fucking lived for it.

"Absolutely fucking not," he answered.

My gaze flickered to his crotch, spotting his hard-on. "Yeah, but you're so hard it looks painful," I said, pressing my thighs together to ease the fervent need between them.

"That's normal. I'm intoxicated from a pill that gets me high and horny, you're touching my thigh, and we're talking about sex. I'm bound to be aroused."

I noticed the change in his breathing, the way he couldn't keep his gaze from falling to my mouth.

I removed my hand from his thigh and slid Dog's jacket off me, arching my back a little. The action had his eyes dropping to my chest, and I was positive he was looking at the outline of my pierced nipples.

What the fuck am I doing?

Blame it on the drugs.

I watched Elio swallow before tentatively raising his gaze to lock with mine. "Zahra—"

I moved. Rose from my position, and straddled his thighs, angling the heat between my legs over his erection. A shivering breath left me when I settled my hands on his shoulders and pressed my throbbing clit against his arousal, the fabric of my panties and his pants the only thing stopping skin-to-skin contact.

"Fuck," Elio breathed out, voice edgy and hoarse, and I felt myself grow wetter at the sound.

Our gazes locked, and Elio's big hands covered the space between my hips and waist, holding me in place and stopping me from moving as his chest heaved. "Stop, we can't." Was it possible for someone to sound like sin and lust, because that was exactly how this man sounded, and it was fucking with my mind.

Our warmth was one, bodies connected, heat joined. And I was scorching with need, the need to move, rub my clit against him, create friction, and fucking get off because, damn hell, he felt so good against me. So thick, long, and hard, fuck—I wanted to see him and touch him.

"This is a bad fucking idea, Zahra," he grunted.

"I have a thing for bad ideas."

"My brother, he—"

I leaned closer to him, my chest pressing against his, nipples sensitive against his warm chest.

Elio's gaze dropped to my lips as I responded, "Makes it even hotter."

His hips jerked, and I hissed at the spike of pleasure that shot through me from that little friction.

One of his hands remained firm on my hips while the other left to cup the side of my face, his fingers curling underneath my ear and the back of my neck, holding me in place, almost like he was stopping me from kissing him.

"I don't want to do this," he rasped.

"I don't want to either," I whispered.

Our breathing was loud, faces only inches apart. His grip on the back of my neck tightened, and he leaned in.

"My brother's going to kill me," he said breathily against my lips.

"Who's gonna tell him?"

"Fuck . . ." He breathed. "You're a bad influence, Zahra."

"So I've been to—"

Warmth covered my lips; a soft, tentative, sweet heat that made my senses tingle in a wave to suck all the air from my lungs. My heartbeat staggered a millisecond, like a glitch—a glitch caused by the firm press of his lips to mine.

It was embarrassing how fast I melted. Kisses meant nothing to me. But this—fuck—a kiss had never abruptly stolen my breath—no, not stolen, it had sucked it out of me.

Almost like he had been testing the waters, he removed his lips from mine, his unsure gaze flickering to mine.

I shamelessly took in oxygen like I was starved for it, the taste from his lips supplying me with a dazed edge.

That's not enough.

I gripped his shirt, pulling his body back to mine as I joined our lips together again.

My stomach flipped at how plush, warm, and perfect his lips were, and the moment he parted them, I wanted a taste so desperately that I darted my tongue into his mouth, seeking his, which carefully came to brush and curl around mine.

A soft moan left my throat at the same time a groan vibrated from his chest.

Fuck me—kissing this mouth was an addiction waiting to happen.

Our tongues rubbed against each other for a bit before it materialized into a kiss that felt so intimate and exquisite.

He tasted like the beer he had drunk: hot, mature, and intoxicating. My senses, aside from the one between my legs, head, and the fiery feeling peppering my skin, were nonexistent.

His hand on my waist pulled, urging me to move against him, and I did, grinding on his erection and creating hot friction that sent shivers up my spine and compelled goosebumps on my skin.

His hips moved, and I moaned at the added pressure. This was not enough; I wanted to feel him for real.

God, I was so wet, so horny for a man who wanted to slit my fucking throat open. This was sick. I was sick. But fuck it. I didn't want to be healthy if this was what sickness felt like.

I rubbed against him, his hand gripping my waist.

We broke away from the kiss, and I took a small breath before tilting my head to the other side, connecting our lips again while we dry humped each other.

Body grinding against body, chasing a high that would take us over and under the edge.

I increased my pace, breaking our kiss and thriving on the feverish breath he let out, his lips parted in ecstasy and lust as his hand lowered to my ass, trying to control my movement.

"My pace," he gritted out, holding firm on the back of my neck.

"No . . . *my* pace," I countered.

His hard stare held mine, and I felt a sharp pain on my ass.

He fucking pinched me, and the pain had me soaking wet for him.

"My fucking pace," he repeated, hand back to my waist, stopping my movement.

I gave in.

We went at his pace; he controlled my hips, and my eyes rolled when he ground his erection into my heat. My nightgown rode up altogether.

I didn't know someone could be good at dry humping. What the fuck was this . . . "Fuck . . ." I breathed in a moan, throwing my head back at the sensations hitting me.

I'd never wanted to come so bad. I knew the pill could get you horny, yes . . . but I didn't think it could make you feel this good.

Elio grunted deep in his chest as he cursed, a breathy moan escaping him afterward.

The sound sent tantalizing flutters to my stomach, and I felt myself reaching the edge.

Our heated gazes locked again, and I didn't look away from him, not wanting to miss how beautiful he looked right now, brows pinched, eyes in a daze, lips parted in lust.

At this moment, I wanted more than anything to see how he'd look in the heat of skin-to-skin pleasure. At the edge, about to come.

The thoughts and the pressure of his hard length had my toes curling with tantalizing sensations, and I was almost fucking there; the buildup was quickly ramping up for release . . . fuck, *we* were almost—

The roof door pushed open. "Marino, are you out here!"

I scrambled off him instantly, pushing my gown down, my panties soaked and uncomfortable. Annoyance gripped my bones at the interruption that slapped reality back into our faces.

My heart was racing. Unsatisfaction still thumped between my legs, seeking warmth and a little friction I knew would get me off. But thank you, fucking orgasm-restricting universe!

Elio adjusted himself, and I tried to calm my breathing as footsteps stopped. I looked to the side at Angelo, who stood frozen upon spotting us.

The man beside me was as calm as a dove. His breathing was back to normal, face void of any indication that we'd both been about to get each other off—what the fuck?

My pulse was still thudding abnormally.

"Uh . . ." Angelo started, ". . . am I—am I interrupting something?"

"Ye—"

"No!" I spoke over Elio's voice, shooting him a glare as I staggered to my feet, grabbing my jacket and slipping it back on. "I was just leaving."

Elio's head snapped up to look at me. "What?"

I glanced down at him, catching the displeasure lining his brows, his calm façade shifting.

I swallowed, my heart hammering as I forced a very strained smile at Angelo, before walking quickly towards the roof door.

I stopped halfway through and turned sharply to a still-stunned Angelo, whose eyes were wide and unsure, as if he was trying to put two and two together, but the results were impossible.

"He's high on drugs, and it will wear off probably in a few hours," I informed.

"What the—"

"Anything he says is a lie. Night, Angie."

"Angie?"

I scurried out the door and down the anxiety-raising staircase without waiting to hear what else he would say.

Note to self: Never take Dog's pills near Elio Marino's dwellings. My heart was still crazy—because what the fuck had just happened? And how the fuck do we come back from that . . . Devil—oh shit . . .

It's the pill, my mind assured.

Even though I felt very fucking sober right now—

It's because of the pill.

Blame it on the pill.

CHAPTER THIRTY

Elio

I *have lost my mind.*

I had always prided myself on my ability to wield control. To pull back when I knew I was breaching a line I shouldn't and couldn't cross. But tonight, my sense of reasoning had drifted into the open sky.

The moment my mind decided it was okay to pull down my walls and let that pestilent woman see a side of me I reserved for people who knew little of my world, I knew I was compromised.

Sex was sacred to me because I knew how many men in my field had fallen due to the body of a woman: her smiles and curves, the soft voice that would make a man wonder what exactly she would sound like when he buried himself inside her.

For years, I had deprived myself of the intimacy that came with sexual activities.

For precisely three reasons.

One was distraction. I couldn't afford it. The fear of missing out on something important while doing something as measly as fucking a woman was very close to home. I couldn't afford a mistake like that again.

Two: my attachment issues. Becoming attached to a woman who would only want me for what my body had to offer was as useless as the act of *fucking* itself. I would not delude myself and say that as a new adult, I hadn't longed for the intimacy that came with being in a relationship or the absolution that grew with the bond of marriage.

Three: respect. Seeing how my father had handled the issue with Elia's mother and how he had disrespected my mother countless times afterward, flaunting the women he practiced infidelity with, I'd vowed never to be like him. To respect women. It was why I was never with the same woman twice, why I could finger-count the very few women I had been with in my whole existence.

Grace, the woman from the art exhibit, being the fourth and second to last. I'd only been with her once, and I made sure it never happened again because I knew if it did, I'd most definitely enter into a relationship with her because I wasn't about to fuck a woman more than once for the sake of pleasure. It would have to mean something.

I didn't just act out of pure lust. My actions were continuously measured and calculated before even carrying them out.

This was precisely why my mind was spiraling.

I was aware that it wasn't the drug.

On several occasions, I had admitted to being attracted to Zahra because I conceded that it was normal. I was a full-blooded man, always finding myself in the presence of an aggravating, attractive woman who was sharp-mouthed and provoked useless emotions in me.

Seeing her walk to that railing, wearing that sorry excuse for a nightgown, which exposed tormenting legs and thighs that delivered sinful images to my mind's eye, I knew I had to be on guard.

But the minute she sat beside me, opening that mouth to talk to me and ask me questions no one had ever bothered to ask, I just couldn't shut up. I couldn't stop myself from bringing out the Elio Marino who lived outside his head, and far away from the chaos his last name compelled.

Her presence was hot and cold. Sometimes she drove me to the brink of wanting to actually go through with killing her . . . and sometimes, like tonight, she pushed me out of my head into a comforting place where I had no reason to hide or pretend I was a well-packaged psychopath.

It scared me.

She scared me.

I should be thanking Angelo for interrupting and stopping me from doing something I wouldn't be able to take back, but I surprised myself by picturing his body mysteriously falling over the railing, with me standing behind it, watching him plummet to his death, for choosing this time to check on me.

And the way she had rushed out, separating herself from me like it would end the world if anyone found out we'd been that close, had me feeling . . . strange.

I was annoyed, yes.

But I was confused even more than I was annoyed.

I liked kissing her.

I had done it because I momentarily forgot the meaning of control, credit to her heat against the strain of my crotch and those pierced hard nipples pressing against my chest. But more than anything, there was an aching I needed to please, one that tugged deep in my stomach, one I had never felt before.

Her lips called to mine, and I wanted a taste, even though I knew it was a cretinous thing to do.

But she had run from me . . . why?

Did she hate it?

Did the intoxication of the drug fade from her eyes and show her who exactly had kissed her? Was she appalled by it? By me? Was she worried about what Elia would think? Goodness gracious—what would he think?

He would kill me, of that I was certain. She was his, and I had just ruined that.

But it was terrific for me; I won't lie.

It was intimate and rapturously addicting, but was I the only one who felt it? Did I do it wrong?

It was inescapable. I knew I would obsess over this until I got an answer. I would waste precious time dissecting the look of irritation and discomfort in her eyes the moment she rushed to her feet.

Women had tried to kiss me a couple of times; if I had succumbed and kissed them, would they have looked at me the same way, or was this because Zahra hated me?

But why would she stop me from hurting myself if she hated me? Why would she ask me questions about why I couldn't sleep?

I was treading through a territory I knew I shouldn't cross. All through the day, this woman refused to leave my mind. I'd asked myself similar questions to the ones plaguing my mind now.

Did she care, stopping me from ending it all? Why didn't she get nervous and scared around me? Why didn't she drive away from me? What was she up to today? Did she tell Elia about what happened?

When she'd told me she had to get away from everyone, I had a burning desire to ask, and I would have asked what happened, but I knew I couldn't get invested.

I knew little about her.

I'd found she had some history with some self-made mobster in Sicily, but I didn't know how deep it ran or how she came to be here in Milan. I knew nothing. I needed to stop wondering and asking questions, but a part of me also knew it was too late, and if picturing Angelo's death wasn't proof, I didn't know what would be.

"I most definitely interrupted something, didn't I?"

I blinked, looking up at him. "Every human has two angels, the good one that rests on the right shoulder, and the bad that rests on the left."

Angelo frowned. "I don't . . ."

"You're the good one. The one always giving advice that I would never follow and popping in when I don't even need you. The one I'd love to squish, but I can't because I happen to like you. How fortunate for you and unfortunate for me."

He opened his mouth to say something—closed it, opened it again, before finally closing it.

My lips lifted in irritation as I watched him try to find an excuse.

He cleared his throat, standing straighter, his hair rough, as if he had just gotten out of bed. "I didn't know you wouldn't be alone, Marino, and—the girl was the last person I expected you to be with. Are you fucking her?"

"I beg your pardon?"

"I mean—something was happening, the way she rushed—"

"And how is any of that your business?"

"It's not, but it's unlike you. I mean, you did try to drown her before, so . . . it's just—you don't, you and women—I've never . . ."

"Go on, Angelo, I've heard you form consecutive sentences before. You can do it."

He sighed. "You're right; it's none of my business. But if you are . . . involved with her or . . . want to be, or would soon be? I can ask my people to carry out intensive research on Manuel Conti—"

"Leave it to me," I said, getting to my feet, surprisingly without staggering. I felt very sober but still a little light. "No one does any research on her. I doubt you would find anything useful."

Angelo's eyes widened with surprise as he watched me. "My God. You didn't deny it."

"Deny what?"

"That you're involved with her, or would want to be, or will *soon* be involved with her."

I bent to pick up the empty beer bottle on the ground, straightening before walking to the end of the chair and leaning on it. "Why? Are you interested in her?"

"Of course not."

"In me, then?"

He gave me a blank look.

"What? You are awfully invested in this. I only want to confirm."

"I am not interested in you, Marino."

"Okay, why are you so concerned then?"

"Because I *am* concerned. I don't trust her. I'm usually not this skeptical about people. But—something about that woman ticks me off the wrong way, and I don't want you . . ." He trailed off.

"Carry on." I urged with my hands.

He sighed. "I've never seen you with anyone, not since Grace. So I know if this thing with Zahra is a thing, then it might be serious for you, and we know little about her to conclude if she is to be trusted."

"No one is to be trusted, Angelo. Besides, as far as the situation is right now, there is nothing between her and me. I appreciate that you care, but I am not a child. If I need relationship advice, I will come to you, but I don't need it."

He nodded. "All right."

"Good. Now, about that phone. I was hoping to discuss it when it's daytime, but I might as well tell you now. I need one."

He blinked at me like he hadn't heard me well. "You . . . you need a phone?"

"Yes. What is wrong with you today? Why are you lagging? Should I be worried?"

"No. I'm just surprised. I've been trying for years to get you a phone, but you've always refused, so I'm a little shocked that you want one all of a sudden," he said, and when I didn't respond, he rearranged his previous blabber because he didn't exactly ask a question. "Why do you want a phone all of a sudden?"

"Someone might be expecting my text."

"Someone . . ."

"Yes." I leaned off the chair, walking past him. "A very kind woman who gave me a ride in her car. She gave me her number and asked me to text her. She's my friend. Her name's Gemma."

"So . . . a stranger is the reason you're getting a phone after all my efforts over the years?"

"Yes," I said, opening the roof door.

"That doesn't hurt my feelings at all," he said, following after me.

"I'm glad it doesn't."

"That was sarcasm."

"I'm afraid I am under the influence; I can't tell the difference. Minutes ago, the moon was smiling at me," I said, climbing down the stairs.

"I want to push you," he said.

"You'd be doing me a favor."

He groaned.

"Oh, before I forget. Arrange a meeting with Street when the sun is up. I have a job offer for them."

"Noted."

The chihuahua painting was lying flat on the board table the next day.

Before the group arrived, I discarded my suit jacket and left just my black button-up with a tie. I had paced the length of the multipurpose space on the casino's top floor, solely because I was restless.

Casmiro had begrudgingly asked what the matter was with me, but I couldn't exactly explain to him that my always controlled nerves had gotten the better of me because a certain woman had walked away from me after I kissed her. So, I just settled for doing what I do best, lighting up a cigar and ignoring him.

The moment Street walked in, my pacing stopped as I blew out the smoke I had drawn in. My gaze zeroed in on the entrance as they filed in.

Something seemed off.

Milk had an anxious and wary look, Dog looked pissed, Upper looked sick, and Elia wore almost the same look as Zahra, completely blank.

Angelo followed behind them, locking the door as they settled like they had the last time they'd been here.

My gaze briefly locked with Zahra's, but she didn't give anything away. Instead, it looked like she was staring through a transparent wall.

The silence in the room was deafening until Dog broke it.

"Well, that's one ugly dog. It's even uglier in person; how's that possible?" he remarked, eyeing the painting.

"Angelo said you had an offer for us; we'd like to go straight to the point, please," Elia voiced.

Casmiro glanced at me, and I could read the question in his mind. *What the fuck happened to them.*

I walked back to the head of the table, took my seat, and assessed the group. I should have asked Zahra why she left the house last night because whatever it was, it was ruining their typical demeanor.

I searched inside me for the satisfaction of this new development but couldn't find it, so I chose to ignore it altogether. The matter at hand was more important than their off day.

"I am well aware that you all know about the dealings with the painting. About Arturo Garza's quest," I said into the silence, waiting for any of them to chip in with a response, but there was just . . . silence.

"That's a shock," Casmiro muttered, relaxing back on his chair beside me, watching the group with a smile of amusement.

"I'll take your silence for a yes," I added. "A lot of men like me are on the hunt for the original painting, and—"

"Why are you on the hunt for it?" Elia asked.

"The gold, why else?"

"Bullshit," Zahra muttered with a scoff, but she didn't look at me. Her jaw was locked, and her index finger circled the table, eyes focused on the painting.

"And why would you insinuate that?" I asked, still looking at her.

I expected her to give me her infamous challenging look, but she didn't even look up once as she said, "Everybody in this room knows that you don't give a shit about the gold. You have a thousand times the amount it promises to fetch resting in your bank account, Marino."

Marino?

Discomfort claimed me.

"All right, since we're going to be working together—"

Her head shot up, eyes locking with mine. "Working together?"

I held her gaze. "Yes, Zahra. I plan to hire you for a job. You and the rest of your team will help me find the original painting."

Milk's eyes widened as she looked around the group.

The confused look in Zahra's eyes quickly changed into a glare. "I'm sorry to break it to you, but we're already planning to go after it on our own."

Dog scoffed. "I wonder how that's gonna work when no one is talking to anyone. Might as well get out there and get fucking killed," he muttered.

Elia aimed a glare his way. "Maybe shut the fuck up?"

"Me?" Dog sat up. "Oh, you're asking for a fucking punch because you caused this whole motherfucking bullshit."

Upper spoke into the tense silence. "Fellas, not here."

Dog turned to him in his seat. "Don't even get me started on you, you little shithead."

"Don't talk to him like that," Elia warned.

Zahra sat up, turning to Elia with wide eyes as she clapped her hands together once, shooting him a mock appreciative smile. "Wow, you're one to talk about *how* to talk to him."

Surprisingly, Elia leveled her with a glare. "I wasn't fucking talking to you."

A gasp left Zahra, and she gritted out, "Somebody fucking hold me because I'm about to punch a motherfucker in the face."

"Before you do that," I cut in, blowing out my smoke calmly, pressing the lit cigar to the ashtray beside me. "I was wondering if maybe we can all return to the matter at hand; that would be splendid."

Silence fell on them, but I could still see withheld anger from Dog, Zahra, and Elia while Milk and Upper sat there in utter discomfort.

"It was getting good," Casmiro said, straightening his suit, leaning on the table, and joining his hands together. "But yes, the matter at hand is important. I don't know what you and your crew were thinking, Zahra, but if I remember correctly, you are under Marino's command, so even if you wanted to hunt for the original on your own, it wouldn't be possible. You answer to us."

"We're not going on a suicide mission unless we know why you want the painting so bad," Zahra said.

I released a breath, weighing my options before coming to a decision. I motioned to Angelo to explain.

"There are very important flash drives kept with the gold," Angelo informed. "These flash drives contain intel regarding some of the wealthiest men in and out of this business."

Elia perked up. "By intel you mean . . ."

"Self-incriminating."

Dog whistled. "Well, ain't that something."

"What's in it for us?" Zahra asked this time.

"The gold," Angelo responded.

Zahra shook her head. "Oh no, we'll get the gold, I know that. But you're hiring us for this . . . what do we get out of it?" She directed the question to me, and everyone waited for my response.

There was always a catch with this woman.

Smart.

"All right." I bit my tongue hard before I let my next words through. "You get your freedom—all of you. If you find the painting, get the gold and the flash drives. You're free."

Dog spoke up. "Now, that's a fucking deal."

Zahra still looked skeptical, like she was thinking it through. After a while, she shook her head. "I say yes to the freedom, but . . . I want something more. Apparently, we're not the only ones hunting for this painting. We might be good, but some people have been looking for this thing longer than we have. We might get one-upped; we might lose our lives," she said.

"She has a point," Upper said.

Zahra leveled me with a stern professional stare. "A hundred million dollars, and we'll consider helping you find those flash drives."

I frowned. "You already get the gold."

"We're risking our lives on a 'maybe we'll find the original painting and get the gold.' It's not certain. The payment guarantees that even if we don't find the gold, we're not risking our lives for nothing." She turned to her group. "Is that all right with everyone?"

"That's perfect," Milk said.

"I'm game," Dog agreed.

Upper shrugged. "It's better than five thousand dollars."

Elia looked like he couldn't care less.

"So"—Zahra looked back at me—"do we have a deal, Marino?"

"This is ridiculous." Casmiro's voice was soaked with disbelief. "They're in no position to be cutting deals. We already agree to grant them their freedom; that's quite enough, in my opinion," he said when he realized I was actually thinking about it.

"I agree with Casmiro," Angelo said.

Their freedom was inevitable.

The money was nothing. I wouldn't need it where I was going. This all would be nothing if I found those flash drives. Casmiro didn't know that.

After a few minutes of pondering, I sat up straighter, clearing my throat. "We have a deal, Zahra."

"Are you fucking kidding me," Casmiro hissed, relaxing back in the chair with a look of annoyance.

Zahra gave a curt nod. "I would like that to be stated in a certified contract to avoid future misinterpretations."

"As you wish."

Casmiro shot me a bewildered look, leaning towards me while he said quietly, "Tell me there's an explanation for this."

"Have you ever known me to do things without reason, Casmiro?"

He shook his head.

"Good. We'll talk at length later. For now, trust me."

He sneaked a look at Angelo, who shrugged.

"Fine."

I turned my attention back to the group. "From your interactions, I believe there are issues that need to be solved amongst your group. I am not hiring a bunch of children who can't air out their disputes and separate them from their work; I'm hiring the people who stole from me and claimed to be shadows of Italy. You're dismissed in hopes that I'm not making a mistake. When I have news for you, you'll be informed."

Elia was the first to shoot up from his seat, walking out like the room was on fire. Dog followed suit with a curse.

"Zahra, will you stay back a minute, please?" I said, gesturing to Casmiro and Angelo to excuse us.

The question in Casmiro's eyes was evident, but he didn't ask it. Angelo, though, shot me a familiar look, the one he had worn when he told me not to trust her.

Zahra stood up but did not attempt to leave.

I got to my feet when everyone left, and it was just us two.

"What is this about?" she asked, crossing her arms against her chest. "Do you want to add something to the contract?" She eyed me suspiciously.

"It is unrelated to work," I said, walking to her.

When I got close, she raised her chin, locking her jaw—determination in those stubborn eyes.

I leaned on the table before her, a foot's distance between us.

Mirroring her actions by crossing my arms, I watched her swallow, her eyes glazing over momentarily.

"Did you tell my brother? Is that why there's animosity between you both?"

Mock confusion brought down her brows. "What are you talking about? Tell Devil what?"

Annoyance prickled in me, but I tamped it down. "Do not pretend you don't know what I'm talking about."

"Maybe you just need to be specific."

She stared me down, and I honestly did not want to waste more time on this. "The rooftop, last night."

Mock realization filled her eyes. "Oh, that. What's there to tell? It was nothing."

"I beg to differ. We need to talk about it."

She sighed, dropping her hands. "There's nothing to talk about, Marino—"

"Stop. Stop calling me that." My annoyance and irritation flared as I cut her off.

"It's your name."

"That's not what you call me."

She shrugged. "Well, get used to it, Marino."

I frowned. Not many things threw me off guard, but her attitude right then was answering all the questions that had been taunting my mind.

"What happened?" I asked in Spanish carefully; you might have even thought there was a genuine softness to my voice—maybe there was.

Zahra's eyes widened, showing that she hadn't expected me to ask. But she collected herself quickly, and I saw how she locked her shoulders, raising her guard.

"Whatever happened is none of your business," she responded in English. "Like I said," she continued, "there is nothing to talk about, and honestly, I'm in a very terrible mood right now, and I can't dissect whatever happened on that rooftop or why the fuck you would want to talk about it, but get this, we were high out of our minds, okay? It was a fucked-up night, filled with raging hormones, and we shared a stupid fucking kiss and tried to get each other off until we were interrupted; thank God for that."

It was silent for what seemed like a long minute. I had nothing to say. No—my mouth felt too dry, and I had the strongest urge to drink water.

She shifted on her feet. "So, if you'd excuse me, I'd like to go back to that house and pretend like the people I call family don't exist until I have to work with them again."

I tried to find thoughts, but they were very silent at the moment, so I just swallowed, nodded, looked away from her, and motioned to the door as I said, "Of course."

She hesitated to leave for a bit, and when I looked back at her, I caught what seemed like regret in her eyes.

She sighed. "Listen, Elio—"

"You've cleared up my concerns. You can leave now."

She let out a shaky breath before nodding. "Okay . . ." Her eyes searched mine for a few seconds, and then she turned on her heel and left the space, closing the door behind her and subjecting me to silence.

I stood staring at the closed door.

For how long, I had no idea.

But finally, after so long, I had one thought.

No—one affirmation.

I had wasted valuable time asking questions I should have seen the answers to up front, and I should probably have punished myself for how useless the last ten hours had been and for losing control like that on the rooftop.

But I knew I would also be wasting my time punishing myself, so I'd learn the lesson from this experience instead.

It was a *"stupid fucking kiss."* Therefore, it was something I'd never repeat.

Probably for as long as I breathed.

CHAPTER THIRTY-ONE

Zahra

Through my headphones, I could hear the soft knocking on my door, which I'd been ignoring for almost five minutes now. I pressed my eyelids together, a flimsy attempt to block out my thoughts and center my mind.

I wasn't in a good place. I was too in my head. A lot of thoughts plagued my mind. I didn't know which to focus on. Devil and Upper being involved in some way. Milk knowing about it, Dog suspecting and not saying anything to me. The incident on the rooftop with Elio, which hadn't stopped replaying in my head . . . the warmth of his lips that had me pressing mine together every time to remember how it felt subconsciously.

I couldn't stop thinking about it and him. Which was very fucking inconvenient because I didn't need this. It wasn't just that I was attracted to him, I cared. As much as I loved to deny it, I fucking cared. This wasn't predetermined. It just happened, and I hated it, and him.

I'd have loved to think that it was centered chiefly towards guilt, but it wasn't; because I panicked—when he asked me to wait behind, my heart jumped because I was hoping he wouldn't remember—I didn't want to talk about it. I should have known he would address it because he didn't seem like a man who would shy away from something like that.

This man was exactly like the people I had fought tooth and nail to escape from. He had hurt a teenager, for God's sake, tried to drown me, shot and tortured me. He'd threatened to kill me more times than I could count, and yet, *yet* I couldn't help but be drawn to him. I didn't want to overthink it or give it importance, but the look on his face when I'd written it all off as nothing . . .

I groaned in annoyance, snapping my eyes back open and staring at the ceiling for a second too long before my gaze settled on the door.

The knocking continued, and I took off my headphones, sighing.

"It's open," I called out, sitting up as the door opened an inch. Upper was peeking in like I would jump off the bed and attack him if he so much as breathed the same air as me.

"What do you want?" I asked him, taking off my headphones.

"I just . . ." He fumbled. "I wanted to—" He stood upright, swallowing. "Can we talk?" he asked, unable to shield the nervousness in his voice.

I hesitated, locked my jaw, but nodded all the same.

He walked in cautiously, closed the door, and settled a few inches away from me on the mattress, his movement gentle as he watched me. "Hey," he started.

"Hey," I responded, watching him struggle with what to say next.

His dark brown hair was rough, and circles were underneath his eyes; even his infamous one pair of earrings was missing, and his neck chains were gone too; it was weird seeing him so . . . bare. He looked so stressed.

"Listen, Zahra, I know . . . I know my apology would mean shit to you—"

"Actually, I'd take an apology," I told him honestly.

His eyes went wide, even though they were filled with uncertainty. "You're serious?"

I nodded. "You both fucked up, and the least either of you could have done was to actually apologize for treating me like the damn fool in all this."

His lips parted, and he shifted closer to me, eyes pleading. "I promise you; it was not my intention. I swear on my life and everything I hold dear that I never wanted to hurt you with this revelation. The first time it happened, I—I wanted to tell you, but I was scared that this whole thing would happen, and now that it is happening, I feel like a pound of bloody arseholish-shit, and I, I am *so* sorry, Zahra."

I blinked at him, shocked a little by the sincerity in his words, but what surprised me more was how his accent had gone more profound; he sounded almost elegant, even with the—weird curse word.

"What the fuck is a pound of bloody arseholish-shit?"

He breathed out a laugh, and I joined in with a chuckle.

He looked down, but before he did, I caught the glassy haze in his eyes, and when he sniffed, I shifted closer to him.

"Hey," I called, trying to catch his gaze.

He shook and raised his head, sucking in a shaky breath as he wiped off his tears and forced out a laugh. "Sorry, I know this is not—this is not the Upper version of myself." He swallowed, refusing to meet my gaze as he mumbled, "Whoever the fuck that is."

My heart melted there and then, and I couldn't believe I was slightly mad at him.

"Upper—"

"I promise I'm not some crybaby."

"I happen to love crybabies," I said, ruffling his already-ruffled hair. His teary eyes met mine, and he smiled sheepishly at me.

"I'm usually not a mess like this . . ." he said, looking down again. "It's just—this whole thing has dredged up awful memories from before, and the last thing I want is to be the reason why a family like ours gets separated. I always fuck things up for people I care about, and my biggest fear is . . . is doing that to Street."

I wanted to ask what he was talking about because it seemed to really be bothering him. "You're not fucking up anything."

He shook his head. "No, I am. Look at us. I know it's just been a day, but—we've never gone this long being hostile with each other, and it's all because I couldn't stop myself from feeling."

"No one should ever stop themselves from feeling what they want to feel, Upper. You're one of the best people I know; you couldn't even ruin a family if you tried."

He went silent for a long moment before he swallowed and said, "I could."

"What do you mean?"

"I did it . . . almost ruined a family . . . a big one. It's the reason why I'm in this bloody country. Away from everyone that I—" He stopped, the thickness of tears in his voice blocking his next words from coming through.

I rubbed his back. "Hey, I know you. Whatever happened, I'm sure it's not your fault. I'm positive it's not."

He smiled. "I want to believe that. But you should have seen how I was packaged like an abomination. All that happened when they didn't even know my sexuality; imagine how they'd treat me if they knew."

"Upper—"

"I can't stay, Zahra," he blurted, and my hand movement on his back stopped.

"What are you talking about?"

He worried his bottom lip with his teeth. "I can't stay here . . . with Street. I—not after what happened; it's too fucking close to home, and I know I shouldn't tuck tail and run, but that's how I was able to stop my family from breaking apart the first time."

I dropped my hand, frowning. "Upper—"

"I will go after we get the gold, and I'm not saying this because I need the money or anything like that. We started the mission together, and we'll end it together. After that, I'm leaving Street."

I swallowed down the lump in my throat. "You don't have to leave, Upper."

"I know, but I want to. I need to."

"Is this because of Devil? Do I need to knock some sense into him?"

He shook his head quickly. "No, no, don't—don't tell him anything. In fact, don't tell anyone anything."

"That's—"

"I'll tell them after we get the gold so it will seem as if I was selfish, and now that we have gold, I want to leave. That narrative suits me."

"No, it doesn't."

"I'll make it suit me."

"Upper." I stopped him. "Is this because you like Devil, and he won't return your feelings? I can talk to him. Maybe he's just conflicted."

He shook his head. "Me and Devil, we're very impossible. I like him, yes. I really do, I more than like him, but it's not going to happen."

I frowned. "How long has this been going on between you two."

He sighed. "The dare happened four months ago, and the other stuff just—happened along the line, we didn't generally hook up, just like—three times, and that's it. It was nothing."

"Did you tell him that you liked him?"

He shook his head again. "There's no point. I mean nothing to him. And that's okay. I think he really does love you, Zahra. I confused him. On his behalf, I'm sorry."

"Don't." I held his face in my hands. "None of this is your fault. It happened because it was meant to happen. Do you believe in reasons, Upper?"

"I don't know."

"Well, believe in them. Because there's a reason this is happening, and whatever it is, I'm sure it didn't just push you into Devil's path so that you could force yourself out of it. Maybe Devil loves me in his own weird way, but I am certain that he feels more for you than he does me."

"I don't think so."

"I think so. He wouldn't be trying this hard to run away from it if it meant nothing. I'll talk to him—"

"No, please—"

"I'll talk to him. I won't tell him you're planning—planning to leave; a decision I'm hoping you'll change your mind on because you're a part of this, you're the fucking Elegant in Street. Without that one 'E,' we're incomplete."

He smiled through tear-filled eyes.

"Come here, you crybaby."

He melted into me, burying his head in my neck as I held him close.

Eventually, we both settled properly on my bed while he dozed off in minutes. I was still holding him, staring up at the ceiling and thinking of ways to convince him to get the thought of leaving out of his mind.

But somewhere along the line, I drifted off to sleep too.

Upper was still dead asleep beside me when I woke up, so I slipped off the bed and out of the room. He looked like he hadn't slept a wink the night before, just like me and probably Devil and the rest of us.

Walking down the passageway, I bumped into Milk, who let out a somewhat loud yelp.

"Jesus fucking Christ, Zahra." She blew out a breath, her hand on her chest.

"Have any idea where Devil is?"

"I saw him out back from the kitchen window."

"Thanks." I was about to brush past her but stopped, leveling her with a firm stare. "Why didn't you tell me?"

She blinked. "It wasn't my secret to share—"

"We're supposed to have each other's backs."

"I know, but I was—I was having both Upper's and Devil's backs by keeping my mouth shut, and I was having *your* back by bugging them to tell you or I'd spill, and I didn't want you to be hurt, and I also didn't want them to be hurt too, and it just got so confusing and delicate so fast that I—I'm sorry. I should have said something."

I chuckled, letting out a sigh. "We all suck because I would have also wanted to protect them if I were in your shoes."

"I don't think five people can be best friends. Because when one person has a secret that concerns another person, it's flipping hard to keep it because you're considering everyone's feelings and the fucking pressure is choking."

"I think we're trying. And I think this whole day has been shit."

She let out a loud sigh of relief. "I know! Dog refused to cook, so yes, it has been shit, and now I gotta bake. I guarantee a burnt dinner; sorry in advance."

"I don't care if it's charcoal, I'll eat anything, cause I'm starving. I'll come to help soon, just gotta talk to Devil real quick."

"Go easy on him."

"I will," I said, making my way to the backyard.

When I opened the door, I was greeted with golden hour sunlight and cool weather that seemed to draw me towards Devil's somber figure, sitting on the back porch as guards walked by here and there, with cars entering and leaving the compound.

I walked over to him, sitting by his side.

I stifled a yawn as I bathed in the sunlight before looking over at him. His skin, the same shade as Elio's, glowed under the light with a natural ease that had me comparing his eyelashes to his brother's. They weren't as long, but they were thick and had the same shadowing grace.

I could spot some resemblance here and there, but I looked away before said brother started plaguing my mind again.

"You look like a vampire under this light." I broke the silence.

He scoffed a chuckle, and I caught him stealing a glance my way. "Why? Do I sparkle?"

I looked at him. "No . . . you glow."

"Real smooth, Z. A for effort."

"Thank you, I'm glad," I said with a smile, and he turned to look at me.

"Sorry about the boardroom—I was just pissed. You didn't want to talk to me, and the time you did, you called me out on—Upper." He sighed, looking away and ahead. "I'm sorry about everything. I was—I didn't handle it well; this thing with Upper is . . . confusing. I don't—I don't know how to separate it from my feelings for you, and I know that's a shitty thing to say in this situation because I don't want either of you to get hurt, and I—"

My hand covered his. "Hey . . ."

He sucked in a breath, intertwining our fingers before turning to look at me.

"It's fine . . . I'm not angry anymore."

His eyes searched mine. "No, it's not fine. I am angry. I am angry at myself and my feelings and how badly I fucked up. For hurting you. I love you, I know I do. It's just—"

"It's different when you're with him," I completed.

He looked down at our hands together. "I'm sorry."

"It's okay." I laughed lightly. "I don't know how I didn't see it. You both spend so much time together, but when we're all together, you barely talk to each other. I should have seen it."

"Milk caught on first. It's not her fault she didn't tell you. Upper and I wanted to tell you—but then I freaked because I feel something for you, and I didn't want to throw that away because being with Upper is so consuming, like—I fight for breath whenever he's near, and it fucking scares me, Zahra. Because it was so sudden. We've known each other for years, and I've never once thought that—I've never once seen him that way, and now it's—now I've fucked it up."

I didn't know love. I thought I did until the person who made me believe *I* did explained how he felt when he saw me, and I realized I didn't feel that way; I realized I was scared, not in love.

What Devil had just described sounded an awful lot like the words of someone in love . . . It was crazy.

I wanted that . . . someday. A dream, I knew, but—it wasn't bad to dream it.

"What are you gonna do about it?" I asked.

"Nothing," he said.

"Nothing?"

"I don't know, Z. I still need to work out some things, and I—what about this—us."

"I know it's not going to happen, and I'm okay with that. It doesn't change the fact that you're my best friend and that I love you and will always be there for you. Our promises remain the same. You can cry if you want, I'd never tell anyone. You can tell me how bad you can't stop staring at Upper; I'll keep it till I'm six feet under—"

"And you'll always have me in line?"

"Of course." I smiled softly. "Always."

He wrapped his arms around me, pulling my body to his as he pressed a kiss to my hair.

A comfortable silence settled between us as we watched the sun go down.

"Why did my brother want you to stay back?"

I froze, and he noticed because he was already pulling away from my body, leveling me with a look.

"Nothing," I blurted.

Devil frowned. "Why . . . are you lying?"

"I'm not; he just wanted to know what was up with everyone."

"Why would he be asking *you* that?"

I shrugged. "I guess we—we're kind of, like, friends?"

His frown deepened. "Yeah . . . no."

I laughed it off, backtracking. "I'm joking. He probably wanted to ask you, but you stormed off early, and he knows I know, and well—yeah, nothing serious."

He eyed me. "You'll stay away from him."

"Are you asking or telling?"

"Neither. It's a given. You don't get close to someone like that."

I became surprisingly uncomfortable. "You yourself said he wasn't that bad."

"Yeah, *wasn't*. That's until he tried to drown you and almost killed you; why are we even debating this?"

I blinked. "We're not. Just—he's your brother, and I thought you wanted to get closer to him."

"Not anymore."

"He cares about you."

"He pointed a gun at me."

"Devil—"

"Why are you defending him, Z."

I hesitated. "I'm not."

His eyes searched mine. "You will stay away from him, right? We do this one mission, and we're out, right?"

"Yeah."

"Zahra—"

"I will stay away. I have—I have no interest. I promise," I lied.

He let out a sigh of relief. "You scared me with the whole defending-him thing. He's not a good guy; he's just very good at making people think he is."

"Mmm."

"Yo, quick team meeting, you shitheads!" Dog yelled from the window, and I snorted, glad for his interruption because I was close to getting the air sucked out of me with this damn conversation.

We both joined the rest in the living room. Upper was there, curled beside Milk, who was stroking his hair.

He still looked sleepy, like Dog had dragged him out of my bed.

Upper eyed us with a frown, but I smiled to let him know I said nothing. He visibly relaxed.

When Devil and I settled on a chair next to each other, Dog clapped his hand once, standing in the middle of the room.

"Great, the whole family's here together. We have two options we can go through to clear the air and get our shit together."

"What's the first one?" Upper asked, and I knew it was to indulge him because we'd already cleared the air.

"I'm stoked that you asked. The first one is to talk. It's very fucking boring, I know, but it might help if we all just—talked in the sense that—we tell each other one thing we've never told each other to rekindle our bond. We don't ask questions; we just tell."

Devil relaxed back on the couch, throwing his arm around my shoulder and pulling me back with him. "And the second one?" he asked.

"We have a sweaty, steamy gang bang that centers very close to a very sweaty orgy. We let out our frustrations by fucking each other's brains out."

"My God, you're such a man-slut," Milk said, her nose scrunched up in disgust.

Upper spoke up drowsily. "That's not a bad idea."

Dog pointed his hand in Upper's direction with a grin. "See, Upper gets it."

"Upper is sleep-deprived," Devil pointed out.

"Yup." Upper snuggled closer to Milk. "That's bloody right." He yawned.

"I say we give the first option a theme, like the truth behind our names?" Milk suggested.

We all nodded in agreement.

"Okay, so the first option, who's going first?" Dog asked.

"No one asks questions, right?" Devil inquired.

"Yup. No questions."

"Elio Marino's my half-brother. He's The Wicked, and I'm The Devil," Devil said.

There was silence. A very long silence.

Upper and Milk shared the same wide-eyed look.

Even though I knew, it didn't stop me from freezing beside him, seeing as he had just blurted it out.

Just like that.

"Are you serious?" Upper asked.

"As a heart attack," Devil responded.

"Dude," Milk breathed out.

Dog slowly took a seat on the single-seater couch. "Now that's a fucking foul; how can you expect us not to ask questions, motherfucker."

Devil shrugged. "You made the rules."

"My fucking God," Dog muttered. "I'll go next. Since we're starting with the heavy shit." He squared his shoulders.

We all waited for him to speak, and I braced myself.

"I had a dog named Dog. I mistakenly shot him when I was seven. With my mom's stun gun. She was a cop. He didn't wake up."

Silence settled.

"That's—that's awful," Upper said, straightening.

"I'm sorry," Milk whispered.

"Yeah, thanks." Dog offered a tight smile.

"I'll go next," Upper said. "Kinda glad we're not asking questions because . . . yeah."

He swallowed. "I . . . I am a bastard prince."

"I fucking knew this bitch was rich," Dog said with a grin that showed he had been suspecting.

"So you didn't climb up ventilators to get an education," Milk mused. "Wow."

Upper shrugged.

Dog slapped his knees. "No wonder he's Upper, cause . . ."

"Upper class," I completed.

"Got to keep some of it," Upper said.

"Still doesn't make sense," Devil said. "Just saying."

I jabbed him in the ribs.

Blowing out a breath, I sat up. "I'll go next."

The room went silent, all eyes on me.

"I—" My throat clogged, and I cleared it. "I put that anklet on myself. To remember who I am. I forget sometimes."

"Oh damn," Dog said.

"Sucks that I lost it," I said with a chuckle.

"You don't need it anymore," Devil said beside me. "We're here to remind you every day who you are."

"I agree," Upper said with a smile, and Milk offered me a reassuring nod.

"My turn," Milk said with a cautious smile.

We all waited for her to speak, and for a moment, her eyes glazed over like she was remembering what she was about to divulge.

"I found my mother hanging from her bedroom ceiling when I was nine. I didn't call for help, didn't leave the house. The guy who delivered milk to us every day was the one who noticed my mother never came to open the door. I survived on milk while her body grew rotten in her bedroom. On the fourth day, he was concerned, so he came into the house and saw her. Still hanging."

This time, the silence was heavy.

"That's . . ." Dog said. "I'm sorry, Milk."

She nodded with an appreciative smile.

"You're strong," I told her. "Literally, every time someone calls you Milk, you have to remember."

She shrugged. "I don't want to forget."

I'd never felt closer to every single one of them than I did now. Everything just had . . . meaning.

A comfortable silence settled, and a smile crept up my lips. "I love you guys. More than anything."

They didn't need to say it back; I saw the response on their faces.

"We should do this more often," Dog said, "because I'd really love to know how the fuck he's related to Marino." He motioned to Devil.

"And how rich Upper is," Milk added.

"Maybe next time when we fight. For now"—I got to my feet—"I'm fucking starving, and I need food."

Upper sighed, holding his stomach. "Me too."

"Come on, baby, let's go see what Milk burned." I reached towards him and outstretched my hand. He grabbed it, and I hurled him up as we headed to the kitchen.

"I haven't even started yet!" I heard Milk's voice close behind me.

"Nobody can do anything without me," Dog muttered.

"You gotta admit. It was a dick move to deny everyone food." Devil aimed the jab at him.

"I was hoping you guys would settle for the orgy option. All the food we need."

"Get the fuck out." Devil laughed.

I smiled from my position behind the counter.

We're okay.

No.

We're more than okay, even better than before we had the fight.

I knew in my heart that we'd always be okay.

My gaze traveled in Upper's direction to find him bickering with Milk over a tray choice.

I hoped this new development was enough reason for him to want to stay.

CHAPTER THIRTY-TWO

Elio

I haven't used the phone.

It had been three weeks since Angelo got it, and it remained sealed inside the box.

I couldn't explain why I couldn't open or activate the device. Probably because it had been over a decade since I last owned one, and a lot had changed within that time. I mostly didn't have the zeal to own one or set it up.

I was not a Luddite, but I wouldn't deny that it would sting to ask a smug Angelo or Casmiro for help in understanding how exactly the item worked.

But I knew I would have to break that barrier sooner or later. Aside from sending Gemma a text message, the device was necessary.

It could have been beneficial during the times when Zah—

I shook that thought out of my head, picked the box up from the table, and tucked it safely inside one of my drawers.

Work. Yes, focus on work.

I ignored the emails and went straight to the folders I'd gotten from the mayor of Turin; thanks to Edoardo's over-trusting personality and his love for loyalty, Marino had gained control over the state affairs in Turin, and with that came a lot of brain work that I'd been putting off due to another project for Milan. I didn't want to attend to both at the same time, but I was falling behind, losing focus on . . . essential things.

It was careless.

I can't be careless.

It had been three weeks since that boardroom meeting, three

weeks since I'd last seen Street, though Angelo made sure I received updates on their progress.

A new painting had been released, and they had traveled to Tunisia to fetch it. According to the report, some other group had beaten them to it, but it was later confirmed that the painting was also a fake.

I wasn't surprised.

There was obviously more to it. We were missing something, and my little artist was the key to finding that thing.

Except, according to my people in charge of getting the answers out of him, he wasn't opening up.

This was when I usually succumbed to taking matters into my own hands, but I had been hesitating. If I interfered, someone would die . . . and I didn't have time to see through a wipeout, so I put the artist's fate in the hands of professionals who could torture the truth out of him.

That way, nobody dies. And I still get my answer.

I should also probably stop Street from wasting their time searching for the fakes. But what good would that do me?

I wanted to keep them busy, away from me. I needed to focus.

I needed *her* away from my space.

I couldn't afford the distracting feelings that came with my thoughts trailing to her—damn it.

I flipped a page open in the folder, my eyes perusing the words as I read—correction; I *tried* to read, to understand the words, and I did understand them, but they made absolutely no sense.

Three weeks.

Three weeks of me trying so hard to school my thoughts, to block out the voice of the witch, to erase the strange feeling of dissatisfaction, and the nonsensical craving I had to hear her speak to me. To have her ask me questions that would require me to *talk* to her. To have a conversation where she threw out sarcastic jokes, and I pretended to hate them.

Pathetic.

The woman probably doesn't remember you exist, and if she does remember, what then? She had made her feelings clear. And even if she hadn't, even if by an opportune chance she actually wanted to talk about it, what would happen afterward? Did we explore? Did I ask her to enter into a relationship with me? Did I fuck her—

That is a very nefarious thought, Elio. She is with your brother, for God's sake.

I was getting ahead of myself here. Why would I think of a relationship with someone I still fantasized about killing?

What is wrong with you, Elio?

I didn't like this.

This fucking distraction—I banged the folder on the table, the blow from my fist causing a rattle as I shot to my feet, walking around the desk while rubbing my brows and pacing back and forth in the study.

"Focus, focus," I chanted. "These are all useless thoughts, not beneficial; it's not aiding your goals, it's not important, it's rubbish . . . She's rubbish, she's nothing, she's a woman, she's just an element made up of skin, bones, and a soul, she's only matter, a substance put together with numerous particles that occupy space. Nothing more, she's—"

"E, are you fr—"

I stopped and turned towards the door to see that it was opened slightly with Casmiro peeking in, brows drawn down in a frown.

"Were you talking to yourself?" he asked.

"No."

I shoved both my hands into my pockets, watching him.

Slowly, he walked into the study, eyes going around the space like he was trying to seek out who I was talking to; when he couldn't find anyone, he looked back at me with a frown, and I kept my expression blank.

"I heard you mumbling something."

"You heard nothing."

"I heard something—"

"What is the reason for your visit? State it and leave. I am busy."

"Talking to yourself?"

"State it. And leave."

He sighed, dropping it. "It's about your artist."

That caught my attention. "Did he speak?"

Casmiro shook his head. "No, I'm beginning to think he's never going to. We need you down there; maybe your presence would change something."

I locked my jaw. "Are you telling me that my professional team is incapable of torturing answers out of a simple artist?"

"They've tried all the methods; his fingers have been chopped off; I'm guessing his inability to work has made him incompliant."

"Ah . . . I see. Poor thing."

"It has been three weeks. He's wasting our time, and Street hasn't gotten any new leads for the next painting yet."

"Hm. How unfortunate."

Casmiro glared at me, standing straighter. "Be serious, E. If we go on like this, the artist will be dead before we pull out any answers from him."

"You want me to speak to him."

"Yes. He will talk when you . . . do your thing."

"My thing?"

"You know . . . The Wicked thing that works for people."

I wanted to laugh, but my expression remained blank as I said, "There is no such thing as *The Wicked thing*."

He sighed. "I think you should show your face once, so he knows we mean business."

"I'm sure he knows we mean business. The team chopped off his fingers. Cruel. Impressive. But I have work to do. We should be traveling to Turin in a few days for the dinner—"

"We still have time for that. This is important."

I suppressed the urge to groan, doing away with my unseriousness. "I know it is important." I stopped to think, my brain issuing me ugly ideas. "He should be taken to the hot room. Open his wounds, and leave him there for an hour; I'll visit him afterward."

"Okay." He moved towards the door, eyeing me . . . "I can leave you alone, right?"

"Hm."

He stood there, staring at me like he needed another confirmation. When the silence dragged on, I sighed, motioning to the door.

"Get the fuck out, Casmiro."

"Right." He cleared his throat. "See you in an hour."

And then he was gone.

I shook my head, returning to my desk drawer to take out the phone box. Without a second thought, I opened it, turned it on, and spent the next few minutes setting it up. Some things took a few minutes for me to get used to, but I quickly mastered it.

I saved Angelo's number, followed by Casmiro's and Gemma's, before clicking on the messaging icon next to her name.

The screen switched to a blank message space.

I hesitated, knowing it had been almost a month since she had given me her number. I didn't want to give the wrong impression by proceeding to use the number, but she had been kind to me, oblivious of my world—from what I could tell, she didn't care if I was covered in blood. It was strange.

But I was inquisitive; it took quite a lot for another human to have me *curious*. It was effortless with Zahra because I became a completely different person when it came to her. But with Gemma, I simply wondered why she had chosen to ignore my bad and focus on the good she could see, the good I seemed to have.

Why haven't I forgotten our encounter? What is there?

I was not one to ignore something my mind refused to forget, and my gut feeling had never once led me astray, so . . .

> **Me:**
> **Hello.**

I stared at the phone screen, wondering briefly if she would respond.

If I had gotten a text like this, I would probably have ignored it. Upon getting this phone, I informed the people with my contact info that they could only call the number for significant emergencies. *Not* for emergencies.

No texting.

The phone vibrated in my grip.

> *Gemma (blonde car highway):*
> Hi? Who is this?

My fingers drummed on the table as I read the message.

Why am I hesitating? I have no reason to hesitate.

I admit that I subconsciously and physically made sure I cleared up the incident on the roof with Zahra. In fact, I'd had three weeks to think.

This was lust, pure carnal lust I had no way of getting rid of, but I shouldn't dwell on it because each time I allowed my mind to wander in that direction, I forgot the crucial detail of her involvement with my brother.

She did say they weren't in a relationship. But they were involved.

The act on that rooftop weeks ago went against every set rule I had in place for myself. It felt even worse knowing I had grown oddly fond of her in a way, a fondness that allowed the feeling of care to creep in. My phone vibrated multiple times.

> *Gemma (blonde car highway):*
> Uncle Rod?
> If it's you, again, I told you I'd pay you

back. Gran Louisa is my priority now; she
still thinks she will die soon.
AND FOR THE LAST TIME.
I DID NOT USE THE MONEY TO GET THE
CAR.
Don't believe everything Luigi tells you.
He's out for my life.
I swear I will kill that little shit!

I waited for the next message to pop in, but nothing came after her spamming, so I typed a response.

Me:
Why is Luigi out for your life?

Her message came instantly.

Gemma (blonde car highway):
BECAUSE!!
I'm poor and still managed to do better
than him. I even have a car *smirking
emoji*
Granted, I stole it from my last relationship.
Remember Giacomo? The stripper you
disapproved of? Yeah, he owns the car, and
he's never getting it back.
Luigi would never be successful enough to
get it, so he's out for my life.

Me:
Do you want Luigi dead?

The bubble popped up immediately, but then it disappeared. It did that a couple of times before a response finally came.

Gemma (blonde car highway):
You're not Uncle Rod, are you?

Me:
No.

Gemma (blonde car highway):
Are you Giacomo?
Serial killer guy?
OR FUCKING LUIGI.

I was amused by the capital letters; I could hear her voice yelling the words at me. It reminded me of my sister.

Me:
It's Elio.

The bubble disappeared and appeared several times, and then it disappeared for minutes; I didn't think she would respond until she did.

Gemma (blonde car highway):
I'm just gonna sidestep my embarrassment with everything I typed and pretend I'm the cool blonde who gave you her number at a drugstore.
You can just block me now if your image of me is ruined. I'll accept that.

Me:
I have no intention of blocking you, Gemma.

Gemma (blonde car highway):
Honestly, I would block me.

My eyes flitted to the time above the screen before I typed in my response.

> **Me:**
> **I have to go. I will pick this up when I return. Luigi sounds like an exciting topic of conversation.**

Gemma (blonde car highway):
The little shit is the bane of my existence.
Where do you have to go . . .
Does this involve torturing your victims?

> **Me:**
> **Something like that. Speak soon.**

I exited the messaging app, slipped the phone into my pocket, and left for the hot room.

Casmiro and Angelo, alongside three other soldiers from my torture team, stood inside the room. I didn't acknowledge any of them as I entered. My attention was trained solely on the person I wanted to question.

When I stepped forward, every man in the room, including Casmiro and Angelo, straightened while discreetly inching back even though they were already standing at a convenient distance.

The artist sat in a mid-back iron chair with his back bending in a way that made him look more uncomfortable; his hands were strapped to each arm of the chair. No fingers. Cuts here and there on his arm. Although the wounds were treated and covered, I could still smell burning flesh.

I bottled my irritation, reaching the man, who was breathing heavily, head cast downward, clothes bloodied and dirty.

I admired his strong will. Anyone else would have killed him at this point, registering that he knew nothing and could give no useful information.

But I'd brought him here based on a gut feeling. He wasn't leaving until I got my answer.

"Look up." I spoke into the stale air.

His shoulders stopped moving. His breathing ceased for a second before it grew more frantic. His head snapped up, and red-rimmed brown eyes coated in fear stared at me.

"Handling you is already inconvenient, and I wouldn't like to waste even more of my time because I have a conversation to finish in about"—I looked at my wristwatch—"thirty minutes. So, I will ask the question, and you will answer me. Not with a lie. Not with a half-truth and not with a dismissal. If you do any of these three things, you will lose more than your fingers."

His chapped lips pressed into a thin line, determination in his eyes.

He was going to do one of the options I listed.

"What's his first name?" I asked no one in particular without taking my eyes off him.

"Fio," Angelo answered.

"Fio," I repeated, "it will be in your best interest to cooperate with me."

"I know nothing, and even if I do, and I do tell you, you will kill me either way. I know who you are."

"It is good that you do. That's why you will not waste my time."

"My response remains the same. Mr. Garza wanted me to paint the damn chihuahua, and I painted the damn chihuahua. The rest were printed fakes."

"Yet, millions of US dollars went into your bank account after you painted the original."

"It was valuable."

I nodded. "It was. I have spoken once with Arturo Garza. And just like me, he's a strategic businessman. He wouldn't make you set for life with a huge amount of money for one original painting. Not when each painting has the same intricate brushstrokes and the distinct smell of dried paint and . . . pine wood."

He swallowed, panic working its way to his eyes as I continued.

"You disappeared for months. Into a very convenient safe house a few states outside of Mexico City; the said safe house was made out of the pine woods surrounding the area. Am I correct?"

"I don't know what you're talking about."

"Strike one. Dismissal," I announced, straightening. "The safe house I speak of was registered in Arturo's name. I believe that is where you decided to paint?"

Fio let out a shaky breath. "Yes, Mr. Garza had given me that safe house. He didn't want me in the city while I worked on the original painting—"

"Strike two. Half-truth. You'd already painted the original. Arturo gave you that safe house so you could paint the duplicates of the original, am I correct?"

He hesitated, shifting slightly on the chair as he shook his head. "No, you are not. The duplicates were printed."

"Strike three. Lies."

He swallowed. "I know fucking nothing, I swear to you. When Mr. Garza gave me that project, my life changed, and I—"

"I will care about your life's achievement when pigs grow wings and litter the sky."

He clamped his mouth shut.

"I warned you about wasting my time. Apparently, you are one of those who gets curious to see what I will do next. You might think since your fingers and source of livelihood are gone, there's nothing else we can take."

"I have no family you can hunt down. I have nothing. You might as well kill me."

I watched him for almost a minute, and he squirmed under my stare, discomfort straining his posture.

I brought one hand from my pocket, rubbing my jaw as I

looked away from the man to everyone else in the room, watching the scene with curiosity, also wondering what I would do next.

I looked back at the artist. "Last chance, Fio. I insist you tell me what you know about the original painting. What is the tell? What would make finding it easier?"

"Like I said, I know nothing."

The silence grew—one minute.

Two.

Three.

Four . . .

Well . . . I warned.

I bent to his level; both my hands covered his wrists on the arms of the chair as I looked him dead in the eye. "Do you want to hear a story, Fio?"

He swallowed, the sound spelling fear.

"About an artist. He *was* an orphan, drew little sketches of people in the streets of Paris, wore rags for clothes, but had a brown hat given to him by a respectable sailor after a wonderful sketch he made of him. The artist was so happy. He wore it daily; even when he went to sleep, he would hug it to his chest, his first achievement."

Fio's eyes grew wide in horror.

"That little hat seemed to have given him so much hope, and then he started sketching for coins. People would stop by in his open corner, dropping coins for a sketch—couples, families, tourists . . . He felt like he had found a calling. It made him save up. He then bought watercolors and brushes and started adding colors to people's clothes in his drawings. He gave them smiles that reached their eyes, even when the smiles didn't."

Fio's lips parted, breathing noisily.

"He made so much money, grew up, and traveled to Mexico. He got a part-time job at an antique store and changed his name from Yves to Fio so that he could blend in. The owner of the antique store never paid him a dime, but the basement beneath the store was spacious and had an aesthetic feel; he *loved* painting there. Made a couple of thousand dollars through online ordering and delivering."

Fio shook his head slowly, tears gathering in his eyes.

"Through that means, he met a beautiful woman, Sofia. She *was* also an artist, but she was more into digital art. They fell madly in love. She had red hair and the most dashing smile he had ever seen. They met physically on a sunny summer morning, and her beauty enchanted him; he couldn't stop smiling at her. She became his muse, and he painted a beautiful portrait of her, which caught the eye of many collectors. Eventually, they got married."

"No." His voice trembled.

"Oh yes, they did."

"No, please." His breathing shuddered, and his tears dropped.

"It was a small wedding. Only four attendees. But it was the most important day of their lives; they would finally live their dreams and grow old together as man and wife."

"Stop—"

"Fio got an amazing offer worth millions of dollars about a year later. It was so huge that he got a lovely bottle of wine to celebrate this good news. Sofia was his biggest supporter; together, they took a renewed honeymoon to a little cabin outside Mexico City."

"Stop, please . . ."

"The air was fresher, the smell of pine wood and raw earth, the sheer luxury of peace and freedom. It was the best time of Fio's life. After six months, he finished the job and returned, receiving extra money for his efficiency. Fio was indeed set for life."

"I will tell you all you need to know . . . just don't finish the story."

I ignored him. "Years later, his wife gets pregnant."

His shoulders shook with sobs.

"Unfortunately, she was only six months in when he got kidnapped."

"Ask me any question; I'll give you your answer."

"He was kept in the hands of terrible men, tortured every day, his fingers were chopped off, and he knows he'll probably never be able to hold a brush to paint ever again, so he decides to be stubborn. To take the truth to his grave."

"Jesus Christ, I beg of you. There's a tell, okay! There's a fucking tell in the original painting!"

"He tried to tell the truth when the bad guys told him a story of himself, but it was too late. He shouldn't have been stubborn. The bad guys didn't have time for a story, you see, but he made them tell it anyway. So, they got very annoyed. Irritated . . . And they brought in his pregnant wife."

The sound of the door opening had him jolting. Soft whimpers and footsteps reached my ear, and I didn't have to look to see the red-haired pregnant woman by the side of the room, next to probably a stunned Casmiro and Angelo.

I couldn't care less about what they were thinking because my eyes were solely on Fio, whose body started to thrash at the sight of his blindfolded wife.

"Sofia!" he yelled.

A sob racked out of the woman. "F-Fio?"

"When Fio caught sight of his crying wife, he yelled her name, so loud, so fierce the bad guys felt it right in their guts, and when sweet Sofia responded with a stutter, they wanted to feel pity, but then they remembered they had given Fio a chance to talk, and he didn't."

"For the love of God, she's pregnant; she has nothing to do with this. We have nothing to do with your search; I'm just an ordinary artist who got paid for a fucking job—please—please just let her go," he cried.

"Then Fio tried to bargain and make the bad guys see reason. To let his pregnant wife go, but no one said this was a romance story or a happily ever after . . ."

A shiver of fear ran through Fio's body. "Th-there's a little white s-stroke underneath the eye of the chihuahua in every fake. It is absent in the original. Mr. Garza sent out ninety-nine of those paintings after I had them delivered. The original—the original was only with me until I painted the first duplicate. I don't know, but I think he hid the original himself; he went on a trip outside of Mexico, I don't know where, but I bet that trip was to find a perfect s-spot to hide the original. Maybe at a family landmark, I have no fucking idea—but I swear—I swear this is all I know."

"Fio, in a state of panic, told the bad guys all he knew about the painting, and since the bad guys had gotten all they needed from him, they decided to let him go . . ." I let a pause ring through, and I could feel every breath in the room pause with my last statement. "But then, the bad guys thought, if we let him and his pregnant wife go, what would happen if someone else got to them?"

"No, please." Fio choked out a cry at the same time Sofia let out a sob.

"The bad guys took pity on pregnant Sofia and removed her blindfold so she could see her husband alive one last time." I didn't look to see if the blindfold had come off, but the gasp from Sofia and the loud crying that followed told me it had.

"Fio . . . amore . . . p-please, sir—don't hurt him; he hasn't done anything. He hasn't hurt anyone in his life—he hasn't caused any trouble; he's innocent, sir."

"Sofia tried to beg the bad guys, tried to save her husband, but the bad guys knew it wouldn't be possible. If Fio could break so easily, someone else might do even worse, and he'd spill the truth to that someone else, and the bad guys couldn't have that, so they decided . . ."

I turned my gaze from Fio for the first time, looking at Angelo, whose eyes showed wariness, and then Casmiro, who looked uncertain, but remained firm in support of every decision I'd made, no matter how cruel.

I looked back at Fio, whose eyes remained pleadingly on me.

"I beg you, do whatever you want with me, but please let her go, ple—please."

"Fio begged." I raised my hands from his wrists, placing them on both sides of his face. "His eyes, once hopeful for a bright future, his eyes that had shined in happiness after he received that hat on the streets of Paris, now flowed with tears, knowing the very thing he loved the most was now the one thing that would put him under."

Sofia's heart-wrenching cry met my ears.

"It was so sad a scene. Too . . . emotional for the bad guys to spend even a second in the room, knowing how it would all end. They decided to snap the neck of Fio, and they probably should have asked Sofia to look away. Still, the bad guys were so bad that they derived pleasure from the scream the wife gave afterward . . . They knew they would derive even more pleasure when they buried her six feet under . . . alive with her husband." My eyes searched his as my grip tightened on both sides of his face. "A very tragic end to a beautiful story."

The room went quiet.

"Did you like my story, Fio?"

"No, no . . . I want to hear more," he rushed out.

I pressed my lips together, shaking my head. "Unfortunately . . . that was the end."

"Please, n—"

I twisted his neck in a sickening snap.

The wailing-like scream from his wife pierced the air, almost making me deaf.

I withdrew my hand from his head, and it fell lifelessly at an odd angle.

And like that, Fio died.

I rose to my full height, turning to see Sofia holding her stomach as she cried, her face scrunched up in pain as her body shook, crying out her husband's name.

Angelo brushed past, beelining for the door, looking like someone who wanted to throw up.

When I looked at Casmiro, his jaw was clenched tight. His eyes weren't on me; they were on Fio.

Of course they were on Fio. He'd just witnessed his life from start to finish.

I could have just killed him. I didn't have to make anyone *know* him before I did. I didn't have to make them care . . . I didn't have to make Fio relive his life and see his death before it happened.

I didn't have to make his wife watch.

But I did.

Why?

Because I am sick in the head.

Because I'm The Wicked.

Because I . . . I liked it.

My hands shook. I balled them into fists before releasing and shoving them into my pockets.

The cries from Sofia attached themselves to my brain, resounding in echoes.

I stepped closer to her and ground my teeth as I said, "Shut up."

She didn't seem to hear.

"Shut. Up," I repeated, and she snapped upright, pressing her lips together to try to stifle her cry. Her body shook, tears streaming down her face as she held her stomach, body tight with withheld tears, eyes unable to meet mine.

I turned to Casmiro.

"See to it that she's taken care of," I stated, making him look up at me with guarded eyes.

"Taken care of . . ." Something like hope lingered in his voice.

"Six feet under. Alive with her husband."

"No . . . ¡por favor!" Sofia cried out, hand grasping my arm. "I don't care what you do to me, but let—please! Please let me have my baby first. She's innocent. Please, sir."

My gaze settled on her hand on my arm before I slowly looked back at her. "Get . . . your hands off me."

She drew back in fear, almost stumbling, but Casmiro held her upright.

Tears streamed down her face as she clasped her palms tightly under her chin in a praying posture. "Let her live, please; she doesn't—she doesn't know anything about the painting; she's not even born yet, sir." Her lips trembled. "When—when she's born—you can take me—kill me, butcher me, I don't—I don't care at all, but just—let her live, sir, please."

My gaze flickered to her stomach, then back to her tear-stricken face.

I dusted where she had touched me on my suit, gathering my composure as my gaze briefly flickered to Casmiro, whose expression resembled a plea.

"... *Grief is normal. You can't stop people from feeling it by killing them.*"

I glanced at the other soldiers in the room before looking back at Sofia.

"... *You're stopping them from a future they could have had. A life. Maybe even better than the one we have.*"

I tried blocking out her voice.

I was suffocating.

I loosened my tie, trying to free its hold around my neck. "Then"—my gaze flickered to Casmiro, silently telling him to do the exact opposite of what I'd ordered, and then back to Sofia—"take the easy way out, Sofia."

Her eyes widened as she looked up at Casmiro, then at me.

The air was suffocating me.

I looked away from the crying woman. "You know what to do, Cas." He nodded in understanding. Then I turned and motioned at the other soldiers. "Clean up the mess."

With that, I was out of the room, taking a lungful of clear oxygen, but it wasn't enough.

Go back in there. Finish the job.

I brushed past men who cleared the way for me.

You're making a mistake, boy; she will come back for you. Finish the damn job.

I chased the entrance like I chased death.

Go back now, Marino, yo—

I got out of the building, letting out a gasp of breath.

Releasing my shaky hands from my pockets, I flexed my fingers, walking towards my house in the compound with a fast-thumping heart.

I looked up when I rounded a corner and halted at the sight before me.

Zahra was there, wearing a black dress, pacing back and forth and glaring at the soldiers standing in front of my building.

She did a double take in my direction, almost folding over in relief.

"Thank fucking Jesus." She looked back at the guards. "Please give me permission to kill these motherfuckers. I've been standing here for almost an hour, and I don't think Street bought my 'need to relax, headache' story." She looked back at me. "And I bet one of them is planning to burst into my room to find arranged pillows on the—" She stopped midway, her gaze searching my face as her eyes slowly widened in concern. "What's wrong?" She advanced towards me.

But I met her halfway before she could reach me, taking her hand in mine.

"You're coming with me." I pulled her towards my house, right past the guards and into my space.

CHAPTER THIRTY-THREE

Elio

For a woman with a sharp mouth and a bold personality, her hand was small against mine, warm and soft, addicting to touch.

You would think her palm, which I was certain had held a gun one too many times, would be calloused, but it felt the same as the first time I'd held it—soft, warm, and delicate. I wanted to sever my hand; I wanted to sever that small connection, but I did the complete opposite; my grip tightened, and I led us towards my room without pause.

What was I doing? Why was I doing this? What was the purpose of taking her with me? My mind could not fathom an answer; all I knew was that she had to undo whatever mutilation she had summoned into my mind.

"Will you fucking slow down?" she gasped, practically running after me. I didn't care.

An infinitesimal part of my senses was actively trying very hard not to acknowledge the fact that she was in a dress that hugged her body like a second skin; curves I had once noticed were now accentuated to drive home my attraction towards her.

I pulled her past the passageway, down to the last room on the left.

I'd never brought anyone here.

Casmiro never came here; if he ever was in the house, his destination was my lounge area and study, never my room. Angelo, though, my ever-loving shadow, dropped by my room once in a while to check if I was still breathing.

Letting Zahra cross into this space when I still knew nothing about her was by far the most careless thing I'd ever done. But then again, my reasoning barely functioned when it came to her.

I was either too blinded by anger to see reason, too taken by curiosity to see what lay behind her eyes, too irked by irritation to see past her behavior, or too driven to comprehend the other things I had just mentioned.

She caused this. She would solve it.

I pushed open the door to the room, locked it behind me, and then let go of her hand before finally looking at her.

Wide eyes shone with annoyance and somehow looked brighter than usual. I could tell it had something to do with the dark straight line across her eye—makeup, she was wearing makeup.

"What is the matter with you?" she asked, looking from me to peer around the space.

"Stay here, and don't move," I told her, making my way to the bathroom while I shrugged off my suit jacket, hanging it carefully before I entered, closed the door behind me, and headed straight for the sink.

My hands still shook when I opened the mirror compartment and picked up the small bronze bottle filled with pills. I uncapped it, filtered four atop my palm, and threw them into my mouth, swallowing dry.

They were tasteless—or maybe I was just used to it.

I covered the case, putting it back and closing the hidden cabinet, coming face-to-face with my reflection.

I held both sides of the sink tight, eyes on my reflection as I began inhaling and exhaling—

Sofia's scream pierced my head suddenly. I winced and pressed my eyelids together before opening them, trying to blink my thoughts back in order as I shook my head sharply.

I let her live.

I shouldn't have.

It was unfinished business, and I hated it. It made me feel

incomplete. I knew I would suffer for it; I knew the voices would triple in number.

In my dictionary, there was no such thing as right or wrong. There had been once, but my life hadn't been fair, so why should I be fair? Why should I understand something no one had cared to understand when it came to me? Why should I do the right thing?

What exactly *was* the right thing?

Letting her suffer for the rest of her life, raising a baby alone without a father? Or ending her suffering before it even began?

Why does it seem like I have just made a colossal mistake?

My breathing wasn't calming. I was getting angrier by the second, my mind was getting sharper, and the pills were doing absolutely nothing.

Had Zahra's voice not entered my mind at that very moment—I would have moved on with my day. Had Zahra not entered my life *at all,* I wouldn't remember what it felt like to be guilty; all these unwanted, weak emotions and thoughts wouldn't be singing a fucking elegy in my head.

I wouldn't be a torment to myself. My skin wouldn't feel like that of a stranger's. I wouldn't want to peel it off or get out of myself or my body. I wouldn't—

I swung my hand, knocking off all the items on the counter; they fell with sharp clashes.

Jittery, I exited the bathroom, my gaze finding Zahra's wary one from where she stood in front of a dressing table.

Her lips parted like she wanted to say something, but I was already walking towards her with a glare that I couldn't even hide or morph into indifference.

"Elio—"

Her words ceased when I caged her with my body, locking her against the dressing table with one hand on either side.

I caught the sound of her breath hitching in her throat with a small gasp. "Whatever you think I've done—"

"Fix this," I cut her off, my skin sucking in the warmth from her body.

She blinked, her brows dropping in genuine confusion. "What are you talking about? Fix—fix what?" I hated and loved the concern in her voice.

"Fix this!" My voice shook with withheld anger, and then I said between my teeth, "Fix me."

Her chest heaved, and her frown deepened. "I don't—"

"Don't fucking feign innocence right now, Zahra. You know what you did."

"What did I do?"

I drew in a shaky breath, leaning away from her, from the damning sweet smell of her hair and skin, from the familiar tightness in my chest that grew from the fondness of seeing her face and hearing her voice.

I brushed my hair back with a sharp, painful tug as I looked away from her.

"You have ruined my mind."

"What—"

"Three weeks, Zahra." I looked back at her. "I have not been myself for three weeks, and I don't understand why because, believe it or not, I truly *really* want to see you dead. I don't like you, I don't like you as a person; you have all the qualities that I despise in a woman and a person, you have qualities that mirror who I am, and I don't want to be near it, I don't want to want it, but—you did something to me. Somewhere between when we were being chased by the Russians and now, you did something to me; I know it."

"I didn't do anything to you; what are you talking about?"

"You are messing with my head!" I yelled. "I can't—I can't focus on anything; I can't think properly because all I fucking see, think, and breathe is the thought of you for no goddamn reason, so fucking fix it!"

"Elio—"

"I am spiraling, Zahra. For the first time in my life, I am questioning my actions, I am seeking morals I have never once cared for, and it's all because of you. I might have just made a mistake because of your voice in my head, so take it away. Now."

She didn't speak for a long time, like she was trying to assess my situation in her head and come up with a solution.

After a while, she stood straighter. "Okay, breathe—"

"I am breathing."

"I know, I just need you to calm down—"

"I am calm," I snapped, knowing I was a long distance away from calm.

"What mistake were you talking about?" she asked carefully.

I bit the inside of my mouth, taking three steps backward before I turned and started to pace, trying to center my mind and my thoughts, wondering why every fiber of my being thought it was okay to confide in her or let her see this side of me. We weren't friends, or were we?

"Elio—"

"I let someone live." I dug my thumb into the palm of my other hand, trying to stop the shaking as I glanced at her, seeing her confused expression. "She's pregnant, and I ruined her life and let her live. She should be dead."

"Who are you talking—"

"The artist's wife, Sofia."

"What artist?"

"The one who painted the chihuahua. Damn it, Zahra, keep up with me."

"I don't know what you're talking about; I'm trying to understand you!" she yelled in frustration.

My attention drew back to her when she let out a sigh. I watched her eyes grow unfocused before she outstretched her hand towards the bed. *"Let's sit and talk,"* she said in Spanish. *"Your pacing is not helping your case."*

"It helps me get my thoughts in order," I responded in the language.

"Well, sitting helps me sometimes, so we're going to do what I want because I don't think you're in the right state of mind to think," she

continued, her tone curling softly around her accent, and I succumbed, settling on the edge of the bed while she took the space beside me.

"So, you didn't hurt her; what would you have gained if you had hurt her?"

"Peace."

I could feel her stare on the side of my face as she asked, "Are you certain?"

I dug my thumb even deeper into my palm, but my fingers still shook; the veins on my hand were so visible, and my fingers grew so cold.

"Are you certain that's what you would have felt afterward?"

I dropped my brows in a frown. "I don't know."

Zahra's hand covered mine, eradicating the vacant cold and replacing it with a warmth that stopped the shaking instantly. "Elio, did you want to hurt them? The artist and his wife?"

My head turned towards her, and our gazes locked as I answered, "Yes."

"Because you thought you had to?"

"Because I wanted to. I killed her husband right in front of her. And I told him—I *warned* him not to dismiss my question or supply me with a half-truth or a lie, and he did just that. I didn't want it to come to that. I gave him a chance to survive, but he didn't take it; they never take it."

"Still, you didn't kill her—"

"I *wanted* to. I wanted her dead; I wanted her buried, I still do, because if it doesn't happen, I will lose my mind."

She removed my thumb from my palm and held my hand. "Why do you think you'll lose your mind?"

"Because I didn't finish the job, Zahra. I always finish the job, no matter how bloody or gruesome; I leave no stone unturned, my word is law, and if I go against it, I lose myself," I said, but it came out monotone, like a pledge.

She frowned. "Are you reciting that from a memory, or do you really mean it?"

I paused.

Her question sank in with a cold shiver tickling my neck and my feet, and for a second, *I was out of this room, this space, this time. And I was watching myself, strapped to a chair, my neck against cold metal; my eyes opened wide to be burned by the sharp blue ray of light that kept zooming in and out of focus, dropping me in a hypnotic state. A state that had me feeling numb in my feet, buried inside a large container of ice.*

"Repeat the word, soldier!" My commander's voice boomed in the echoing room.

"I always finish the job . . ."

My eyes, wide and unseeing, stared above as my mouth, thirsty and dry, forced itself to move, repeating after him. I didn't want to, but my mind wasn't my own anymore; somehow, he managed to control my vocal cords. It was violating, but I couldn't help myself.

"Louder, soldier!"

"I always finish the job . . ."

"Continue," he said like we had done this a thousand times before, and I would know the words.

Surprisingly, I continued talking. ". . . No matter how bloody or gruesome; I leave no stone unturned, my word is law, and if I go against it, I lose myself."

"Elio."

I blinked. Coming out of my head.

"Did you mean that?" she said, concern and question in her eyes.

Goosebumps littered my skin at that flash of . . . memory?

"Elio—"

"I—I don't know." I shook my head, looking away from her. "Yes, I wanted to do it, but I didn't want to, *want* to do it because I don't think that's who I am—"

"Who are you?"

My grip tightened around her hand. "I don't know. I am a different person when I'm with Casmiro and Angelo; I am different when I'm with Elia; I am different when I'm with my soldiers and associates; I am different when I'm with normal people outside my world . . ." I looked at her. "I'm different when I'm with you."

Her eyes widened, and I caught her pupils dilating in reaction to my words.

She had captivating eyes.

I looked down at our hands together, my thumb absentmindedly stroking her knuckles. "There are so many versions of myself that I don't know which part of me is real anymore. I don't know who my name belongs to."

"I think your name belongs to the person before me, trying to find who he is."

"Hm."

My mind flashed to the memory I had somehow seemed to have forgotten. The man questioning me had been in uniform, which meant it was from my time in the army. Did I make up that memory, or did it . . . happen? Why had I forgotten it if it happened?

My father had sent me there after I was diagnosed with what my mother had . . . He said he was going to fix me . . . Did he have them do something to me?

"Where's your mind?" she asked in Spanish.

I met her gaze. *"Nowhere,"* I lied, then frowned, my eyes searching hers. "Why are you sitting here, willingly talking to me?"

"What?"

"Why do you care—" I stopped and reworded the question. "Do you care?"

She looked caught off guard by my question, and I watched her draw back from me, subtly taking her hand from mine, leaving it cold. I had the strongest urge to take her hand back, but I didn't want to cross a boundary or scare her away, so I just clasped my hands together instead.

Zahra swallowed. "I—I have a hero complex. I think. I'm not a monster; even though I do not like you, I won't leave you when you're clearly going through stuff you need to talk about."

"So . . . you care?"

"That's not care; that's me. I'll do it for anyone, even if it's a stranger on the fucking street." She looked uncomfortable, tucking her hair behind her ear as she added, "It's who I am."

I said nothing; I just sat there staring at her while she squirmed.

"I mean—you kind of did blame me for your state, and part of why I talked to you was because I didn't like you accusing me of your unstable state of mind."

"Oh, you are a huge part of the reason, Sport."

She opened her mouth to counter my statement but closed it again like she had forgotten what she wanted to say. I took the liberty to continue.

"From the moment you left that boardroom till now, I've been unable to stop thinking about you."

She sucked in a breath, looking away from me to stare ahead . . . it was faint, very faint, but I caught the slight flush in her cheeks before she turned.

"Jesus fucking Christ, why are you so blunt with your feelings," she muttered.

"I'm too old to beat around the bush."

She turned to me with a smug look that almost washed the flush from her cheeks, but I could still see the ghost of it.

"I thought you said thirty-three wasn't old?"

"I meant that I'm not a sixteen-year-old boy who would deny his feelings because of his pride."

"Well, I have learned that it's better to keep your feelings to yourself, or they will be used against you."

"That begs the question of why I saw you pacing outside my house like seeing me would break the barrier for whatever troubled you. Why did you come to me?"

Her lips thinned, pressed together like she was biting the inside of them.

I wanted to reach forward and use my thumb to stop her from worrying them . . . but that would make me want to kiss her—I wanted to kiss her—but unfortunately, that was never going to happen again, so I clasped my hands tighter, banishing the thoughts.

"You really want to know the reason I'm here?"

"You might as well state it now that you have my attention."

Her gaze flickered between my eyes, so guarded, so cautious about letting slip what she had wanted to tell me. I wondered what made her this way, locked in herself, beyond reach of anyone who wanted to reach.

"Fine. You—maybe haven't been the—the only one who's been a mess these past weeks. I've been screwing shit up for Street, and Dog is ready to rip my head apart. A few hours ago, we were at a brunch, and I completely forgot the fake name I had told the guy who was supposed to have information about the next painting, and I had to fake a faint to avoid it. It was a disaster because I can't fake a faint to save my life." She breathed. "The silver lining is that you were right; I think we need to talk about the—the incident on the rooftop."

"Incident?"

"I don't know, okay? Occurrence, situation—"

"You don't think it was a fucked-up night filled with raging hormones? Your words."

"I—" She sighed. "I wasn't in a good mood when I said all that. If we're going to be mutual—or friends or whatever—you should know that I say things I don't mean when I'm in a mood. And that day, I was in a mood."

"In a mood," I repeated.

"Yes, Elio, are you slow?"

I tilted my head, staring at her as I recalled when I'd asked her the same question in that car right before the chase.

I curled my lips into a smile that turned into a small half laugh as I looked away from her, shaking my head.

It was silent for three beats before she spoke up. "Did you just—did you just laugh?"

My smile died, and I turned to look at her again with a frown. "No."

"But I just—" She looked unsure. "Stop fucking with me."

"You are not making any sense," I said with the same stern look.

"I just heard you laugh, and you literally smiled. It was charming and beautiful, do it again."

"You are delusional."

"I am not," she said, uncertainty in her eyes. "God, you're so good at this shit."

"No, you're probably going crazy with all the drugs you take with your friend." I tilted my head slowly, watching her with a mock concerned frown. "Maybe you need help. You're hallucinating; I don't want a sick person looking for that painting. You'll drag the others down."

"Damn, you're good." She slapped my arm excitedly. "You're making me think *I'm* crazy. How the fuck do you do that? Teach me."

The urge to smile tugged at me, but I bit it back. "You're a case, Zahra."

I missed this.

She laughed. "Okay, back to the issue on ground," she said, angling her body to face mine. "We're both distracted. It's obvious there's something here"—she motioned between us—"something we don't want—"

"How do you know I don't want it?"

"You said you didn't like me—"

"I don't want to but—"

"Great, I don't like you too, but there's obvious physical attraction, and for us to get it out of our systems, I suggest we fuck it out and resume this animosity without compromise."

I jumbled her words in my head, imagining her beneath me, atop me, beside me, sweaty and undone. It was very shameless and odd for my mind to conjure such vivid images but—

"How can you suggest this when you're involved with my brother?"

"That's history. It ended recently . . ." She frowned before continuing. "Scratch that; it ended a long time ago. I just didn't know it—still, even if it does happen, between us—no one can find out. Devil can *never* find out; I made him a promise."

I raised a brow at her, moving closer until I could feel her breath on my face. I lowered the tone of my voice like it was a sin for a third party to listen in. "A promise you want to break with a man who has only ever broken promises when it comes to him; some friend you are."

She glared at me. "I don't want it, okay? But—I feel like if we cross this off, it'll disappear."

"I don't feel the same."

"So you don't want to fuck me?" she asked with a taunting smile.

My eyes roamed her face, down to the swell of her breasts caged inside that dress; an image of me taking it off filtered past my brain before I locked eyes with her again. "I do, but I also want to talk to you."

"You want to be friends . . ." she drawled. "Friends who fuck."

"No. Friends don't do that, but whatever definition you think suits our . . . *one-time compromise.*"

Lust stained her eyes. "You're still on my shit list, and I'm still going to kill you."

I nodded, unable to comprehend how I could manage an erection after literally breaking in front of this woman. "If you annoy me, I still won't hesitate to slit your throat."

Her gaze centered on my lips. "Good."

"Good," I responded.

She leaned in, aiming to kiss me, but I drew back. "No."

She frowned. "No?"

"Ground rules."

She rolled her eyes. "Jesus Christ, Elio, it's just sex, and no, I'm not saying we should do it now—" Her gaze dropped to my crotch, where I was sure she spotted my need for her. "Unless you want to." She looked back at me. "You're—"

"Not now, but I still want to set ground rules."

She sighed. "Right, fine, let's hear it."

"One: No kissing."

Her eyes widened. "What?"

"Two: It only happens once. No more. You don't touch me sexually without my permission."

"Yeah, but—"

"Three: You don't forget either of the first two."

"Why no kissing? We kissed on the rooftop, so—"

"For reasons best known to me, I don't want to."

Her gaze dropped to my lips longingly before she shook her head. "Fine," she said half-heartedly.

"Hm. Before then, I'd like you to accompany me to a business dinner in Turin."

"Why?"

"That . . . I don't know yet; I would like you there."

"And what do I tell Street?"

"You're a liar; I'm sure you can come up with something. Or you could tell them the truth. You're accompanying a friend you want to kill to a business dinner."

"I don't even know why I'm agreeing to this."

"Makes two of us," I lied.

Her eyes searched mine. "How are you feeling now?"

"Hard, uncomfortable."

"I meant about your . . . earlier state," she said cautiously.

"Oh . . ." I'd completely forgotten about my earlier state, and even with her reminder, I didn't feel the heaviness. "Better."

It was no secret that she had a negative effect on me. Still, the positive effects intrigued me: She brought me back from a raging ten to a calming zero, and I still couldn't remember how our conversation had slowly shifted from a serious discussion to this.

Then again, that was how it was with her.

I lost sense of my mind and surroundings; the feeling was new, and like every new feeling I got, I wanted to explore it.

CHAPTER THIRTY-FOUR

Zahra

"It doesn't make any sense."

I refrained from looking at Devil, who watched me pick up the small black glitter purse I'd snagged from Milk's collection. Something to go with the ankle-length black dress I wore with a slit that reached my mid-thigh.

"Are you totally sure about this?" Upper asked from his leaning position on my bedroom doorway. "What if he wants to take you somewhere it'll be easy to—I don't know—chop your bloody head off?"

I rolled my eyes, letting out a tired sigh. "You guys are like brothers I didn't ask for."

"There's nothing *brotherly* about this," Devil said, and the edge to his voice made me glance at him, spotting the scowl of disapproval on his face. "I don't like this, Z."

He had been in a shitty mood since I told them about the business dinner I was attending with Elio. While I had expected instant disapproval from all of them, Devil was beginning to get on my fucking nerves.

Also, maybe there was a small bite of guilt in my stomach every time he reminded me how terrible a person his brother was.

Fine, Elio was bad . . . he was terrible, but he was good company, most times; but if I presented my narrative about him to Devil, it would raise questions, so I did the next best thing; I agreed with him.

I pressed my lips together, checking my reflection one last time before I responded to him. "I don't like it either. But to study your enemy, you've got to get close to them."

"He already gave us a deal." Devil uncrossed his arms while leaning away from the wardrobe door. "We signed a contract. We don't need to cross their path any more than we already have. This whole dinner thing makes absolutely no sense. Why did you even agree to it? When did you two talk?"

Thankfully, Milk appeared in the doorway, brushing past Upper with a jewelry box in her hand. "This goes perfectly with the dress."

"Zahra," Devil's voice called, sharper this time.

I breathed out sharply and pinned him with a frown. "You know him more than anyone, Devil. You know what he's capable of, and you also know he is a man without morals, a man who doesn't honor loyalty. Do you think a piece of paper will guarantee our freedom out of here or the promise of a hundred million dollars, which, mind you, they just agreed to give us on a whim? No negotiation? I am going to make sure he sees us as business partners and not pawns on his chessboard."

"That's why you're leaving without any disguise? You want people in his political setting to see you both together? And then what? You accompany him to other business dinners?"

"I think Zahra's right," Milk said as she helped me put on the earrings and necklace. "It's not exactly safe to go anywhere with Marino, seeing as we don't know his intentions, but don't you think it's stupid to believe that when all this is over, and we find the gold and his flash drives, we'll be free to go? Just like that?"

"It never happens that way in movies," Upper supported. "The bad guys always find a way to fuck the good guys over. It's the bloody rule of heroes and villains. You ought to earn the villain's respect if you ever want them to trust you enough to let you go when all is said and done."

"Thank you, Upper," I said with a sigh of appreciation before my gaze settled on Devil, who still looked very uncomfortable. "It's going to be fine. I have my phone with me; Upper installed a tracking app earlier. If by chance the app stops working, I have Dog on speed dial."

Almost as if I had summoned him, Dog popped his head behind Upper. "I'd probably leave you to die. You should really stop calling me first when there's trouble. Also, Casmiro is out front waiting for you—and why the fuck is that purse shining?"

"Glitter, idiot," Milk muttered in annoyance. "You're good to go, Zahra."

"Thanks."

Because I knew Devil was still frowning and fuming with disapproval, I didn't say anything as I exited my room and the house. And, of course, they all followed behind me like ants.

I took in the car parked outside the building; Casmiro was leaning against it, a stern frown on his face as he waited.

Adorned in a gray fitted suit, with hair combed to perfection, he screamed dangerous wealth and annoyance. An emotion I was certain came from the fact that I was going on this trip with his boss, who hadn't come to fetch me himself.

Why did I think he would be the one standing here and not Casmiro?

I brushed the thought of Elio from my head and focused on the car. It was the same Lamborghini I had watched drown over a month ago.

Someone brushed past me, and I didn't have to look to know it was Upper.

"Holy bloody fucking shit, I thought you said it drowned!" Upper threw an accusatory glance at me.

We reached Casmiro, and I eyed the car and then him. "Yeah, it did. Did you get a new one, Cassie?"

Casmiro straightened his suit. "I don't see how that's any of—"

"Oh my God, please, can I touch it? Just one graze," Upper cut in with haste, staring with pleading wide eyes at Casmiro, who eyed him like this was the first time he was seeing him.

"This motherfucking princeling 'bout to get nuked," Dog snickered, earning an elbow blow from Milk.

I wanted to cut in when Casmiro did the honors by asking, "You like cars?"

"Are you joking, mate? I'm obsessed." He looked from Casmiro to the car. "This is—she's bloody beautiful," he gushed.

There were literal stars in Upper's eyes, and I watched Casmiro's gaze travel up and down the length of his body; it was subtle, but I caught it, and Upper probably did too because he was clearing his throat, taking a step back from the Lamborghini, cheeks turning bright red.

"Sorry," he said nervously. "I lose myself when I'm—when there's a beautiful car around me."

"That's no crime, Upper. Maybe you can take her for a spin when I get back from the airport."

Upper's jaw dropped. "What—seriously?"

It was slow, but I watched how amusement grew in Casmiro's eyes. I'd only ever seen him frown, so it was pretty strange . . . to see him lose some of his guard just because Upper wanted to touch his car.

"I admire people who admire cars," Casmiro said. "They are one of humanity's most phenomenal creations."

"Yes—it's—God, thank you, Casmiro."

"You can call me Cas," Casmiro said, his lips lifting to the side in a small decent smile.

Upper blinked at him. "Ye— Thank you, Cas."

And just like that, the rest of us standing here were background noise, and I took that short period to steal a glance at Devil, whose scowl had dropped as he watched the two of them, chest heaving slightly in what I could tell was withheld anger.

At the sight, I cleared my throat, and Upper flinched.

"We should get going."

From my periphery, Devil had already turned, making his way back to the house without a second glance our way. I made a mental note to check on him with a text later in the day.

A few minutes later, I was heading to the airport beside Casmiro.

His usual frown was now back on his face. I didn't like silence, and I didn't know why the man disliked me. I am very likable; at least, I like to think so.

"So—"

"Don't speak to me. We're almost at the airport; just shut up until we get there, and you get the fuck out of my car."

I wanted to leave him be. I did. But I was curious and had a thing for poking angry bears. And right now, Cassie right here was very fucking angry. "You seriously don't have to be so rude."

"How I decide to relate with you is my choice."

I shifted with a frown, genuinely curious. "Why do you dislike me so much?"

"What?"

"You're always rude to me. You look at me like I kicked your rabbit to death. You don't even know me."

He glanced my way briefly, ignoring me.

"I thought you were this way with everyone in Street, but you interacted kindly with Upper, so why are you unnecessarily rude to me."

"It's not unnecessary."

"Really? Pray tell, Cassie, what did I do to you?"

His jaw clenched and unclenched. "I don't trust you."

"Awesome, I don't exactly trust you either, but you don't see me being a raging bitch about it."

His grip tightened on the steering wheel like he wanted nothing more than to reach over, open my side door, and push me out.

"I'm usually not a *raging bitch* to people I don't know, but I just don't like you, Zahra. I think you're full of shit."

Or I could reach over, open his side door, and push him out.

He stopped at a red light, looking over at me. "I read people, and I'm pretty sure Marino is good at reading people too, but for some fucked-up reason, he's blinded when it comes to you."

"Or maybe he's just a kind person who doesn't judge."

"I'm not judging you, Zahra. It's something I see. You have

so many layers, so many secrets; your eyes are so insincere, even with Street. I don't trust you because I know you're hiding something. And whatever it is, it has to do with Manuel Conti."

I scoffed out a laugh, relaxing. "Seriously?"

"I'm not an idiot. Marino isn't an idiot either. So, I'd advise you to stop whatever shit trap you're trying to make him fall into; he's not a saint. He will figure you out if he hasn't already."

"Oh, Cassie, why are you looking for answers where there's no question? Manuel Conti used to be someone I worked for. What if I told you I was one of his housekeepers? I have scrubbed blood off wooden floors and stubborn rugs since I was sixteen—"

"I would ask you if I had *stupid* tattooed on my forehead," he said with a glare and turned his attention back to the road when the light turned green again. "Like I said, you are full of shit, and I'm going to figure you out."

I watched him for about a minute before looking ahead. "I wouldn't advise that, Casmiro."

The tension inside the car thickened as my thumb absentmindedly stroked my purse. "The person who said curiosity killed the cat wasn't delusional when he said it," I mused aloud.

He glanced at me, and I caught his stare without a smile or a frown as I said, "Stay out of my way, and I'll stay out of yours."

"Is that a threat?" he asked, looking back at the road.

"I have a job to do, Mr. Valerio. Find the gold, find your fucking flash drives, and then get the fuck out of Marino's compound. I despise compromise; that's why I'm giving you a subtle reminder that if you try to compromise my mission, I will not hesitate to retaliate."

"That sounds like a threat." There was a warning in his voice.

"Take it however you want to. If you have no intention of finding common ground as I have done with Marino, then I am happy to make you my enemy."

"The feeling is very mutual. I won't fall for your bullshit like everyone has, Zahra. I'm on to you, and when I find proof, I'll put you down myself."

I ground my teeth together as I looked ahead, biting my tongue to stop myself from saying anything more, but I was certain about one thing.

He might be a problem.

Angelo collected me the moment Casmiro dropped me off at the airport. Unlike Casmiro, Angelo had greeted me; even though it wasn't warm, it was something.

"Nice dress," he said, leading us to the private-plane area, three guards behind us as we walked into an elevator.

"Thanks. Do you think I'm overdressed? Or underdressed. I'm not really used to fancy gatherings without being someone else," I said, adjusting the dress as the elevator moved down.

Angelo glanced my way, giving me a subtle sweep. "Yeah, you're perfectly dressed. It's a business dinner that includes pompous men and their wives, girlfriends, or mistresses."

"Oh . . . makes me wonder why your boss wanted me there."

"Does it?" Angelo said, looking ahead. "I thought you shared an intimate relationship with him. The rooftop—"

"What did he say?" I rushed to ask.

"He didn't have to say anything," Angelo said, voice straight as he looked down at me. "But I'm watching you, Zahra. One wrong move against him, and you're out."

"Why the fuck does everyone seem to think I have some grand ulterior motive? Cassie almost chewed my head off in that car. Now you?"

"I have nothing against you, Zahra. All I care about is Marino. He doesn't do things like this, so it only means whatever you both have is serious to him. The other day I caught you leaving his house. I'd like to think whatever you both are doing isn't one-sided from his end. I will haunt you if you hurt him. That is not a threat but a fact."

I swallowed. "I have no intention of hurting him . . . unless it is completely necessary and I have to protect myself. Then yeah."

"You're in no position to make comments like that; it makes it hard to trust you."

"The last thing anybody should do is trust me, Angie. Besides, it wasn't a comment. Just a fact."

The elevator doors opened, and I walked out, spotting the plane right ahead, soldiers everywhere.

My heels clicked and echoed on the ground as I walked, and I could also hear Angelo's footsteps behind me.

Eyes were on me when I approached the private plane. Apparently, Elio Marino never took dates to events like these, and I was an exception because he loved my company.

Bullshit.

He was up to something.

Or maybe he does like my company?

I hate compromises, and that was one of the main reasons I was putting up with his weird idea of foreplay. I needed to get him out of my system. The fact that this wasn't me was the most daunting part.

I'd never outright wanted anyone's touch like I wanted Elio's. Devil was convenient, Manuel was necessary, and the selected few others were mainly by choice.

But Elio . . . God, he evoked what I could only name as pure desire, and yes, the feeling scared me.

A soldier led me inside the plane, which was minimal, very clean and private, like an en-suite lounge area with golden lights and white leather seats. It smelled divine and had a warm, cozy feel to it. I couldn't stop my eyes from roaming around the space as the man led me down a small compartment until he pushed open a door, and I was in an even more private room. It was the same design as the other area we had just come through, but the smell was different, familiar. And I soon registered why after seeing Elio's figure in the corner, an unlit cigar between his lips, book in hand, wearing a black men's turtleneck and black pants.

He didn't look up, even as the soldier announced my presence and left me alone with him.

I took the liberty of settling in the chair opposite him, appreciating the comfort of the leather and how appetizing the man sitting atop it was.

My God. He was handsome; it was so unfair. He had an engrossing aura, which was doing funny things to my stomach and the back of my spine.

"Zahra," he said in greeting, his eyes going over the page.

"Marino," I responded, and he looked up finally.

"Don't call . . ." He trailed off, eyes taking me in slowly before he completed his statement: ". . . me that."

"Okay, *Dad*."

His stare hardened, and he looked back at his book. "Stop," he muttered.

I smiled at him . . . genuinely. "Any reason your cigar isn't lit?"

"Still figuring out if I should light it."

"Right." My gaze dropped to a black device on the table. "I thought you said you didn't have a phone?"

"It's new," he said, discarding the cigar.

"Oh, what made you get one?" I made conversation because, yes, sue me, he might be infuriating and might end up at the end of my barrel when push came to shove, but I liked talking to him too.

Despite what Casmiro felt about me getting close to Elio, I knew something was there. If we did away with the inconvenient physical attraction, we could be friends . . . cordial, at least.

His gaze flickered to me and then to the phone.

I raised a brow at the conflict in his eyes, and then he closed the book, placing it beside the phone as he said, "Because almost everyone I know has one."

"Cool . . . want my number?" I asked.

His eyes took me in again, and he seemed confused. "What for?"

I shrugged. "I don't know, we could be text buddies since we're like—trying to be friends—"

What's wrong with my voice?

"Thank you, but I have no use for your number."

It was like someone had punched my chest in. "Ouch."

"I meant that politely. If I ever need it, I'll ask for it."

Forcing on a smile, I shifted uncomfortably. "Right," I said, looking out the side window, seeing everyone gearing up for the flight to take off.

His response had rattled me. I didn't know why it stung, but it did.

This was a sign. Maybe we were spending too much time together. Maybe I was in over my head thinking he actually did want me here because he liked my company, and wanted more than just the physical.

I mean I'm "just Zahra," and he's way above "just Zahra." He's more into Grace from the exhibit, not "just Zahra" from . . . the streets. I'm pretty sure he'd have use for her number.

God . . .

My eyes remained fixed on the window, watching the men going this way and that, making sure everything was intact because they were carrying someone important.

Elio. Not me.

Why did I agree to come to this again? And why am I suddenly missing my friends?

Maybe I should have come with a disguise, maybe I would have felt more confident with one . . . but I knew he had asked *me* to accompany him, not someone else. I was also maybe . . . eager to spend time with him.

Foolish Zahra.

But God . . . I was not supposed to like him or be *fond* of him. I should have noticed it whenever I had the powerful urge to defend Elio from Devil's trash-talking.

Elio was growing on me, and this was not because I really wanted to fuck him. No. This was something else.

"I feel like I've said something wrong." He voiced his concern, making me look back at him.

"What?"

"Your guard is up again. Is this because I don't want your phone number?"

I was transparent to this man, and it was dangerous.

"I'm a big girl; I'll get over it," I said with a tight smile I'd wanted to be carefree, but my mood wasn't shifting or lifting.

He sighed, picked up the phone from the table, and got to his feet.

For some unknown reason, my heart skipped a beat.

I often knew how to predict people, but I raised my guard for this man because he was the most unpredictable person I'd ever encountered.

He crossed the space between us and sat beside me, clouding my senses with his cologne. I couldn't think straight for a good minute.

"Here." He outstretched his phone to me. "Put in your number."

I blinked at him. "What?"

"Your number," he repeated.

"I thought you didn't want it?"

"I don't," he stated. "But apparently, that upset you, so if putting your number in would make you feel better, then here. We can be—" He clenched his jaw like he didn't want to say it but cleared his throat and completed, "Text buddies."

My eyes searched his and then dropped to the phone.

The normal Zahra would brush it off, raise her chin up, and never *ever* give him her number, but this Zahra, whoever the fuck she was, was collecting his phone and saving her number.

When I was done, I gave him the phone back, and his fingers tapped on the screen for a short moment. I briefly wondered what he was doing until my phone vibrated inside my purse.

I glanced at him, and he gestured with his chin towards the purse in my lap. I took my phone out swiftly and smiled when I saw a message from an unknown number. It was a simple "Hello." With a freaking full stop at the end of it.

"Happy?" he asked, making me look back at him, the color of his eyes causing me to hold my breath for a few seconds.

"You are weird," I told him.

"I know," he said, gaze flickering to my hair before his hand moved, and he grazed the ends softly with his fingers, feeling the texture but not overdoing it, as if he didn't want to scare me away. "I love what you did with your hair."

I couldn't look away from him, which made it hard to hide the evidence of the heat that rushed to my cheeks. "I—just brushed it."

"It's beautiful."

"What's your angle?" I asked.

His gaze seemed like he was drinking my face in.

"Elio."

"Hm?"

"What's your angle?" I asked in Spanish.

"I have no angle. You look outstanding. I like the dress too, and the purse. We're matching."

What the fuck?

"You wear black every day; I'm sure you match with tons of people in this world who wear black."

He shook his head. "No, it looks different when you wear it."

"Are you flirting with me?"

"I don't flirt. I tell."

"Right."

His attention remained solely on me; while it was unnerving, it felt good.

"So, anything I should prepare for with this dinner?"

"I do not think you need to prepare." His eyes looked between mine. "I have a gut feeling you know precisely what to do at events like these."

"So, you're trusting me based on a gut feeling?"

"Exactly."

There was a challenge in his eyes, and I knew if I tried to deny anything now, he would pick out my lie, so I let it be.

And minutes later, as the plane took off, I wondered briefly if Devil had been right.

Was I walking into a trap?

We had gotten to the business dinner quite fashionably late. The event center was large, with different wafts of expensive perfumes in the air, expensive menus, and an elite orchestra band at the far end of the table where Elio and I sat.

When we arrived earlier, Elio had headed straight to the mayor of Turin, and while I didn't pay attention to the conversation, I could tell the mayor held the man on my arm in high regard.

Elio had surprisingly introduced me as his friend, using my name. I didn't mind; I was prepared for this evening. I had also been getting looks from women around me. Some were mostly curious, and others judged with their eyes.

Elio might not have noticed or pretended not to, but he held me to his side with pride and asked Angelo to move around and mingle.

About an hour later, an announcement and speech were made. We were seated at a dinner table with the mayor, his wife and son, Angelo, a neighboring local mayor and his family, and some minister whose name I'd forgotten, along with his wife and daughter.

Elio had gone quiet beside me, but conversations passed freely around the table.

Bringing my wineglass to my lips, I looked around the large room where conversations, laughter, and clanking of forks to plates resounded in the air.

My gaze connected with a gruff-looking man at a far-off table; it stayed for two seconds before he looked away. I took a sip of my drink, glancing at the table two steps away from him; two men, one in a maroon suit and the other in a striped black-and-white one, turned my way before subtly looking away. I swallowed the wine, looking up to the railing where two men stood with drinks in hand, conversing before they glanced my way, and averted their gaze seconds after.

I returned my attention to my table, stopping short when I caught Angelo staring at me. The suspicion in his eyes was so evident that I couldn't help but curl up one side of my lips in a smirk while raising my glass to him before looking away to a tense Elio beside me.

His attention was not on the table, and when I followed his gaze, I found he was staring at a woman who sat at the table next to ours. She was laughing loudly at what someone at her table had said.

I frowned.

He was staring intently at her, which made me size her up. She was a gorgeous model-figure beauty, with a pretty feminine smile, long curly light brown hair that reached her back, and soft painted lips that could be considered charming, to say the least.

My frown deepened as I looked back at Elio, whose attention had utterly left the woman to another table.

I followed his gaze, and lo and behold, he was staring at another woman. This one was a platinum blonde, long hair straightened to perfection. She wore a strapless dress. She had a heart-shaped face and a Cupid's bow mouth. Minimal makeup. Really beautiful.

His fingers on the table drummed absentmindedly. My gaze dropped to his knee beside me; it was bouncing rapidly underneath the table.

He seemed so tense.

I looked back at him to see his gaze on yet another woman; this one had auburn hair pulled up in a ponytail, loose strands falling down her face as she smiled at the conversation going around their table.

I wasn't his girlfriend or anything, but fuck if I didn't want to bash his head on the table.

But it was also strange because Elio didn't seem like the kind of man to be this blatantly rude.

Subtly, I shifted my chair near his and placed my hand on his knee. "Hey."

The shaking stopped, and he turned to look at me, gray eyes locking with mine.

I ran my hand up his thigh. "Focus on me, will you?"

His gaze dropped to my hand on his thigh, and I noticed how he grew more tense upon my touch.

At that moment, the mayor called his attention with a question. He looked away from me and didn't say anything about my hand on his thigh under the table; he just conversed with the mayor with complete control in his voice.

My hand rubbed his thigh smoothly, my thumb brushing against the inner side, trying to calm his nerves . . . or . . . making it worse, because he wasn't getting calm. His body was growing more tense, and I had an inkling that he was hard, though his voice was steady as he spoke.

I almost cursed myself for the idea that crossed my mind, but my brain had stopped transporting reasonable thoughts to my hand as it moved further up his thigh under the table until my finger brushed against his crotch.

My stomach jumped with excitement when I felt his semi-hard-on.

I should stop.

I was going against his rules.

Rules? Pfft. I'd never been one to abide by them, and I sure as hell wouldn't start now.

So instead of stopping, I felt him up, rubbing against his erection, which grew harder by the second, thanks to the stimulation coming from my hand.

I could feel the defined outline of him, and I was grateful that his trench coat was long enough to shield any eyes from behind and in front of us.

The mayor asked him another question about something that had to do with a small town near Milan. Elio responded, voice still level, all attention on him, including mine.

I marveled at his level of control and decorum. The look on

his face didn't give away the fact that he was getting strokes from my hand underneath the table.

He went on to explain some talk that had to do with citizens' data.

My hand skillfully brushed the outline of his cock, squeezing a little as I gave one tight rub.

His breath hitched loudly—in fact, he stopped talking altogether, and our table went silent, waiting for him to continue while wondering what had happened.

Slowly, ever so slowly, his head turned towards me, and he placed me under his very calm stare as he said in Spanish, loud enough for everyone at the table to hear, *"Don't start what you can't finish."*

My eyes widened in surprise, and I felt my cheeks heat up as he turned back to the mayor, who looked between us with amused confusion; it was almost the same look everyone at the table threw at us.

I removed my hand quickly.

Elio continued what he was saying as if he hadn't just stopped the whole conversation to scold me.

I wasn't embarrassed. Fuck, I was turned on. *I've never been so turned on like I am right now.*

When the conversation shifted from Elio, he stayed for about six minutes before he excused himself to the bathroom, not before sending a pointed glare at me.

I bit the inside of my lip, waited for exactly three minutes after he left, and then I excused myself too, walking the same direction he had gone.

Was that subtle? No. Did half the table know I was going after him? Yes. Did I give a fuck about what they thought?

Hell.

Fucking.

No.

CHAPTER THIRTY-FIVE

Elio

I was thinking with my dick.

I never think with my dick. I never think or *use* the word *dick*. It was no consternation that I was gone. Too far gone into whatever fog the thought of Zahra brought to my head.

My thought process around the time I'd set those rules could be considered laughable at this very moment. Zahra Faizan wasn't a woman you could touch once and be satisfied. She was slow poison, sinking and slipping into your veins with an alluring sensation that could turn any active brain to mush.

Unfortunately, I'd fallen victim to this sensation.

When she entered the plane earlier, my mind had already predicted that she would come in disguise. I never thought she would arrive without one. It took me by surprise. I couldn't help but stare like I'd never seen a beautiful woman. God . . . from that moment, I knew I was done for. Her hair had been styled so beautifully. I relished the feeling of sinking my fingers into the mild curly waves, getting my fill of its fullness and softness, melting into the abyss of how beautiful it smelled, and then pulling until her neck craned and became mine to kiss, lick, and suck until I bruised her clear skin.

The flight had been spent with me fighting a battle with my mind, my brain, and my hand; and back there at that dinner table, I allowed Zahra to touch me, which was the most unprofessional I'd ever been.

Zahra had woven her webs so thick around the body of my mind. I couldn't help but compare every woman in there to the one by my side. It was absurd. I do not compare women. I do not spend time letting my thoughts control me, but apparently, my common sense had vacated.

I let her touch me.

I *wanted* her to touch me.

Back at that table, I knew nothing else but the warmth of her hand on my thigh.

That simple touch ignited a fire inside of me. One I couldn't control, one that had made me envision myself pulling her with me to a place where no one would catch a glimpse of her bare skin when I fucked that attitude right back to a place she'd never be able to reach.

These thoughts were very foreign. They had never once grazed my mind when it came to other women.

I thought I was mad, but Zahra Faizan was driving me to the brink of what absolute madness felt like.

Now I was hard, uncomfortable, and frustrated.

I pushed into the men's washroom. Thankfully, it was empty. I had to calm down, get my head in order, and hope for the erection Zahra had coaxed to settle.

I walked to the sinks and shrugged off my coat before placing it on the neighboring sink.

I knew exactly what to do to get myself back in control. The only massive turn-off I could ever get was the sight of myself.

Not the best method, but I needed to start thinking with my head and not my—

The door opened, drawing my attention from the mirror to the last person I needed in my presence right now.

The witch wore a sly smile as she closed the door behind her and leaned on it, both hands behind her in an innocent pose, bottom lip tucked under her teeth.

I clenched my jaw; the sight of her tightened the knot in my chest, and the strain in my pants.

Control.

Control, Marino.

She released her bottom lip, drawing my attention to its flush redness.

"Hi there," she said with a taunting smile, her eyes flickering to my crotch and back to me. "Got anything I could help you with?"

"No. Get out."

Her smile drew up as she leaned away from the door, twirling left and right with hands behind her as she walked towards me.

"You don't really mean that," she said.

"Get out, Zahra; this is the men's washroom," I said, my eyes flickering to the door, knowing anyone could walk in at any second.

"I don't mind." She smiled.

"I mind," I gritted out.

Instead of leaving, she advanced towards me.

"Leave, Zah—"

She pressed her palm flat on my chest.

Her touch charged warmth down my stomach, straight to my cock. I wanted her to touch me. But not here . . . not here.

Her eyes were bright with lust, and seduction, embodied with a dark pull that made her pupils dilate. I was 100 percent positive I mirrored the desire on her face, but this wasn't—

Her hand ran down my chest, down to the hard ridges of my stomach. My muscles tensed against her purposeful exploration.

I swallowed.

"Leave, Zahra."

"No."

Her hand glided up from my stomach to my chest in defiance as she brushed past my shoulders, and then I felt her fingers smooth past the side of my face before burying themselves inside my hair.

I bit back the hum of relief from her soft touch against my scalp.

She massaged gently, eyes searching between mine. "Let me

kiss you." Her voice at this moment could be compared to that of a siren song, compelling men to do her bidding.

Control . . . control.

"No," I said.

Her gaze flickered to my lips as she pressed her body to mine. "But I want to."

"And I want you to leave."

"Do you?" she asked, her fingers tightening their hold on my hair; not too much, just enough to pull me down so that we breathed the same air. "Do you really, Elio?"

"Ye—yes."

Her eyes narrowed in amusement. "You don't sound so sure."

A strained noise rumbled from my chest, my control on the verge of slipping. "Why are you doing this?"

Her hold softened on my hair, her other hand trailing up my arm with her index finger. "Because, Elio, I want nothing more than to see you lose yourself in pleasure."

"Zahra—"

"I want to please you." She leaned up, bringing her lips to the underside of my ear. I first felt the warm wetness of her tongue before her lips closed around my skin, sucking on a kiss that sent shock waves down to my hard length, still locked inside the strain of my briefs.

I clenched my jaw hard.

"You're so tense," she whispered.

Her hand, which had been trailing up my arm, went back down as it disappeared between us. She rubbed against the bulge lining my pants before bringing her gaze to mine. "Let me help you." Her fingers moved up to my belt in an attempt to undo it.

I held the left side of her hip, a move I made to push her away from my body, but I found myself pulling her closer.

"No," I rasped.

"Give in, Elio."

"No."

I let her undo my belt buckle, her eyes still on me as she said, "You're so hard; let me fix it."

"You fucking caused it."

"I merely touched you; you got hard because your body clearly needs the relief." She unzipped me, and I groaned closed-mouthed when she palmed me, her sinful eyes peering up at me. "A relief only I can give."

She carefully rubbed me, and my forehead settled against hers, my breathing feverish. "You undo me, *Zahra*."

With hooded eyes and wet lips, she swallowed. "I like that."

"Anybody could walk in," I said.

"Even better. Imagine the mayor walking in and getting a show of me sucking your cock?"

That should have turned me off, but I grew rock solid against her touch.

Her eyes widened. "Oh shit, you like that, don't you? The thought of getting caught?" She grinned. "You big whore."

"You little slut."

She chuckled softly, the sound bouncing inside my chest. "Now, now, slut-shaming is bad."

"So it's okay when you do it?"

"Are you admitting you're a whore?"

"Zahra," I warned, and my breathing mirrored the pace at which my heart worked. "We shouldn't—"

"Come on, don't you love the thrill?"

Frustration stained my feelings red. "Fuck, Sport, this is unethical, it's risky, it's stupid—"

Her hand left the inside of my hair as she smirked. "Live a little."

And then she pushed me lightly until my back was against the sink, and she was going down to her knees, separating the slit on her dress for easy settlement; then the little witch smiled up at me from underneath her lashes.

Beyond sinful.

She looked back down; anticipation sizzled through me, but

I still managed to catch the slight tremor in her fingers as she moved.

I reached down, putting a finger under her chin and lifting it so she could look at me.

"You don't have to."

"I want to." She gulped, shaking her head. "No, I'm *dying* to. I've been dying to since that time in the woods when I suggested it," she said, and I let her be.

I felt her fingers on me, and then she let me out of my briefs.

I watched her take in my size, her lips parting as she looked up at me. "How do you have a pretty face and a fucking pretty—" She looked back down, and my breathing grew ragged as she held me. "Fuck me, you're—you're huge."

"You don't have to voice it. I am not blind."

I bit my tongue at the sensation of her soft palm trying to encircle me—it made the heat not enough, but at the same time, drove me to the edge.

"Not too late to turn back," I told her.

"You should know by now that I take everything as a challenge," she said breathily, the heat from her mouth bathing my hard length, and I wanted inside that mouth.

I'd never longed for anything more than the wet heat her mouth would provide to my cock.

She stroked me once, and then I caught her pink tongue strutting out of her mouth, licking from the base of my length to the tip, which leaked out pre-cum.

When was the last time I had relief or gratified myself sexually—I couldn't remember—but right now, I was a starved man, and I needed that relief she so wanted to give me.

She locked her gaze with mine as she spread the pre-cum against my shaft, seeking easier friction, and then she licked me, taking her time, teasing me.

My mind had shoved the thoughts of being caught to a place where it didn't bother me but made the act even more daring.

Her thumb brushed the slit at the head of my cock, and I

groaned, my hand smoothing her hair from the side of her face as I held it at the back of her head. I didn't pull.

"Is this okay?" I asked.

"Anything you do is okay," she said.

"I—"

She spat against the head of my cock, and her tongue and hand worked the lubrication around my shaft.

Edging me.

"We do not have time for foreplay, Zah—"

Her mouth covered me.

For a second, I forgot to breathe. My chest stopped heaving until I felt her twirl her tongue around the head of my cock, coaxing me deeper into her mouth.

A soft, breathy groan rumbled from my chest, and I parted my lips, letting the sound out.

I was throbbing so hard inside the wetness and delicate tightness of her mouth, my head was filled with equally sinful thoughts, like how badly I wanted to grip her hair and take control, fucking her mouth like it was my personal property.

Control.

I ground my teeth together, holding back.

Zahra took me deeper, her tongue giving me equal attention as she moved her head, stroking, sucking, and licking at the same goddamn time.

How the fuck is she so good—

I felt her soft grip at my base, and she squeezed lightly, removing her mouth from my cock, and looking up at me from underneath her lashes, lips swollen, eyes glassy with lust as she said, "Fuck my mouth."

"What?"

"Do it." She shifted closer to me, eager. "Please."

My grip tightened on her hair, and I tilted her head back to the angle I preferred. I moved my other hand, wrapping it around my length, stroking a few times while I angled the head against her lips.

"Open up for me."

The moment she let her lips part, I slid into her mouth, filling it up.

Fuck.

I lost control. My crazed habit took over. There was no stopping this now.

My fingers buried themselves into her hair, and I gripped and pulled her head further back.

And then, I fucked her mouth.

Pumping in mercilessly, past the limit where she had taken me before. I hit the back of her throat, still didn't bottom out, but the tightness hugging the head of my cock at her gag doubled my need for release.

Her choking and gurgling sounds as I tamed her mouth swarmed straight to my head, causing chaos in my chest and bringing haste to my movement.

"Fuck, Zahra." I caught her eyes tearing up at the force with which I used her mouth.

I was close. So fucking close.

Zahra held both my thighs to steady herself, and I wanted to savor this moment, record it in my head and never let it leave, but I knew we still had to go out there, and I'd already made a mess of her hair.

Oh fuck . . .

I had to take back control but damn it to hell and under—her mouth felt so good wrapped around my cock.

My need for release tightened to the edge.

"Ah—" I breathed out. "Swallow?"

She answered positively with a small throaty sound, and I thrust into her mouth a few more times before my movements turned sloppy. One of her hands left my thigh as she wrapped her hand at my base; the short stroke she gave had my release spurting into her mouth and down her throat as she swallowed.

My movement slowed, and I let her lick and suck the aftershocks out of me. I was still semi-hard and hated that we weren't in a more private area.

I wanted to bathe her face with my cum, revel in the fucking sight for sore eyes I knew she would be. But we couldn't be messy. Not here.

I slipped out of her mouth, letting go of my hold on her hair.

"I want more," she said, her tongue running over her glistening bottom lip as she watched me tuck myself back into decency again.

"Get up."

She did, wiping the corners of her eyes as she squirmed on her feet, most definitely due to the discomfort between her legs.

Her lips looked like I'd fucked the subtleness out of them; they were swollen, pink flushed, fucking kissable, and I wanted to do it, close the distance between us, taste my cum on her tongue—but I couldn't.

I hated that I couldn't.

So I pulled her by her waist, and her body fell against mine.

The piercings from her nipples pressed against my shirt, and my tongue ached to lick them back to softness.

I raised a hand to her hair, brushing the short length as I asked, "Are you okay? Did I hurt you?"

"Not in a bad way," she said.

"Hm." I arranged her hair as it was when she entered the washroom.

"You might not believe it," she said, and I dropped my gaze to hers, "but this was the first time I've let anyone near my mouth since I was fifteen. Just in case my skills were—"

"You were perfect," I countered immediately because, yes, she was. I'd never been so undone to the point that it affected my breathing. "I thought you said your first time was seventeen?" I asked, even though I knew it had been a lie.

She looked away from my face to my shoulder. "I lied," she said. "I was fourteen . . . my first time."

My hand froze on her hair; she noticed and quickly added to her previous statement.

"It was nothing. I barely remember it." She shrugged, but I knew she did remember. Her lie was transparent.

"Hm," I said in response.

Her gaze met mine again. "So . . . this no kissing thing. Can we just take it away?"

"No."

"Why?"

"I never go back on my words or my affirmations." I dropped my hand from her hair, trailing the naked skin on her exposed thigh. Unable to keep my hands off.

"But you do," she pointed out. "We just broke one of your rules."

"Which you will pay for." My hand moved.

A giddy look crossed her face. "Oooh, why do I like the sound of—" She gasped when my hand cupped the heat between her legs, my touch intense and possessive because it was precisely how I felt.

A glint of pride bloomed in my chest at how soaked and hot she was for me. I wanted nothing more than to make her pay for the interruption she had caused today, for the rules she had made me break.

Just as she had made me lose my damn mind a few minutes ago, I wanted her to lose hers too.

She sucked in her bottom lip to stop the soft hiss that had been about to escape.

"You don't know what you've signed up for, Querida."

Her eyes brightened as she released her lip. "I could say the same for you." She smiled. "As you said, we're alike in so many different ways. I want to unearth you as much as you want to do the same with me. It's what makes this fun."

"You shouldn't hoodwink yourself by thinking there is anything *fun* about this. It is incommodious at best."

"Incommo-what now?"

I took my hand off her, settling both on her waist before I hesitantly pushed her away from me.

"Inconvenient," I stated in much simpler terms.

Grabbing my trench coat, I brushed past her towards the door and slipped it back on, turning to face her.

"And . . . he's back." She took my previous position, leaning against the sink as wide lustful eyes roamed my body.

I eyed her. "I have a small house downtown. That's where we'll be settling tonight."

Her eyes spoke dirty thoughts as she watched my fingers fasten two buttons of my trench coat.

"Sport."

"Yeah?" Her gaze snapped to mine.

"Did you hear what I said?"

"Honestly, no. Your fingers are—distracting. Why are they distracting?"

By habit, I shoved both hands into the pockets of the coat. "I said I have a small house downtown, and we'll settle there tonight."

"Small house?"

"Yes. Angelo will be at his mother's, and by the morning, we'll be back on a flight to Milan," I informed.

Hopefully, an enclosed space housing the both of us would be enough to get in her head and discover why her eyes held so many secrets.

"Okay, when you said small, I was thinking like a—smallish fancy house with black-and-white design and classy shit—" she said.

I could see what she was seeing now: the small living room with three yellow couches, soft beige wallpaper, decorative flowers on the walls, bookshelves lining a small space by the far end of one of the couches, and a soft, comfortable rug that added a homey feel to the house.

There was one kitchen, bathroom, and bedroom, and no passageways. The doors to the bathroom and bedroom were to our left, although the bathroom had another cojoined door inside the bedroom.

The kitchen was visible from where we stood, a small cozy space with a brown marble counter, one gas cooker, an oven, and one small fridge with picture stickers of my brother and sister, Elia, and my mom.

Some of the pictures were cut out; a face was missing—my face.

"The more I look at it, the more it feels . . . personal," Zahra voiced.

"It is," I told her, pulling off my coat and turning on more lights.

The room was now bathed in white, brown, and yellow.

I caught the look of discomfort in Zahra's eyes as she turned to look at me. "Elio, why did you bring me here? We could have gone to a hotel or something."

I took off my wristwatch. "It would be illogical to spend money on hotels when I have a house here."

"You're rich."

"Yes, but I am not wasteful."

"It's—" She paused, exasperated and jittery. "Elio, what do you think we're doing here?" She motioned between us.

"What?"

"What do you think this is? You can't bring me to your space . . . You shouldn't trust me so much."

"I don't trust you."

"Yet you bring me here. To this house that looks like your safe space. I'm pretty sure you've never brought anyone here, so what makes me an exception?"

She was right. No one had been here but me. This house was a delusion. I didn't like flashy or extravagant things. I was born from wealth, but I wanted the most minor things that came with life.

Well, for now . . . while I'm still inconveniently breathing.

"I don't want anything to get mixed up or blurry, okay? This feels too personal," she said.

"I think it's just a house. Why are you overthinking, hm? Is this stemming from guilt because you do not have pure intentions?"

"It's not guilt," she countered . . . *She lied.* "I'm just—I'm just not used to this. Maybe I'm overthinking it."

"Or maybe you need a shower and a change of clothes. And food, because you eat like a horse, and the dinner served today was subpar."

"Hmm." A smile broke out on her face. "Look at you, knowing the right buttons to push."

"Okay."

She laughed, walking around the space. "Are any of your soldiers around?"

"Why? Do you aim to strangle me in my sleep?"

She turned to me, a smile curving at her lips. "Don't give me ideas."

Zahra Faizan was a beautiful disaster. A cunning woman. An entity as discreet and suave as me.

Her only mistake was her utter transparency.

"I'll shower and wear your clothes while you order food. Or cook—can you cook?"

"I don't know."

"Ordering it is, then."

"Hm. The bathroom is the one on the left. Everything you require is easy to find. It's a small space. Nothing is hidden."

"Roger that."

I watched her walk towards the door I had pointed out and disappear behind it.

My eyes were still on the door when my phone vibrated in my pocket. I pulled out the device, seeing Angelo's name on the screen.

I answered. "Significant emergencies, Mancini."

"*I'm calling to check in. You didn't inform me if you arrived at your place yet.*"

"I did. Did you find them?"

"*Yes. They are from Sicily. Manuel Conti's men.*"

"Manuel Conti," I drawled. "Hm. Dig up all you can. Not about her; her information in the database is useless. But Conti. I want to know everything."

"Noted. Are you being careful?"

"Yes, I have condoms, Papà."

"That's not—Jesus. I'm just saying be careful around her."

"Hm. Say hi to your mother and Lisa for me. Don't forget the prayer pamphlets; she would feel offended if I didn't ask for them."

His mom was religious, and each time Angelo visited, he always returned with pamphlets she had picked out for me. His mother, my mother, and his aunt, Lisa, had been close back in the day. But then my mother's case worsened, and she withdrew from everyone until . . .

"I'll do that." Angelo's voice reached my ear. *"See you tomorrow."*

I hung up.

Earlier, I hadn't cared enough to look into Manuel Conti. I was not one to meddle with growing families. Let's say our level differed in rank. But his name had been mentioned one too many times, and his connection with Zahra evoked a gut feeling I couldn't ignore. It might not concern me, but it was happening right in my territory.

And that . . . just wouldn't do.

CHAPTER THIRTY-SIX

Zahra

Elio Marino was wearing white.
Although that wasn't the subject matter here, it was just one interesting fact. The man had been entirely unashamed, walking into the bedroom he knew I was in, wearing nothing but black boxer briefs, with wet hair, which he towel-dried right in front of me.

His body—fuck me sideways and back—he was rough, invisible scars covered by ink, taut muscles built from pure hard labor and, well—the gym? But it really didn't look like gym muscles or sex muscles. From every rip in his arms to his defined-as-fuck stomach, there was something intricate about each flex as he moved.

And that particular thing pushed me into a trance-like state, staring at him when he turned to find new clothes. His broad back and shoulders flexed erotically as he moved to slip strong legs and thighs into black sweatpants.

Another thing that caught my attention was his tattoos. I had always been curious about where the ink flame led, but I found out today, and . . .

It had me feeling wary.

A well-detailed drawing of burning flames drove up his forearm and shoulders, over to his neck, and then half his chest. I caught something like a church tower and a crucifix sign above—at first, I didn't realize it, but then I noticed the fire was aflame in the church, and when he turned, my stomach dipped.

The Chinese he had ordered had threatened to come back out

of my mouth; even the raspberry I was currently munching on temporarily became unappetizing.

It was a drawing of three faces amidst the flame. Hollow eyes wide with tears streaming down sunken cheeks, mouths wide open in a wail. The three faces seemed to float between the fire—a little boy, a young girl, and a woman.

I was so caught in it that I had to blink my thoughts back in order when he slid an oversized white sweater on, covering the tattoos.

Then without looking my way, he went to the dresser, dried his hair a little bit, and then brushed it down. Seeing him in another color of clothing was—strange; it didn't seem like him, but I wouldn't lie and say that he didn't look good.

Honestly, I would have preferred him without anything. One reason was that he was pleasant to look at, and the other was because I wanted to study the ink on him. I felt like if I kept looking, I'd find something new to give me further insight into the story behind those faces.

I took my mind off him, glancing at the calm darkness outside the window in the room.

Last I'd checked the time, it was almost 12:30 A.M.

Elio had been reading while I ate the food he had ordered for me, and when he decided to shower, I decided to retire into the room with a bowl of raspberries.

I shifted on the bed, leaning against the headboard, wearing a white shirt with writing on the front. I had found it folded in the dresser, amongst other mundane things that didn't scream the Elio Marino I had gotten used to.

Underneath, I wore a pair of his boxer briefs, my legs on full display as I ate.

I could tell someone had dropped by to clean up the place and stock up the fridge, meaning he had spent time planning this whole thing, but I didn't comment. Commenting on it would have made it seem real. It would have made me acknowledge that he had put in effort . . . for me.

I backtracked as he walked towards the bed, phone in hand, before he pulled the duvet to one side, attempting to lie down.

I swallowed the last raspberry I had taken in, eyeing his movements as he settled beside me on the bed. "Uh . . . what are you doing?"

He pushed the duvet further down with his legs. "What do people do on beds?"

"They—"

"Either sleep, get intimate, or just relax. The last option is what I'm doing," he said, settling into the pillow, about to use his phone.

"Won't you at least be a gentleman and take the couch?"

He turned to look at me for the first time since he came out of that bathroom. "Why, in all consciousness of the mind, would I take the couch when there's a bed?"

I shifted the bowl of raspberries towards me. "Because *I'm on* the bed?"

"Oh . . ." he said, blinking at me while trailing off as if thinking deeply. "I have no problem sharing a bed with you. It is big enough to accommodate two people, but I understand if you have a problem sharing a bed. You can take the couch."

My jaw dropped, and I laughed lightly. "I seriously don't understand you. Pick a side. Are you a gentleman or an asshole? Stop confusing me."

He pursed his lips, eyes searching mine before he moved, raising himself to my level, as he propped up on one elbow, now facing me fully.

He reached for a raspberry in the bowl, watching me while he put it into his mouth, tongue collecting it first before it disappeared inside his mouth and he chewed delicately.

A little thump made itself known between my legs, and I pressed them together and shifted as I looked from his lips to his eyes, quenching the thought of wanting to kiss him.

"I am not an asshole. I am just very straightforward. The

sooner you learn the difference between the two, the better," he said, dropping his phone in the tiny space between us.

"Why are you so comfortable sharing a bed with me?" I asked. "Aren't you wary I'd hurt you in your sleep?"

"No."

"Why?"

His shoulders moved. "I won't sleep. So it's useless worrying about a situation I can control."

I picked up another raspberry, watching him while I chewed.

The man didn't take his eyes off me either, and I could tell there were questions within their depths.

But I knew I needed to ask him questions before getting into character.

"I thought you only wore black because you despise other colors?"

"Hm." He nodded. "When I'm in the compound, yes. Outside the compound, I do whatever I desire. I also like to collect items I'll never wear, like the shirt you're wearing. This sweater, though, was a birthday gift from Angelo's mother. I liked it. I kept it. Now I'm wearing it," he said, reaching for another berry.

"When's your birthday?" I asked him, genuinely curious.

"December first. When's yours?"

I didn't think he'd ask, but then again, he had been behaving suspiciously since I got on that plane.

"I'm surprised you don't know . . . since you're supposed to have run a background check on me."

"Hm. We did run one, but now I'm asking. I want you to tell me."

I nodded. "It's January third, according to certificates and documents I've seen; I don't know how true it is."

He watched me.

"What? Did you see a different date when you ran your check?"

He shook his head. "No."

I looked away from him to the bowl. It was quiet for about ten seconds before I broke the silence.

"Can I ask a question?"

"I thought we were already doing that," Elio responded, still watching me.

He got more comfortable, shifting closer to me, his chin on his palm, his gaze unnerving. The same way it had been on the plane when he looked up for the first time.

Like he was in awe.

No one had ever looked at me like that.

Whenever Manuel looked at me, all I saw was controlled obsession, lust, care, and anger.

There was also lust in Elio's stare, but that wasn't really what was shown. It was something else.

He looked at me like I was something shiny and new, something worth looking at. The awe in his eyes didn't exactly spell care, but it gave the definition of wonder and curiosity. Like he wanted to know me, sink into my head, and decipher my thoughts gradually.

He looked at me like I was the only thing in this room that could keep his attention.

Those eyes, intense and beautiful, looked so soft right now. It made me want to confide in him, tell him every secret I'd kept hidden since I could make sense of this world. I knew he wouldn't judge; I knew he would listen.

But I still held back. I was willing to give him my body and nothing else.

"I'm listening, Sport; ask your question."

The space was warm between us, and I could hear him breathing, just as I was sure he heard me.

"I couldn't help but notice your tattoos. Are those your family?"

"Yes." He answered with no subtle blink to show he was lying, no hesitation, no hiding; he just blurted it like he was prepared for my questions.

"Your mom—I thought you stabbed her to death; why was she in the fire?"

"Because she was."

I frowned. "I don't understand, didn't you—kill her?"

He didn't respond; he just stared.

I bit my bottom lip, rephrasing my statement and testing a theory I had about him. He never responded to assumptions. Only questions.

"Did you stab your mother to death?" I asked.

"No."

I pressed more with another question. "Did she burn in that fire?"

"Yes."

I nodded. "Why did you set them on fire?"

No response.

I realized I had assumed while asking the question—this man.

"Did you do it? Did you kill your family?"

He swallowed, eyes searching mine as the silence after I'd asked that question lengthened. I knew he wasn't taking his time because he was thinking of a lie. The look in those tormented eyes told me he wouldn't like to continue this topic of conversation. I was about to tell him it was okay until he spoke.

"No. I didn't kill my family." His voice sounded gruffer, deeper, rough.

It sent a pang straight to my chest.

"Then why don't you tell people the truth?"

"No one has ever asked."

I had the strongest urge to shift even closer to him. "So . . . why do you tell people that you did."

His jaw clenched and unclenched. "I have never told anyone I killed my family, Zahra."

"Why does everyone think—"

"My father. He created the narrative to protect his image and build mine, rumors turned to rumors, and I became—the monster who went wild after a year in the army and killed my family the day I got back just because I'd found out they weren't exactly my family. My mother had been a whore and a cheater who sold out family secrets. So, I burned them all in a fit of rage, and I'd do it again to anyone who is a threat to our family name," he said.

I didn't know what to say, so I let him continue.

"A very embarrassing narrative, to be honest; my father was never creative. I could have come up with something better. Then again, it seemed to do the trick. I was named The Wicked and reigned amid assumptions people make of me. I must admit that it is fun sometimes."

I breathed out, taking the bowl from between us before stretching to keep it on the bedside table. I shifted closer to him.

"Hey," I said softly, and he gave me his attention. "I think it's not too late to start changing the narrative."

He shook his head. "It is too late. The narrative is who I am. It might not be who I am now, right in this moment with you. But the minute I walk back into that compound, it's who I am."

"But that's not fair. To yourself, or the memory of your family."

Something softened in his eyes; his stare grew deeper, more meaningful, and I almost shrank into myself at all the emotions it carried and how he didn't make any move to hide them.

"You believe me," he said, lowering his pitch.

I lowered the pitch of my voice too, keeping our conversation locked between us and nowhere else in the room. "From one liar to another, I think it's pretty easy to spot our truths just as much as our lies, Elio."

"That might be the wisest thing you've ever said since I met you."

I let a small laugh bubble out of my chest. "Come on, I have said wise things . . . a lot of them, actually."

"Your sexual innuendos?"

I shot him a deadpan stare, struggling not to smile. "Now you're the one bringing sex into the conversation."

"I'm only stating facts."

I smiled. "Well, what can I say? Sexual innuendos come with my whole package."

He raised both his brows. "Oh, you're a package now."

"Mm-hmm. I know people who would kill to have me stand by their side," I said with a proud smile.

He switched to Spanish. *"With you offering them what?"*

I loved his accent when he spoke in the language. It rolled naturally and deeply off his tongue and throat. It was seductive, even though I was positive he didn't mean for it to be that way.

I responded in Spanish too. *"Words of advice, strategic planning, ways to get information because it is the most valuable thing you could ever hold against your enemy."*

"Is that what you offered Manuel?"

I knew he was going to ask, and I thought I knew the answer I would give, but looking at him now, I didn't know how to lie . . . so I just went with the first thing that came to mind.

"It wasn't like that, at first . . . I was just living with him, helping with chores here and there because I'm all things but a freeloader."

"Why were you living with him?"

I swallowed, looking away from his face. "I-I can't really remember much about those times, but . . . I think he saved me. Um—from my buyer in the trafficking business, and he brought me to Sicily. I was sixteen. I thought I was finally free from the life I'd had, but—"

"It wasn't freedom," Elio pointed out, and I nodded.

"It wasn't . . . It was worse."

"Did he hurt you?"

I bit the inside of my lip. "He didn't do anything that I didn't want. At least I thought I wanted it because I thought he—loved me."

I looked at him, expecting to find his eyes judging me, but there was nothing; he just listened.

"But he didn't love you," Elio said, gently urging me to divulge more.

"Maybe he did . . . in his own weird way, but it was unhealthy. I was underage, and he was an adult—and I was stupid to think it was real from my end. Manuel was obsessed at best. I started living when I left him."

"When was that."

"I was nineteen."

"And he just let you go?"

"Yeah," I said, finally looking at him. "He woke up one morning and told me that I was free to leave if I wanted to."

"Did you want to?"

I shrugged. "At that time, I didn't really know—it took me a month to make the decision to leave. I needed to find myself, you know. He didn't give me any money to fend for myself when I left, and I was stubborn as hell, so I just told myself that I would be able to do it, and well, here I am, in bed with the guy who kidnapped my family and me."

Elio didn't say anything; he just stared, eyes deciphering, cutting down each of my words, looking for loose ends, anything that would signify a lie.

"Hm. You still have your freedom."

"In a twisted, fucked-up way, yeah."

It was quiet for a while, and then he spoke. "I have a vague idea of what it feels like to have your freedom taken from you. I had mine taken when I left for the army."

"Why did you leave?"

"My father. He thought I was going crazy like Mother, so he forced it on me. I was nineteen. He wanted to rid me of my depression, and to him, the army was the answer. I respected him too much to say no. I had to leave everyone I loved behind . . . It was horrible out there." His throat bobbed. "When I came back, they, I didn't get there on time, the fire—my mother—she—my siblings—well, they were gone."

Something melted inside me. "I'm so sorry to hear that."

He nodded. "Going to the army . . . it didn't just take away my freedom; it took my family, destroyed what was left of it, and it was all because my father thought I was crazy."

I frowned. "He was the crazy one," I said, then paused. "Wait—is this by any chance the reason you left Devil?"

He nodded. "There would have been no one to take care of him when I left for the army. I couldn't trust anyone, not even Casmiro. So I had to send him away."

"But it was only for a year, right? You could have reached out when you got back."

"I wanted to. I went to Los Angeles a few months after I got back. I watched him from afar for a few days. He was happy, or he seemed happy and normal. I didn't want to ruin that. So, I left and have watched him from afar ever since."

"Then tell him this; I'm sure he wouldn't hate you as much as he does now. Devil might be stubborn, but he's understanding, and deep down, I know he cares for you."

"I don't want him to. I can't be there for him. I can't promise to be when I know I might not live past thirty-three."

My frown deepened. "Don't fucking say things like that."

"Does it upset you?"

I shot him a look of disbelief. "Yes, it does."

"Then I'll stop."

"You'll stop thinking it too?"

"I am afraid that is impossible. It's not something I can control."

"Then seek—"

I could tell he suppressed a groan. "I have repeatedly told you why I can't seek help. Repeating myself is not something I am fond of."

"Okay, fine, I'll drop it."

"Thank you, Sport."

"Why do you call me that?"

His brows twitched, and his gaze dropped from mine.

Silence fell between us.

"Are you gonna answer or—"

"You challenge me. You're sharp-mouthed; you don't fold easily; you keep me on my toes. You're just as stubborn as me. You're a little thing, yet a big force of nature. You're like my personal kind of sport. Except I don't like to play, I just derive pleasure from watching."

Like it had the time he kissed me, the little glitchy stutter attacked my chest to the point that my response was a simple "Oh."

"Hm," he hummed, eyes still on me, and I wanted to ask him why he was staring, but his phone screen lit up with a vibration and a text sound.

My gaze flickered to it, but I couldn't see the texter.

He looked down at his phone but didn't pick it up. He just brought his attention back to me.

"So tell—" He stopped when his phone blared up again. Three times consecutively. He sighed and then picked it up.

I watched him unlock the device. It was shielded from my view, but I watched how he typed back to whoever texted him.

I frowned again.

Was it Casmiro . . .

The sound of him sending the text filled the space between us.

It wasn't even up to a second before the sound of a response from the texter came through.

He was typing out another reply.

Elio's face gave nothing away, and it only fueled my curiosity.

The back-and-forth continued for about a minute before he dropped the phone.

"Cassie?" I asked.

"No."

"Angie?"

"No."

"Who was—"

"I'm curious to know you, Zahra," he cut me off.

My gaze went to the phone again, unable to detach my mind

from how he had wholly stopped our conversation to text this person.

If it was Cas . . .

I could feel his eyes on me when he spoke again. "Tell me, what is it you desire?"

The question had my gaze snapping to his, and I couldn't help but snicker. "Okay, Lucifer Morningstar."

"What is a Lucifer Morningstar?" he asked.

"He's a character from a show—like a TV—never mind." I couldn't deal with explaining it to him; I felt I'd spend hours doing that. "That, though, is a very dangerous question to ask a woman like me."

"I think it's a pretty normal question. Do you plan to be a thief for the rest of your life, or is there something more that you want?"

I parted my lips to answer the question, but nothing came.

Elio waited patiently until I sighed and decided to be honest about myself for the first time tonight. "Honestly, I haven't thought that far yet. Maybe it's because I don't like to dwell on my future when I could just have it all in my present."

"That's careless thinking."

"I never said I was careful." I curled the side of my lips.

A small scoff left him as he raised his hand to my hair, and I stiffened. He stroked gently before tucking it behind my ear; the warm tips of his fingers brushed the skin at the back of my ear and down my neck. I couldn't hide my visible shiver.

"Your actions show how very careless you are, Sport; you don't have to say it in words that you're not," he said, his voice lower than before, gaze dropping to my mouth.

God . . . I wanted him to break that one rule, close the space between us, and just . . . do it.

Why the fuck was I waiting for him to do it?

Fuck this.

My palm rested flat on his chest, and I was genuinely surprised to feel how fast and hard his heart thumped.

I pushed him flat and settled atop him in a straddle. He didn't stop me when I brought my head to his neck, breathing him in as I kissed his hot skin.

His hands came to hold my waist in a firm grip.

I kissed from his neck to his chin, then up to the corner of his lips, before I pulled away slightly, connecting my gaze with his—his hot breath fanning my face, his eyes showing how completely resigned he was to this situation.

He would let me kiss him. I knew it.

"I want to break a rule, Elio. I know you want it too."

"I do," he said, swallowing while his heart hammered against my palm. "But I can't." His whisper brushed against my lips.

"Yeah, I know. It's a good thing that I can, then."

Without thinking about what he'd do next, I leaned in to satisfy that ache in my chest and the desire to feel the warmth from a kiss and—

His phone blared up in a ring before I could even press my lips to his.

"Are you fucking kidding me," I muttered through clenched teeth. "Don't answer—"

He was already reaching for the phone, bringing it to his view while I got off him with a glare.

"Who the hell is it?"

"Angelo," he said, watching the phone ring.

I rolled my eyes. "Why am I not surprised."

"It's almost three A.M. He wouldn't be calling if it wasn't important," he said, sitting up.

Wow—did we talk that long into the night? It hadn't even seemed like an hour.

Elio picked up, placing the phone against his ear. "This better be important."

I couldn't hear what Angelo was saying, but it sure as hell made Elio grow tense, though his face gave nothing away.

"How," he stated in question. Angelo's response came, and it made Elio completely stiffen.

"Is he okay?" he asked.

I bit the inside of my tongue.

Elio shifted away from me, getting off the bed. "When did this happen?" he asked, moving to the dresser while I sat there . . . just watching.

"Share the location; I'll be there."

Then he hung up, dropped the phone on the flat surface of the dresser, and took off the white sweater hurriedly before quickly fishing out a black one.

I got off the bed. "What happened?"

Elio slipped on the sweater, turning to face me with furrowed brows. "Casmiro was shot."

"What? When?" I asked, putting on a concerned frown.

"About thirty minutes ago. He's here in Turin." His phone vibrated on the table, and he picked it up from the surface, glancing at the screen, and then he started heading towards the door. "Angelo just shared the location—"

"Let me come with."

He paused, turning to look at me. I spotted the hesitation in his stare.

"I won't get in your way. I just—don't want to be here alone."

His jaw worked as he scanned me from head to toe and said, "Change."

"On it."

"I'll wait outside; do *not* take your time."

"Got it." I was already heading to the dresser when he left the room.

I found a black sweater identical to the one Elio had put on and then slipped on one of the pairs of sweatpants I found in there, grabbed my phone, and left the room.

A few minutes later, Elio and I were driving to the location.

CHAPTER THIRTY-SEVEN

Zahra

He wasn't taken to a hospital, but one of the Marino safe houses in the city. It was a penthouse in a hotel near Elio's building. All through the ride here, Elio hadn't said a word; the man had been deep in silence, probably buried in his thoughts. I wanted to assure him that all would be well. I had no idea why I felt the need to talk him out of his head; I didn't give a shit about Casmiro, but I cared about Elio, so I guess that's why.

When we entered the elevator, I glanced at him, noticing his tense shoulders; his face was etched in a frown that made him look unapproachable. He was worried, and even his strong front couldn't hide it.

"I'm sure he's fine since he wasn't hospitalized?"

"The medical team is here."

"Oh," I said as the elevator rode up, the silence tense and deafening. "What was he doing here in Turin, anyway?"

"Business."

"Then why didn't he come with us earlier on the pla—"

"I'm not in the mood to talk, Zahra," he snapped.

I parted my lips to say something but closed them again, shifting on my feet as I looked ahead, grateful that the elevator stopped and slid apart, revealing a large living room.

Elio walked out quickly, and I followed behind him, but my steps faltered for a second when I spotted Upper and Angelo talking with some soldiers; two nurses were checking a file at the far end of the living room. Soldiers were all around the space; there was also a table filled with weapons as if they were preparing to head out once information about the shooters came forward.

"Where is he?" Elio asked as we approached Upper and Angelo.

Real fear gripped me when my eyes scanned Upper from head to toe, and even when I confirmed that he was okay and the blood on him wasn't his, the fear remained.

He could have died tonight.

"In there," Angelo said. "It's not looking good."

Elio didn't wait to hear anything else, he just disappeared behind the door Angelo had pointed to, and when Angelo followed him—not before shooting me a distrusting frown—I pulled Upper by his wrists, away from the other soldiers, who kept their eyes on us.

"What the fuck are you doing here?" I asked in a panicked whisper.

He frowned. "Glad to see that's the first thing you care about."

"What? You—where's everyone else?"

"Back in Milan, at the compound. I just informed them about what hap—"

"Why are you here?" I bit at him.

Upper looked tired. There were fading bloodstains on his hands and some smudges here and there on his face; his hair looked a mess. "We were together when we got attacked by some real crazy gun-ninja a-holes. Casmiro took three bullets, and we barely escaped that building alive."

I eyed him. "Why were you *with him?*"

Upper eyed me cautiously. "He invited me to come along? When he got back from the airport, we went for a drive, and I was still in the car when he told me he had a company here that dealt with racing and car shit. He asked if I'd like to tag along, and I did, we drove here a—"

"And you didn't think to tell me you were *tagging* along?" I gritted out.

"It slipped my mind, okay? I figured I would surprise you,

and you wouldn't have to be alone on the journey back—but fuck, that isn't important. These people stormed the company un-bloody-announced, and he got shot, and there was so much blood, and I freaked out because they were gunning for him, Zahra. They wanted to kill him. Not me. Or anyone else in that building."

I was *furious*.

"I don't give a shit about Casmiro, Upper. You made a fucking mistake tonight, not telling me you would be here; you could have fucking died just by being with him. You don't *tag* along with people like that."

Upper's eyes widened in disbelief, looking at me like my face belonged to a stranger. "What in bloody hell's name is wrong with you, Zahra? Do you not get it? He might die, and you're here worrying about the measly fact that I didn't shoot you a quick text?"

"Upper—"

"He took a bloody bullet for me, and he's in there fighting for his life because of it; you should be worried about *him,* not me. I'm fine; he's not. And he's not a fucking bad person, okay? Just because he's in a crime family doesn't mean we automatically wish him dead."

"I get what you're saying, and I'm glad he took that bullet for you—"

"What?"

"You would have died otherwise; spare me if I care about you and not someone I know absolutely nothing about."

"Jesus Christ, Zahra, at least show some sympathy."

I scoffed, relaxing my shoulders as I looked towards the window. "I have no sympathy to give. Not even a tiny drop of care. He probably pissed off some people, made threats here and there, and talked more than he should. That's what these guys do; they run their mouths because they think they have a title that makes them untouchable. But karma is a bitch, not our problem."

Upper shook his head. "Are you high right now?"

"Completely sober. How many were they, the men."

Still frowning at me, he crossed his arms over his chest. "I couldn't exactly count. We were being chased around the building, and I practically dragged him to a car, where I drove and informed Angelo."

My brain worked. "They didn't follow?"

Concern filled his eyes. "No, they didn't . . . it worries me that they didn't because they were hell-bent on making sure they emptied their bullets in him. Whoever sent them must be influential because . . . What are you doing?"

I rushed to the window, quickly pulling the curtain aside as I looked down.

Three cars were pulling up, all tinted windows. Armed men started filing out, and people rushed in different directions, evading the unknown gunmen.

I closed the curtain and turned. "They followed. They just waited to make sure there was no room for escape."

Upper's eyes widened as he rushed towards me, pulling the curtain.

"Bloody fuck."

"We need to secure the building," I said. "Or we're all dead."

The door Elio and Angelo had walked into pulled open, and Angelo stepped out. "Secure the building, shoot to kill on sight. Leave one person for questioning."

Soldiers moved, talking on comms, grabbing weapons.

"Hey," I whispered to Upper. "Stay here; on no account should you leave this apartment."

"Where are you going?" he asked, confused.

I didn't answer as I moved to the weapons table, Upper on my tail as I grabbed a handy gun. The weight was perfect in my grip.

"Zahra, I don't think this is a good idea; these people, they know how to work a gun—"

"Awesome, I happen to be perfect at working a gun too."

He shot me a strange look as I cocked the weapon expertly before slipping the gun into the back of my sweatpants. "Listen, I know you're confused, but there's no time for me to explain why and how I know how to work a gun—"

"That's not it. Ever since you arrived with Elio, you've been a completely different person."

"I'm in men's clothing; what the fuck do you expect?"

"That's not—"

"Stay here with Elio and Cas and the doctors, and I will—"

"Do nothing." Elio's voice had my head snapping to the side.

He reached us, his face void of emotion, attention settling on Upper. "I will never be able to repay you for saving Casmiro's life. I owe you."

Upper nodded. "It's all right; he saved mine too."

Elio gave a firm nod before looking at me. "You will banish whatever thought you think you have at this instant; you are not getting in that elevator."

"I'm of no use here. I can help out there."

His eyes hardened. "I don't need help; I have enough people to handle this."

Goddamn it.

I frowned, leveling Elio with a glare. "Upper would have died today. Understand? Those fuckers invading this building would have touched one of my own. I want nothing more than to bring down the people responsible for that and—"

"Upper, can you give us a moment?" Elio said, cutting me off.

Upper's eyes narrowed as he looked between us, confusion and suspicion lacing his assessing stare. His gaze dropped to our chests like he was looking at our outfits before he blinked and shook his head, settling his attention on me, seeking my approval.

"It's fine," I said.

He nodded before walking over to Angelo, who was on the phone.

Some of the soldiers were already filing into the elevator.

I felt Elio's hand on my arm as he gently turned my body to face him.

Our gazes locked. "I have to be out there, Elio."

"You sound desperate."

His remark caught me off guard. "What?"

He looked around the room, conflict in his eyes, before he looked back at me. "Why do you want to be out there so badly?"

"To help?"

"You don't care about any of this or Casmiro."

"I care about Upper, and he almost died."

"Yes, but he's alive, and he's fine, so why do you want to get involved in a fight that isn't yours?" His eyes searched mine with confident suspicion. My stomach clenched, and I bit the inside of my lips till I tasted blood. My brain was working so fast.

"I just—"

"Unless it's your fight . . ."

"What?"

"Unless, one way or another, this is your fault."

"What the fuck are you talking about?"

"Casmiro was attacked by Manuel Conti's men," he stated. "You knew him."

"Yeah, years ago . . . I have no idea why—"

"Be honest with me, Zahra."

I blinked at him. "You think I'm responsible for this?" My eyes searched his. "Are you fucking kidding me, Elio?"

He closed his eyes briefly, jaw clenching as he opened them back up. "I wouldn't make an accusation if I had no reason to, Zahra."

"How—when the—why would I want to hurt Casmiro?"

"*That* is what I am hoping you will answer for me."

I shook my head slowly. "This is insane. I'm trying to help, and you think that I'm involved? That I would put Upper in danger just to—kill your underboss? How the fuck do you think I would have access to men like that? Or—or—kill someone I know nothing about; why would you even have a thought like this?"

He looked as uncomfortable as I felt.

"Zahra, you have given me no reason to trust you but more reasons to question everything you do. Casmiro informed me about the conversation you two had yesterday."

The air was leaving my lungs. "I can't believe this is happening right now."

"It is. You were so desperate to go out there. Your friend might not see it, but I see it. I see all your lies and all your tells. Every question I asked you tonight, *every response* you gave was *fucking bullshit.*"

"What?" His words shot through my chest. "They were not."

"Maybe they aren't, but you weren't completely honest with me," he stated confidently. "I went bare for you today." He lowered his voice, looking me right in the eye. "I told you things I never thought I would ever tell anyone; I confided in you and took your advice; I have shown you more of myself than I have ever shown anyone. I trusted you with my feelings; all I'm asking . . . is that you be honest with me for once tonight. Do you have anything to do with Casmiro lying in that room on the brink of death?"

A small, humorless laugh left my throat. "Wow . . ." I said, almost out of breath. "The first time I actually opened up to someone about Manuel, and this is what I get—an absurd accusation."

"Don't do that. Don't try to manipulate me."

My frown deepened. "I'm not trying to—your claims are beyond wrong."

"Zahra."

I stepped closer to him, my eyes fixed on his. "You say I wasn't completely honest with you. You're right, I wasn't. That part of my life is hard for me to talk about, and I opened up to you about something I have spent years of my life trying to forget."

His brows drew down in confusion.

"Street has no fucking idea about Manuel. I don't even plan to ever let them know, but you—just like you showed me a part of yourself, I did too. Because I thought maybe as we got to know each other, I might finally have someone I could talk to about this stuff."

"Zahra, I know you weren't sincere."

"Of course I wasn't sincere; you don't expect me to bring down my walls completely just because you told me you didn't kill your family."

He frowned. "Don't bring my family into this."

"You are the one accusing me of attempting to kill Cassie; he might be an asshole, and yes, I might have wanted to push him out of the car on our way to the airport, but I would never just wake up one morning and hire assassins to finish him off."

He sighed. "Zahra—"

"I don't know what you think you see, but remember, you were the one who invited me here. I don't know anyone in Turin but you. I didn't even know Casmiro would be here. Upper never told me shit; you can ask him if that's what you're thinking. I don't know who those men are."

He looked away from me, eyes moving around; I mirrored his action to see some eyes on us, including Upper's.

I looked away at the same time Elio's gaze locked with mine. "I am giving you one pass, Zahra. Come clean, and I promise I won't hurt you. I won't let anyone harm a hair on your head. I need to know—"

"Jesus fucking Christ, Elio, you were with me throughout—I can't even believe you're falsely accusing me without any proof—"

"My gut is all the proof I need."

I blinked at him. "You're pinning this on me because of a gut feeling?"

"Yes."

I locked my jaw, a breathy scoff leaving my chest as I stepped back from him. "Well, you're wrong. You couldn't even be more wrong—and we don't have time for this. I'm going down there."

He straightened. "No, you're not. It might be dangerous."

"You know more than anyone here that I can fend for myself.

And maybe when I shoot a man or two, you will be convinced I had nothing to do with this." I turned to leave, but he grabbed my arm almost immediately.

"Zahra—"

A ground-shaking explosion shocked the building, and screams and loud gunshots quickly followed the sound.

I looked back at him, my gaze flickering to his grip on my arm and then his heated eyes. "Are you gonna let me go? Or are we waiting for the next explosion to take us all under?" I asked.

Elio cursed, letting go of me, grabbing a weapon from the table, and gesturing to the elevator. "Stay by my side, always."

"Why? So you can see if I'm giving the shooters eye signals?"

"We'll talk about this later."

"Fuck you."

I had something to prove.

So I didn't exactly *stay by his side, always.*

It was chaotic when we got down. Bullets ricocheting, bystanders running to leave the building, most getting caught in the crossfire or being used as human shields for the assassins, but I was prepared, managing to take down one of them in two missed shots and one hit.

At first, we were a little outnumbered. But thankfully backup had rushed into the evacuating building, and Angelo had pulled Elio over to some of the new soldiers, who were now working towards securing the building's perimeter.

At the little distraction, I took the opportunity to chase down two of the shooters I'd spotted taking the stairs to get to the emergency elevator, seeing as Marino's people had secured the main elevator.

It was foolish to disappear alone with these guys scattered around the building—but I saw an opportunity to end this, and I took it.

I spotted both guys coming off the stairs and approaching the elevator, their backs to me.

I had an advantage because while the guns outstretched in their hands moved this way and that as if someone would pop out and jump them, I held a gun in each hand. Aiming one barrel at the calf of the guy on the left, and pointing the other to the top shoulder of the guy on the right, I calculated my next moves in my head. Then I pulled the triggers as I ran towards them, my feet slamming into the calf of the guy on the left.

He went down sharply with a loud grunt, turning swiftly to shoot at the same time the other one collected himself, holding his wounded shoulder as he snapped back, aiming the gun at me, but I already had my gun aimed at him.

He shot the same time I pulled the trigger, but I'd anticipated his move and dodged as my bullet pierced through his hand, his gun falling the moment my feet swung, knocking the gun from the guy whose calf I had shot.

It all happened in an adrenaline rush as I quickly kicked the guns far away from their reach, standing where I could face them, my weapons aimed directly at them.

The one whose hand I'd shot bared his teeth in a groan, about to charge forward.

"I would hold off if I were you." I kept my guns aimed at them, looking up around the top corners of the hallway and then back at them. They made no further move to attack. "Who sent you?"

They were alert, faces hard in pain.

"We are not here for you," one of them said with a thick Italian accent.

"Obviously, but you almost killed my friend, you fucking idiot, so here's how we're going to do it." My grip tightened on the gun. "I will kill one of you and hand the other over to Marino's people. Who is willing to die? Discuss amongst yourselves; make it snappy."

"Go to hell," the one whose shoulder I had shot spat at me.

"Nice choice."

I aimed my gun at the guy I had shot in the calf, pulling the trigger.

His body dropped to the ground.

"Zahra!" Elio's voice rang into the space, and I turned to see one of the assassins right behind me, a barrel pointed right to my head just before a loud bang pierced through the air. My whole body shook, and I stared wide-eyed as the assassin's gun clattered to the ground before his body followed.

Elio stood there, fuming, gun pointed right at me before he lowered it.

I swallowed. "Well, that could have been bad."

He rushed to me. "What part of staying by my side don't you *fucking* understand?" he gritted as his men rushed upstairs.

"I thought I'd bring you your man for questioning; you can ask him if he's seen me before."

"Right, because you didn't spend enough time disarming and killing one of them. Many words could have been exchanged."

My heart dropped. "Are you—"

"Shut up," he said before turning to his men. "Clean this up," he ordered before gesturing to the other man. "Take this one in. Inform Angelo that I'll contact him."

Elio took the guns from me, handing them to one of his men, and then he grabbed my hand. "You could have been killed just now."

"Better that than being in the same space with you at this point."

His jaw clenched as he pulled me back down the stairs with him.

"Let go of me." I tried to wrench my hand out of his hold, but he held firm as he pulled me past a back room, out of the building, and towards the parking lot where he had left the car earlier.

He opened the door and finally let go of me. "Get in."

"And what about the others?"

"We have the building secured, get in."

"No."

"Get the fuck in the car, Zahra, or I'll force you into it."

I ground my teeth, glaring at his unwavering stare. I knew he would do it, so I got into the car and bottled my pride, clenching my jaw hard.

He slammed the door beside me and rounded the car. My eyes followed his movements as he entered; he looked at me while he started the engine and then looked away when he drove out of the parking lot to the private road twenty minutes away from the main road, I'm guessing to avoid any of our lingering attackers.

I let out a sharp breath and shook my head, looking out the window, the anger in my stomach spiking at intervals. The frown I had worn before entering the car didn't let up. I needed to let it out, yell, bash his head against the steering wheel. "I shouldn't have told you anything about myself. If I'd known you'd treat me like this afterward . . ."

"Don't play the victim."

I snapped my head to him. "I *am* the victim! I'm the one getting accused of attempting to kill your underboss. If anything, he was the one who threatened to kill me before dropping me off yesterday."

"Casmiro would never threaten you unless he had a good reason to. You knew he was on to you, so you ordered the hit."

"What the fuck? You're delusional, Elio—for someone who's running a whole fucking criminal family, you are so fucking shortsighted."

"Am I?"

"Yes. Now I see why your father sent you to the army; you needed to get your fucking crazy head in check."

He glanced at me, a fire in his eyes like none I'd ever seen before. He looked away, swiveled the car to the side of the road, stopped the engine, and turned to me. "What the fuck did you just say to me?"

I shoved my middle finger in front of his face and quickly exited the car, slamming the door harder than he had slammed it before, then I walked down the road.

I would get a fucking bus ticket and head back to Milan if I had to.

I heard the car door opening and closing, but I didn't turn back, even as footsteps came behind me.

He caught up quickly, a strong hand encircling my arm, pulling me back and swinging me around to face him. "Where do you think you're going?"

"If you don't let me go, I swear to God, I will hit you."

He didn't respond to my threat but dragged me back, and I tried to free my hand. "I'm warning you, Elio."

When he got us back in front of the car, he let me go. "You don't—"

I swung a blow at him, but he quickly shifted his head, catching my wrist and pushing me away like a bug in his face.

The action only made me more furious, and I charged for him, hoping to land a kick to his stomach, a blow, or a slap, but fucking hell, he wasn't playing either; he avoided every one of my attacks with hard pushes that only fueled my anger.

On my last attempt to get my fist to the side of his face, he grabbed my wrist and pushed me forcefully, slamming my back into the side of the car. A sharp pain exploded at my side, but my adrenaline dulled it.

I moved to push back but he'd already pinned me with his body, one knee between my legs, the other successfully caging me.

My breathing was just as ragged as his, and my gaze flickered to his parted lips. "Get off me."

"Why do you have to be so stubborn?"

I pushed at his chest. "Get off me or I'll—"

"Or you'll what, hm?" He brought his face closer to mine, drawing his knee up till I felt it brush against me. The friction made my hips jerk forward. The heat, the adrenaline, the fight, everything rushed to the pressure his knee applied between my legs.

"Can't speak?" he whispered in a fevered breath, moving his knee and pulling a reluctant whimper from me.

I wanted to gut him; I really wanted to make him bleed, but why the fuck was I so turned on instead? Why could I feel him pressing against my stomach like this was as arousing for him as it was for me?

"Tell me, what will you do?" he whispered against my lips.

"I'll—"

He buried his head in my neck, his warm breath and lips sending a spike down my belly to the pressure between my legs.

"You'll . . ." He trailed off, lips brushing my neck.

"I didn't . . ."

His knee moved, hands gripping my waist, pulling me flush against him.

"You didn't . . . ?"

I wanted to push him, punch him, slap him, kiss him, feel more of him. I wanted to get very far away from him, his warmth, the pull of him, his lips on my skin, our breaths falling in sync. I wanted to be mad at him, to be above the effect his body had on me.

But . . . there was this rush from our push and pull, this pump that had me falling into his warmth and . . .

Fuck me, I couldn't remember how to form words, or—I did remember how to form words, just not the ones my anger or brain wanted to say; my body and the desire wreaking havoc between my legs were the demons behind the words that left my mouth next. "I need you," I whispered, gripping the front of his shirt in my fist. "Now."

A strangled noise left his throat. "I hate your effect on me; I want to kill you for it."

"Unfortunately, we are both suffering from the same illness."

His heated eyes burned fiercely into mine, and he pulled back. I missed the pressure his knee supplied until he opened the car's back door. "Get in."

Excitement and anger sizzled through me as I rushed to the back seat, and he followed closely behind before slamming the door shut beside him. "Take off—just take off—"

He didn't have to tell me twice; I was already taking off my clothes with fast, shaky, anticipating fingers, while he undid his belt and took off his pants, but left his briefs and shirt on.

I wasn't wearing anything underneath the clothes I wore, so my breasts came free, and his eyes were glued to them.

"On me," he breathed.

A smirk curled at my lips as I wasted no time getting on his lap, his back to the door, with me straddling him, bare breasts in his face.

He buried his head in my neck, his hand going into the depth of my hair, fisting as he sucked kisses down my neck while I rubbed against him.

Feverish hot lips peppered kisses down to my collarbone.

His other hand squeezed my ass before his palm drew up my back; the warmth from the smoothness of his touch set my body ablaze. My stomach tightened.

I could tell he felt some of my scars, and his touch, though it lingered to feel and explore, didn't stop his lips from moving down to my left breast. My nipples hardened, ached, and tingled as his tongue flicked up and down the pierced bud before his mouth closed around it.

"Oh," I breathed out in a moan; the heat from his mouth and the wetness of his tongue twirling and sucking my nipple had my legs squeezing against both sides of his thigh. The sensation was mind-numbing. I breathed out the words that left me. "I don't like condoms; I'm clean and on strict pills. You?"

"Yes. Clean," he mumbled before returning to his licking and sucking.

"Fuck me, please," I begged.

He took his mouth off me. "Your begging is pathetic."

My hand went to his hair and pulled so I could look into those pretty eyes. "Revel in it now because you won't hear me beg for it again."

"Lies, like the rest you've been telling tonight." He lifted himself and pulled down his briefs a little, his hard cock coming free;

he was thick, and fucking veiny; the thought of him inside me scared and excited me at the same time.

"You don't know what the fuck you're talking about."

I went to touch him, but he swatted my hand away while his went between my legs, rubbing me as if to gather my wetness and coat his fingers with it, but his hot, warm touch sent my stomach tightening immediately; my clit throbbed like it needed just one stroke to let go.

Elio removed his fingers and brought them to his lips; a very sinful tongue came out, curling around his fingers as he licked my wetness, closed his eyes, and hummed in appreciation. "Hm, very . . . interesting."

Yes. I would never get this man out of my system.

"Better than any you've tasted?"

"You're my first. I don't like a mess, but I'll take yours any day."

My breath hitched at his words.

His hand left my hair and gripped my waist, lifting me slightly. "You hear that? That was me being honest. You might want to learn a lesson or two from it."

"For the thousandth fucking time," I supplied breathlessly, feeling the tip of his cock at my entrance. "I am not lying to you."

He glared. "My gut tells me you are."

My grip tightened on his hair as I gritted out, "Your gut is fucked in the head, and it's making your inhuman lie detector malfunahfuck!" The feel of his thrust made me scream out at the pain and the pleasure that followed. "Oh fuck," I breathed, a blinding wave of pleasure igniting deep within me. Fevering through my body. I writhed atop him, toes curling.

My walls hugged him tightly, and he let out a breathy moan-groan thing; I wasn't sure I heard correctly because he steadied my body, pulling out and thrusting deep again, hitting me where I most craved him.

My body had turned to the softest of jelly atop him, and my palm slapped against the window above his head to get a balance on myself as he fucked me into a mess of moans, my breasts bouncing at the force of his malicious fucking.

Each of his thrusts sent shuddering shivers that had me writhing—it was too much—he was too much, and I was so fucking full I couldn't breathe properly.

I didn't care that I was probably gripping his hair so tight; the sound of his hips slapping against my ass with each thrust he gave had me on the brink of release. It filled the hot car, our breathing loud and so fucking intimate. Deep in my chest, I felt the effect of each breath I took and released.

"Everything you said tonight told me—nothing," he said between breaths.

This man went even deeper with each thrust.

"Fuck—" I hissed. "No matter what I say—you'd never believe me."

"Then give me something," he ground out, voice heavy with lust and pleasure. "Anything," he breathed. "Anything to ease my doubt. Just one truth."

"Mmm—Elio—fuck," I whined in a moan.

He didn't let up, didn't slow down. His grunts, so deep and hot, did something enrapturing to my stomach; I wanted to hear it all day, every fucking day.

I rode him as he thrust into me, deepening the intense warmth he ignited all over me.

My clit strung tight into a painful bud, my stomach tightened in knots. I was at the edge.

"*Zahra.*" He moaned my name, his hot breath fanning against the skin on my collarbone.

The sound of my name on his lips had my thighs trembling and clenching tightly to his, my release rising to the peak as it shattered me completely. "Elio, oh . . . ohfffuck," I cried, coming so hard that my vision turned white for a second.

With three hard, sloppy thrusts, he stilled inside me, and I felt the warmth of his release coat my walls. The feeling made me shudder as we rode it out and came down from the high together. My hand slipped from the window, leaving a draggy imprint as I relaxed against him, my head on his shoulder. The thick smell of sex and sweat lingered around our space.

My grip loosened from his hair as I caressed it softly, an attempt to ease whatever pain I might have caused.

Our breathing slowly settled and aligned in sequence.

"Are you okay?" he asked.

"Hmyeah," I voiced, lifting myself, my gaze connecting with his dazed but hard, confused one.

I leaned in, my lips just a few inches from his, as I moved to kiss him.

He turned his head. "Good, get off me."

I laughed tauntingly, hiding the discomfort of his rejection and hating that it even affected me.

"Why?" I moved against him, and he hissed. "The best sex you ever had?"

"Get off." His voice hardened, and I got the message loud and clear.

Rolling my eyes, I eased myself off him, a little pain pinching between my legs as his cock slipped out of me.

I didn't look at him as I quickly got myself back to being decent. My chest felt heavy at the sudden awkward quiet between us. It had to be the first awkward silence we'd ever shared.

I glanced at him. He was pulling his pants back on. When he was done, his hand moved to the handle of the car.

"Wait—" I said immediately, making him stop. "You're being weird because you think I really hurt Casmiro."

His throat worked before he turned to look at me. "Didn't you?"

I smoothed my hair from both sides of my face, tucking it behind my ears. "Listen . . . I know you think I'm lying because you believe there isn't an honest bone in my body. Sometimes I think so too," I said, not taking my eyes from his. "I have lied and cheated my way through life to the point that being dishonest became my default. So I understand why you can't trust me. But I need you to give me the benefit of the doubt. Don't look at my eyes or my expression; hear my words. I didn't fucking hurt Cassie. I didn't. I promise you."

He was silent for a few beats, just staring at me like his head was struggling to come to some kind of conclusion, but after a few tense seconds, he nodded.

"Okay."

I drew my brows down, tilting my head slightly to catch his gaze. "Okay?"

"Hm." He breathed out. "I believe you."

Gulping down and breathing out, I nodded. "Thank you," I said, rubbing my sweaty palms on my pants. "If you need help finding who did this, I'm on board."

"Hm." He didn't take his eyes off me.

"Right. We should—head out."

When he said nothing, I shifted to leave through the other side, but his hand encircled my wrist, tugging me back and stopping me from leaving.

I looked down at his hand and then at him. "What."

"I want to break a rule."

My chest grew heavier than it had been before. "Which one?"

"The one that says this has to happen only once. I will not be able to follow that rule, Zahra."

I drew in a breath to try to calm the sudden increase in my heart rate.

"Would you want that?" he asked.

I swallowed. "I've never been opposed to it as long as it stays between us," I said. "No one can find out."

He didn't say anything.

"Would *you* want that?" I asked this time.

He hesitated. "I've never done anything like this before."

"I know," I said.

His gaze moved around my face, and I just knew he was

thinking too hard about it, weighing consequences, advantages, and disadvantages . . . but after a short minute, he nodded. "Okay. I'm not opposed to that either . . . for now."

I nodded, suppressing a smile as I responded.

"For now."

CHAPTER THIRTY-EIGHT

Zahra

I'd always been able to tell whenever someone was about to die.

This was probably because 75 percent of my life had been spent with death surrounding me. Some by my hands, and some by people around me. It had gotten to the point where it stopped bothering me.

I used to hate it—the thick smell of gunpowder, capable of making you gag once a bullet hit a living person; the scent of blood and fear tainted the atmosphere before you saw the person falling to the ground. I used to hate all of it, even if the victim deserved it. But it had been years since I flinched before pulling a trigger or slitting a throat; and it didn't take long enough to attune my senses to the nearness of death. Right now, standing in front of the room Casmiro was lying in, I knew death wasn't around the corner, and the feeling that came with that realization didn't exactly sit well with me.

I knocked twice before I opened the door and stepped in.

Upper was the only one there when I closed the door behind me, the sound making him look up from his phone.

Casmiro still wasn't awake, and according to what I'd heard when Elio and I arrived after the sun came up, his vitals were looking good, and he was responding well to treatments.

"Hey," Upper said with a small smile.

"Hi . . . Still here?"

He thinned his lips, looking at Casmiro's still form, the heart monitor beeping steadily by the side of the bed. My gaze lingered on it for a second before I looked back at Upper, who blew out a breath, getting to his feet. "Where else would I be? I tried calling; you never came back last night. What happened?"

"My phone was dead."

He gave me a disbelieving look. "Yeah . . . and you just randomly disappeared with the boss?"

"No. We went back to his house here because he was upset about Casmiro. But the building was secured, and he passed out after taking a pill since he has sleeping problems, as he said. They took one of the shooters in for questioning, though."

"Yes, Angelo informed me." Upper eyed me, and I knew he wanted to probe. His suspicions about Elio and me were written all over his face.

To hell if I'm going to divulge anything.

"I'm sure Devil would have blown up my phone with worried texts. Did he text you?" I asked, changing the topic.

Upper's curious stare turned into discomfort as he answered, "Yes." His fingers brushed Casmiro's bedpost. "He couldn't reach you either, so he texted. We never text—but like, yeah, he wanted to ask about you," he said, gaze flickering to mine. "But I told him you were okay."

I nodded. "Okay . . . Are *you* okay?"

His head snapped up to look at me. "What?"

"You look like you've barely slept," I pointed out.

"Yeah, the whole, um—anxiety over what happened with Cas and those gunmen and everything. I'm all right though; I probably just need to bathe in coffee." He let out a shaky laugh that didn't reach his eyes.

I glanced at Casmiro's sleeping figure and then at Upper. "You can go get coffee; I'll stay with Cassie while you're out."

He frowned, hesitating as his gaze flickered between Casmiro and me. "You're sure? I know you're not his biggest fan," he said wearily.

"Yeah, about that." I blew out a breath. "I was insensitive earlier—and like, just in the heat of the moment, and I wasn't expecting to see you here. I had so many thoughts run through my mind . . . What could have happened and not? But I'm glad he didn't die."

Upper smiled at me. "I know, it was scary. We've done crazy jobs, but never one that had us running from stray bullets. These guys do that on a regular basis."

"And now we're working for them." My tongue poked the inner side of my cheek.

He eyed me. "You know how to work a gun, so I'm not too worried."

I opened my mouth to say something.

"It's okay." He chuckled. "Your secret is safe with me, and it's all good if you don't want to elaborate."

I really did not want to elaborate, so I smiled in appreciation instead. "Thank you."

"That's all right; I kind of owe you one for keeping the secret about me leaving Street after we find the gold."

"Upper—"

"I'll go get that coffee," he cut me off. "Want one?"

A small smile grazed my lips, and I dropped that topic. "Yeah, I could use a cup."

He nodded before walking past me and out the door.

I watched the closed door for exactly five seconds before looking back at the man on the bed. The room was silent, save for the beeping of the heart monitor.

I walked over, taking the seat Upper had been in, as I soaked in Casmiro's unconscious state. The rise and fall of his chest, his breath bouncing to the top of his oxygen mask as he breathed out, and dropping as he breathed in. The sound steady and in sync with the beep of the machine.

I sighed in exasperation, looking up and around the room.

No CCTV cameras.

"Are they stupid, or are they stupid?" I muttered, only to be met with silence.

Tentatively, I sat up and leaned in, shifting the chair closer to his bed, before lifting my hand and removing his oxygen mask.

I leaned back and watched, tilting my head to the side as his lips parted slightly, his body unconsciously seeking oxygen assistance. It took mere seconds for the sound of the beeping sequence to falter a little.

Seconds for my mind to wander and bring to my mind's eye different scenarios that could take place after cutting off his oxygen . . . His heart could fail without the assistance; his body could go into shock, and the machine would beep like crazy before it drew a flatline.

I shook my head free of those thoughts, leaned back in, and placed his mask back on, dropping my hands to my thighs and watching him. "Oh, Cassie, you are one stubborn motherfucker," I mused. "I was hoping you'd die. It was three fucking bullets, damn it." I rubbed the side of my head, feeling the faint headache grow more profound. "What a mess."

I willed my brain to stop thinking about this and my heart to stop freezing every second with the fear of Elio walking in here and giving me that look of suspicion—

No, I am not thinking about this.

Not thinking about the man I'd spent all night thinking about. The fact that he wanted to break that rule, how he had looked at me before he said he wanted to break the rule, how he had dropped every suspicion, believing me on the spot.

While I was thankful for that, it still had me a bit wary. He was unpredictable; he saw right through and beyond me.

I wondered how he'd question the idiot they caught; I wondered what the idiot would say in the heat of Elio's torture.

I knew Casmiro and Elio were close, but not this much, not so much that it kept him up all night, restless. He wanted to go back but had changed his mind for some reason. He didn't tell me, didn't speak much. When we arrived, he told me to stay here until he returned from wherever he, Angelo, and a few of his soldiers went to interrogate the idiot.

Angelo had only supplied me with a silent nod as a greeting.

Like Casmiro, I knew he didn't trust or like me, and it bothered me because I hadn't exactly done anything to warrant that... aside from messing around with their boss. Talking back at him or diverting his attention from what really mattered—that was it, and I didn't do all of that because of some *ill intention*. I just genuinely liked toying with him and getting him to loosen up and get frustrated.

Not my fault that he looked insanely hot when he frowned or yelled... It was fun messing with him... fun seeing him lose himself buried inside me... fun hearing him moan my name, so hot and breathy as he came inside me and I collapsed against him... God, he really was good with his cock and his hands.

His touch, every single fucking graze, had been deliberate, like he wanted to explore so that he could see the way I'd react when he touched a part of my body.

The sex was more like a quickie, but goddamn, did I feel it right to the tips of my toes. The impact of his thrusts, his grip on me, the pure fucking need in his eyes as he owned me and fucked me into delusion.

I closed my eyes, shaking my head. This might not be the first time playing with fire, but it would most definitely be the first time I'd been burned by it; the only concerning thing was how much I didn't care about that burn.

Hours later, we arrived back in Milan. Casmiro was transferred to the hospital within the compound, and Upper followed.

Elio hadn't said a word to me yet, and I waited for Angelo to finish talking to him before I approached. He didn't turn to me even after he finished; he just walked towards his house. If he wanted me to stop following him, he said nothing about it.

I took my time to study the interior of the ample space, having not had the time to really look around the last time I'd been here. It was pretty basic, nothing homey, just a dead quiet capable of sending chills down your spine. The couches had no color, just a plain smooth black that seemed like no one had ever sat on them.

Unlike the house in Turin, this one had no pictures, almost like the space wasn't his, and he had just been placed here because it was convenient.

I followed him to another corner of the house; this place harbored one couch, a center table, a floor-to-ceiling window, and an elegant bar area filled with different expensive-looking drinks, a closed glass shelf with packs of cigars arranged perfectly inside, and another one filled with different kinds of wineglasses—

"Any purposive reason you're following me?" he asked, shrugging off his jacket, glancing at me before properly hanging it, and moving to his collection of vinyl. A few seconds later, some ominous classical music filled the air.

He moved to the bar area.

"I wanted to find out what happened with the guy you questioned; did he say anything?"

Elio went behind the counter, brows down as he fixed himself a drink, pulling out a cigar when he was done.

I reached him and leaned on the counter, waiting for his response.

He carefully—like he had all the time in the world—placed the cigar between his lips as he spoke. "We did not ask him anything. He has been moved to the compound. I was in no mood to torture, so I only have him locked up."

I frowned. "No mood to torture the guy who knows the person responsible for Casmiro's condition?"

"Hm," he voiced, lighting the cigar, sucking smoke in, and blowing it out, sending that erotic smell of vanilla my way.

"Elio, what—don't you know you're wasting time? These people could be recruiting more men to attack again as we speak."

He nodded, picking up his drink. "Maybe." Then he frowned and looked at me. "My manners—would you like a drink?"

Why the fuck is he so calm?

"No." I gave a humorless laugh. "I would not like a drink when we are sitting ducks and might probably be blown to crisps at any second." I grinned.

"Okay," he said, cigar between his fingers as he picked up his whiskey glass and brought it to his lips, downing the contents in one go before he put it down and got the cigar between his lips again.

"What is going on, Elio?"

His gaze lifted to mine, and his brows dropped as he stared at me with confusion and blew out another smoke streak. "We came back from Turin, I talked briefly with Angelo, I came home, you followed me. I asked if you would like a drink, you gave an odd laugh and refused, and I said okay, and now you're asking what's going on. That is what is going on."

I blinked at him, my mouth gaping open, lost for words. "You are like a fifteen-year-old teenage boy who just can't help but be annoying, just for the sake of being annoying."

He paused as if thinking about my statement, and then he nodded. "Okay."

Jesus—

"Elio, can we get back to this time and this day and age when Casmiro is still unconscious and you're not actively trying to find the people responsible?"

"We are indeed in this time and day and age. And I will find them. I do not rush. I take my time because I like to enjoy it, Zahra. What is the best way to inflict worry on your enemies?"

"I don't know, torturing them?"

He shook his head. "Let me tell you a secret." He placed both his elbows on the counter, bending and leaning in so he could look me right in the eye, his cigar burning away. "I do not like to torture physically—"

"You shot me."

"Your voice bugged me. And I didn't like your tone. Don't interrupt me again."

I rolled my eyes but let him continue.

"When I said I do not like to torture physically, I did not mean that I refrain from doing it entirely. Sometimes I like to do it, but ninety-nine percent of the time, I enjoy playing with the minds of my victims. I love painting images and scenarios in their heads. I don't seek fear; I seek terror. Fear is so little compared to the pure smell of terror you can get from a human body when you meddle with their mind."

I gulped down a bitter taste in my throat.

"I left the man to his mind. I want him to think of all the things he will go through, all the questions he'll have asked, all the *lies* he'll have prepared for them. I want him to second-guess *everything*. I want him at the peak of his mind, thinking of the first words I'll say, the first question I'll ask, and the first look I'll give him; I want him to get very comfortable with his situation. I want him to prepare, to be ready . . . Only then will I visit him." He said it all with his eyes flickering between mine, searching, waiting, learning.

I swallowed again, my throat beyond dry. "And what if his people are recruiting? What if—"

"They would never dare it. Not without thorough preparation. Not without starting a war that would most likely affect each man and those who share his last name, not without ensuring they can take down this empire. I would like to think it would take years of preparing. Because if it doesn't, and they storm in here with guns and bombs at the ready . . . existences would be wiped out; they know that, and this reason alone is why I will win."

A cold chill ran down my spine. "Why do you have to be so intense."

"I am under the influence, and I am in your presence, so yes." His eyes searched mine.

"What has my presence got to do with your intensity?"

His lips lifted a little at the sides. "You arouse me, Zahra. Mind, body, and soul. I am always ready to talk when you're here; your influence on me is . . . highly delectable."

Something was melting in my chest, sinking and rubbing against the walls of my stomach with a tickle that made my insides feel excited.

This man is fucking with my mind.

And I . . . like it.

"Have I finally succeeded in shutting you up with something other than my cock, Querida?"

I swallowed, clearing my throat and straightening.

Amusement lingered in his eyes as he watched me. "You didn't shut me up," I lied. "As embarrassing as it might sound, I was trying to understand the meaning of *delectable*."

"Mm-hmm." He hummed mockingly, still watching me.

"I'm being dead-ass serious."

"Did I counter it?"

"Not with words—your little *mm-hmm* sound did all the countering I needed to hear."

He nodded, bringing his cigar to his lips again, sucking in smoke before placing the cigar on the ashtray, letting the lit end burn away, not once looking away from me.

He turned his head to the side a bit, dark gray eyes still on me as thick white smoke danced out of his mouth, caressing my cheek and increasing the dull thumping between my legs. "You need to talk to your team members; they might wonder why you are not back."

"They don't—"

"I am going to try to get some sleep. Things blur when I've been awake for more than seventy-two hours . . . I get a little . . . light in the head."

I nodded, my teeth pressing on my bottom lip before I released it and spoke. "When do we see each other again?"

His lips twitched as he watched me. "I will call."

"Or I could just sneak out whenever I can? Cause you have so many drinks, and your house is huge?"

"Would dropping by now and then make you satisfied?"

I nodded.

"I will let security know you're allowed to come in whenever."

Just like that . . .

I chucked aside the feeling of unease for later as I grinned instead. "Awesome." I placed both my hands on the counter. "I'll go now, and I would have kissed you if it wasn't *'banned,'* but yeah, you have your *'reasons.'*" I put air quotes around *banned* and *reasons*.

"Hm." He didn't take those eyes off me.

I shook my head, leaning away. "I'll see you, weirdo."

With that, I turned and walked away, knowing his eyes followed my every move.

My mind slipped back to his words to me in the car after I'd asked him to give me the benefit of the doubt.

When I was out of the house, I let my mouth and brows fall into a stern frown as I pulled out my phone and muttered, *"I believe you,* my ass."

I knew something was wrong the moment I entered Street's quarters.

Everyone except Upper stood in front of the kitchen, speaking in hushed voices. They were arguing about something, their faces etched with hard frowns.

"What's going on?"

The argument stopped, and they all looked up at once. The deer-in-a-headlight looks I caught on their faces calmed down when they saw it was me.

"Thank fuck you're back," Dog said. "Shit went down."

Milk nodded hastily. "Big shit."

"Where's Upper?" Devil asked, eyes narrowing behind me.

I walked up to them. "He's with Casmiro; he's fine. What's going on?"

Devil sighed. "When you both left, we got an anonymous email."

That got my attention. "What?"

"Yeah," Milk said. "Dog tried to trace it, but it was fruitless."

"What was it about?"

"The damn chihuahua," Dog supplied. "They sent us a location with a short note that said, 'The package you find is the key to finding the original painting.' *There,* that look you're giving right now is the very one I had after reading it."

I frowned. "Who the fuck would send us that? Or try to help?"

"That's not even the worst part," Milk said.

I narrowed my eyes at them.

"We went to the location, and we did find something," Devil said.

Oh . . .

"What did you find?"

They all exchanged wary looks; the silence stretched, doing wonders to heighten my already heightened nerves. "What is it? The suspense is killing me," I urged.

Milk backed towards the kitchen. "Right here in the kitchen; promise you won't freak out."

"I can't promise when I don't even know what it is."

"Well, come on." Devil gestured with his head as we went into the kitchen. Milk stopped behind the counter, her gaze on the spot by the fridge and the cupboard a few inches above the ground before she looked at me.

I approached, preparing myself for the worst as I followed Milk's gaze and looked—

A gasp left my parted lips, and my whole body went completely frozen.

CHAPTER THIRTY-NINE

Zahra

We steal, we cheat, and we piss off bad guys, but we don't usually . . . kidnap people.

Even if we held someone against their will, we always wore masks and never brought them to where we lived. We didn't leave a trace of ourselves for the victim to recognize, and we most definitely did not kidnap guys in cream-colored dad khakis and a sky-blue polo shirt with a chef's hat logo on the left side and a name tag that said "Saucy Chika."

I blinked, staring at a dark-skinned, brown-eyed, scared man whose head moved frantically between us as he tried to shift further away. His breathing became loud, and he was humming his words because his mouth was covered by a strip of wide silver tape; his legs and hands were tied in what looked like a complicated knot that made it difficult for him to move.

His eyes were wide in fear, and I couldn't—*couldn't*—think of a reason as to . . . why this stranger was tied up in our kitchen or how the fuck they were able to get him in here.

I nodded slowly and then turned to my people. "Let's step outside for a bit." I ushered them with my hands, a smile on my face.

When we were a reasonable distance from the kitchen, I turned sharply to the three people in front of me. "Who the fuck is that?"

"We have no idea," Devil said.

"You have—" My hand covered my mouth as I looked around as if people would charge in any minute to get us for this. When my eyes settled on Street again, I leaned in and whisper-yelled.

"You have no idea why a guy who looks like a nine-to-five counter boy at an upgraded version of McDonald's is tied up in our fucking kitchen?"

"Yeah," Milk answered this time, eyeing me. "Devil just said that."

I leaned back. "He didn't—what is happening right now? Did you guys tie him up?"

Devil shook his head, crossing his arms to his chest, his biceps straining against the Henley he wore. "We found him like that at the pickup point under some bridge, very secluded. He was in some truck. Knocked out, and we brought him here."

"This is bad. What the fuck does he have to do with the chihuahua?" I asked.

"I'm guessing that's what we need to ask him," Milk said.

"I personally just want to know why his name tag says 'Saucy.' What the fuck is that about?" Dog voiced.

Devil shot him an annoyed frown. "I'm more concerned about the people who dropped him off and reached out to us to pick him up."

"Yeah, me too," Milk joined in. "If Saucy Chika knows anything about Arturo's chihuahua, why would the people who dropped him off want us to decipher it? Why us? And why Saucy Chika?"

"You just love saying 'Saucy Chika.'" Dog smirked at Milk.

"What? It's a sexy combination and flows well with my accent, and now I think everyone should have at least one sexy—"

"Guys, can we focus on the real matter here?" I cut in. "We gotta find out who he is and let him go before Marino finds out and this all goes to shit before it even starts—"

The front door opened, and Upper walked in, attention on his phone as he closed the door behind him. He looked up in a double take and slowed to a stop as he peered at us, his brows furrowed.

"What did you fuckers do now?" he asked as he reached us, pocketing his phone.

"Kidnapped someone," I informed.

"We didn't kidnap anyone," Devil injected immediately. "He was already kidnapped before we . . . took him from the car where he was tied up and . . . brought him here."

Silence befell us as we stared at each other.

"If we're being logical, that's still kidnapping," Milk said.

"Worse than kidnapping," Upper supported. "It's double kidnapping; we've taken kidnapping to a level that borders on diabolical because we took a kidnapped person and kidnapped them, which means we are the kidnappers of the kidnapped."

"That doesn't make any fucking sense, Upper," Dog said.

Milk shrugged. "It made sense to me."

"Of course it would; you're . . . *you*." Dog frowned.

"I hope you didn't mean that in an offensive way," Milk said, turning slightly to face him.

"Please, by all means, take all the offense because that is what I was aiming for."

I sighed. "Guys, back to Saucy Chika—"

"Who is Saucy Chika?" Upper asked, confusion in his tone.

"The guy we kidnapped," Devil answered, and then silence fell again. He closed his eyes for a second before snapping them back open. "No, we didn't kidnap—he was—you know what? It doesn't fucking matter; let's go untie him and get answers."

We all seemed to agree with that as we returned to the kitchen. Saucy Chika's eyes were wide, and his hums of protest became frantic as Devil tore off the tape not so gently from his mouth.

"Fuck!" Saucy Chika cursed, breathing harshly with his mouth as he looked frantically around at us. "Who're you lot?" His thick roadman accent coated his words.

"Your worst nightmare," Dog whispered, dragging it out dramatically.

"My what?" the confused man asked.

"Ignore him," Devil said, undoing the knots on Saucy Chika's legs. "He was diagnosed with idiotism a while back."

The man frowned. "Is that actually a thing?"

Devil extended his hand to help pull him up. "It's now a thing; he was patient zero."

"Oh." Saucy Chika eyed Dog warily like the idiotism thing was contagious. "Why you lot letting me out, though?" he asked no one in particular, rubbing his wrist while Devil gave him his space to collect himself.

I took a step forward. "Because we didn't kidnap you."

"Yeah, we just took you from your kidnappers. Which makes us worse than them," Upper said.

Devil settled his gaze on Upper. "We got an anonymous email that a package they would send would answer questions about Arturo Garza's chihuahua. We got to the location and found him."

"Oh." Upper frowned. "Anonymous email . . ." He looked at Dog. "Were you able to track it?"

"No luck; I was hoping you'd have some."

Upper nodded. "On it." He left the kitchen.

I studied the victim in front of me; his brows were drawn down in confusion, his eyes unfocused.

"What is it? Does the name Arturo Garza sound familiar to you?" I asked him.

His throat bobbed. "Bruv, I don't . . ." He trailed off, swaying on his feet; I quickly rushed towards him, holding him steady while Devil took care of his other side.

"I think we should get him to a chair," I said to Devil and then looked at Milk. "Can you arrange a quick sandwich and maybe some milk with sugar?"

"Sure."

Devil and I led him to the living room, and Dog followed right behind us.

We settled Saucy Chika on a chair, and he rubbed his head as a groan left him.

I took a chair opposite him, and Dog settled on the arm of the chair while Devil stood at the side. Upper walked in with a laptop, settling on a chair as he worked on finding who sent that email.

"What's your name?" I asked him.

"Chika," he answered as Milk came out with a sandwich and a glass of milk, which I was sure was mixed with something that would give him his energy back. "Thank you," he said with a smile, which she returned before taking the space next to Upper.

"Why is there 'Saucy' right before 'Chika,' though," Dog asked.

"Dog," I groaned in a warning.

"What? Don't pretend like you don't want to know too."

Chika drank half of the water in the glass before dropping it down and picking up the sandwich. "It's company protocol," he answered before taking a bite of the sandwich.

"Company protocol to . . . put in something sexy before your name?" Dog asked.

"Bruv, my boss is tapped," Chika muttered with his mouth full. "My name's calm compared to the madness they got here. Man's got Busty Chloe, Sex God Mason, COCK-ey Christian, and the worst one, Glistening Pink Candy. It only gets worse from this point."

"Why do you *work* there?" I couldn't help but ask because that protocol was shit.

"Bruv, you try cuttin' from a job that pays a thousand pounds every two days, just cause man's gotta wear some dead name tag and serve wastemen in London. You think my uni fees and rent pay themselves?"

"A thousand pounds every two days—that's amazing! What name do you think I'll get?" Milk asked with an excited grin.

"Creamy Milk, definitely Creamy Milk," I said with a wide smile, nodding with Milk.

"Come again. Did you say London?" Devil cut into our distracting exchange.

"Yeah—hold up, where is this?" He looked around.

"Italy . . . Milan."

Chika almost choked on the sandwich he was eating. "Say what?"

"Yeah, you are far from home, Spider-Man," Dog said.

"What day is it?" he asked with wide eyes.

"Uh . . . July eleventh? Tuesday, the year 2023?" Milk said.

"Holy shit," Chika mused aloud. "Holy fucking shit?"

"Is he having a seizure?" Dog asked.

Chika dropped the half-eaten sandwich and picked up the glass of milk, gulping everything down loudly before he finished and set the glass on the center table.

"I'm sweatin'." He untucked his polo. "Nah, I'm sweatin' bad. I need air, fam."

"The aircon's working perfectly," Milk answered.

"Bruv, I'm sweatin' tears right now. I just lost my job, yeah? And—fuck, I didn't even do that big quiz for that class I'm failing. Man was on my knees beggin' for a retake, fam! And I still missed it. Plus, I skipped that school competition where I was meant to chat about fire and water or some shit—"

"That's dumb," Upper said.

"I know," Chika said, blowing out a breath and, well—freaking out. "This is fucked up. The last time I was proper awake was the seventh. After I got attacked? It's just dust, fam. Can't remember shit."

I sat up, longing to get to the point. "What happened? Tell us what you remember."

He sighed. "Bruv, I was at work, normal ting. Stepped out to chuck the trash, yeah? Then I hear footsteps. Before man even turns 'round—boom—white handkerchief on my face. Next thing? I'm here."

"They kept sedating him," Devil said.

"Yeah, kept him somewhere clean too; that's why he still looks fresh out of a shitty situation," Dog said.

"Do you know Arturo Garza?" I asked.

He scoffed. "Do I know him? Even in death—even in fucking

death—the old man still finds a way to fuck up my life—him and that godforsaken chihuahua."

"So you *do* know him."

"Yeah, man was my dad."

Upper frowned. "Arturo Garza didn't have children."

"So says everyone who *knows* him." Chika laughed humorlessly. "I was his adopted mistake. Never knew why he took me in, just to bin me off." The hate in his voice told me he knew why, and when he spoke again, we all knew why. "Maybe he just wanted a Nigerian son cause his old ting back in the day was from there. Thought he could get that feeling back through me—in a platonic way, obviously—then he washed his hands off me when he saw it didn't work," he said in one breath, looking around at us before clearing his throat. "But he's no longer in my life, so whoever thought it was fun to kidnap me cause they think I have some info on him just wasted their fucking time."

"So, you don't know anything about the painting?" Milk asked.

"Or the quest?" Devil added.

"Yeah, that dumbass quest. Man's whole life was just plottin', schemin', actin' like some mastermind of his own fucking hype. Long ting, bruv."

"So you are wealthy; why work in some make-believe McDonald's?" Dog asked.

"Because I told Arturo to keep his help and his money. Man tried throwin' me a cut when he was turnin' all his shit to gold, yeah? I told him to give that to his real kid and get the fuck out my face."

"His real kid being the chihuahua," I noted.

"Yes. And he did, and I was free until—now."

Devil frowned. "The people who took you must have a valid reason for doing so or else you wouldn't be here. You know something about the quest. It's only a matter of time before the other people find out and you're hunted. We can offer you protection if you tell us all you know."

Chika's eyes scanned us uncertainly, his stare saying that he did know something and was holding back.

His gaze locked with mine, and I nodded encouragingly at him.

Chika sighed. "Listen, I don't wanna get caught up in Arturo's business. I have spent years, *years* tryna forget that I had someone like that as a parent, and I did. I moved to London, started fresh, and got a banging job that pays a lot of money so people can say Saucy Chika every time they see me while my sadist of a boss wanks on it while he watches like a creep from the computers in his office."

"That is gross," Milk said.

"Bruv, the money's worth it. Only thing I know 'bout the painting is that every piece was kept in one place. Here in Milan, yeah? Some heavily guarded 'sock' company. They move 'em bit by bit to different regions and countries. No clue how the timing works with all the shipping madness, fam. I just know the spot where all the paintings are. And I only clocked that by accident; I overheard him once chatting to himself and his dog, plotting like some mad scientist. I thought he was going crazy."

I smiled to myself. "The location would be perfect. Just tell us what you need in exchange for this info, and we'll provide it."

"You offered to give me protection."

"You don't want money?" Dog asked.

"I don't want his money, your money, or no dirty gang money, fam. I don't want none of it; man just wants to go back to my life, innit."

My gaze met Devil's, and he nodded with a shrug.

I brought my gaze back to Chika. "You're in luck, Chika. I happen to know someone who can provide you the kind of protection you need until all this is over."

He let out a breath of relief. "I can cut now, yeah?"

"No," I said.

Upper looked up and shot me a frown. "No? We are letting him go."

Chika's eyes fell on me. "Listen, if I even wanna save my job, or keep my boss off my neck, I gotta cut now, fam."

I shook my head. "I am sorry about your job, school, and life, but you're in this now. You are part of the narrative, and you'll go with us when we want to get the paintings."

"You want him to put his life on hold for us?" Milk asked, looking at me with disbelief.

I got to my feet and paced the room. "I know it's insensitive—"

"It's beyond insensitive, Zahra," Upper said. "He has been kidnapped for days."

"We didn't kidnap him. We don't know who did. We need more time to study our situation before we let him out with our protection." I looked at Chika. "It's for your safety and our gain, Chika. A win-win situation."

"I see a point in that," Dog said.

Upper shook his head. "What about Marino's people? If they catch wind of this—"

I shrugged. "They won't; we'll be careful."

"A word, Zahra," Devil said, heading for the kitchen.

With a sigh and a disapproving stare from Upper and Milk, I followed Devil to the kitchen.

"Let me guess; you don't agree with me," I said.

Dark eyes watched me. "It's not that, Z. I just need to know why you're brushing away the fact that some unknown person out there gave us this much means to get information about the painting. Something big is obviously at work here."

"Devil—"

"They kidnapped someone, Z. All the way from London and dropped them in our laps, for free, just like that. It doesn't happen. It's above our damn pay grade, and as much as I hate to say this, I think we should tell Marino."

"No."

"Zahra—"

"We are not telling them until we confirm the source is legit. Until we find the paintings."

He frowned, confused. "Why? Is there a loophole I don't know about?"

I bit the inside of my lips. "There are no loopholes; I know as much as you do, D. Just trust me on this; if there's one thing we can hold against Marino to guarantee our safety out of this, it's our leverage with this information."

He didn't look convinced, but he didn't counter it.

"Guys," Upper's voice called from the living room. Devil and I locked gazes before we exited the kitchen.

"What happened?" Devil asked as we watched Upper frown at the laptop screen.

"I didn't get the person who gave the info, but I traced it down to a region."

"In Italy?" I asked.

"Yeah . . . Sicily, that's where it came from. Everything else is blocked by an adaptive firewall, and it would take me forever to bypass it because it just keeps regenerating."

"I don't know about this, guys. Who the hell knows us from Sicily?" Milk said.

"Or maybe it was a cover route?" Dog asked.

"No, their cover route was China, but I broke it. It's Sicily. Real name unknown, direct location unknown, almost like it's not even on the map," Upper said.

My spine straightened. "It doesn't matter where they're from or who they are," I said. "We need to find the original painting. And get the gold. Whoever they are, we are one piece of information richer, and that's all that matters right now."

When I got nods of approval, I released a breath.

"Come on, guys; we have lots of planning to do."

CHAPTER FORTY

Elio

I might have overdosed again.

In all honesty, I could not be certain, but from the moment my heavy eyelids opened, I knew I had been benumbed for a long time, a day or maybe two. It was all murky. The last thing I remembered was telling Zahra I needed to rest and that I'd call her.

I groaned—thinking felt like the most difficult task my brain had ever had to do, and it took great effort to turn my head towards the side of the bed to check the time. It was 10:57 P.M.; I turned away, my eyes settling on the plain white ceiling above me.

The quietness around me was disturbing, and the room was dimly lit, the windows closed; the air conditioner worked at an average level, not too cold, not too hot. The covers were drawn up to my mid-stomach, and the curtains were closed.

Angelo has been here.

I could discern that from the lit lamps around the room. I never turned them on before I filled myself with pills and passed out. I also didn't close the curtains and windows or use the duvet.

I sat up and rubbed my eyes, ignoring how lightheaded I felt, how tight my muscles were, and how tired I was for no reason.

I had a transcendent urge to fall back against the bed and never get up until I exigently had to. But doing that was equivalent to signing myself up for a depressive episode that I would be very willing to let overcome me.

I didn't have the time to be reposed. There was work to do—a painting to find.

I stretched my neck from left to right while removing the thick covers and dragging myself out of bed.

My stomach ached with pangs of hunger, supplying me the substantiation that I had been out for hours on end, forcing rest when I should be out there doing something worthwhile.

I headed straight for the bathroom, catching my reflection in the mirror. The instant burn of irritation I felt in my chest was not erasable. My eyes were sunken, white, and lifeless, my skin pale, hair a mess—

I held both sides of the sink, my grip hard as I tried to fight off the unnecessary self-disappointment weighing on my shoulders like ancient rocks.

I shook my head and proceeded to brush my teeth and then shower.

Taking my time, I scrubbed my skin with the primary aim of washing myself *off* myself. But like the many times I'd tried, it was impossible; my gaze kept shifting to the bathtub, and it took every bit of my willpower to stop myself from approaching it and using it for all the wrong purposes.

I shook my head yet again and made haste: finished showering, moisturized my skin, and put on a fresh loose black T-shirt and black slacks, even though I really wanted to wear sweatpants, which were more comfortable. But I was home and it was nighttime, and the T-shirt was already a stretch out of what I knew to be my comfort zone.

I quickly brushed my hair and exited the bathroom like I was being chased out. Many items in there were triggering, and I was physically, emotionally, and mentally incapable of dealing with the aftermath of my weakness.

All I needed now was a book, a cigar, food—if I had enough zeal to even stomach anything—and some peace and quiet outside . . . maybe at the rooftop, which I could no longer go to without thinking of the one woman who had plastered herself in my mind before I lost all sense of consciousness the last time I was awake.

Right now, I couldn't afford to have my train of thought directed back to her. It would most definitely bring back the mind-numbing conflict I had been battling with myself since I caught every bit of the lies she had woven into truths.

She confused me—yet, she didn't.

Zahra was playing a game, one that I couldn't decipher or break down on my own. Her dishonesty was disappointing. I had shared my baggage, opened up to her so she could feel free to do the same without having to walk a path where she'd openly betray me, and I'd have no choice but to kill her for it.

But apparently, like me, she treated trust like a possession too hard to let go of.

I wasn't sure if she had anything to do with Casmiro's situation. I didn't want to jump to conclusions and make a mistake based on the way I felt—she made me doubt it; for the first time in my life, I doubted myself, just because Zahra had looked at me some kind of way, just because she had shut me up by letting me have her in a way that had made me ache for more since our time in that car.

Never in a million years did I think a woman would be why I temporarily lost my senses or broke a rule I had put in place with the intent to follow it.

Caring for Zahra Faizan was not on my agenda, and as much as I would love to deny it till I believed the lie, the thought of her would never let me.

I could be fucking the enemy, and the only thought in my mind—the only thought that had been in my mind that night was the fact that I longed for the next time I got to experience being that close to her again.

The heat, the obscene connection that had me wanting to tear off my outrageous affirmation and kiss her back into arousal, the burning need still lingering in me even after I'd had the most mind-altering sex in all my thirty-three years of living.

I'd had orgasms with the few women I'd been with, but I never thought it could feel like that . . . I never thought the feeling could soften every nerve ending in a human body and make them feel content with just the sight of the person who had caused it.

If she had been my first, I would have waved it off as the normal way it should feel, but she wasn't my first. She wasn't the first woman I'd desired, but she was the first to elicit such emotions from me.

I was craving a forbidden fruit that might very well drag me to the darkest pits of hell—but this was also where my gut feeling kicked in; if she had been trying to harm me in any way, I would have picked it up by now, but I had a feeling that whatever game she was playing had nothing to do with me. She was only using my name and the protection and connections I had to offer.

I wouldn't have cared. Zahra wasn't the first to use me or the power my name held. I had no desire to stop whatever she was doing; as long as it didn't alter my goal, she was free to use me however she pleased. Maybe she would open up later on . . . or perhaps I was just delusional, and my gut feelings were broken, and she was indeed after something that could alter my goals and stop me from burning this hell to the ground; maybe I should kill her, kill her before I fell deeper into this obvious hole I had been conveniently ignoring . . . Maybe, I don't know . . . maybe I was finally losing my mind. Maybe I should stop thinking about—

A sharp beeping sound, followed by a vibration, had my attention turned to the lit-up phone screen by the bedside table.

It was connected to a charger I didn't remember putting there.

Angelo, with his creepy behavior, was beginning to crawl his way up my nerves. I made a mental note to have a lengthy discussion with him about the importance of my privacy . . . *again*.

I settled on the side of the bed, unplugged the phone, and unlocked it.

There were four messages from Gemma, nine from Zahra, and one from Angelo.

I opened Angelo's first.

Today

> *Angelo Mancini (Ex-consigliere):*
> Casmiro's awake and doing all right. I didn't want to call because I knew you were on your pills. I stopped by yesterday afternoon to check on you. I'm about to call again, if you don't pick up, call me whenever you get this message, or I'll stop by again.
> 1 min ago

In the next minute, he was calling. I picked up on the first ring.

"*Finally. I was about to stop by with a doctor.*"

"How is he?" I asked, ignoring his remark.

"*Looking good. He's resting now.*"

I closed my eyes for a few seconds, reveling in the relief that flooded through me. "Did he ask for me?"

"*Yes. I told him you weren't in the compound. He thinks you're out there with soldiers actively looking for the people who did this. He also chewed me a new one for not going with you.*"

"Tell him I'm back and will come to see him soon. Thanks for covering for me."

Casmiro could not find out about this. About my mental health problems. He was better off not knowing—one less person to worry about.

"*Will you ever tell him? About your—*"

"Thank you for the information, Angelo. Do not text me next time unless it is for a significant emergency. The keyword there is *significant*. Am I clear?"

I heard him sigh from the other end of the line.

"*Okay, Marino.*"

"In addition, I think it is very weird for you to walk into my bedroom and change its setting to make me feel comfortable. While it is very much appreciated, I would not like it to happen again."

"What—"

"Goodbye." I ended the call, exiting his message box to click on Gemma's.

Yesterday

> *Gemma (blonde car highway):*
> Hi, my love! I'm thinking of getting a
> tattoo; which do you think suits me best?
> An eagle or a dove?
> 1:34 P.M.

> *Gemma (blonde car highway):*
> I think I'm going to go with a dove; it's
> more fitting. I'm gonna have it under my
> left boob. I'll send a picture when it's done!
> 2:01 P.M.

> *Gemma (blonde car highway):*
> It's done! Omg, it's gorge!
> (Sent a photo)
> You like????
> 5:55 P.M.

The dove drawing was really beautiful, larger than I imagined, and it suited her skin complexion.

I was impressed.

Today

> *Gemma (blonde car highway):*
> Are you okay? You didn't read this or

respond. Did your victims finally fight back
and kill you? Omg! Do I need to call 112???
Fuck, I don't even know your address.
Hope you're okay. TEXT ME BACK SO I
DON'T DIE WITH WORRY!
11:28 A.M.

I shook my head. It was good, the kind of friendship we shared. She texted every day, and I responded whenever I wasn't too busy. Gemma was a free-spirited woman who reminded me so much of my sister. While their personalities might differ in several ways, I shared a closeness with this stranger that had me adding her to the list of people I had to make sure were okay before I reached my end goal.

But first I had to figure out why I was drawn to her.

Me:
Hello.
Me:
I apologize for the delay in
response. I had a rough week.
Me:
The dove tattoo looks perfect. I
like it. The artist did a good job.
Me:
If it's no trouble for you, I would
like to see you again, maybe at a
restaurant of your choosing. Not
tonight, but sometime between
tomorrow and next day. Let me
know your schedule.

After I sent the message, I reread it, hoping I didn't pass across the wrong subtext. I wasn't well-versed in the world of texting, and it was worrisome how one text could be interpreted into many meanings.

I exited her message box and let my thumb hover above Zahra's message.

Something bizarre happened at that moment. I felt a small squeezing burn in my chest; an odd—out-of-place—nervousness gripped me out of nowhere, and I hesitated for a long time before clicking on her name.

Yesterday

> *Zahra:*
> Hey Dad
> 2:35 P.M.

> *Zahra:*
> U know, when u said u'd call, I didn't think it would take u so long. I'd love to believe u are not blowing me off
> 4:42 P.M.

> *Zahra:*
> Are u blowing me off?
> 7:50 P.M.

> *Zahra:*
> Wait, this is not delivering, did u fucking block me?
> 9:02 P.M.

> *Zahra:*
> Fine. I get the message. I'll delete ur number too. Asshole.
> 1:42 A.M.

Today

> *Zahra:*
> Listen, I'm not much of a texter, and I obvs did not delete your number. I was kind of high when I sent that, anyway. Is this really you blowing me off and changing your mind about that rule? Cause you can just come clean and say it to me instead of ignoring me? It's kind of a dick move.
> 12:56 P.M.

> *Zahra:*
> My God! I can't believe I'm being ghosted by YOU of all fucking people
> 4:08 P.M.

> *Zahra:*
> Is something wrong?
> 6:31 P.M.

> *Zahra:*
> Text me when you wake up.
> 9:26 P.M.

I frowned at the last message and looked around the room as if I'd spot a trace of her. There was nothing.

But she was here. A few minutes ago.

I clicked on the call icon above the screen without thinking.

Drumming my finger against my knee, I felt another squeeze in my chest when the first ring came through, and then the call was declined.

I frowned, my brain already taking a route down its familiar overthinking lane. This was why I was not too fond of phone calls, receiving or initiating them. They never came with a positive outcome. Either something was wrong, or the person you were trying to reach didn't respond, or, in my case now—declined the call.

I didn't know if I should feel anger or worry.

The first time I willingly initiate a call, it's rejected almost immediate—

The phone buzzed in my hand, Zahra's name flashing on the screen. I watched it ring for a decent stretch of seconds, and then I picked it up.

"*Hi?*" Her voice came through uncertain, soft, far away.

"You declined my call."

"*I called back,*" she said, voice low like she didn't want anyone to overhear her.

"Why did you decline it?"

There was a slight shuffling sound at the end of the line. "*My phone was on the center table, and Devil was there. I didn't want him to see that you were calling.*"

"I thought you were smart enough not to save my number with my actual name."

"*I didn't. It was saved as Dad. How the fuck would I have explained that to him. I don't have a dad, and it's—I can't tell him it's you because then he'd ask what that is about, and then he'd wonder why I have your number and why I didn't save it with Marino or Elio and I—*"

"Zahra."

"*Yeah?*" she breathed out, and I could sense a twinge of nervousness in that small gesture.

A calm settled within me. "Your voice . . . it's different on the phone."

I think I heard a small laugh. "*Of course it is; you're hearing it through signals from a satellite in space.*"

"Fascinating." I relaxed back on the bed. "I didn't know that; enlighten me on satellites and space that I definitely know nothing about."

"*And he says I'm insufferable.*"

"We are alike in so many ways. Therefore I concede that it is normal for both of us to be insufferable."

"Smart-ass."

"I have an IQ of 170, so yes. I am smart."

"You weren't supposed to respond to that. For a man with an IQ of 170, you lack basic conversational skills."

"Being academically intelligent is not equal to being socially intelligent."

"Fine, I give up."

"As you should."

Silence stretched.

"So Cassie's awake." She broke it.

"Indeed."

"Did you see him yet? Any valuable information he might have to pass across about the people who did this?"

I sighed. "I don't want to talk about Casmiro."

"Oh . . . What do you want to talk about?"

"Food. I think I'm hungry."

I could hear the smile in her voice as she said, *"You're in luck. I haven't had my dinner yet. In fact, I was about to eat when your call came in. Give me a second. I'll be there, and you can eat me—I mean, eat with me. With me. Jesus fuck—bye."*

The line cut off abruptly, and I stared at the screen, unable to stop my lips from curling at the side.

After a few useless seconds of replaying our conversation, I fixed myself a cigar and grabbed the book by my bedside table, put on my reading glasses, and settled as I drew in a lungful of smoke.

It burned my chest, sending the breath out of me in an instant and clogging my windpipe; the feeling compelled a cough out of me.

"That's a first," I mused aloud, blowing out the smoke while stifling the cough.

I cleared my throat, ignoring the feeling as it subsided. Somehow, the pain the cigar caused pushed me to take another drag, expecting to feel the burn—nothing happened.

Disappointment weighed heavily on my shoulders.

I fought off the thought and focused on the book in my grip.

About forty minutes into the book, the cigar had been discarded, my hunger forgotten, and the sound of my door quietly pushing open became a background disturbance.

I looked up briefly to catch Zahra walking in.

"Your idea of a second is worrisome."

"Shut up; I had to make sure it was safe enough to sneak out."

I memorized the page number and then dropped the book on my bedside table.

Unintentionally, my gaze took her in, sweeping from her head to her toes and then back to her head. She was in a different silk nightgown, bloodred, with a robe over it. I watched her drop the food bag on the two-seater couch before she turned to me, her short hair brushed to curly perfection, and she watched me like a package handed to her on a platter. She was in awe for some reason. It would be quite embarrassing to admit that the look had me feeling the same way compliments made me feel—flustered.

"It's late already, you shouldn't be walking around the compound dressed like that," I said, and she looked down at herself innocently.

"Dressed like what?"

"In a nightgown."

She shrugged. "Well, I told you, it's all silk inside my wardrobe."

"Why do I have the urge to see your wardrobe?" I asked, and her eyes widened and sparkled beautifully in mischief, lips curling to the side in a smile as she approached the bed like she had done this particular action many times before.

"Maybe because you are a fucking weirdo," she said; her sly smile turned genuine as she got on the bed. "And a creep with serial killer genes."

A twitch in my cock told me I liked the way she gracefully climbed onto my bed, and how perfect she looked on it. "There's no such thing as serial killer genes, Zahra."

"I saw a TV show once. One of the main characters had serial killer genes."

"Fiction."

Her perfectly shaped brows drew together. "Yeah?"

"Yes, if you must know, a lot of things can be created in fictional works. Like transportation tubes, Holophonors, and the What-If Machine in *Futurama* in 2000; DNA altering in *Gattaca*, released in 1997, which was said to help children not contract genetic diseases from parents; and the Skin-Healing patch from the film *Aeon Flux*, made in 2005. That one is self-explanatory," I said, expecting her to respond, but she just stared. "I can understand why someone like you would mistake the serial killer genes for—don't give me that look, Sport."

"What look?" She blinked, her eyes brighter than before, staring lustfully at me.

My index finger gestured in circles to her face. "*That* look."

She grinned. "Your intelligence is a huge turn-on, I'm not gonna lie. Besides, only a creep would want to see my wardrobe."

I took off my glasses, dropping them on top of the book without taking my eyes off her. "If we want to talk about creeps, your name should be included on the list."

She angled her body towards me, her nipples reflecting against the silk nightwear she wore, tilting her head and baring her neck for me to see how suckable it was. "How so?"

"Turning on my night lamps, closing my windows and curtains, drawing my covers up my body as if you don't plan to kill me in the near future."

She rose to her knees, fingers raking her hair back from her face. "You were shivering."

"I never shiver."

"And how would you know that? Do you set cameras around your room like a creep who loves to watch himself sleep after he wakes up?" She crawled to me, straddling my thighs and making breathing extremely difficult.

"Are you asking about cameras so you know which to take care of when you sneak into my room to slit my throat?"

"I already checked. There are no cameras or bugs. For a man who preaches about carefulness, you are very careless."

"I am not. Getting killed in my sleep is one of my fantasies."

She drew her body closer to mine. "Weirdo."

"Creep." My voice was hoarse as her long fingers brushed down my shoulders, stealing my breath with the warmth of each graze through my shirt.

"Asshole," she whispered.

"Greedy thief."

Her lips found my ear. "Psycho killer." She bit my earlobe.

My lips parted. "Witch."

She chuckled, lifting her face from my neck, then her lips aligned with mine, a breath touch away from brushing, and then she whispered, "Whore."

My breathing fevered against her lips. "Slut."

Her teeth clamped down on her bottom lip, her fingers disappearing underneath my shirt, her palms feeling up my stomach muscles, which flexed at the tantalizing burn from her touch.

Her gaze locked with mine.

Beautiful.

I switched to Spanish. *"You do not want me obsessed with you, Zahra."*

"Funny," she also said in Spanish, *"I was about to say the same thing."*

"Really?"

"Yes, I can be really scary."

My hand moved to the back of her neck, fisting her hair, not enough to cause pain, but enough to bare her neck for my hungry tongue.

"I am hungry," I whispered in the language. My tongue and teeth dragged up her collarbone to the top of her neck, below her ear, the warmth from her skin feeding me in more ways than one. *"But not for food."*

In a swift movement, I flipped us over until she was beneath me, her lust-filled eyes peering up at me.

"It's all your fault," I said, tightening my grip on her hair.

"What is?" she asked when I released my hold, watching me take one of her hands from underneath my shirt.

"Putting the idea of eating you out in my head," I answered, gesturing for her to keep her fingers up as I removed my rings one by one, slipping them down her fingers for safekeeping. "Now you'll have to hold these for me."

Her chest heaved in anticipation. "Thought you didn't like the mess?"

"Apparently, Sport, you have not been paying attention to the things I say to you."

"What do you mean?"

"Do I need to fuck you to bring back your memories?"

Her pupils dilated.

My hand, free of the rings, was ready to inflict torture.

"I'm sorry, but the last thing I want to do right now is think," she said, frustration leeching into every rise and fall of her voice.

The smile I allowed to curl at the sides of my lips did not promise safety; it was created from the intentions buried deep inside my head, intentions that I finally felt comfortable putting into play.

My eyes searched hers as I repeated my words from a few days ago. "I don't like a mess, Zahra, but I'll take yours any day."

"Oh, that."

"Yes . . ." I trailed off, gaze dropping to her lips, my heart thumping harshly. "Allow me to give you a chance to tap out now before it's too late," I said.

The smile that touched her lips mirrored mine.

"I never tap out, especially not from your challenges."

I was amused yet again. Immensely impressed by her confidence. I tilted my head, watching my living, breathing addiction as I responded, "That, Querida, is one of the many reasons I like you."

CHAPTER FORTY-ONE

Elio

Zahra Faizan's body was equivalent to a serum created to ignite a strong dose of fever into a healthy body.

Warm, soft, and ready, this woman was mine for the taking. She was mine to own and claim tonight and as many nights as I saw fit. She didn't know it yet, but she'd signed away a lot the moment she agreed to my rule break.

My addictions had always been centered on want, and at first, I wanted Zahra—to be close to her, to hear her speak to me—but now, the need to touch her played with my reasoning. She had me daring myself to act without thinking. To be careless. I had never been careless, but she made carelessness seem like the new carefulness. I was blinded, and I was aware that my indifference towards this was reckless; but this, *this* moment, here and now, was worth every risk of recklessness.

Her eyes were as bright as my desperation. Her brows, shaped to perfection, had me admiring the smooth sweep of the hair lining them. An uncertain smile tugged at her lips. "You . . . like me," she stated.

"Have my actions or my words shown anything otherwise?"

She chortled. "You having a fantasy of slitting my throat doesn't exactly spell out how much you like me, sir."

Sir.

I had been addressed that way often, but it had never made me feel so . . . desperate.

"I like it," I stated, watching her face go from smug to interested.

She raised a brow. "Like what?"

"*Sir.* I like how you say it."

She raised her hand, her fingers disappearing into my hair, the feeling as exhilarating as the first time she performed that very action. "And I like how transparent you are with your emotions. It's new. Men are always—"

I shook my head. "I don't care about what men always do. I feel it; I say it. Like I once told you, beating around the bush is for children."

She smiled, eyes softening, fingers caressing my scalp. "The world would be chaos if everyone had the same reasoning as you."

"I know." I leaned close to her until my nose was buried in the crook of her neck, my tongue strutting out to lick her warm skin before my lips sucked on the tender spot. I felt her body arch slightly from the bed, shuddering breath leaving her parted lips. Pride filled me. "I'm mostly this way because I crave the chaos," I muttered before moving higher, my tongue exploring before I left a bruise.

There was an aching strain against my briefs, bringing the annoying realization that I still had my slacks on. But I loved the pleasuring pain created from the anticipation of making her moan and writhe beneath and atop me, making her brand this moment to memory for as long as she breathed.

"You keep leaving hickeys like that, some people might put two and two together," she said, voice breathy.

"Their funerals if they have enough courage to voice their suspicion," I mumbled as my hand brushed the side of her thigh, up to the curves of her hip, and then settled on her waist, her nightgown creasing and lifting, exposing skin, and fueling my addiction.

I loved the way she tasted, the way she smelled, the little breaths that kept escaping her lips, the soft tugs she gave my hair when my lips traveled down her neck to her collarbone while my hand fisted the hem of her dress, pushing it up until her bare chest was left on full display for me. I allowed my eyes to trail down her body, wondering how the fuck I had seen her for the first time and had zero attraction towards her.

Something changed. Maybe it was her smart mouth or those freckles scattered here and there on her skin, some covering scars, some forming constellations, some just being alone, waiting for a lover's kiss.

Her body was meant to be worshipped—a religion to remain unseen to all but me.

The red thong she wore was begging to be carelessly handled and ripped apart by me, but a light glint of metal drew my attention to her perky nipples, and my need to rip off her underwear was halted when I wrapped my lips around one pierced nipple. The metallic taste condemned me to a subject that answered silent commands from her moans of pleasure.

I fucking loved the sounds she was making; they did unsanctified things to me.

My tongue swirled around the metal, sucking and drawing out a moan and a tug of my hair from her. My other hand moved from holding her gown to cupping her other breast, my thumb teasing her nipple as she held the dress up.

I gave her nipple a punishing suck, and she hissed after I released her. I watched her lust-filled eyes regard me with flimsy malice.

"Motherfucker." She cursed me.

I squinted. "That's a far cry from *sir* or *Dad*."

"It's not a far cry from *asshole*."

My gaze moved to her shoulder, settling on the scar from my bullet on her skin. "That's a fine-looking scar," I reminded her.

"I'll be sure to return the favor in the near future."

"I like the way you keep making me look forward to the future."

Before she could comment, I kissed the underside of her breast, feeling the fast beating of her heart as I pressed heated but feather-light kisses down her stomach. The moment I heard the hitch of her breath and felt the flex of her stomach when my lips explored, my hand traveled ahead of my mouth.

Softly, I traced my finger along the hemline of the thong. I licked and pressed my lips into every contour of her stomach.

An overwhelming desire bellowed through me. I couldn't stop my hand from disappearing between her legs, touching her soft heat that begged for attention, attention that I was eager to give . . . then take away . . . and then give.

You wouldn't blame me; I was curious to know what other names she would call me aside from "motherfucker" and "asshole."

My fingers took time to explore her waist before they trailed down to her middle, cupping her soaked underwear, while my lips kissed down her navel and to the line of the red material covering her from me.

I lifted myself a little, reaching to pull it off her, and she helped, rising as I dragged the thong down her legs and threw it to a corner.

Zahra was quick to take off her robe and then the nightdress. "You really love being naked," I observed.

"And you have too many clothes on."

I went above her again, my eyes soaking in the brownish bruise on her neck, before dragging my gaze back to hers. "Would you love to see my tattoos while we do this?"

She smiled. "I don't have a problem with your tattoos."

"You don't?" I asked. "The first time Casmiro saw them, he screamed like a girl. And don't think I didn't see the disdain in your eyes when you first saw them."

"I didn't know what they meant," she said, her hand raising to stroke my cheek. "Now that I do, I want to study every stroke, every ink; I want to see it through your eyes, and aside from the tattoos, you have a good physique. Who wouldn't want to see that?"

"Grace. She hated it."

The immediate frown that touched her brows had me wondering what I had said wrong, but it was gone as soon as it came, replaced by a more sadistic smile as she rose a little on one elbow, cupped my chin, looking straight into my eyes. "Never speak of another woman when I'm naked and beneath you. My rule." She smiled, tilting her head and tugging me down to her, our lips nearly touching. "Is that clear . . . sir?"

My cock hardened at the domineering tone of her voice, and I felt the urge to take control but, at the same time, let her have it so she could wield the knife and stir this.

My knees drew up, separating her legs as I responded, "Yes, ma'am."

"Good."

"Hm." My palm pressed flat on her stomach, pushing her back down gently. "Now relax."

Her teeth clamped on her bottom lip. "Why? You wanna take care of me?"

"Whatever gave you that notion?"

This time, the frown that touched her brows was plagued with confusion, which I reveled in as my hand traveled down her stomach to the wetness between her legs. I rubbed slowly at her swollen clit, wet and fucking soft to the touch; I knew for a fact that I could play with her all day if for nothing but to feel her softness on the pads of my fingers and to hear her breathy moans now erupting with a lust-filled voice.

If my mind had a face, it would be grinning right now.

I tapped her clit, and she gasped, eyes widening in surprise at the impact. I could only begin to imagine the pain and pleasure she got from that action.

My gaze locked with hers, dropping to those lips, the bottom one swollen and red due to how hard she had bitten it. I wanted to suck it, kiss her, and feel her tongue against mine.

I moved to stroke between her slit, spreading her wetness all around her core, basking in the way her thighs shook. I allowed my mind to drift off to how wonderful it had felt to kiss her, how intimate and connected I had felt to another person.

The moment that sealed the deal for me.

The moment she ruined afterward.

I massaged the pulsing bud of her clit, earning small moans and whimpers from her, teasing and making her squirm in waiting to be filled up. I slipped a finger into her, and her walls immediately stuck to my finger, tight and pulsing.

"Fuck," she let out, her head pressing further into the pillow, eyes almost shut but still in a heated daze, looking at me while my finger worked its way inside her, curling and freeing, searching, seeking, and finding. She felt so good.

I pushed in another finger, and she lifted her hips, her hand fisting my shirt around my shoulder, her walls clamping to my fingers immediately.

This woman was naked before me, and I was still thinking of the next opportunity I would get to fuck her. It felt like the first time all over again.

I hated how my body had never longed for anyone as much as it did for her. It made it seem like a first. I already had so many firsts with her. Things might not end well if we kept going at this pace.

That right there—that thought—was my rational thinking, but unfortunately, I was now blinded by every irrational circumstance that came with being with this woman.

I pumped my fingers in and out of her, and her body arched. I palmed her stomach, pressing her back to the bed, the sound of my strokes heightening and lessening, filling the space between us.

I added a third finger, stretching her. The hiss that left the space between her teeth was accompanied by a throaty moan that had her thighs quaking. "Mmm, fuck, your fingers are . . ."

"What."

"They feel so good . . . so fucking good, sir."

My lips fell to her nipple, hiding my smile as I satisfied my craving for another connection with her body, one I knew I couldn't get from kissing her. I flicked the erect bud with my tongue, twirling with the same pattern and pace my fingers pleasured her.

I felt warmth from inside her, and I knew she was close, the way her body gave in entirely to me, submitting as I increased my pace, the heel of my palm rubbing against her clit with each stroke.

"Fuck . . . Elio . . . I'm close."

I maintained my pace, and she held the back of my neck, her hips lifting.

I released her nipple, pressing my palm flat on her stomach, halting my movement and hers.

"What the—"

With three fingers still inside her, I stroked her clit with my thumb, circling the swell of her arousal sensually and shutting her up, letting her growing high dial back down into something torturingly sweet.

She rolled her hips to the swirling of my thumb, probably enjoying it.

I stopped.

She whined. "Seriously, what—"

My fingers moved inside her, thrusting and curling at a faster pace than before. Deeper until I felt her shiver when I touched that part of her that had her shivering when I entered her the first time.

I hit that spot with each thrust. She squirmed beneath me, writhing and heaving, wholly undone.

"Oh, please don't stop."

I stopped.

"Fucking hell, Elio. I swear to all things holy; I'll be slitting your throat before you get to slit—mmph." She whimpered, then I pulled my hand out and dragged my fingers up and down her slit. "You don't plan on making me come, do you?"

"I do. Just not through my fingers."

"What—"

I lifted myself off her. "I want to taste you. No—I apologize—I have been craving to taste you since that time in the car; I can barely control the urge."

She blinked. "Then go ahead . . ."

"I will. But I also remember when you told me you could get off on my face; I've wanted to test that theory."

Zahra's brows rose; her lips curled into a sly smile as her tongue ran across her bottom lip. "This is one of the rare moments I appreciate your attention to detail."

"That so?"

She nodded, quickly switching our positions until she was straddling me. "We really are a match made in hell."

"A mistake."

"One I'm pretty sure you're grateful for."

"You think so highly of yourself."

"No one else does, so I gotta do it for me."

"I think highly of you," I told her, and it was the truth.

She looked genuinely surprised. "You do?"

"Hm. I like that you're smart. That you challenge me."

Her hand moved to the hem of my shirt as she pulled it over my head, throwing it to the side. For the first time since I became obsessed with cleaning, I didn't focus on the mess we were making in my room. I was close to her, and she was the only thing that got my attention.

Her fingers trailed my chest. "I'm curious now; what else do you like about me?"

"You complement my being."

She nodded, looking impressed with my statement. "What else?" She leaned in to kiss my throat, which bobbed at the contact.

She was lighting a fire I had no desire to quench.

"You're interesting."

"What else?" Her lips feathered down to my chest, licking me like there was vanilla coating my skin.

"You're beautiful, and I love your freckles and hair."

I felt her smile against my skin before she looked up at me. "What else?" she asked again, and my eyes memorized every speck of color in her irises.

"You," I voiced, and raised my hand, stroking her hair away from her face and tucking it behind her ear. "It's near impossible to pinpoint why I like you, Zahra. I have tried, denied it, and given it an overthought, but I can't find a specific reason. It's just you." My hand trailed down her arm to her forearm and then to the dip in her waist. "All of you."

Her smile was small and genuine now. "I am wrong, Elio. My whole existence is wrong."

"My life is wrong; what would one more wrong do to the other boatload of wrongs?"

She tilted her head. "It could tip you over."

"Maybe that's exactly what I want."

"Or maybe it's the sex talking; *maybe* you're delusional."

I wanted to tell her not to downplay what I had just confessed, but I didn't. I was unknowingly giving her too many weapons. I didn't want to cross the limit, so I said, "Hm. Maybe."

She grinned, the topic forgotten.

"Can I test my theory now?"

She answered by moving, and I shifted further down as she got in line with my face; the sight of her glistening slit had me aching to be inside her. I had to remind myself that she wasn't here to gratify me; she was here so I could do the gratifying.

Her hands latched onto the headboard, and mine went around both her thighs, pulling her down to my face as I licked between her slit, drawing my tongue up until I reached her clit and gave it a good suck.

"Mmmm," I groaned, loving the way she tasted, *like fucking addiction*.

I sucked on her, twirling my tongue on her clit, French fucking kissing her flesh like it was the only kissable part of her body.

"Oh fuuuck," she moaned, grinding on my face as I ate.

My tongue flicked her throbbing bud a few times before I satisfied her with a deep suck that had her breath hitching in gasps as her moans grew louder.

My tongue stroked down her clit before curling and thrusting inside her, fucking her, licking her, sucking her, feeding the Zahra addict inside me.

I loved it. *I love this. I want to do this every day. Every hour. Every fucking second.*

"Fuck, it feels so good; you're doing so fucking good, sir."

The little praise and nickname had my grip tightening on her thighs as I relished the taste and feel of her. I fucked her to unfinished sentences with each stroke of my tongue.

Her moans were unrestrained as her thighs shook, and she was coming, her warm release filling my tongue as I drank and licked her clean of my torment.

I didn't want to stop, but her sighs sounded tired, and I allowed her the space to get off me.

I lifted myself to one of my elbows, watching her settle beside me, her head to the pillow, hair a mess as she blew out a breath and turned her head to look at me and then my lips.

"How are you so good with your tongue if you don't have sex often."

"I don't know. I'm glad you think I'm good. Want to do it again?"

She laughed, the sound bubbling out of her in waves as she looked away from me, her eyes on the ceiling as the laugh died down.

"Usually, we like to recuperate," she said, turning her head to me again. "You know, catch our breath?"

"Hm." I couldn't look away from her face as my hand went to her stomach, fingers grazing her skin.

"You have a tub?" she asked.

"Hm."

"I'd like to use it," she said, her hand rising while her fingers grazed my jaw. "Join me."

"No."

She frowned. "No?"

My eyes locked with hers. "I meant . . . I don't often use the tub."

"Let's go use it together."

I shifted. "I don't want to."

"Why?" she asked, lifting herself with an elbow, making my hand drop from her stomach. "Are you shy to get naked with me?"

I drew a blank look.

She chuckled. "What else do you want me to think?"

I looked away from her, my hand grazing my ring on her finger. "I don't like too much . . . water . . . being under it. I only go under when I'm . . ." I trailed off.

"Yeah, your fucked-up father," she voiced into the heavy silence, but then a frown touched her brows. "But you were in the pool with me."

"Yes. That was because someone was drowning," I said. "I was distracted because you were there, and I was trying to drown you."

"What if I promise this time would be different?"

"It won't—"

She scooted closer to me. "I'll be there, you'll be there, and there will be no drowning. Just me and you, in a tub . . . naked and wet."

I tried to suppress a groan, but I could see myself raising a white flag.

The scene she just painted played in my head. It was amazing, but the nervousness at the pit of my stomach refused to yield.

Her finger trailed down my naked chest to my stomach. "What do you say?"

I didn't need to speak. The look in my eyes must have told her I was agreeing to it because she was pulling me out of bed to the bathroom with her.

Surprisingly, my nervousness wasn't as copious as the anticipation I felt when I saw her naked body standing right before me.

She was beautiful, and I was privileged enough to be standing here right now.

"You don't plan on entering with your pants, do you?"

My gaze moved to the bathtub, and a small spike of nervousness rocked me. I didn't let it stay as I dragged my gaze back to her.

Without overthinking it, I started to undo my belt, slipping it off and dropping it on the sink. I undid the buttons, zipped down, and slipped the pants off me before setting them on the sink too.

Zahra's teeth bit down on her bottom lip, stopping a smile as she took steps back towards the tub and motioned for me with her index finger to walk towards her.

I watched her turn on the water, and quickly, the tub began to fill up, the sound of the water numbing my senses for a second, but they became clear soon after when I watched Zahra step into the tub big enough to fit two people.

She released her teeth from her lips, letting a wide grin spring through. "It's like Dion's, but bigger." She tilted her head as the water rose to her stomach level. "You getting in?"

I watched her relax, her hand coming to caress her breast. "The water is a little bit cold; it needs you to keep it warm," she goofed. "Cause you're so hot."

"Very mature," I stated, finally freeing myself from my briefs; despite my inhibitions about this tub, her body seemed to be all the distraction I needed.

She giggled before she relaxed, resting her back at the tub's edge and closing her eyes as the water covered her chest and I stepped in, resting opposite her.

My muscles coiled at the feel of being underwater without going under. I gripped both edges of the tub as if I wanted to jump out at any second. For a moment, I wanted to, but then Zahra's head went under the water, and I just watched. I could see her eyes closed underneath. She was holding her breath but still letting herself go.

I removed my grip from the tub's edges, letting my hands fall into the water, just when Zahra came back up for air, her hands pulling her hair from her face as she smiled at me. "It's cool underwater. You should try it."

"I should have known this was a ploy to drown me."

She laughed. "No, it's not. It's a ploy to tell you that being underwater doesn't have to be a death sentence. Think about it: You wouldn't be alive if it were. You would have died the first time your dad tried to 'baptize' you."

I frowned. "I didn't die because he didn't want me dead."

"So why is it a death sentence to you."

"It's not."

She raised a brow, moving closer to me, her legs grazing mine. "Right. But you refrain from getting underwater because . . ."

"To punish myself."

She nodded. "Why would you punish yourself?"

"I fuck up sometimes."

"We all fuck up sometimes, but we don't punish ourselves in our bathtubs, not unless we're a little crazy in the head."

"I'm not crazy," I gritted.

"But you call yourself a psychopath."

"There's a distinction."

"Is there?"

My jaw clenched. "Is there a point to this conversation?"

"Yes." She drew even closer to me. "You claim not to be crazy, but your father treated you like a crazy person, and you're still following his methods. You're proving him right."

"Zahra—"

She straddled me, my cock pressing against her stomach underneath the water. She cupped my face in her hands, clear brown eyes looking directly into mine, wet lashes making them seem like she was in a daze. "I'm trying to make you see that it's all in your head. It's embedded deep in your mind, and you have strange beliefs and affirmations you were made to believe. I don't know how the bastard did it, but I know one thing."

She lifted herself, her hand wrapping around my cock in the water, stroking me once before guiding me to her entrance and sinking on my length. My heart pumped faster than ever before; I could hear the sound of the thumping in my ears.

She smiled, her thumb stroking my cheek. "You and I? We're alike in so many ways. That's how I know you're strong; that's how I know you can't be scared of getting into a fucking bathtub; that's how I know that this fear you feel is all in your head."

My hands landed on her hips as she moved against me, riding my cock in the sweetest way possible, pulling out a groan from me.

"You fell in that pool with me," she breathed, rocking her hips. "I'm sure as hell you didn't think about the water when you spoke to me seconds after you came up for air. It wasn't because you wanted to drown me. It was because you didn't *think*."

My hand moved from her hips to the small of her back, aiding her movements as she rode me, rolling her hips in a circular motion that had my head spinning.

"You were too focused. On me. Not the water. You didn't punish yourself then. You punished me. Now you're not punishing me; you're fucking me."

"Ah." My chest heaved out the sound, her tight walls hugging my cock in an intense vise as she rocked back and forth, her back arching skillfully as my hips lifted to meet her strokes, drawing out a moan from her.

Her soft lips kissed the underside of my ear. "The problem here . . . isn't the water or the tub; it's your thoughts, your mind," she whispered before raising her head and locking gazes with me. "Let me be your only thought."

She was my only thought; the water and the tub were the last things on my mind.

We were going slow . . . this moment was therapeutic and intimate. I pulled her closer, her pelvis rubbing against mine as she rode me, feverish breaths escaping both our lips, gazes locked, the lust and intensity in her eyes luring my release.

"Feel me," she whispered, hand cupping my neck and the underside of my left ear. "Feel only me, see only me. Forget your old memories from this tub. Make a new one of me riding your cock, looking into your eyes, telling you how fucking pretty they are when filled with lust for me. Only me, only Zahra."

"Only you."

"Yes," she moaned.

My skin heated up, her movement dialing up, riding me with the intent to get off; our lips were parted, breathing through our mouths, said breaths mingling to form the most intoxicating sound I'd ever heard.

She was divine. This was divine. This was everything.

"Fuck, *Sport*, I love being inside you."

Her other hand came around my shoulder, hugging me as her hips rocked with mine, a rhythm created by a connection I never thought I would feel with another human being.

I always thought I was a man without feelings. No—I had believed the projection people had imbued in me about not having feelings. I thought it to the extent that it took a great deal to make me feel something—anything.

But right now, all I was doing was feeling.

Her skin melded with mine, a blend that gave the word *perfect* a run for its money, her moans and mine highlighted to speak languages to the ears of the very element that fueled our attraction. The thumping of my heart followed the same rhythm as hers. A rhythm that spelled eagerness, intimacy, lust, and need.

I came with a groan, the same time her hips pressed around me tightly, and her release joined mine, a high we were climbing together, the feeling weakening every bone in my damn body as hers fell flatly on mine, our breathing the only thing to be heard.

This woman had just ripped up a page in my book, taking the liberty to write her own paragraphs.

I stood corrected; Zahra Faizan's body was equivalent to a serum created to ignite a strong dose of fever into a healthy body.

This healthy body being mine, and this fever, too far gone to be cured.

CHAPTER FORTY-TWO

Zahra

I may have overdone it.

Trickery and manipulation were my things, but it had never gotten to the point where I'd used this particular skill to help someone else. Especially not someone like Elio Marino, who saw words as affirmations. Passing on the wrong notion might be terrible, but if I was honest with myself, would it still be considered wrong if I actually wanted to do it because I cared? Not really. But denial was sweeter than acceptance. We might be alike, but I sure as hell was not ready to confront my conflicting feelings, at least not when my intentions were a little . . . sideways.

There was a benefit, though. Having him by my side was for the best. It was better to be in the good graces of this man than the opposite.

One thing I had come to learn in this game was that trusting impulsive and unpredictable people could lead to your downfall; so no, I didn't trust him, and he didn't trust me either, but there was a truce somewhere in the middle, and I had to admit that it was better than nothing at all.

We were settled back on his bed, and I'd gotten dressed again; after wanting to bolt, immediately I had my clothes on, but then I remembered dinner, which was not as hot as when I first brought it, but warm enough to be eatable.

It wouldn't have cost me a second to leave it all for Elio to eat, but I was hungry too, and I never said no to food, no matter how awkward the situation might be. Who was I kidding—I was more uncomfortable because the situation wasn't awkward. Elio was quiet, on his phone, looking more relaxed than he had been before I got here.

I was the problem.

I didn't deal with aftermaths, and our aftermath wasn't supposed to be so . . . comfortable.

I opened the bowl I'd put the food in. The smell of fried potatoes, sauce, garlic, and something that could only be described as whatever Dog's secret ingredient was filled my nostrils and transported me to a setting where food was the main character, and humans were its supporting cast for it.

His patatas bravas were his brand signature, my personal favorite after his pasta and showstopping tortillas.

Elio dropped his phone by his side, looking into the bowl with a surprised glint in his eyes. "Hm. Impressive."

I took in a deep breath with my eyes closed, a smile spreading on my lips as I opened my eyes again, hypnotized by the aroma and garnish. "Food prepared by my best friend, Dog. Always phenomenal; one bite changes your life, never to be eaten for free because we at Street believe *nothing* this good should come easy, and one day, *one day* we will have our own restaurant, with Dog as chef and all members of Street getting access to eat for free for the rest of our lives, and we will make history, endless meals, endless—"

"I believe I have gotten your point now," he cut me off, and the imaginary soundtrack in my head ceased. I rolled my eyes as I passed him a fork.

"My mother loved this dish," he said. "She never prepared it, but she had this recipe book. *Patatas bravas* was highlighted with a pen. Although this is the first I'm seeing one that's made with beef."

"Ah, Dog loves experimenting with his dishes, but I'm glad to know your mom loved it," I said, shoving my fork into a potato and then a small hunk of beef and some of the sauce, raising it to my view. "Let's eat this with her, yeah?" I grinned.

"I don't know how that would work. She's been dead for years," he stated.

My grin died. "Jesus—you know what I meant, you blunt fuck."

"Oh," he said, but then went quiet with a frown before his brows went up. "You meant that in a figurative sense."

I shook my head. "Something tells me many people have died because you thought their statements were literal."

He dipped his fork into a piece of potato. "You're probably right." He ate the potato, and his eyes widened a little.

I ate it too, and I almost melted on the spot. It tasted like a good orgasm. My mind took a second to fly into space and back. "So *delicious*!" I moaned. "What do you think?"

He shrugged. "It's not bad."

My frown was immediate. "Not bad? Do you have . . . Hold on." I reached for his phone, about to tell him to unlock it when it opened on its own. Upon his not stopping to question me, I searched for the Safari icon and, in the search bar, typed out: *What's it called when someone doesn't have a sense of taste?*

The results filed out, and my frown deepened. "How the fuck is this shit pronounced? Ageu—wi-usia?"

"Ageusia," he corrected fluently, taking his phone from my hand and dropping it beside him. "My sense of taste is perfect."

I felt offended for Dog's talent. "If it were perfect, you wouldn't refer to this awesomeness between us as 'not bad.' You should be jailed for it."

He took another forkful into his mouth while nodding at my statement. "I never said it was bad."

"You didn't say it was good either."

"Baseless argument."

"I swear, you—"

"Keep talking, and I'll finish it all." He lined his fork with three potatoes and almost all the sauce before shoving it into his mouth.

"What the fuck—"

He was diving for another round, determined actually to finish it all.

I'll show him.

I shoved my own fork in, stabbing as many potatoes as I

could carry, alongside portions of beef, shoving it all in my mouth. It got so full that I had to use my other hand to support my jaw.

Elio had taken two more forkfuls during my struggle. I had the urge to scream, but my mouth was too full, and it wasn't easy to chew. The man was eating like he was the only one destined to eat from the bowl, like it would help stop the apocalypse or something.

After a few minutes of me trying to swallow and fill up my fork at the same time, the bowl was almost empty.

No, this won't do.

This time, he didn't take any potato because there were only a few left; his focus was on the beef. I didn't know how he did it, but he managed to gather almost everything on his fork. When he took it up and into his mouth, I grabbed the bowl quickly and got off the bed, heading to the far corner of the room as I managed to swallow. "You're a fucking food bully; what the fuck!" I shot with a glare.

"I don't like sharing," he said, bringing the fork in line with his mouth as his tongue came out to lick the metal, somehow making me feel jealous of the nonliving thing.

I got ahold of myself. "It was *my* food that *I* decided, out of the *kindness* of my very *subtle* heart, to share with you. *My* food. I should be the one to eat most of it."

"You speak as though your name was carved into the bowl."

"Never again. I'll never eat with you again; you're one of those kids with wide mouths and throats, always bringing the biggest spoon so they can eat more than the little people. That is mean, no one should do shit like that."

Amusement danced in his eyes. "I was eating like I normally do."

I scoffed. "And he calls me an animal. You're a beast, the worst of your kind, fucking asshole."

Elio chuckled, getting off the bed while I hugged the bowl to my chest possessively.

"Relax, let's get water in the kitchen. I'm full; the rest is yours."

"You ate almost everything; there's no . . . *rest*."

He dished me a disapproving look. "Follow me."

We reached the kitchen some minutes later, and he washed the fork he'd used before getting himself and me some water and settling on a stool opposite me.

"Thanks for dinner," he said. "Both dinners."

I gave him a fake wide smile, getting on a stool. "Real smooth."

"Hm," he said, ring-free fingers thumping on the table, biding his time to ask me a question. When I returned his rings earlier, he didn't bother to put them back on.

I sneaked a glance at him as I ate the last bit from the bowl, not nearly enough to make me satisfied. "What is it?"

"I'm curious," he said. "How many languages do you know?"

I picked up the cup, bringing it to my lips before speaking. "Nine." I drank a few gulps before dropping the glass back down. "Italian, Spanish, English, French, Korean, Russian, Vietnamese, Polish, and Mandarin."

"How did you learn?"

I shrugged. "I was little. As you've seen in your background check, we didn't have a normal school where I grew up. But our guardian was a linguist. When I had the chance to study more, I decided to focus on languages. There's just something beautiful about speaking and knowing that not everyone around you understands. You could be selling off someone, and they'd be smiling and thanking you."

He nodded. "It's a good skill."

I smiled.

"Can you read and write in those languages?" he asked.

"Nope. I only speak and understand."

"English too?"

I paused, my eyes searching his as I shifted uncomfortably. "They didn't really pay attention to what we studied and how far we'd learned where I grew up . . . Um, I try though, with English, but mostly the basic stuff."

He nodded. "Hm."

"Well, I should get going; it's midnight."

"Stay; leave when the sun comes up."

"No, can't do that," I blurted. "There's no staying overnight in this arrangement."

He frowned like he didn't like what I just said. "We don't have to do anything."

I forced out a laugh, giving him a wary stare. "What, you want me to stay back so we can . . . *cuddle?*" At *cuddle*, I made an irritated expression, anything to show him we weren't there and would never be there.

He didn't respond.

"Pfft, get real, Elio. That's never going to happen."

He shifted like he was uncomfortable. "I don't know where your mind traveled to, but no. I recall the other day in Turin, you mentioned this TV show about a morning star, and I—" He stopped abruptly, and it seemed he was looking for ways to frame his words. "I have a cinema room. We could watch it since, well, most of my knowledge about TV shows is from before I went to the army and you seem more, more . . . up to date in that area."

I blinked, completely frozen, while I watched him, my stomach flipping. Unannounced. I wouldn't have been able to stop the way my heartbeat had increased because it seemed as though this man . . . Elio Marino . . . The Wicked . . . incapable of feelings, who never smiled, never had a girlfriend, didn't often have sex, a psycho killer, wanted to spend time . . . with me.

Even if I succumbed, accepting that he wanted to spend time with me, there was still the fact that, for some reason, I wanted to spend time with him too. I bought the idea.

Why the fuck am I buying the idea?

Backtrack, Zahra, backtrack.

I gathered the bowl, his fork, and my fork. "Right . . . that sounds cool, but I'm gonna have to pass. I might doze off, and I don't want to have to answer questions from Street about why I'm coming from the front door and not my bedroom, so . . ."

"Okay," he stated.

"Yeah . . . but you can totally go and watch it alone—"

"I'll read."

I nodded. "Cool."

"Hm."

"See you in the morning or . . . whenever."

"Okay."

I gave another awkward nod and then turned on my heel. I could still feel his eyes on me, but I didn't look back. I couldn't.

If I did, I might succumb and stay.

And that was an action I couldn't and shouldn't take.

I was probably making a mistake not informing Angelo's people of this new development. Still, I needed to see it for myself, find the original painting first, and be one step ahead before letting their people in on the intel. This might sever any trust we had so far formed with them, but we worked better without supervision, and this was the first legit lead we'd gotten in months; we couldn't risk sharing that intel with people who might be careless with it.

It was why we were staking out a school close to the sock company, Dog looking through binoculars as we waited for the guards to change shifts again.

Devil and I remained in the back seat of the SUV we had taken out while Dog and Chika were in the front seat.

We'd waited a week to head out, dishing out a perfect excuse for our movement; it was a bonus that we'd garnered a little bit of freedom working for, no—*with*—Elio, through Angelo's supervision and team.

Milk and Upper had stayed back, but they were in our ears and also had eyes on us, thanks to the direct link Upper had created from the surveillance cameras around this area and the whole district back to our quarters in the Marino compound.

We had a solid plan to infiltrate the building. It was late in the afternoon, schools were very close to ending for the day, and I silently prayed that they changed shifts again when all the students had gone home from school. Although we had tried to master their shift change, it didn't have any order, so it was difficult to predict a set time frame.

It was not a big, structured building, it was just a small company that produced socks—the perfect front for the paintings being shipped.

Apparently, Arturo's great-grandfather had attended this school by the side of the sock building when he was little; no one knew this because, according to Chika, Arturo's great-grandfather hadn't spent more than three weeks in the institution.

I squared my shoulders, looking to my side to find Devil's quiet gaze on the weapon he held. I bumped my shoulder into him, and he looked my way.

I tapped my comm, turning it off while indicating that he turn his off. He did.

"You good?" I whispered into the space between us, not wanting our other companions in the car to get wind of it.

"Yeah, why?"

"Because you don't seem like you're good. You've been quiet all week."

He looked away from me. "I'm fine."

I wanted to drop it. That was the cue to drop it, but I decided to press. "You know you can talk to me."

"Yeah."

"Then talk to me."

His lips went into a thin line as he looked out the window, like sitting beside me was suffocating him. "There's nothing to talk to you about."

I didn't like how difficult he could get sometimes, bottling up his thoughts and dying safely in silence. It was unhealthy.

"Devil, I know we—"

He looked at me with dark eyes showing how badly he

wanted me to stop trying to get to him. "I am fine," he said. "Just don't have a good feeling about this. It seems too easy, and you're not seeing it, or listening to me, so I'm fine; we're following your lead."

I sighed. "I get it; you don't like this—"

"You're working on your own terms. We're supposed to be a team."

I frowned. "Everyone agreed to it."

"Because you forced it on them; you gave no room for any other opinion, acted like you have some other personal shit to deal with."

I looked up at the rearview to catch Chika's gaze on us.

I looked back at Devil and said quietly, "We're doing this for us, for our freedom."

"A freedom we already have?" He raised his hand. "Look around; we're fucking free."

"Devil—"

"Maybe next time, leave room for other opinions because this isn't your 'freedom' alone; it's for everyone in Street. Something is going to go so fucking wrong today, I feel it in my gut, and all casualties will be your fault because you choose to blindly trust a stranger rather than the people you've lived with for years."

"I'm not—"

"Hey." Dog turned his head to the back seat. "I'm going out for a smoke. Zahra, you coming? Monitor me and shit?" He stared at me pointedly.

"I'll be right out."

He glanced at Devil and then left the car.

I turned to Devil again. "Just trust me, okay? I know what I'm doing."

He looked away and muttered, "You always do."

I sighed, opening my mouth to say something, but thought better of it, deciding to get out of the car. My leather pants stretched as I closed the door and walked to the back of the vehicle, seeing Dog leaning against the trunk.

"What," I snapped.

He turned off his comm and lit the cigarette between his lips. "He's right, you know? Keep going at this pace, and you'll run whatever race you're running alone."

"Oh, so you're the reasonable one now."

"Don't pick a fight with me; I'm tryna help."

I leaned on the trunk right beside him, staring at the school bus by the side of the school building. "I'm not running any race."

"But you're going faster than we normally do; we might be unable to keep up."

I shook my head, clenching my jaw. "I just feel guilty."

"For what?"

"For this," I said with a sigh, "all of this."

He looked at me with a frown. "What's there to feel guilty for? We all want this gold. We all want to go after it. As fucked up as it sounds, we love our new home too. No one's complaining."

"What about the vacation? Taking a break from stealing, traveling around the world, giving Milk her American dream? All our plans, cut short, just like that. If I hadn't thought it was a good idea to steal from Marino, we might be on some faraway island, drunk off our asses in some fancy beach house, wearing nothing but colorful bikinis with dried puke at the side of your lips because you can't hold your damn liquor."

He laughed. "Yeah, that's fucking accurate."

"I know." I smiled, but it died down as quickly as it came. "I just feel like if we can do this, find the gold, and the flash drives, we'll be set for life; we wouldn't have to steal or commit crimes. We could do whatever we want, go wherever we want, marry a stranger in Las Vegas, and laugh about it the next day."

"But we don't have to rush," he said, looking down at me as he threw the cigarette away. "We don't have to lose track of ourselves. If we're careful, we'll have a lifetime to fuck with life."

Something twisted in the pit of my stomach. "Yeah."

"Awesome, so fucking take us along. We work better when

we do shit together. With Devil's gut, your determination, Milk's charm, Upper's brain, and my fuckery, we got this."

I allowed a smile to curl against my lips. "Yeah. You're right."

He nodded, looking around us. "Perfect timing, cause some other car just came by."

"What?" I followed his line of vision, spotting the matte black car with all-black tinted windows.

"Shit, turn on your comms," Dog urged.

Upper's and Milk's voices filled my ears when I pressed the small button.

"Guys! Get the fuck out of there; it was a bloody trap!" Upper yelled.

"Why aren't they responding?" Milk's worried voice filtered in at the moment I locked gazes with Dog.

Fucking hell.

Dog and I both turned to return to the car, but Devil was already coming out, disarmed, hands in the air as Chika followed, holding a gun to Devil's head.

I grabbed my gun from the holster, pointing it right at Chika while Dog did the same.

"The fuck, Chika? You're a bad guy?" Dog sounded genuinely surprised.

"I'm literally dressin' as Guy from *Free Guy*; how the fuck did none of you clock that?"

"We don't watch a lot of movies, better things to do and all," Dog said.

"Yeah, whatever; you're surrounded. Drop your weapons, or I'll blow his brains out," Chika said.

"Bloody fuck," Upper's voice rang through.

"Wait," Dog said, "I have a question. Do you really have a job in London where they sexualize your names?"

"No. God, no," Chika said, looking like he was surprised we were having this conversation.

Dog blinked. "Oh, so that means no one has done it yet. Folks, we can make my future restaurant with that theme. It would rock so hard; we could go all dark, maybe not like the dad-pants costume, something sexy?"

"Could work; I like it," Milk said.

"It would totally sell in a city like Miami. Oh fuck, the beaches and titties."

"That sounds amazing," I added.

"What is happening right now," Chika asked.

"What would you call it, though?" Upper asked.

"Probably something sexy too, attractive to the eyes. Itsy, bitsy titty," Dog said.

"Too wordy," I said.

"Yeah, guys, I don't think this is the right time for this conversation," Devil said.

"Oh right, Sauce Boy," Dog said. "Where were we? Lost track back there with the whole future-planning thing."

Chika looked just about ready to explode. "You lot are just like him. Never taking me seriously, and they ask me why I grew up with so much malice."

Dog stepped up. "Okay, Daddy Issues, you got a problem, blow your brains out and go settle it in hell with Daddy Dearest; we don't give a shit. You either drop your weapon or—"

More cars pulled in, drawing our attention, but staying clear away from people and the school. Men in black coveralls got out of them, guns in hand, pointed right at us.

Chika smiled, eyes coming to settle on me. "You're done, Street."

My grip on the gun tightened, gaze burning into Chika's. "It seems like you have a death wish."

"One that's gonna get passed on to you and your man friend if you don't drop your weapons and do as we say."

"Man friend? Who says *man friend*?" Dog asked.

"I'm not on no jokes, fam!" Chika yelled like a psycho. "I'll shoot him!"

"Nah, you're a chicken; you can't do it," Dog taunted.

Chika angled his gun towards Dog and pulled the trigger; the sound of the bang was so sharp that the comm in my ear gave a piercing high pitch.

"Fuck!" Dog staggered back, the arm of his shirt torn from the graze of the bullet, blood seeping out of the wound. He glared at Chika. "Motherfucker! You shot me!"

Chika directed the gun to the back of Devil's head again. "Try me, Bruv. Next one's in his brain, no cap."

Gritting my teeth hard, I gestured to Dog to drop his weapon while I slowly dropped mine.

Three men took the liberty of cuffing our hands in front of us, denying us free movement, and probably straining Dog's wound, based on how he winced.

Chika pushed Devil to us, and Devil righted himself, turning to Chika with a question. "Why agree to help if you had your motive? Why stage your own kidnapping?"

Chika's gaze fell on me, and he smirked. "Guess I picked up a lil' somethin' from Arturo, innit. Who don't love a bit of dramatics?"

"Why bring us out here at all? Contacting us when you could have gotten all the pieces on your own?" Devil asked.

"*Street,*" Chika said, "shadows of Italy. Running around the world looking for the original painting. I gotta say, I was disappointed. You lot didn't know shit about it."

"Yet you told us."

"The original ain't even here, bruv," he said, a twinge of annoyance in his voice. "I have spent years searchin' for this shit. To think Arturo wasn't decent enough to let me in on the quest after years of ignoring me during his schemin'. The gold, all that money, and them flash drives fucking belong to me."

"Daddy didn't leave a will, so you decided to be delusional and make your own," Dog egged him.

"Shut the fuck up, dickhead! He left the quest. He wanted me to find it." His glare pinned on me. "Not you, Zahra. And not Marino."

"You've been following us," Devil noted.

"You lot have been the only ones to make real progress. I

thought there would be something; maybe if I helped, I'd get a piece of that information too. But I was wrong. I will make sure none of you ever know shit. Because I won't let it happen."

I gritted my teeth. "I would think before acting if I were you. Measure your options. Know who rules the city you're in."

The man dared to laugh. "Oh, I know all right. Do I look scared?"

Devil's gaze met mine, asking a silent question. I shook my head. He looked just about ready to go against my wishes anyway, but he held himself back.

"Turn around," Chika demanded.

"Got a thing for ass, Sauce Boy?" Dog asked.

"Dog, quit it," Milk snapped.

"Should we contact Angelo's people? We didn't exactly have a backup plan," Upper asked.

"Don't contact anyone," I said as we turned around.

"Move," Chika urged.

"We don't know what he has planned," Milk said.

"We've survived worse."

"I don't like this," Devil seethed, and I looked over at him.

"Trust me."

He shook his head, turning away from me as we walked towards the school bus in time to see two men in black jumping down from it and another man lying face down on the ground, fingers shaking. It was clear he was the bus driver.

No.

My footsteps faltered.

"I got a next-level plan for you, *Street.*"

"Why does he keep saying our name like that?" Dog asked.

We ignored him as we stopped in front of the bus.

"Get in. All three of you."

We exchanged glances amongst ourselves before I looked back at Chika. "What are you doing?" I asked.

"Get the fuck in!" Chika yelled.

With a grunt, Dog went in first, mindful of his arm, with a rough assist from one of the men holding us hostage.

"Ah shit," Dog cursed.

Devil climbed in next, and I followed behind, seeing why Dog had cursed.

The bus was filled with children, scared, wide eyes staring right at us.

My head snapped towards Chika, who had a smug smile, taking two steps back from the bus. "What the fuck is this?" I seethed.

He didn't answer, but he gestured to Devil. "You. Start up the engine, and drive."

"With my cuffed hands?" Devil glared.

"Pretty sure you can pattern that, easy," Chika said. "No stress, we tested. It works."

With a flare in his nostrils, Devil got in the driver's seat after stealing one glance at the children on the bus.

"What are you playing at? Let the kids go!" I yelled.

"It's all part of the game, sweet."

"Don't fucking bring children into this, you bastard."

He dipped his hand into his pocket, pulling out a small remote. "There's a bomb installed and attached to the bus, just there, on your right."

My gaze flickered to the beeping device by the first passenger seat.

"Bro, what the fuck?" Dog bent to inspect it.

"It's a very special bomb, you see." He smiled.

"This isn't funny, Chika." My voice shook.

"You don't drive, it goes boom; you drive, it counts and eventually goes off, but still gives you an hour's worth of minutes to count your friggin' blessings."

"Let the kids go."

"You stop driving, it goes off. You drive too slowly to preserve fuel, the time reads faster; you drive too fast to alert the authorities, it reads even faster. Either way, it'll go off but will buy us enough time to be out of sight."

"You're fucking crazy bringing innocent children into this!"

"How else will I make you sweat . . . *Faizan*."

"You motherfu—"

"I'd start driving now if I was you, fam!" Chika yelled at Devil. He clicked a button on the remote, and a beeping sound went off inside the bus. Cries of panic from the children, not more than ten to twelve years old, filled the bus.

I glanced at the bomb; the time was counting down rapidly, faster than a second at a time.

"Shit, Devil, drive!" Dog yelled.

"Fuck," Devil cursed, stepping on the gas as one of the men slammed the bus door shut, leaving me staring at Chika's smirking face while he raised his hand in a slow wave, and the bus started to move.

"Permission to contact Angelo's people, Zahra; that shit doesn't sound funny," Upper said with an edge to his voice as the bus pulled into the road, past the car we brought to the scene.

"Don't contact anyone."

"You gotta be fucking kidding me," Devil gritted out.

"What on God's fucking earth do you suggest we do then?" Dog looked as angry as Devil sounded.

My gaze landed on the children. Scared eyes locked on me like they were also waiting for what I would say next.

I looked back at the bomb, the beeping going steady now.

"Devil drives. You try to talk to the kids without swearing at them. Upper, Milk, and I will play with the wires on that thing until it stops beeping, and we remain breathing afterward."

"That doesn't sound like a solid solution," Dog said.

"You got anything better than contacting people who might not give a shit about the children?" I asked, glancing at him and Devil.

Silence reigned, and then I nodded.

"Awesome." I looked back at the bomb. "We stay calm, and then we get to work."

CHAPTER FORTY-THREE

Elio

Gemma Parisi's house was normal.

A modest bungalow in a neighborhood that was exceptionally peaceful. The lawn was neatly mowed, drawing attention to the white picket fence that stood unblemished, just like the building, which stood out from the other cream-brown houses with its dark sky-blue and white paint design, along with the beautiful flowerbeds that lined the corners of the house. It brought me to the realization that this house was either just remodeled or just built. Her red car was parked right in front of the black tinted-windows minivan I had brought.

My gaze checked along the corners of the house, the little pathways leading to the other street in back. All clear. No suspicious movements that would have me on guard. It was normal.

Just like the woman I had come to see.

The woman who would invite a mere acquaintance to her house rather than meet at a public restaurant where people could see if something were to go wrong or inauspiciously.

I sucked on the almost burnt-out cigar, allowing it to warm my chest while I discarded the lit end, then blew out the smoke.

Removing my gaze from the house, I looked down at the phone in my hand, still on the page that showed Zahra's name and contact number. My thumb hovered on the call button like it had been doing since the night she refused my invitation.

I had battled with the need to call her and the pull to ignore her. To slap on the mindset that she was just another woman—*yes, another woman, but also the first woman you slept with twice.*

Twice. The first woman you can't get enough of. The first woman you confessed to.

Very convenient, this situation I found myself in. Quite fucking impressive.

I sighed and pressed the side button.

Grabbing the black cap on the passenger's side, I slipped it on my head before getting my gun, engaging the safety, and getting out of the car. While looking around, I shoved the gun in the back of the black jeans I wore. I allowed the jacket to fall over it as I shut the van door, going around it till I was face-to-face with the house, but a lawn's distance away.

I'd started walking towards the entrance when the door pulled open, revealing Gemma in a beige-yellow tank top and dark gray sweatpants.

A genuine bright smile crossed her face as she approached me, enveloping me in a warm hug that had me standing very still.

She pulled away with a grin. "It's good to see you again, cutie. You look . . ."

"Casual."

Gemma's brows went up as she looked at me from head to toe. "*This* was your attempt at casual?"

"Yes."

She laughed, shaking her head. "Oh God, my love, you're wearing a cap and a black . . . eh . . . well, a black everything, and you drove here in a small minivan? With black tinted windows? That's not a casual look; that's an 'I want my victims to know they will never survive it if I successfully catch them' look."

"I see," I stated. "I must have misinterpreted casual, then."

She leveled me with a smile. "You're good. Gran Louisa has been dying to meet you."

"Has she?"

"Yup!" She jumped on her feet, interlocking her arm with mine as she pulled me towards the house. "Hope you haven't had lunch! And I hope you like Italian?"

"I am Italian, Gemma."

"Even better because Gran Louisa made something extra spicy!"

We got into the house, which was as normal as the outside. Beige, white flowery wallpaper, light brown couches, picture frames on all the walls, the smell of a homemade meal lingering in the air. A ginger cat—Sailor, whose pictures littered my phone gallery thanks to Gemma being obsessed with it and wanting me to be too, for some obscure reason—was lying peacefully on one of the yellow bean bags in the living room.

"Welcome to my home!" She untangled her hand from mine, twirling around with a grin. "What do you think?" Her eyes twinkled with eagerness for my response.

"I think it is well put together," I said. "Homey."

I didn't think it was possible, but her grin widened, and her blue eyes shone with pride. "Thank you," she said. "I put literally everything into this house: my savings from all the jobs I did, and this face modeling gig I had a couple of years back. I saw the neighborhood in some real estate flyer back in the hood we used to stay in, and I said to myself, *Gemma, you're going to work your ass off and buy yourself a house in this neighborhood.* And here we are, my very first property."

"That is truly impressive. I am sure Gran Louisa was proud."

"Oh, she was." Gemma chuckled fondly. "Wouldn't stop talking about it. Every Sunday, I swear, she tells everyone her granddaughter bought a house in some fancy neighborhood. They think she has dementia."

"Being happy about something enough to repeat it is a far cry from dementia."

Her eyes widened. "Right? They just don't get it! The jealous ones always think she likes to brag about it, but she believes she will die soon; she has been saying that for two years now, and she's still very much alive and healthy, kind of. But she's the sweetest thing."

"You seem to love her very much."

"She's my only family, and I believe family is . . . everything.

I'm sorry you don't have any, but that doesn't mean Gran Louisa can't adopt another grandchild." She grinned, taking my hand and pulling me further inside the house. "Let's go see her in the kitchen."

My eyes took in the small hallway that held two doors I was sure were the rooms, but my view was taken away as she pulled me to a short corner, and we were in the most colorful kitchen I had ever seen.

Yellow countertops, different colors of plates and kitchen utensils, a huge bowl of plastic fruit atop the counter, and a bowl of real fruit on the dining table.

Spanish music was playing from a speaker in the kitchen, and beautiful, colorful flowerpots lined the windows, looking like someone went to extra lengths to care for the plants every day. It all just felt so normal.

Then my eyes settled on her grandmother, her hair in a netted bun, wearing a pink sweater and jeans; even though she was a little bit hunched over, she still looked smart as she cooked, moving her body to the beat.

She looked like one of those people who would hug you to sleep like my mother used to do. The instant craving for that affection made me feel cold and empty.

"Nonna," Gemma called her attention. "Elio's here."

The woman turned immediately, soft blue eyes settling on me before a wide smile overtook her face, and she was wiping her hand on the apron around her waist.

"Oh, at last!" She laughed, walking over to me. Without warning, she threw her arms around me like we had known each other a long time. "Good meeting you, Elio." She patted my back. Her hug was warm. Friendly, motherly. It made me yearn to stay there and forget that I had a responsibility somewhere.

When she pulled away, she smiled warmly at me, her short arm raising to squeeze my cheek. "Ah, look at you. Pretty man. Eyes like steel, created to woo women." She laughed.

"Nonna, knock it off," Gemma said, going to stir what her grandma had been cooking.

"What? I never see fine men like this when I was young."

"Even Nonno?" Gemma threw from over her shoulder.

The woman rolled her eyes. "Maurice had beauty on the inside," she said, and then turned to me with a blank look, shaking her head slowly like she didn't believe a word she just said, and she had only said it to appease Gemma. "But you see beauty like you, Elio." She smiled at me. "Hard to see."

"Thank you."

"Yes, yes, remove cap. You are inside now; cap is for outside. Why you wear one? Are you a paparazzi friend?" she asked.

"No . . . it was for me to look casual." I removed it.

"Remove jacket too. Gemma is bad house guest. Never ever remove the jacket, and she ask why Luigi hate her, foolish girl."

Gemma laughed, shaking her head. "Luigi doesn't hate me, Nonna; he's just bitter."

Gran Louisa rolled her eyes as I removed my jacket and let my shirt cover the gun instead. She collected it from me, leaving me in just my black shirt.

"I hang this for you." She smiled. "And yes, feel at home; my Gemma bought this place, so no landlord coming to bang and say, pay rent. Fucking Paolo," she said before walking out of the kitchen.

My gaze settled on Gemma to find her leaning on the oven, a fond smile on her face. "She's a handful, isn't she?"

"She's wonderful," I answered.

Gemma nodded. "She also loves having people over; it makes her feel like she's made a new friend. The first day we met, I told her about it, and she was excited that I helped a stranger, and then when I told her we were texting, she was glad I finally made a friend."

"You don't have friends?"

Her smile dimmed. "I used to, back in our old neighborhood," she said, turning off the stove. "It wasn't as peaceful and spacious as this, and nobody minded their own business. When I saved enough to move, they just stopped talking to me. They have this notion that anyone who moves away stops being part of the community, and well, since I dared to move into the middle-class area, I'm now one of the people they think oppresses them." She sighed with a sad smile.

"You haven't talked to any of them since you moved?"

"Aside from fucking Luigi and Uncle Rod, no."

I nodded. "You're doing well, Gemma."

A smile brightened her eyes. "Thank you."

"Anything I can help out with?" I asked her, rolling up my sleeves.

"You can help out in a kitchen?"

"Yes, Gemma. I had a mother and a very mean sister."

She smiled at me. "Well, you can help set the table."

I got to work, and was setting the table like she had asked when she called me.

"Hey."

I turned to look at her.

"I just want us to be clear about something first, before Gran Louisa comes in."

"What is it?"

"This thing between us, it's just friendship, right?"

"Yes."

She blew out a breath of relief. "Great, because I'm not really looking for a serious thing, and you seem like someone who wants a serious thing. I'm not even sure if I want another boyfriend after Giacomo, at least not so soon . . . I just really need a friend."

"I can say the same."

"Okay, that's a relief. Thank you for coming today."

"I'm glad I did," I told her with a nod before going back to set the table.

Gran Louisa reappeared. "Ah, handsome, and know how to set table; your girlfriend very lucky."

I suppressed a smile.

"Nonna," Gemma's voice warned.

"Shut it. You have girlfriend, Elio? You are fine man; you should have lover."

I allowed a smile to slip onto my lips as I arranged the utensils beside the plates.

"Tell us," Gran Louisa urged, excitement in her voice.

I caught Gemma's curious stare on me, and I could tell she had grown very interested in the topic.

I cleared my throat. "It's—I, yes, I have someone, but not a girlfriend, just—"

"A fuck friend," Gran Louisa said.

"No," I blurted immediately, and Gemma choked out a laugh. "She's not a . . . *that*, Gran Louisa; she's a friend that I—"

"Fuck?" Gran Louisa completed again.

"It is complicated." I settled with that.

"Ahhhhh," she and Gemma drawled at the same time.

I shook my head, setting the final plate and utensils while Gemma placed the covered bowl of food in the middle of the table, and from the look of it, they had made fried spaghetti; I could smell the hot sauce even from the covered bowl.

She placed a jug of water by the side of the fake plastic fruit bowl at the center of the table.

"Let us settle, say prayer, and ignore table manner as we talk about Elio fuck friend but complicated."

Gemma chuckled as we three sat around the small table like a religious Italian family, saying our prayers before we ate.

The nostalgia hitting me from left to right when we finished praying had me soaking in this moment.

"I hope you have a warrior's tongue," Gemma said excitedly and worriedly.

"I don't know yet," I responded.

"No worries, it is only spaghetti," Gran Louisa said as Gemma began plating the food.

"Yeah, Nonna, spaghetti all'assassina. With extra Nonna spicy ingredients. Nothing much."

"What. You suppose to eat every meal like it is your last."

"And that is why I never let you cook," Gemma said, settling when she was done plating.

"Okay, children." Gran Louisa grinned. "Dig into hell."

We did dig in, and after three forkfuls, I couldn't feel my tongue. Gemma's face had gone red, and Gran Louisa's lips trembled.

"Okay . . . I think . . . I think we stop now," Gran Louisa said. "Too . . . hot."

Gemma dropped her fork with a loud clank, getting off the chair and to the kitchen sink before a gurgling sound filled the space.

I refilled my glass of water for the third time and gulped it all down.

It still didn't help because I was sweating like the spice was all over my body.

"I will . . . order pizza and increase air conditioner," Gran Louisa said, getting up from the table and heading to the living room.

I blew out a breath, checking my phone to see that I'd spent close to an hour here, and I didn't even want to leave yet.

Standing up, I decided to clear the table, even though my head felt woozy and my stomach was hot.

"I'll help out," Gemma said, and I almost laughed at how red her eyes were. "My grandmother is crazy."

"I agree," I admitted as we cleared the table together, and as time went by, the spice started to fade into a dull tingle, thanks to the change of temperature in the house and the fact that we had stopped very early into the meal.

As she washed the dishes and I rinsed and dried them, she asked, "So, this girl . . . how come you never mentioned her?"

I shrugged. "I didn't know how I felt."

"And now you do?"

"Hm."

"And this girl—"

"Zahra," I told her.

"Zahra, do you know where she stands with it?"

"Yes." I placed a plate in the holder, picking up another one to dry. "It is one-sided."

She stopped washing for a second before continuing. "And you know this, how?"

"When you tell someone you like them . . . they are supposed to respond if they like you too; she didn't."

Gemma nodded. "Maybe she just wasn't ready? You know it takes some people a lot of time to catch up to their feelings? Maybe it's like that with her."

I glanced over at her. "Are you saying that with certainty?"

She shrugged. "Not really, I'm just saying it based on what I think. I don't know her, so I might not know what could really be going on in her head, but I think if you really like her, don't stop doing what you do. Sometimes, some people want you to give them a reason to show that they like you too."

I paused. "That . . . makes sense."

"I know." She smiled. "And it's cute," she added after a pause.

"What is?"

"The fact that you like her. The tips of your ears are redder than my face right now."

I raised a brow at her, keeping a plate. "If I don't see it, then it never happened."

She laughed, proceeding to inform me of the different shades of skin flushing and what they meant.

About thirty minutes later, we were settled in the living room, the pizza had arrived, and Gran Louisa had popped open a whiskey bottle.

"Sorry about food, Elio," she said.

"It's okay—it was spicy, but I enjoyed it," I told her, now recovered from the attack of the meal.

"My dead husband like spice. He always say it is real men food. That is why he die early."

"Nonna," Gemma chided.

"What. I cannot speak truth?"

"It is always advisable to speak the truth," I supported, and Gemma pinned me with a look as she changed the channels on the TV.

"So, Elio, how come no family? Cousins. Uncle. Aunty, no one?"

I drank from the glass in my grip, about to give the usual response I delivered to anyone who asked me that question. "Actually," I started instead, "I have a brother, half-brother."

"You do?" That caught Gemma's interest.

"Hm," I said.

"Why didn't you say?" she asked.

"We aren't close. He doesn't see me as family."

"Ah . . . bad relationship," Gran Louisa pointed out.

I nodded. "I abandoned him. Although he is closer to where I am now, but—"

"You're not his favorite person," Gemma completed as if she understood what I was saying.

"Yes."

"So, what are you doing to fix problem?" Gran Louisa asked. "What is plan to make you his favorite person?"

I blinked. "Plan . . ."

"Yes, foolish boy, you think relationship will fix by itself. You have to draw him back to you. Life is not two, is one. You have to make peace with family because you don't know when death come and take them from you," Gran Louisa said. "Or you from them. You see, the same thing I always tell Maurice before he die. Make peace with family. He never listen; now they cut us off because of Maurice. All of them in France, living rich, happy life. While we are here, making do with what we can," Gran Louisa said, a hint of sadness in her voice.

My gaze went to Gemma, and she offered me a sad but encouraging smile before turning her attention back to the TV screen.

"So, make peace with brother. Do not allow pride make you regret it. Okay?"

"Okay," I responded with a nod, placing it in my mind that I would try to talk to him when I—

"Oh my God." Gemma's worried voice got our attention.

She increased the volume of the news station. A news anchor was standing in front of a school with reporters all around, a little bit of chaos outside the school.

". . . Information reaching us is that there are three military mercenaries inside the school bus, trying to defuse the bomb; surveillance footage from the school was sent to local authorities, showing how these mercenaries were handcuffed by some unknown gunmen and escorted onto the school bus holding a total of twenty-three debate students who had just returned from a successful educational debate. This is Elena Colombo from Direct Regional News." The screen cut to parents around the school building.

"Holy Mary, Mother, what this world has come to," Gran Louisa said.

Gemma changed the channel to another news station. They were airing the same news, but this showed footage of the school bus driving down a main road, cars stopping and changing directions via a mass announcement from police cars behind the bus, urging other drivers to give the bus space.

A male news anchor from a helicopter filled the screen. "The school bus can now be seen driving on the main road of Monte Napoleone. The mercenaries are said to be communicating with outside help, trying to defuse the bomb and make sure it doesn't go off. The authorities are organizing help a few kilometers from the bus, clearing the roads, and creating a safe corridor—"

Channel change.

". . . Parents are camping outside the school waiting for updates on their children—"

Channel change.

"... Milan, Italy, has never seen a crisis this massive, and prayers are being said all around the city and the world, seeking a safe return of the children and heroes trying to stop the bomb and bring the children home, now showing you direct footage of the school bus. Evelyn Arrow, BBC World News."

Gran Louisa stood up. "I will go pray for their safety, poor children," she said before disappearing down the hallway.

Channel change.

"... The mayor of Milan has been asked for a sitting with the president regarding a possible terrorist attack after viral footage of military mercenaries entering a school bus caught the media—"

Channel change.

"... Just in, authorities have raided a small private sock-producing company just by the school after an employee suspiciously fled the area; a couple of paintings of a chihuahua were found in this raid." A photo of the painting was shown on the screen alongside the employee who was trying to flee. "Locals are astonished after the employee revealed that the company was put in place to ship these paintings all around the world."

I shook my head, knowing the disaster this was about to cause.

Channel change, this time with a frown on Gemma's face.

"... ro Garza, a popular philanthropist and art collector in Mexico City, being the owner of the painting; a secret source says it is all part of an art quest that quickly turned criminal in the span of a few years." A picture of Arturo and the painting was displayed on the screen.

"Hold on a second," Gemma said. "I think I've seen that painting before. I don't know, but . . . I have seen this same painting and heard that name . . ."

My gaze snapped to her. "What do you mean."

She quickly fished for her phone by her side, her hand tapping and scrolling as she got to her feet and made her way over to me, settling on the armchair as she brought her phone into my view, scrolling through pictures of dogs in an album called "dogs." "I dog-sit from time to time, and I love dogs so I always take pictures of them, and here . . ." She stopped on the painting. "There it is," she said.

I took the phone from her hand, zooming in on the painting.

I couldn't find the tell. The little stroke that had been in every fake was missing, and I was genuinely impressed when the realization dawned on me that I was staring at the original painting of the chihuahua.

"Where did you take this?" I asked, understanding why my gut feeling had pushed me towards her.

"Mexico," she said, getting to her feet again as she paced the living room.

"Where in Mexico?"

"It was a year ago. Uncle Rod had sent for me, and Giacomo and I took a road trip to the manor in Mexico where Uncle Rod and Luigi worked in maintenance . . . shit." She stopped. "That's the name! Garza! Arturo Garza, the dead guy who owns the manor. Luigi was being a prick, and I was mad, but then, Giacomo told me that I should take a tour of the manor to cool off while he talked to Luigi, and I was just roaming around when I saw the painting, just sitting there, peeking out from behind a shelf in some abandoned storeroom. It was covered in dust. I cleaned it and took a picture because it was very peculiar, but I never got to post it."

Arturo, you mad mastermind.

The original painting never left the manor.

"Where did you leave the painting afterward?"

"I covered it and slipped it back behind the shelf. I don't think anyone goes in there."

"Hm."

"Do you think we should contact the authorities? Maybe it would help in some way?"

"No. Don't get involved. Send this picture to me. I'll handle it."

She frowned. "What would you do?"

"Problem-solving."

My phone vibrated in my pocket, and I brought it out. Angelo's name was plastered on the screen. I handed Gemma her phone, getting to my feet. "Excuse me; I'll take this."

She nodded, eyeing me suspiciously but choosing to trust me, as she returned to her seat and watched the news.

I answered the call. "Significant emergencies, Angelo; when will you learn?"

"This is significant. The mayor has reached out; he needs your help. I don't know where the fuck you are, but everybody's looking for you." His voice was frantic.

"That so?"

"Marino, there's a school bus—"

"I am aware of the school bus and the chaos and the quest going live—"

"Are you also aware that the so-called military mercenaries are Devil, Dog, and Zahra?"

I stopped. My breathing halted for about a second or two, slow panic ensuing gradually. "Elia . . ." I whispered.

"We are doing damage control over that, but the mayor is seeking your help smoothing things out with the president. We don't have fucking time on our hands, okay? Zahra, Devil, and Dog's lives are on the line, and the bomb is not fucking stopping." He breathed. "I didn't want to say anything, but I know who Devil is to you, and I know you probably don't give a fuck about the kids, or Dog, or Zahra, but your brother might die today, Elio. That should be a significant emergency."

A wave of blinding anger overtook my mind to the point that I couldn't get a breath out properly.

"Who led the operation."

"What?"

I grabbed my jacket and cap from the hanger. "Who led the operation for Street. Who led the fucking operation, Mancini!"

I heard him sigh and hesitate. "It was Zahra."

"That *fucking*—I'm on my way."

CHAPTER FORTY-FOUR

Zahra

I do not work well under pressure.

I avoid situations I can't control, and this situation—fuck, I didn't know that bastard was going to pull a stunt like this. I didn't think he was capable of pulling this off or devising a plan like this. I underestimated him, and that one mistake might cost us our lives today. I was sweating; my clothes felt tight, and the cuffs around my wrists dug into my skin, leaving a red bruise that became visible whenever I moved my hand.

My heart had stopped functioning at its normal pace the moment I caught sight of those children.

To think, I was the one preaching about staying calm.

All the sounds around me were delivered in distant echoes; the sound of a helicopter above the bus, which heightened my anxiety when I first heard it, the little whimpers and cries from the children on the bus, the noise in my ear from the comm: Milk's and Upper's staticky voices trying to communicate with me, and the people around them.

"Zahra."

The sounds . . . God, they were all mixed together in shadowy echoes, seeing as my breathing was the loudest thing I heard, the *only* thing I heard.

"Zahra."

My chest was tight, it felt like I had a fever, and the ominous beeping of the bomb tickled my head.

"Zahra."

I needed to breathe, to relax, to stay calm, be in control, but with this fucking noise around me, the honks from passing cars, shouts, helicopter blades, static, the hum of the bus, Dog's cursing, children crying. I needed the world to shut up for one goddamn second so I could think.

"Zahra."

If I could just think . . . then maybe . . .

"Zahra."

My chest was heaving, my mind supplying the image of my body being blown to bits after the countdown reached complete zeroes . . . but not just my body; Dog's body, Devil's body, the children, and the drivers of nearby cars—

"Zahra!"

I could stop it. I could save us all if I just had enough space to breathe and thi—

"Zahra!"

"What!" I yelled back at Dog, nervously bouncing on his toes a few feet away, looking quite pale.

"I've been calling you for fucking ages; what are they saying? The blue fucking wire or the red one? Your comm is the only one connected, remember?" he said between hurried breaths; his panic was adding to mine.

"They don't have any visual on the bomb. My explanation is the only thing they can work with. I was asked to cut off the red wire. They weren't sure, but we have to be sure—"

"The red wire?" Dog's eyes widened. "That's a fucking no. Red is a no, okay? It's in every fucking movie ever, never press the red button, never pull the red lever, never walk through the red fucking door—"

Devil groaned loudly. "I don't know if you've noticed, Dog, but this shit show isn't a movie," he said from the driver's seat, doing his best to navigate the vehicle, not so skillfully.

"Just go talk to the kids, okay? I got this," I said.

"You've been saying that shit since you bent to get a good look at that thing; we barely have fifteen fucking minutes left, Zahra—"

"I'm fucking working on it! Get off my damn ear and let me think, for fuck's sake!"

"Guys, I know adren . . . ne is high right now, but there are children on that b . . . if you could tone down the c . . . ing a little?" Milk said, her voice hiked with nerves, static cutting her off like it had been doing for a while now.

"The last thing these kids need to worry about is bad language, Milk. Any word from the bomb squad?"

"Angelo's people are com . . . ting with them via our line, but it wi . . . ke time because there are no visuals," Upper said.

"Time is the one thing we don't have, Upper. It's running; it's running fast." I swallowed. "How's coverage?"

"It's all over the news; reporters are eating up the . . . bl . . . dy . . . litary . . . story, and cars are being cleared off . . . oad."

I knew it was a matter of time before the media covered the story; that was why Angelo's people covered the news and supplied concrete lies to them. It would have been messier if *we* were the unknown gunmen.

But that didn't erase the fact that we had another problem. Signal. We were losing the signal for the comm. It started when we first set off; Devil and Dog had lost all communication, including me, at first, but then they turned off theirs, and mine picked up after a few seconds; now, mine was cutting out, and my nerves were crawling underneath my skin.

"How about Chika's tracker? Still on?"

"Yes, he hasn't caught wind y . . . He's still in the city. But pre . . . ng to flee."

"Good. That's good."

At least I have something under control.

I wiped the sweat off my forehead with my shoulder, the pounding in my chest making breathing a little difficult.

"Listen, Upper, Milk; we might lose communication—"

"We . . . saying . . . zah . . . ca . . . us?"

"Shit . . . Upper?"

". . . oody fuck . . . can't . . . it's . . ."

The static was hurting my ears.

"What's happening, Z?" Devil's voice was etched with worry.

"We're losing connection," I said, but my voice was small. "Guys, can you hear me?"

Cutting voices and loud static was all I heard.

"Hello? Upper? Still there?"

Static.

"Guys . . ." I blew out a breath when nothing came.

My eyes burned from the stress of the situation as I swallowed. "I think we lost them."

"Just fucking great," Dog cursed, hitting his cuffed hand on a pole in the bus.

I removed the comm from my ear. "I can do it if I just . . . study it a bit more . . ."

Dog scoffed out an annoyed laugh. "We don't have time for you to study the bomb, Zahra. We're fucked!"

The cries from the children doubled in number.

"Dog, come on, there are kids here! Stop fucking around and talk to them. Don't make shit worse!" Devil yelled at him.

"Shit is already worse! Shit is fucked; shit is all over the roof of this fucking bus, calling the angel of death to come for a fucking wine and bread feast with our skin and blood as fucking starters. I ain't about to be delusional right now, and the fucking kids shouldn't have to be either."

"Z," Devil called to me. "Listen to me, if you know there's a way—a chance that we can come out of this alive, please just focus and get to work, okay? Ignore that fuckhead."

"Oh, I'm the fuckhead now, huh?"

"Dog, you do your part, and let her do hers, don't be the fucking prick, all right? Look at how scared those kids are. Do something about it."

"The fuck am I supposed to do?" Dog exclaimed.

"Figure it out!"

"Don't fucking yell at me! I'm already panicking, and my shit is not together right now; you feel me? Your yelling and commanding and the fucking beeping sound from that thing are doing a shit ton of bad to my fucking nerves," Dog let out tightly.

I looked over at him to see that he was pacing up and down the small length of the bus, and had, at some point, made a small bandage with a torn piece of his shirt to tie off the bullet graze wound on his arm.

"Dog," I called, and hysterical brown eyes looked down at me. "Just—breathe, please."

"The fucking irony. In a few minutes, I won't be breathing anymore!"

"Dog, fucking breathe!"

"Okay!" he snapped as he stopped pacing and took a deep breath before letting it out. After doing it several times, he sighed. "Fuck . . . okay . . . okay . . . I'm calm. Zahra, you're calm; Devil, you're calm; children, you're all calm; everybody is calm. We're not on the road; we're in some fucked-up escape room, and to escape it, we have to be calm."

"That's right," Devil said. "Engage the kids, and Zahra, please concentrate."

I didn't know if what I did was a nod or a shake of my head, but I knew my hand had gone back to the beeping device littered with wires, light red, dark red, blue, white, yellow, all wired into the control panel that displayed the beeping red light.

I closed my eyes, trying to level my breathing and manage the noise around me.

The first thing I saw was a gloved hand over mine. A warm chest pressed against my back, and hot breath fanned my ear as he spoke.

"The first thing you do is never to panic; if you panic, you're fucked—"

I snapped my eyes open and shook my head.

"Okay," I breathed out. "I was trained for this a couple of years back. All wires here have a purpose."

"As they should," Dog said.

"There's one for stopping the time, another for speeding it up, another for turning off the device and stopping the bomb, another for slowing the clock, another for setting it off—"

"That's the one we don't want."

"Dog." Devil's voice spelled warning.

"Fine, Jesus, I'll talk to the children."

I saw him walking to the front of the bus from the corner of my eye. I looked at the passenger seats, all eyes on Dog like they were waiting for him to try to talk them out of what he had already fucked up by saying they were all fucked.

"Okay, kids, I'm gonna be real with you. You've seen my worst side in the span of minutes, my panic? Yeah, I figure there's no need to stand here and shit-talk you with rainbows and bumblebees of promises."

"That's starting off great," Devil muttered.

Surprisingly, some cries died down; but they still looked scared.

Dog cleared his throat, looking around. "There comes a time in every man's life when he has to face death."

"Jesus fuck," I cursed, looking back at the device as Dog continued, his footsteps going down the school bus aisle.

"We might all die today, but we must perceive it as normal. Death comes eventually . . ." He sighed dramatically. "Who knows, you with the snotty red nose, you might be crossing the road to get ice cream from that weird old guy who never stops smiling at people, and, bam! You get hit by a car and die. The old man, he was still smiling!

"And you, with the stupid hat, your mom could be slicing vegetables one day, and wham! The knife flies out of her hand and straight into your left eye; she says it's a mistake, but plot twist, it's not; she fucking hates your stupid hat, and she missed."

"My mom's dead," a little boy's tiny, scratchy voice said from the back.

"Oh shit, your dad then. Either way, you somehow die by a kitchen knife."

I heard a few chuckles from the children.

"And you with the tiny creepy pigtails . . . Wait, did your mom make those?"

"My sister," the girl answered.

"Ah shit, she hates you; never let her do your prom makeup or cut your hair, it'll end in a disaster, and you'll never get to date the cute boy in braces who everyone thinks is cool but still sucks his thumb when he sleeps."

More chuckles.

"What? You guys have someone like that in your school?"

"Yes! His name is Alessio."

"Ha! Called it, it's always the Alessios. Ladies, stay away from them Alessios; they're not the cool people. Mommy issues, you don't fucking want that baggage."

Laughter and snorts.

"Right, pigtails, you get eaten by your dog. Horror Movie 101, never get the dog in the first cage with the watery eyes; they're always the dog cannibals, but you didn't listen because it was cute, and it smiled at you, even though you know dogs do not smile!"

"My dog looks at me weird," a kid said. "I got it from the first cage. OMG."

"See? Always skip the first cage."

"What about me? How will I die?"

"And me too!"

"Will my dad kill me; I think my dad hates me."

"I wanna know how I'll die too!"

I shook my head, tuning them out as Dog continued to . . . do whatever the fuck he was doing. It worked, and that was all that mattered.

I blew out a shaky breath as I touched the dark red wire, moving it to the side a little so I could see where it was attached to the control panel.

I shook my head. This was a bomb created not to be defused unless stopped by the remote or by an expert.

I knew I could do it. I just had to remember.

But how could I remember it without remembering him? It was close to impossible.

I blew out another breath and closed my eyes. The red ones

are always to stop or make it fast . . . but sometimes it might be the yellow one. The white is uncertain, a . . . a . . . *detonator.* The voice penetrated my thoughts. I wanted to fight it off, but I ground my teeth together and stopped resisting. *"Or your saving grace,"* the voice continued. *"It all depends on how it was built or who built it. Your call matters, trust your gut."* Gloved hands traced from my forearm to my arm. *"You can do it, Amore mio, you can save them. Focus and think, don't make me do it for you."*

"Let the children go, Manuel; they're scared."

"Only you can save them."

"Not like this. I can learn some other way; put a dummy inside instead . . . please."

"I can't go back in there without setting off the bomb, my Zahra." His lips brushed my bare shoulder. *"You just have to do it the way I taught you. Focus on the sound, where exactly is it coming from?"*

I stopped to listen. "The middle."

"What angle in the middle?"

"Uh . . . I don't know. Left? Or—or maybe—maybe right?"

"Focus."

"I-I'm trying."

"Then try harder!" The voice roared in my head, and I flinched with a gasp, my hand jumping with the dark red wire still in my grip, pulling it from the control panel.

The beeping increased immediately, and the time started going down faster, the same way my panic went from a five to a fucking hundred.

"Shit, shit, shit, shit, shit."

"What! What is it?" Dog asked, his footsteps rushing back until he was crouching beside me.

"What happened?" Devil's voice urged from the front.

"I pulled a time wire . . . I pulled a time wire by mistake. I didn't mean to; I was still studying it. I don't—how—fuck, fuck, fuck."

"Zahra." Dog's hands were on my shoulders. "Hey, hey, you need to breathe and focus—"

I pushed him aside, getting to my feet and shaking my head like the thought of focusing was burning my lungs to crisps.

Dog was up too, trying to catch whatever mumbling I was doing . . .

I knew many people were in attendance that day; anyone could have told Chika how that training ended, how I had failed.

"Zahra, what is going on?"

I shook my head frantically. "I can't—I can't do it. I don't know how . . . I'm sorry, I can't, I fucked up, I didn't think he would know to pull this shit—I can't—I can't—"

"Of course you can. You can do fucking anything; it's just a moment of mild failure. I'm sure if you—"

"No, no, not this . . . I can't—I'm serious. I can't do this—"

"Dog, come over, handle the wheel."

I felt Dog leave my front towards the driver's side. My heart was hammering, the walls were closing in, and a second later, Devil was in front of me. "Hey, Z, look at me."

My throat felt like it was about to jump out of my mouth, alongside my heart and everything in my chest; it was so tight. I was hyperventilating and, at the same time, trying to stop myself from hyperventilating. Trying to take control. It was chaos. I was chaos.

"Zahra—"

"No, I'm sorry—I just can't—I tried, I tried to focus, but I fucked it up."

"No, no, you didn't. Not yet, because we are alive."

"I can't—"

"Fuck, Zahra, I need you to breathe; you're not breathing."

"I should—I should have listened to you, we—we should have planned—I'm such a fucking idiot—under—underestimating people—fuck—I can't—I can't believe—"

I felt him manage to hold my face in his hand, his cuff brushing my chin as he tried to make me look at him, worried eyes searching mine. "It's not your fault—"

I frowned. "No . . . no, it's my fault—I did this, I never

fucking learn—I forgot that I—that I couldn't trust me—I can't trust me—I shouldn't trust myself—because it's not fucking reliable—I am—I am not fucking reliable—I shouldn't have—"

He kissed me.

His lips stopped my rambling and breathing as he pulled me tighter towards his body. Warm. Still alive. Like mine. *I'm still alive. We're still alive.*

He pulled away from the kiss, locking gazes with me as my breathing leveled gradually.

"Are you with me?" he asked quietly.

"Y-yeah."

"Good," he breathed. "Listen, I know how this looks; you want to blame yourself, and yeah, maybe you did make the wrong call, but you gotta remember that you're not the first person in the world who has ever made a wrong call. It happens to everybody. And when it happens, you don't dwell on that shit; you do everything you can to make sure you live to see another day and learn from it."

I breathed shakily, swallowing down the nerves.

"You're one of the bravest people I've ever met, Zahra. You pave roads when we are standing in front of a big fucking wall. You never break. At least you don't show it—"

"But I did—"

"Sometimes, when we break, it's okay to let people see, people you trust. Remember that day when you told me I could cry, and you'd never tell anyone?"

I nodded.

"Great, I'm making the same promise to you. You can break down all you want and have thousands of panic attacks; I'll hold you through them . . . I'll kiss you through them if I have to. Z, you don't have to fucking hide from me."

I held on to his shirt and released another calm breath.

"You can do this. I trust you with my fucking life. If anyone can get us out of this, it's you."

I nodded. "Yeah."

"Yeah?"

"Yeah, yeah . . ." I looked back at the timer; four minutes left. "We don't have much time."

I rushed to crouch in front of it, Devil beside me.

My gaze went to the blue wire. I couldn't take the risk of pulling it now. It could have changed its usual function since I had removed the other red wire.

I couldn't touch the light red one. That was a no. It would most definitely be the trip wire; same went for the yellow one.

That left only the white. It never changed function. But I didn't know what exactly its role was. It could either be . . . a *detonator or your saving grace.*

Manuel's voice reached my head again.

"Do you want to take the risk, Zahra?"

I blinked.

"Where's your head at, Z."

"Here," I blurted. "Here. I'm here."

The timer went down to one minute.

"I'm thinking the white. It has two functions. One guarantees our safety, and the other . . ."

"Yeah, but what does your gut say?" Devil asked calmly as if the timer wasn't getting close to death time.

Forty-three seconds.

"It says I should pull it, but what if . . ." I swallowed, looking at him. "What if I'm not right, what if, what if I pull it and—"

"Hey, if your gut says it's right, then it's right."

I frowned. "What the fuck is with you and Elio on this gut-feeling shit."

He frowned, pausing. "What?"

Shit.

I pulled out the white wire.

The beeping stopped, the red timer turned off, and the bomb . . .

"Holy shit," I said, staring at it.

"Did it . . . did it stop?" Devil asked.

"It stopped?" Dog exclaimed from the driver's seat.

"We gotta wait for the one-minute dramatic silence, or we'll jinx it," I whispered, and we all went quiet.

When one minute passed, and we were still conscious and alive, I breathed a breath of relief. "I think we can freak out now."

The children erupted in screams of happiness.

"Fuck yes! That's what I'm talking about." Dog pressed the bus horn. "I never doubted you for one second, motherfucker."

"Right, you didn't."

Due to the cuff, I turned to Devil, threw my arms over his head, and hugged him. "Thank you. But tell anyone about what happened, and I will fucking skin you alive in your sleep, and I promise you wouldn't even be awake for it. Pass that across to Dog too."

He hugged me tighter. "You got it."

After about three hours of legal necessities that we took care of discreetly, asking for our fake names and faces to be kept out of the news because of our supposedly high-profile military mission, we arrived back at the compound, where we had to report back to Angelo and have Dog's wound properly treated. While he was getting attended to at the hospital in the compound, Devil pulled me aside.

"So, today was wild," he started, and I laughed weakly.

"Yeah, let's never do that again."

"Deal," he said with a smile, as he looked around before his gaze settled on me once more. "Um, so, about earlier . . . in the bus . . . the kiss . . ."

"Oh—"

"I'm sorry, I know we don't have that kind of relationship anymore, I just—in the heat of the moment, that was the only thing I could think to do."

I smiled. "It's okay, I get it, if it wasn't for you—we—let's just say today would have ended very differently, so thank you, for being there."

"Always, Z," he said with a smile. "But just to be clear, we're good, right? This doesn't . . . change anything?"

"No, it doesn't, you're still my best friend, and I still love you; just maybe next time instead of kissing me, you can suffice with a slap."

He laughed, shaking his head.

"No, really, it might be more effective," I said.

"Well, let's hope there's no next time."

"Yeah." I smiled, knowing we were okay and appreciating his clarifications about the kiss. I was glad it didn't mean anything to him, because I felt the same way. It was nothing compared to his brother's—fuck—his brother, who was probably somewhere plotting my murder for putting Devil in harm's way.

Hopefully I would at least get a day off before talking to Elio. I wasn't in the right headspace for that conversation.

When we entered our quarters after Dog was finished with his patching up, Milk jumped from a chair with a scream as she threw her arms around me in a tight hug. "Oh my God, I knew you guys were okay, but—fucking hell, I'm so happy to see that you're okay."

I hugged her back just as tight. "Me too."

She broke away, hugging Devil immediately. "I'm glad you were there with them; if it were just the two of them, that bus would have—"

"Yup, I'm glad I was there too," he said, just as Upper came from the passageway, breathing out in relief.

"You guys scared the bloody fuck out of me after that comm disconnected. I pulled out the Bible and prayed for the third time in my life," Upper said.

"You have a Bible?" I asked as he hugged me.

"Yes. You never know when you will need it."

I watched Milk break away from her hug with Devil before facing Dog. "You just couldn't stop cursing, could you."

"For the record, the kids love me now; I told them how they would—"

She threw her arms around him in a tight hug, mindful of his wounded arm. "I'm so happy you're alive."

He hugged her back with his good arm, letting out a dramatic sigh I knew was probably real. "It would have sucked for you if I died, so I just had to come back."

"You did good," Upper said, stepping away from me and then towards Devil, who was checking his wrists, which were more bruised than mine and Dog's. "You might want to get that checked out."

Devil looked up at him. "Yeah, wanna help?"

"Me?" Upper asked, surprise in his eyes.

"Yes, I was talking to you."

Upper blinked. "Um . . . sure? I mean, I'm not great with the—"

Devil sighed. "Stop being awkward."

"I can't just turn off awkwardness; that is not how it works," Upper clarified.

Milk pulled away from Dog. "I'll get the first—"

A knock on the door stopped her from completing that statement, and whoever it was didn't wait for a response before they came barreling in.

Four soldiers walked into our space, one holding a huge briefcase.

"What's going on?" Upper asked.

The soldier holding the briefcase dropped it on the center table while proceeding to open it.

There were five passports and bundled notes of money. "That is a quarter of your payment for your team's deal with our boss. There's also a check in there for the remaining payment. New names and new identity cards with passports, if needed. From this moment on, you're all free to go."

"What?" Milk asked.

One of the soldiers that accompanied him held my arm. "That is, once the boss questions her."

"Whoa, whoa, whoa, let her go," Devil said, and the soldier . . . released his hold from my arm. "What is this about."

"We were given direct orders to keep her in the compound prison for questioning when the boss returns, Mr. Marino."

Devil's eyes widened. "What the fuck . . . did you just call me?"

"With all due respect, Mr. Marino, we have direct orders from the boss to not engage in further dialogue with you or any of the Street members after passing the message across."

My mind was tuned out of the conversation going around.

The soldier held my arm again, pulling me back towards the door.

"Wait . . . wait, just hold on a second." I turned, the soldier's grip still on me as I settled my gaze on a worried Upper. "Upper, what was your stat on Chika when you last checked?"

Upper blinked. "He arrived in Mexico," he said, and then warily creased his brows. "But we got word about an hour later that he was found dead in some alley close to a busy street."

My stomach jumped.

"Dead," I echoed the word.

"Yeah," Milk answered this time. "We don't know what could have happened; it's still a mystery."

"We have to go," the soldier urged.

"Yeah," I said absentmindedly.

"Hey, Z." Devil called my attention, and I half-heartedly focused on him as my mind raged with questions I already knew the answers to. "When he gets back, I'll talk to him."

"Yeah," I said quietly as the soldiers pulled me out of the house. I didn't even fight to tell them to let me go and that I could walk on my own.

I just had one thought on my mind.

If I don't think of perfectly constructed answers before Elio shows up, I will be wholly and royally fucked.

CHAPTER FORTY-FIVE

Zahra

I underestimated the torture in waiting.

It had an unnerving effect that slowly ate at your nerves, building up uncountable goosebumps on your skin, especially when waiting to receive judgment for a crime you knew you were guilty of.

I was aware that this was Elio's game, making people wait so that they would imagine how the scenario would play out, bite their nails while thinking of what could be happening outside, who could be spilling out truths, fucking up their chance of survival.

As things had—dare I say—progressed between me and Elio, his making me wait was the last thing I was expecting. He had told me countless times that he didn't like beating around the bush. If he had shit to ask, why didn't he just show up and ask me instead of playing with my nerves like this?

I flexed my fingers, trying to stop them from shaking. I would have gotten over the events from the bus if I had been given enough time to relax before this fucking ambush. But the worry of whatever this questioning thing would result in worsened the state of my mind. My hands were still so cold.

I had been here for almost three hours if my calculations were correct. I had no idea how long he wanted to make me wait.

The place I was kept in looked like a prison cell with one window. A small bed without covers, a small table with no chair, dim white lights, faded gray walls, and a quietness that could cut you to the bone. But it was better than the hot room.

With my mind scattered all over the place, I didn't think I could take that much heat.

I stood up from the bed again, pacing the room's length while massaging my wrist.

Chika was dead.

I didn't kill him.

Unless he had enemies I didn't know about, his death was most definitely Elio's doing. And if Elio had reached him first, then I was fucked.

My suspicions had been correct; the original painting was in Mexico City. And going back to the root of this whole fucked-up quest would most likely get me to the original painting.

Arturo Garza had died, and the manor was the only property he hadn't sold off or turned into an asset. It was registered under a privately financed institution tasked with maintaining the building, employing people to clean it, and organizing tours and excursions for little children. The manor would be the first place to look if the original painting could be anywhere.

How I never thought of this before was way beyond me, and I was to blame for that.

I hadn't been focused lately, going off track, making stupid slip-ups like getting kidnapped, and getting myself involved with Elio.

At the thought of Elio, I couldn't help but sigh.

It was no secret that I found him fascinating, a well-sculptured challenge I wanted to win. A challenge that gave me complicated feelings every night. One that had me become as crazy as acknowledging that I might have feelings for him.

I raked my fingers through my hair, pacing around and counting the minutes in my head.

Caring for the victim of my effortless teasing wasn't part of the challenge. Liking how he talked and walked wasn't part of the challenge; staring at him from afar when he wasn't fucking looking was not written in the content list for the so-called fucking challenge.

Maybe my worry didn't entirely stem from the fact that he knew more about me than Street did at the moment; perhaps it came from the fact that I allowed us to get so far with this thing between us, and now it was most likely over.

I would be delusional if I denied the recent shift in the dynamic between us. How he had grown comfortable in my presence, the way he would look at me, without hate or irritation, but like a person he was interested in. A person he could tolerate. A person he liked—as he'd confessed the other day—a confession I had ignored because it meant something I didn't want.

Never in a million years, strapped to that chair, fate slightly uncertain, a bullet in my shoulder and a plea on my lips, did I think a day would come when, with a single thought of Elio, I would feel his gaze on me, his fingers on—and inside—me, his lips marking me and creating still purplish pleasure bruises on my body.

But here we were; my brain had been fucked.

My thoughts had gone soft on a man I wasn't even attracted to the first time I saw him. A man who was in the category of men I judged at first fucking glance, a man who could walk in here any minute with a gun and my life in his hands.

I groaned, feeling that sharp jolt in my stomach with the last thought.

Still . . .

Elio Marino was like a shiny new toy that I didn't like but was stuck with and had to eventually . . . *like* because, despite his similarities to the previous toys I had discarded, he was built a bit differently.

Maybe that was why I understood him when he told me that I complemented his being. He complemented mine too, and it freaked me out in more ways than one.

It was a new feeling.

I didn't like to be shoved into the unknown. Being in the unknown meant being uncertain, and uncertain situations made me uncomfortable.

I should be somewhat glad Elio would be angry enough to call things off between us, but I wasn't. I didn't like the idea of me never getting to tease him, or touch him, or listen to his sarcasm, learning from it, and having him look at me in a way that made me feel different. In a way that showed me he cared . . . like really cared . . . about me.

I despised these feelings, but I couldn't help feeling them.

He had given us the payment and passports to leave. It only meant he had found the original painting or knew where it was; either that or he just wanted to get Street out of his hair after this mess we had caused.

I'd be fucking damned if I let him push me out of the narrative now that things were finally beginning to make sense.

I sat on the small bed again for about thirty minutes before standing up and pacing for another thirty minutes . . . four and a half hours, five hours . . . six . . . seven . . . eight.

In those hours, my nerves flew right through the roof; I was rocking on my feet, leaning on the wall, groaning, cursing, biting my lips till they were swollen.

Waiting . . . waiting and fucking waiting like an animal praying for a knife to reach its neck to end the torture of waiting.

I hated the silence. It made me think unnecessary thoughts, ones mostly centered on him—the last time we were together, how he had let me see him, help him.

Countless times, he'd trusted me with his feelings because he felt like there was no harm in doing that. He knew I wouldn't judge. But I knew he was primarily free with that part of himself because he wanted me to be free too.

But that wasn't as easy as it sounded.

My trust issues ran deeper than I could even fucking reach. In the world I grew up in, it was safer to hold on to your trust, never hand it to anyone else because they would most definitely break it, and then use you to the point that you would lose yourself; believing anything they said, you would mistake manipulation for love, you would be gaslit every second of every single day into thinking everything that went wrong in your life was your fault.

I had been naïve.

Now I liked to think that I had a stronger sense of reasoning, even though I knew, deep down inside me, that the foolish girl still lived. I hoped that she could find someone who wouldn't break and ruin her as the first person did—

The door pushed open, and I gasped at the sudden sound it made as Elio walked in, snapping me out of my thoughts.

When I took in his appearance, I frowned.

He looked . . . disheveled, hair a tousle on his head, shirt-sleeves rolled up to his elbows, the hem untucked from his pants. Head dropped low, studying the file he held, brows drawn down in concentration.

The door closed by itself as he came to stand opposite me, a reasonable distance away.

"I apologize for the delay," he spoke into the silence. "Today has been . . . harrowing, and I suppose I have you and your"—without looking at me, he dismissively waved his hand as if trying to find the right word—"cohorts to thank for it."

He didn't seem . . . angry. But there was a vibe to him that made my stomach churn.

I looked around his body, realizing he didn't carry a gun, so he didn't plan to kill me.

"I won't keep you long, as I have political and business activities to see to after I am done here; I only have a few questions for you and—"

"Would you at least look at me while you address me?"

The silence after I spoke was more deafening than the one that had been in the room before he arrived. It was almost as if his breathing had stopped as he stood ramrod straight—his gaze not shifting from that particular spot on the file, his grip tightening on it a little, barely noticeable, but I caught it, just the same way I had noticed the shift in his false calm behavior.

"It's obvious you're angry, which you have every—"

"Stop talking." He still sounded calm, but that edge had changed from nonchalant to *trying to seek control*.

"Keeping your anger in and trying to be mature about it will only make things worse for you—"

"Stop talking, Zahra."

"You can't shut me up; you've tried a couple of times."

Slowly, he closed the file and dropped it on the table beside him, and then he raised his head, shoving both hands into his pockets before his gaze locked with mine.

I couldn't hide how I sucked a breath in, how my nerves seemed to fly in different directions underneath my skin, seeking shelter from the burning heat in those eyes.

The controlled anger in them had me almost bowing at how in check he was with his emotions—even though I knew he could explode any second.

"What do you want, hm?" he asked. "You want me to hit you?"

I shrugged. "If that would make you feel better, I can take a punch."

He watched me, brows drawing down a little, not in confusion, but in a frown that told me how frustrated he was with me, how he didn't want to be here but, for some reason, had to be.

He momentarily looked away from me to a spot on the wall before shaking his head. "I was sitting on my flight today, thinking about what to do to you," he said, looking back at me. "I asked myself, what punishment could I give to this woman? I scrapped anything physical because, frankly, that would be too boring and a waste of time and energy."

I had a retort at the tip of my tongue but held back as he took a step closer and continued talking.

"And then I thought . . . how about something mental—something that would have her spilling all the truths she guards so fiercely, but I figured that would hurt me mentally more than it would hurt you, and I was at my last straw, so I scrapped it. I thought about it for minutes before deciding there was no point to it. I asked myself why I should dwell on something that might not matter in a few days."

He took another step towards me, and I had to raise my head a little to look at him.

"Some things, Zahra, just do not deserve my attention, but then I had the burning need to get answers to my questions, and that's the only reason you're here."

Another retort pushed at me, but I knew it wasn't time to joke around and mess with him; he was barely hanging on by a thread with his anger.

I might be tough, but I knew when poking the tiger needed to be suspended.

"You already know I plan to let you and your friends go. I just need to know why you did some of the things you did."

"Ask."

His jaw clenched at my tone, his eyes sweeping between mine, withheld anger shimmering in the gray of his irises, pupils dilating and constricting.

If anything, I just wanted him to lash out, yell at me, and let out the anger brewing inside him; maybe then I would feel less . . . guilty.

"For days, you kept someone like Chika in a house with my brother; you staged a kidnapping, fooled your whole team, and kept it from Angelo, whom I put in charge of Street affairs; why?"

The scream I did internally had me wincing.

Fucking saucy bitch!

I gritted my teeth hard, wondering what Elio had done to Chika to have him reveal that information.

"I—"

"When you answer me, Zahra. You do not answer with a lie, a dismissal, or a half-truth. I only want the truth."

I gulped down. No lie . . . no dismissal, no half-truth.

I was screwed unless I told the truth.

He might not carry a gun, but I didn't doubt the ability of his hands to snap a neck. My neck.

Fuck.

I cleared my dry throat, stepping back a bit before answering. His eyes followed my every movement like a hawk, praying for me to slip up so he could attack. Not today. I would surrender to fight another day.

"Fine," I started, "we were behind on finding the painting, and I was agitated. I knew I had to do something, so I contacted some of the people that worked for—for *Manuel*." Saying that name out loud had me shifting uncomfortably, wishing I could bring Chika back from the dead and kill him again for putting me through all he did today. "I asked them for help because I knew they were also looking for the painting, and I know how easy it is to bribe out information from his people."

When he didn't respond, I took that as my cue to continue.

"They told me about Chika, and then I contacted him; he was on edge because some people had already caught wind of Arturo having an adopted son. I offered him protection if he would help us get the paintings and tell us everything he knew. I swear to you that he told me he wanted nothing to do with the paintings and Arturo's business; he said the same thing to Street. I was so focused on the information he would give that I—I didn't listen when Street told me it was a bad idea."

"Continue."

I sighed. "The only reason I staged Chika's kidnapping was because I couldn't answer questions on how I learned about him, seeing as I don't want them to know anything about Manuel, or that part of my life. And I didn't tell Angelo because he would tell his team, and I didn't trust anyone with that information; a lot was riding on it."

He remained silent after I finished talking—just looking at me, his thoughts hidden from his face.

"And the risk you took, getting onto that bus—"

"I didn't think he was going to pull that. If I had known, I would have asked Upper and Milk to contact Angelo's people immediately."

"That's not right. According to what I heard, you still had a few minutes of communications with the rest of your team when you got on the bus."

"Yes. But I am not dumb enough to call your people when shit hits the fan. I had the kids to worry about, and I knew the media would be involved in no time; if your people had come to rescue us, your name would have been caught in the crossfire—"

He took a sharp step towards me, crowding my space, scaring me for a second. "Do I look like someone who cares about some crossfire? You put my brother's life in danger; I could have lost him today."

"But you didn't."

"I almost did!" His voice rose.

"He's alive."

"What if the bomb had gone off, hm?" His jaw clenched, his gaze burning into mine. "What if something had gone wrong, and the bomb was set off."

"It didn't; I stopped it."

"But what if you hadn't? What if you failed? One simple fucking wrong decision, Zahra. That's all it takes."

"I know that!"

"Do you!" he yelled in my face, and I flinched back. "Because when you act without thinking like you did today, it begs the question of whether that was your plan all along."

I scoffed with a glare. "Yeah, because I'm some sociopath who loves to kill little children and herself while she's at it, nothing unusual, just the Sunday fucking special." I turned to step away from him, but his hand came around my arm and pulled me back to face him in one hard tug.

"Don't fucking walk away from me."

"Listen here, motherfucker; I have had the *worst* damn day in all of this year combined, battling with stupid trauma while I tried to stay alive; the last thing I want"—I gestured between us—"is this."

"Oh, sorry, Zahra, I genuinely apologize that you put yourself in a situation that had you battling childhood trauma. Do you want a shoulder pat?"

I was vibrating with anger when I gritted out a "Fuck off" and tried to tug myself free of his hold. "Let me fucking go, or I swear I'll be the one doing the fucking punching."

His hand dropped from my arm. "You think you were the only one who had a *bad day*? Do you know the detestable things I had to do today? The damage control I had to take care of from your immature decisions while fucking worrying about that bus blowing to bits?"

I shot him a sweet smile filled with malice. "I was only doing the job you paid me for."

"Agh," he groaned, raising both his hands as if he wanted to strangle me, his fists clenching and unclenching as he turned away from me, loudly trying to control his breathing, which shook with anger as he kept his distance.

After a few seconds, he turned back to me. "Admit your mistake."

I breathed out a strained laugh. "What?"

"Say that your actions weren't the right ones to take. Say that you could have done about a thousand different things to change the outcome of today; apologize for fucking making me worry about you and my brother."

I blinked, watching him before grinding my teeth together in a clench and standing taller. "I did what I thought was right, and as always, we survived."

"That's not what I asked."

"If you're looking to break me, you might as well get back out there and get a gun to finish me off because I stand by my actions. It might have been a wrong call, but as long as I survived, I know damn well that I didn't make a mistake."

He didn't like my response. It did something to him, something that had the anger leaving his eyes, replaced with a question.

"Why are you really here, Zahra?" he asked calmly.

"You brought me here."

"I know I did," he said with a tired frown, one that resembled disappointment. "But I didn't care when my people found the location of your studio apartment. When they saw the little device in that anklet, and they thought your team was as dumb as they came, leaving something as delicate as that behind. I didn't care what motive you guys had. At some point, I thought Elia wanted me to find him, but then—I got to know you."

His gaze searched my face. "I started to see that this wasn't Elia's doing. It was yours. I was wary at first, but I shoved it aside because I had my goal set, and whatever you and whoever you work for were planning to do to me and the empire wouldn't matter because there would be nothing left to take."

My frown hardened. "I don't work for anyone, and if you really want to know, I'm only here for the gold."

"We both know that is a lie, and I honestly don't care to know why you're really here; or if you choose to remain boneheaded and deny your mistakes from today, I just need to understand why you were fucking with me."

I paused, the glare on my face vanishing. "What are you talking about?"

He narrowed his eyes, pressing his lips into a thin line. "Zahra." His voice was like coal: dense, yet solid. "If all you wanted out of this was the gold, my shelter, and the protection my name provided, why were you playing with me?"

I was confused. "Playing with you . . . what are you—"

"You lied to me, told me you and Elia didn't have anything to do with each other. You knew I wouldn't have crossed that line if I knew, and you fucking lied to me, Zahra."

Gears were turning in my head very fast, spinning, spiraling. "What? No, what are you talking about? I didn't lie . . . there is truly, *most definitely* nothing there—"

"The kids from the bus had something very different to say about that."

My eyes widened. "Oh, oh shit, that was—Elio, they're kids, they see two people kiss, and they imagine they are both in—"

"You knew." He ignored my explanation. "You knew how rocky my relationship with Elia was, yet you lied. You made me touch you, and like you; you fooled me, for what? Hm? Because I shot you when we first met or because I tried to drown you?"

"Elio—"

"You ruined every chance I had of ever building any relationship with him, and that's fine. It's also why I want you all gone. Ever since Street arrived, my life has been inconveniently eventful."

This was going downhill so fast that I couldn't catch the damn rope. "That kiss wasn't—it didn't mean anything; I promise you, it was nothing like that—"

"I already made my decision."

"That wasn't the deal," I snapped. "We were supposed to be here to find the original painting, the gold, and your stupid fucking flash drives."

He took a step back. "I can handle my business. If you want the gold that badly, I'll have people send it to your preferred location when I find it. By morning I expect you and Street to be out of my compound."

"Elio"—*fuck*—"can we please just double back and talk about this? You're angry, I am angry, and we both can't be hotheaded at the same time while we try to find common ground."

"No."

"It doesn't have to be like this."

"It does."

I watched him, and he watched me. For seconds, minutes, I don't know how long we stood there.

I could say many things to fix this, clear his doubt about Devil and me, but I didn't know how to say them. I didn't know if I wanted to say them.

But I didn't like this. Not one bit.

When he spoke next, it was in Spanish. *"You can mess with me all you want, Zahra. I will take it, but involving Elia, the only family I have? That is something I won't take."*

"It wasn't like that."

"I can't choose between you and my brother."

I took a step closer to him, switching back to English. "It really wasn't like that, Elio. I wouldn't purposefully ruin your relationship with your brother; what the fuck would I gain from separating family when I don't even have anyone of my own, nor will I ever?"

"I don't care how it was, neither do I care what your intentions are. This thing between us shouldn't have happened in the first place, and unlike you, I am willing to admit when I have made a mistake."

"That mistake being me?" I asked quietly.

He hesitated seconds too long before he said, "Yes."

I looked away from him, biting inside my lips, feeling like someone had dropped a weight of emotional baggage in my chest and ripped it out along with my heart.

I nodded. "Right." I swallowed, unable to look at him. "When am I—when am I allowed to leave here?" I asked.

"Anytime you want." He gestured to the file. "That's the contract. Whatever clause I didn't fulfill, you can take it up with Angelo; he will pay for it."

"Elio—"

"I wouldn't want to apply force when you and your team do not leave the compound by tomorrow, so make sure to do what's needed," he said without looking at me before he turned and left the cell without a second glance my way.

I let out a shuddering breath, returned to the bed, and sat down when the door closed behind him.

One would think I would jump at the opportunity to be out of this cell, and many would think I did precisely that the moment he left. But no. I sat there for two hours, knowing there were a thousand ways this day and this conversation could have gone, but with the result at the end of the day . . .

I knew I had taken the wrong path.

Acknowledgments

First things first, I want to thank my lord and savior for remembering me when I least expected it, and for giving me experiences I never thought I would ever have.

A huge thank-you to my wonderful agent, Thao Le, for believing in this story and this world, and making this whole process so enjoyable (JSYK, I do a little dance whenever I see your emails). To my brilliant editor Monique, your love for these characters will never not make me smile; thank you for adoring them the way you do and for giving them the perfect shine they needed to glow, you're AWESOME! To the marvelous Mal, your excitement for this book made me excited. I appreciate all the work you do and your efforts in making this book come out so beautifully, you're a gem! To the team at Bramble, and everyone who touched this book in one way or the other, I appreciate you!

To my mom and dad, your prayers and your support for my passion amazes me to this day. I don't know what I did to deserve it, but thank you! Couldn't have done this without your blessings. To my sisters and brothers, I love you for always cheering me on and being there throughout this process, you all are my forever G!

To my friends, Elena, Christine, Amy, Héloïse, Lisa, Riya, Mae, and Mercy. Where would I be without you? I have no idea, and I honestly don't want to find out. Thank you for being here, thank you for never turning your backs on me, thank you for your patience and your care.

To my inner circle at Maniero del Diavolo, your support and your enthusiasm for this book will never not blow my mind! You all are there for me in ways I never thought possible. The work you do, the insights you give, the way you cheer me up whenever I feel low—I don't even know where to start, but thank you.

Cat, Sofia, Lussy, Nono, Djama, Briar, Aleeza, Lea, Lisa, Rumy, Catherine, Dia, Directt, Mariam, and Maryam, I love you sooooo much!

To STREET, the best fandom ever, hello, haha! We made it! Thank you so much for your kindness and your love for these characters, for every reel, every fanart, every post, every edit, every like and comment, every email and private message. I appreciate you more than you know. (Also I lurk in the group chat sometimes while y'all talk . . . so . . . I see a lot of things . . . *a lot of things*.)

And finally, to every reader, thank you for spending time with this story. I appreciate you (even if you want to stab our female lead sometimes—don't worry, I'm there with you).

Thank you, and see you in the next one!

About the Author

REBECCA JOHNPEE has been daydreaming epic, too-good-to-be-true scenarios since she discovered the magic in imagination. Once she found the art of putting those vivid scenarios on paper, she set out to make sure her characters found a home in the hearts of readers. Today, she writes romance across multiple genres, letting whichever story calls to her lead the way. When she's not busy crafting new worlds, Johnpee is planning her next adventure to island countries, where she can indulge in her love for the ocean, meet new people, and immerse herself in different cultures.

rebeccajohnpee.com
Instagram: @therebeccayouknow